MW01134540

To Carla
Enjoy! :)

Deadlocked

A Gina Lindsey Mystery

by

Virginia Ann Work

Virginia Ann Work

Virginia Ann Work

v

ACKNOWLEDGMENTS

Thank you to Dan, my dear husband and friend, for your prayers and encouragement. Thank you, Vicki, for the editing job and for your encouragement. Thanks to all my loyal readers. I promise another book in the series soon!

DEDICATION

To all our wonderful friends in Carter County, MT, for your faith, love, kindness and hospitality. We will never forget the time we spent in your midst. God bless!

Dear Blogger Friends,

The events of last spring changed my life. I feel like a person pulled into a whirlwind and deposited on some distant shore. What happened in those momentous days, how my life changed and the effect it had on me and those closest to me will amaze, astound and confound me for the rest of my life.

While I wrote this blog as I experienced the events, I have also added in what other people told me later so that you would have a better picture of what was happening.

This story is dedicated to a young man who changed my life forever and will always have my deepest respect, gratitude and love. I will let you guess his name.

Chapter 1

Blown Away

Gina's Blog, April 25th, Spokane, Washington

Papers, apple cores, empty pop cans and keys fly in the air as I paw through the clutter on my small, rickety table to find my cell phone. *It's dispatch! I gotta get this one! C'mon, c'mon!* Gritting my teeth, I dig through old magazines and advertisements. Finally my fingers close over the slim blue phone.

I snap it open. "Officer Gina Lindsey."

A calm feminine voice answers. "Backup request. Code Red. North Railroad Avenue in the valley, 5700 block. Two suspects inside building."

"On my way." I glance at my watch. *12:06 am.*

Palming the phone, sending the chair crashing to the floor, I clear the pocket-sized living room in two lunges. I grab my shoulder holster and revolver, tie on my boots, throw on my flak jacket and pull on my cap. My mouth is dry, like someone stuffed cotton in it; my hands are sweaty. I slam the door and lock it.

A sudden surge of adrenalin floods my body. It feels like I could toss a dozen good-sized crooks across the yard single-handedly. *This is it! We've got them!*

Outside, cool damp air smacks my face like a cold shower, bringing with it the smell of wet maple leaves and mown grass. Trucks rumble out on I-90, a siren wails as an ambulance approaches Sacred Heart Hospital, a train whistles downtown. Stars spangle the black canopy of sky like pricks of ice chips. In Manito Park across the street an owl is on the prowl.

It's so quiet! Spokane, Washington has shut down for the night, so unlike my beloved New York. I've worked in Spokane for two years, but I'm still a New Yorker at heart. Yet there are some perks to being in a small town– like the apartment I found above a garage behind one of the grand old brick houses near Manito Park. It was a lucky find – I pay only nine hundred a month rent. In New York, it would cost over two thousand and be twice as small.

As I bounce down the cement steps to the street and dash to the patrol car, I speed dial my partner, Nick Bailey. We're narcotic agents with the federal Drug Enforcement Agency and work in collaboration with the Regional Drug Task Force.

Nick's voice is groggy. "Hey, what's up?"

"This is the big one, Nicko. Get down on Grand. I'll be by in five minutes." I switch on the siren and the lights and burn rubber along the quiet street.

From informants, we'd been closing in on a gang of drug dealers for twenty-three days exactly; I had it marked on my calendar. It was about time something broke on the case. I screech to a halt on Grand where Nick hunches against the cool night air in front of the 14th and Grand Beauty Salon. As he opens the door, I grin at him. "Hey. Wanta lift, handsome?"

He climbs in the squad car and fastens his seat belt. "Sounds like a pickup to me. But I'm game. Let's go." He shakes his wet hair back from his forehead. His uniform is rumpled, his shirt collar twisted inside, his shirt buttoned awry.

I resist the urge to straighten his collar and rebutton his shirt. Instead, I concentrate on navigating the car onto the freeway, then drive east to exit on Sprague and turn north on Fancher. Three blocks from the building, I switch off the siren and lights.

Twenty-one minutes past midnight, I pull up beside an old warehouse near the tracks. A row of dingy buildings the color of dog puke and smelling about the same, lean into one another, deteriorating along with the economy. The narcotics team had scoped out this particular location many times, setting up surveillance, but only came up with cold coffee and sore rears. Two Spokane Police Department officers crouch at the double doors at the end of the building. They're peering into a large empty window that gapes open like the mouth of a dead man.

I step out of the car, my Marui Glock 26 revolver in hand. My voice is low. "What'cha got, Coop? Pete?"

Nick eases the passenger door shut and joins me.

Coop doesn't turn around. "The door's deadlocked. We're going in through the window. You coming in?"

My stomach flip-flops. Time stands still as I remember another case where I'd been forced to enter a dark hallway at the top of a decrepit apartment building in New York. An old man materialized out of the shadows and pulled a gun. I knew he would fire. Instinctively, I shot him point-blank in the face. And even though I'd gone through months of counseling and psychological assistance, I would live with the horror of that moment all my life.

Now terror freezes my limbs and squeezes my throat as I gaze at that dark window and the cavernous insides of the warehouse. I swallow. "I'll circle the building and cover the other entrance. Be careful."

Nick whispers at my shoulder, "Hey, Sarge. Let me go in."

I don't want my partner blown away, yet Nick's eyes gleam in the dim glow of the street light. I sense the tension in his lean body, hear his shallow breathing. I nod. "Go ahead. Give me a call if they head this way."

"Thanks." He flashes a brief smile and clambers over the sill on the heels of Coop and Pete.

Moving to the back of the building, I take a position behind a trash bin twenty feet from the door and brace my right wrist with my left hand to hold my revolver steady. The minutes tick away. Amtrak flies past on its way east. Something rustles in the trash. Dog? Rat? My nose itches, but I hold the position.

What's taking them so long? My legs complain and my shoulder screams. The shot I'd taken in the right shoulder a year ago has healed, but it acts up when I stay immobile for a long time. I scrunch my eyes against the pain and hold the position.

The night is cool with a hint of rain. Beads of sweat slide into my eyes. Here by the tracks, it smells of rust and mold and refuse. Even though the Weather Channel predicted a storm, I'm hoping it will hold off long enough to nail this op. This *has* to go down! *C'mon, you guys!* Waiting is always the worst for me, yet I can't fail. Can't even *think* of failure.

A crash from inside the building reverberates through the night air. One of the officers – Coop, maybe – yells, "Come out! Hands above your head!"

My gun wobbles. I correct it. Another crash, like shelves collapsing. Shouts, thumps, the blast of guns. Nick's Colt MRP Carbine rattles. Then another gun. It sounds like a Micro Uzi. *Oh my god! Whose was that?* No one on the police force has the Israeli-made assault guns, yet I'd heard they were on the street. Bile rises from my gut. If these guys have better weapons – *no. Can't think like that. Focus.*

A man sprints from the darkened doorway, straight toward me. Nick darts out behind him. As I draw breath to shout a warning, an explosion shakes the earth. Orange flames light the sky. The shock wave hurls me backwards; I land hard on my tailbone, roll down the embankment toward the tracks.

Stunned, I try to regain my ability to move. The drug dealer lands only a few feet away. I can see his inert form in the light of the fire that blossoms to life. Nick is lying near the tracks. *My gun. I have to get my gun.*

The dealer lifts his head. He looks around and sees Nick's still body. Is Nick okay? Why doesn't he regain consciousness? About that time, he rolls over, shakes his head and claws through the weeds and rubble for his weapon. The crook scrambles to his feet, clutching his rifle, and draws down, a smile on his face. Time seems to stand still. My heart pounds in my ears.

I rear up to my knees. Maybe I can buy some time. "Hey! You! Throw down your gun and put up your hands! This is the law!"

The man whirls, his rifle swinging with his body. My heart sinks. It's an Uzi SMG, the real thing. *Oh, crap.* Desperately, I comb through gravel and smashed pop cans but find nothing.

The man laughs. "Where's your little toy, pig cop? Think you're hot stuff? Oh, boy, I'm gonna git me a cop."

I scrabble forward through the rocks and weeds. *It has to be here somewhere. Will I die because I lost my gun? What would Dad say of that? Will I bring shame on the Lindsey name?*

The fire fight two and a half years ago in New York is burned in my memory like a hot iron, like it was only moments ago. Even though it hadn't lasted long, Dad took a shot in the chest, and I wasn't in position to help him. There was no excuse for my mistake.

As they loaded him into the ambulance, I saw hurt and anger on his face. "You let me down, Gina. What kind of a cop are you?"

My throat closed as tears streamed my face. "Please, Dad. Please. I tried."

"Trying isn't enough. You have to succeed. Next time you won't be on my team, I swear." He looked away as they slammed the doors.

When he died several weeks later due to complications with his wound, I vowed to never forget or forgive myself. I would go to the grave with his death on my conscience. Maybe it made me a better cop. Maybe it drove me to perfection. Maybe it would drive me insane. In any case, it was part of my life, something I had to live with daily.

Transferring to Spokane had been a desperate attempt to escape the pain and memories. It hadn't worked.

Now my fingers touch something cold and hard. I bring up my Glock and aim.

The dealer snorts, an ugly sound on the damp night air. "Too late, copper. Yur *so* dead." His finger tightens on the trigger.

Chapter 2

Drive-By Fire

Spokane, Washington, April 25

The Spitfire Pub and Eatery on North Trent was dark and smoky, and the noise was so loud it was almost edible. The press of people stifled any breath of fresh air that might find its way inside.

Chris Marshal clambered onto a stool and ordered a beer. As the barkeep tapped the brew into a tall glass, Chris slapped a ten dollar bill on the bar. Glancing up, he glimpsed his face in the mirror. Stringy hair, a scruffy beard the color of sand, a felt hat pulled low over blue eyes, enough grease and dirt and grunge to blend with the worst drunks on the street.

He took a deep gulp of beer, slouching over the bar. What was he doing here? How he hated the city! If only he was home. *Home on the range.* He smiled. The ranch Dad brought near Spokane was everything he'd ever dreamed of, and more. He left the world behind as he worked cattle, farmed the hay fields, assisted heifers in calving, branded, mended fences. The best part was his little herd of horses -- breeding, riding, training and tending them.

He glanced for the hundredth time at his watch. His man was late. He thought briefly of calling him on his cell phone. No, not here. Not with so many ears around.

Someone elbowed up to the bar beside him. He was just about to take his beer to a table when the man leaned closer. "Hello, my friend. Care to join me over there at the window?" He laid a hand on Chris' shoulder.

In the mirror, Chris saw the stranger's reflection – a large, muscular build, a round face that held the look of a bull, and small eyes that gleamed with malice. He was a Mexican with dark skin and hair – a well-connected Mexican. Diamond and gold rings decorated his fingers. He wore a shoulder holster.

The cartel! Here in Spokane?

Chris leaned away from the hand and summoned a smile. "I don't drink with strangers. Ma told me not to."

"I think you can be persuaded." Unobtrusively, the man pulled a gun from his holster.

Dully Chris registered the make of the silencer screwed to the revolver's nose – a GB Tech AAC Scorpion was pressed firmly into his ribs. He nodded. "I imagine that I could."

"Nice and easy does it, then," the man said in a low voice. "On second thought, let's go outside. I hate crowds, don't you?"

Chris made no rejoinder as he allowed the man to steer him through the press of dancers, drinkers and working women. Out of the corner of his eye he saw another man rise to his feet and approach. Two of them. This would be tricky.

Of course he wouldn't allow himself to be commandeered into a lonely alley where someone would find his shot up body early tomorrow morning. He wasn't that dense. Yet he was concerned for the people who packed the room. He didn't want them hurt.

The bouncer stood at the door. Mace was a big man; Chris was glad he'd come here enough times to strike up a relationship with him. He caught Mace's eyes and raised both his brows, moving his eyes to the side with a frantic shake of his head. Warning enough. Mace caught on.

"Hey! You didn't pay for your drink!" The bouncer reached out and grabbed Chris' shirt front.

Chris' head bobbed on his neck like a yo-yo. The next thing he knew, he was flying through the air and landing on a table. A woman screamed. He turned in time to see Mace descend upon the two goons.

"And you!" he bellowed, striking out with a fist to the man's gun hand. "We don't like these kinda toys in here!" The gun went flying.

Chris picked himself up and wondered briefly if Mace needed help. Obviously not. The bouncer heaved the first man out the open door and the second followed his *companero*. Mace dusted off his hands and turned to Chris.

"Sorry about that, young fella. I know you paid yur bill, but it was the first thing that jumped to mind. You okay? I didn't know you had bruisers like that for friends."

Chris summoned a laugh and slapped him on the back. "No friends of mine. Thanks for the help. But I got two guys out on the street now, waiting for me with more than their fists. Is there another way outta here?"

"Sure. Hold on a second." He spoke briefly into a two-way radio and a slim woman appeared. April. What an unlikely name for a business woman.

She grinned and batted her heavily painted eyelashes. "How can I help you, handsome? Ain't nothin' I won't do. Especially for you." She smoothed down her skimpy blouse that revealed more than it covered and slid her hands across her hips.

"Just show me the way to the back door." He pulled out his wallet and handed her a five.

It disappeared down her cleavage. "I kinda like you. Tell you what. I'll give you a special deal. Outta the goodness of my heart, I swear."

He laughed. "The goodness of your – no thanks."

She led him through the crowd. Just as he passed the bar, he felt a tug on his sleeve. Bracing himself for another attack, he sighed with relief when he saw who it was -- his man.

"You dropped this." The short, slender fellow handed him a slip of paper with a grin.

Chris nodded. "Thank you." He tucked the note into his pocket and fished out a card. "Here's my address in case I need to be carried home. Say, I'm feelin' fine tonight. Take this and buy one on me." He pressed a tightly wadded roll of money into the man's hand. It contained more than the agreed amount of one hundred dollars.

It vanished into a tattered shirt pocket. The man tilted his baseball cap. "I thank ye kindly, sir. Very kindly."

The girl tapped her garish red fingernails on the bar. "You ready? Follow me."

He trailed behind her shapely form as she swung down a long narrow hallway, lit only with a bare bulb. Stopping near a door that was marked with a green exit sign, she nodded and with an exaggerated swing of her hips, she swirled around and clattered back down the hall.

Chris let himself out into the alley that led to Trent Avenue. Did the gangsters know of the back door? Trash littered the cement. A cat scittered away on frightened paws. A dog barked somewhere. He heard a siren and the distant hum of tires on I-90. His nerves were raw. Any moment now a gun would discharge and a bullet would crash into his skull.

He crept carefully past a garbage bin that smelled of urine, dog do and rotting fish. *And city people think farms stink!* He'd much rather muck out horse stalls than tread through this filth! The street was quiet. He paused, wondering what his chances were of making a clean get-away to his pickup and to his apartment. About a million to none. The big guys wouldn't give up so easily.

Down the street, a sign above a metal building proclaimed the site to be Mutual Materials. About three blocks away, he saw the blue and yellow sign of Napa Auto Parts. It was closed -- no help there. A breeze lifted a piece of paper and scuttled it down the sidewalk. He watched the cars and trucks that passed. With the information he'd gotten tonight, he'd finish up his business in the city and never return. Sweet!

He crept down the sidewalk, his senses alert, every sound intensified. A drunk on the other side of the street coughed. Footsteps crunched behind him. He looked back. A young kid stopped and lit a joint. The scritch of his match split the greasy night air.

The business district petered out and shabby clapboard houses stood shyly off the street, garrisoned by chain link fences. The Napa Auto store was only a half a block away; his pickup was parked in front of it. His breath came in gasps and fine sweat beaded his forehead. Why had he parked so far from the tavern? *Almost there.*

Suddenly tires screeched on the pavement; a powerful engine roared. Chris dropped to his knees. A black Dodge Ram pickup, shiny in the streetlights, bore down upon him. He glanced left and right. No shelter anywhere -- not even a trash bin. Wait. A mail box. Could he make it, or would the wicked-looking M16 pointing out the driver's window make mincemeat of him before he took two steps?

He pulled his Glock from his inside pocket. *No time!* The truck was on him and the semi-automatic rifle chattered, splaying the sidewalk with deadly fire.

Chapter 3

Wild Goose Chase

Carter County, Montana, April 25

Elton Lindsey was alone the day the last big storm of the season slammed into southeastern Montana. April didn't bring showers to this country – it brought the worst blizzards of the year. They'd called for a bad one on the weather channel, and they just might be right this time.

Driving the tractor slowly through the pasture as a large bale of hay unwound from the trailer on the back, he studied a bank of low clouds building up on the horizon to the south, down along the Powder River.

After he finished feeding, he turned the tractor back to the barn, wondering if Bobbi was okay. Right after breakfast she and Tim left for Miles City. He hadn't wanted her to take the trip, not with the storm threatening, but she said she'd try to get home early. He'd watched her drive the Subaru Forester down the driveway with a nagging worry in the back of his mind. *Something's bothering her -- but what?*

He parked the tractor, finished the chores and headed to the house. As he entered the kitchen, he remembered how preoccupied she'd been that morning, how she didn't hold out her cheek for her traditional good-bye kiss, and hadn't even noticed when he set his mug on her beloved oak table she'd gotten from his mother.

Was she concerned about Tim? The kid had been acting strangely. Wouldn't talk much, and kept to himself in his trailer across the yard, spending a lot of time on his computer. Stayed up nearly all night. Said he was onto a big money making scheme. Wouldn't go to church.

Elton shrugged. *Oh, well.* Tim was a grown man. That's what he kept telling Bobbi. He shook his head. Tim would always be her little boy. Too bad the kid didn't take to ranching, yet he didn't *like* ranch work. Didn't like anything that was important.

He placed his cup in the sink and pulled on his sheepskin jacket. Making his way to the equipment shed, he gathered his tools. Better get that darned fence mended before the storm came or the sheep would find the hole and get out. Sheep had the dangest way of finding the smallest gaps. If there wasn't so much money in the critters, he swore he'd get rid of them.

He loaded the tools into his beat-up outfit, a blue Ford truck, and held the door for Shep. The old border collie hopped in immediately and sat on the passenger seat, grinning with happy eyes and lolling tongue.

The pickup rattled over the rutted dirt road and across the pasture. The fields, variegated greens and browns, were dotted with willows and box elders that grew down on the creek bottoms. The vast dome of the sky arched over head, a cathedral of intense blue. *Big Sky country they call it, and they ain't wrong. We got sky out here like nobody's business.*

At the creek, he counted fifteen head of deer, grazing peacefully. Great. Eating my winter wheat. Well, next fall he'd eat a few of them! Now he knew where they hunkered down.

Around noon, he tightened the wire on the last post and drove home. Back at the house, he knocked dirt off his feet and entered the side door. After hanging up his cowboy hat, he washed his hands, then slapped together a cold salami sandwich, grabbed a handful of chips and snatched a beer from the refrigerator. On the front porch, he sat in his favorite lawn chair and balanced his lunch on his lap. Shep watched with begging eyes. It had turned warm and muggy. The clouds were closer now, piling up over the high plains and grasslands like an omen of doom. He wished Bobbi would get home. Sure didn't want her stuck in a blizzard.

He stretched his long legs and leaned back in the plastic chair. This was his favorite view—the valley spread out before him, a range of buttes to the south, and a spur of the Long Pines to the west. It was all his – every stone, bush and tumbleweed; every cow, sheep and horse; every field of hay and stand of wheat as far as the eye could see. And you could see pretty far in this country – fifty miles on a clear day.

Elton hefted himself from the chair, lifting his head to listen. A truck approached down the long drive. He heard the powerful engine and saw a column of dust. When it roared into sight, he was puzzled. He boasted that he knew every outfit in the county, but he didn't know this one. Who was it? Someone needing gas? Or a nuisance government survey man? A politician? Maybe a religious cult?

The red truck braked, kicking up a cloud of dust. The man who emerged wore a denim work shirt, worn jeans and a dented cowboy hat. Elton groaned and forced a smile. He fought the urge to run out the back way.

A couple of hours later, he found himself with the man on a cliff of sheer rock that bordered a beautiful valley below. Told that there was a vein of silver here, he'd believed the lie. After exploring a shallow cave, he turned back to the opening and faced the business end of a 30.06 rifle. He thought at first it was a joke, but the man who carried it was not laughing.

In that split second, Elton knew two things. He knew why he'd been duped to come up here, and he knew he would die this day. He tried to yank his body away from the blast of the gun. The last he saw before hot lead seared his brain was the leering face of a man he once trusted. And then there was only darkness.

Chapter 4

The Trail Leads East

From Gina's Blog, Spokane, April 25

I throw myself down and flip over. As I hit the ground, a blast of bullets from the Uzi slices the air where my head had been a nano-second before. I find refuge behind an overturned barrel but know the old metal will not stop a slug from an assault rifle. *An Uzi!* What kind of money and connections do these dealers have? Who'd ever expect to find this kind of firepower in this little burg?

Nick yells.

I peer over the barrel and fire a shot at the man who kneels with the Uzi. He twists backward and falls. Then, in my peripheral vision, I see a second man emerge from the darkened doorway. He stands silhouetted against the flaming building and spots me. He brings his rifle around and braces himself.

"Halt, this is the police! Drop your gun now!" My voice ricochets off the metal building and sounds, even to my ears, high and thin. He isn't going to stop, yet still I hesitate to shoot him. It almost cost my life. His shot brushes my hair.

Nick fires twice, shots carefully placed. It catches the man in the doorway, blows him back. He screams and falls. Nick slowly rises and comes toward me.

Fire roars inside the building. It explodes from the vacant windows and finds holes in the roof. I jump up the bank and approach the two wounded men warily. I'd seen "dead" men leap up and run away. Or attack. The heat takes my breath away; I shield my face with one hand. The two crooks lay together, one on top of the other, blood seeping through their clothes.

Cooper and Pete appear from the side of the building, panting, each carrying black plastic bags. They set the bags down near the squad car and run back to help us drag the men from the fire.

I swipe my forehead. "Anyone call the fire department?"

Cooper nodded. "They're on their way, along with the crime team." He peers into my face. "Are you all right?"

I nod and turn to the perps. They are both alive; we'd winged one high on the right shoulder. The other Nick got in the chest. He is worse off, but still alive. Good. Officers who kill people, even pond scum like these, are put on administrative leave nowadays. I don't need that.

"Thanks for drawing fire away from me," Nick says in a quivery voice.

"Sure. You'd do the same for me. Thanks for taking this guy out." I try to smile but my burnt skin only allows a grimace. My nerves are giving away – my knees and hands shake. I fight the urge to crash and burn. Not yet. Job to do here. *Focus, Lindsey.*

We cuff the dealers. Small fry from the looks of them. This isn't the big boss. I wonder where the trail will lead. The deeper we go into this, the bigger it gets. I yank a black coat from the older man's body and rip it into strips, then staunch the flow of blood until the EMTs arrive. The small man, less severely wounded, fights the cuffs and hurls profanity into the air.

Five minutes later, an ambulance screeches to a halt beside us with sirens screaming and lights flickering eerily off the buildings and trees. Following them, the crime team arrives, and shortly after that, the fire engines. After the EMTs load the two men, I report to the crime team and speak briefly with the fire chief.

My knees give out just as I climb behind the steering wheel of my patrol car. I lay my head on the steering wheel and close my eyes. Delayed reaction. It happens. I fasten my seat belt as Nick clambers in beside me. He pours coffee from a thermos and hands it over, concern in his brown eyes.

I accept it with a wry grin. "You did good in there. I'll write you up for a promotion." Nick is a competent man to have at your back. And besides that, I like him. Though I have a policy of not dating fellow officers, we'd gone out several times. But there were limits – I didn't invite him to my apartment, and he didn't push it.

"I can't believe you drew fire for me, Red. That was awesome."

"You brought down the guy who was aiming for me. Turn-about is fair play." I sip the hot coffee, wondering vaguely why I allow him to call me Red. He's the only one in my entire life who jokes about my hair and hasn't gotten body slammed for it. *Oh, gosh. I hope I'm not falling for him!*

He stretches. "It felt fine to cuff those guys. You sure you're okay? Looks like you burned your face."

"I'm fine. I'll slather it with some aloe when I get home. How about you?" I look at him in the swirling lights of the fire trucks. "You got a little singed." His uniform is blackened and soot-covered, his hands red. "What'd you get in there?"

"Don't know, but I bet it's the works." He grins, his white teeth flashing in his sooty face. He nods to Cooper who loads the bags into his car. "Probably a record bust. I figure we got enough to put them away for a while. Good thing we got it out before the fire burned everything. They had it booby-trapped, you know, but we caught 'em sleeping."

I start the motor and pull out into the street. "How about the big boss? You think those two scumballs will squeal? "

Nick shakes his head. "We got ways to make them talk. But you gotta take what you can get, Gina."

"If they talk, we might get a name. Or a location. Wanta bet?"

He glances at me. I can feel his interest level rise. "Sure. What do you suggest?"

"I'm flat broke right now, but if you'll take my word, I'll wager fifty bucks that we get a solid lead. What will you raise?" I pull up in front of his apartment.

He whistles and gets out. "You're out of my league, Sarge. I was thinking ten. But I'll match you. No names, no location, no leads." He slams the door and waves.

At the station the next morning, I pocket five tens and laugh at Nick's woebegone face. "Next time listen to the officer who knows what's goin' down, son."

He shrugs. "We got them talking, Gina. Early this morning. We offered to put them in the witness protection program. Too bad they didn't know much. They mentioned a name. I'm checking it through channels. And they mentioned this place. What do you make of it?" His computer screen shows a map of Montana. "You ever hear of it before?"

I lean closer. "Ekalaka, Montana? Yes, as a matter of fact, I have. My aunt and uncle ranch down there. I visited them when I was in high school. You're saying that the trail leads *there*?"

"That's what I'm saying. Someone put his operation in a remote area where the cops are laid back and the force is understaffed." He grins again. "We got a record bust, Red. Not only weed, but heroin. They must be into the big time."

"Heroin! That explains the Uzis." I tuck some stray auburn strands of hair behind my ears.

He nods. "Quite a haul for one night's work."

"Nick! Gina!" Captain Matthews calls from his office. "Could you step in here for a moment?"

Nick stands. "Maybe we're about to find out where we go next."

Jed Matthews is as hard as iron when an officer makes a mistake, but today he welcomes Nick and I with a wry smile. "Come in. Sit down." He wears a white shirt that's emblazoned with the DEA logo and his name. His blue jacket and cap hang on a coat rack near the door.

I perch on the chair gingerly, nursing my bruised tailbone. My shoulders and legs ache, and my face and hands are puffy red.

Matthews rearranges some papers and glances up, a grin twitching the corners of his mouth. "I congratulate you on your bust last night. I won't shake your hands -- your burns look painful."

"Thank you, sir," I reply. "Now we're gonna nail the boss, right?"

Matthews pierces me with a sharp look. "The drug force team has done well since it was formed. I'm afraid I have some bad news, though. We're facing some budget cuts." He looks down, shuffles some papers. "That means some jobs. After this case is wrapped, we're letting you two go."

"Go! As in, fired, sir?" I sit up and groan from the pain that shoots through my back. "Is this the reward we get for doing a good job?" My voice sounds strident and too assertive, but I don't care. "Why do we have budget cuts when the drug cartels can afford whatever they want?"

Matthews waves away my concern with a negligent hand. "Oh, you'll still have a job. Somewhere. We'll make sure you get reassigned."

"But we're just getting started!" Nick rises halfway, then sinks down. "And this bust shows progress. Sir, the felons mentioned a name. I don't have anything about the guy yet and it might be an alias, but this is a solid lead. I've checked with the FBI and they think he's got something big going on in southeastern Montana. In Carter County."

Matthews raises his eyebrows. "What's the name?"

Nick shakes his head. I can tell he isn't comfortable blurting it out, not even to Cap. "Uh. Butch Wilson, sir.

"Hm." Cap shifts. "So it's in Carter County? I went to law school with the sheriff down there. Mike Crosby." He shakes his head. "It's unlikely that they have anything big down there. You can see a gnat's eyelash a mile away. Check your sources, Bailey."

Nick nods. "Yes, sir. And there's – "

"We can't stop now, sir." I lean forward, anxiety clouding my usual good sense. "Can't you convince the politicians? Pull some strings? Buy us some time?"

Matthews frowns. "I can try, but I can't promise anything."

"Sir, I have an aunt and uncle who ranch in Carter County. Let me go out there undercover and look around."

Matthews shoves back his chair. "Can't afford to have you gone, Lindsey. I need you here." He shoots me a skeptical look, one that says, *don't push it*. "Besides, before authorizing a sting, I'd need to see a definite connection. Bailey, get me some hard facts. Run it through your computer. I could reassign you both to a Mobile Enforcement Team. We've never had one in Montana, but if you find a solid lead, I can requisition it."

Nick gets to his feet. "Okay, I'll check it out. And if we catch this dude it's going to mean lots of political clout for you." He presses his hands on the desk, hands wide apart and leans forward slightly. "You'll have a big name. Lots of publicity."

I'm smiling behind my hand, knowing he's using the old gesture of dominance.

Cap studies his papers, his expression softening. "All right. I'll give Mike a call and talk to him about an undercover operation. You'd be working with the Eastern Montana Drug Force out of Miles City. Mike helped set it up. But we need more proof."

I slowly rise, ignoring the pain in my backside. "Sir, they'll be planting the weed right now. Or they might be growing indoors. Under artificial light, they can grow continuously, no matter what the season."

"Nevertheless, I'm not ready to send you down there, Lindsey. You and Nick come back in here with something solid. In the meantime, have a doctor look at your burns. And take the day off." He looks from me to Nick, a smile creasing his face. "You deserve it."

"Thank you, sir." When I leave his office, I don't know if I'd been complimented or effectively put to the side. I grit my teeth. *I'll show him. I'll show them all.*

In my little cubicle, I lean back in my chair and survey my desk, where my computer competes for space with stacks of paper, an empty yogurt container, and a crushed Diet Coke can. I like it like this, even though sometimes I can't find my keys or an important file.

I turn to Nick, who's hunkering down in front of his computer. "Nice touch, Nicko. *Lots of political clout.*" I chuckle with him. "What're you doing with your day off?"

He shrugs. "Guess I'll watch an old movie and try not to use my hands. Hey, you want to come over? We could order in some pizza."

I appreciate the way his eyes twinkle. "I'll come, but remember I don't get romantic with people I outrank."

He laughs. "No romance, then. I'll be as macho as you want. Okay, I'll email you this information, Red. See you tonight."

That night, after a movie and supper with Nick, I return to my apartment and get the urge to clean. On Friday I'm flying to Mexico with Sue and Bobby, a couple I'd met skiing. For the next three hours, I empty moldy food from the refrigerator, clean the bathroom, vacuum and do six loads of wash.

When I'm finished, I sit down and clean my gun. It's midnight. The phone rings its little ditty – *When the Saints Come Marchin' In* – Aunt Roberta's ring. *Aunt Roberta!* From Ekalaka, Montana! Talk about a coincidence!

I open it. "Hello, Aunt Roberta. How are you?" I can't keep the surprise from my tone. She only calls about once a month, if that. I'm even more startled, though, when she begins to cry. It is not like my feisty, I-can-do-it-all-by-myself aunt to weep.

When Bobbi calms down, her voice holds the tone of one who's reporting a death. "I'm sorry, dear, but it just came over me. It's Elton. He's disappeared."

Chapter 5

Big Sky Country

Carter County, Montana, April 25

It was a steep climb to the top. Sabrina Philips labored up the path to a boulder she'd named the Monolith. Most days she only climbed that far. But today she'd determined to find a canyon she'd seen before where a birch tree leafed out in mint green right beside a willow in yellow. She'd forgotten her camera that day and promised herself that she'd get the picture today. Photography was more than a hobby to her – it was her passion.

Even though a storm was predicted, the sky was clear and it was as warm as a summer day. Just the kind of day to stretch your legs and get a good picture. In fact, some dark clouds looming on the horizon would lend atmosphere to the shot.

Sabrina brushed back her honey-colored hair and climbed over the rocks. She was in good shape and didn't mind mimicking a mountain goat. Just a little further, then she'd be able to see down into that canyon. She paused and looked back over her shoulder. The valley below stretched as far as the eye could see. Quite a sight. She took a deep breath and smiled. Up here was the only place she felt totally alone. And safe from prying eyes.

A crow cawed in the pine tree above her head and a squirrel scolded from a lower branch. Peaceful, just like she wanted. Yet as she approached the lip of the canyon, a low, grinding sound grated on her nerves. What could that be? A second later she knew. A truck. It was getting closer. Why was someone driving up here? Hunters? But it wasn't hunting season yet. Annoyed, she slipped behind a screen of thick elderberry bushes and watched. Maybe it was some lovers, seeking a secluded spot. But why did they have to choose *her* place?

Climbing higher and keeping to the dense cover, she waited. Pretty soon now she'd be able to see the truck on the road below. It stopped just beyond her line of vision. She crept forward and spotted a red pickup. A man, carrying a rifle, climbed out of the vehicle.

He was alone, or so she thought, until he spoke to someone in the truck. Or was it his radio? She couldn't be sure. As she lined up for a shot of the birch tree, she realized the truck was parked right in her line of vision. *Rats.* A door slammed, and she caught a glimpse of another man following the first up the cliff. Why did they have to park in the middle of her picture? When were they coming back? She didn't have all day.

If they were hunting, they were breaking the law. Maybe she could get a picture and report it to the game warden. She hated hunters, anyway. Hated the mounted heads of deer, antelope and elk that decorated their walls. Hated the stories, pictures and drinking that accompanied the sport. Hated the meat.

Sabrina waited. The men did not reappear. She took several pictures of the valley and the tree, thinking she could remove the pickup digitally. And even though the truck looked familiar, she couldn't say who owned it. Everyone drove pickups in this country, and she'd never been good with cars, anyway. She moved to stand behind a big boulder, still studying the red vehicle.

She sighed. It was getting late. She might as well go back.

Turning, she started back. It was then that a single shot rang through the forest. A crow cawed loudly and flapped away. The squirrel disappeared. What had the man shot? Was he target practicing? But, if so, why only one shot?

She paused, listening. Presently the truck roared to life. Tires dug out in the soft dirt as the driver reversed directions, pulled into the track and disappeared. Slowly the motor sounds died away.

She shrugged. Well, he'd ruined a perfectly good picture, the idiot. But, oh well. There were other days and other photos to take. Carefully she descended the steep path and made her way back to her car.

***

Spokane, Washington, April 25

Chris flung himself to the sidewalk, rolled to the curb and fell off it onto the street, almost into the path of the truck. Covering his head with his arms, he huddled into the gutter. Last thing they'd think he'd do – flee for cover right under their noses. It wouldn't take them long to adjust, though -- just lower the rifle an inch and he'd be meeting his creator. He could almost feel the bullets slamming into his body.

A patrol car screeched around the corner, lights blazing and sirens screaming. The deadly rain of bullets stopped instantly and the driver of the truck careened right, rear end wheeling out of control, tires trying to grip the pavement. They turned into an alley and disappeared, the police car hot on their trail.

Chris lay still on the pavement, pain radiating from his shoulder, hip and elbow. He felt something wet on his face and drew back his fingers with blood on them. Shattered cement fragments had lacerated his face, but he was alive. He crawled onto the sidewalk and shuffled as fast as he could to his pickup. With hands that shook, he pushed the unlock button, climbed in and sped away.

Back at his apartment, he threw his few belongings into a battered suitcase, left a note on the kitchen counter and drove off into the night. He didn't really breathe until Spokane lay twenty miles to the south and he saw stars in the black sky.

When he pulled into his ranch, he smiled. Home at last! It wasn't over, though -- he knew too much. They'd come for him again. He sighed and pulled his suitcase from the truck. As he let himself into the darkened farm house, Stan's face drifted into his vision. His younger brother had been gunned down a little over four years ago. Yet still he grieved.

Stan had been his best friend in the world. They'd done about everything together in Bogota, Columbia where they lived. Dad was too busy with his job on staff at the US embassy to pay much attention to them, and Mom died from cancer even before they went down there.

He should have been watching Stan, should have protected him when he got involved with a street gang and started taking dope. But he'd been too busy with his job and school. Now he was dead, rotting in his grave, and Chris only had a slim lead on the man who was responsible. He *had* to find Stan's killers and bring them to justice. No matter the cost.

Chris stuffed his things into another suitcase. Tucked away in a safe deposit box was a fuzzy picture of the man who murdered Stan. No name. Only the picture. In the years since the murder, he'd learned that behind the man in the picture was a powerful drug cartel that operated out of Columbia. Now it was owned by Mexican drug lords.

Chris could feel he was getting close, but time was running out. The killers were onto him. This time he'd have to change his appearance and name; he'd have to nail them before they got him. This time it was all-out war.

Chris jammed the rest of his clothes into the suitcase and clicked it shut. He grabbed up his beat-up cowboy hat and locked the house. Under the light of the stars, he climbed in his truck. *Montana, here I come!*

***

From Gina's Blog, April 26

I pace my tiny bedroom and toss another pair of shorts in the open suitcase while I talk through my ear piece. *"He's disappeared!* How can someone just vanish?"

Roberta's distraught voice comes clearly over the line. "This is big country, Gina. You remember it, don't you, dear? Out here, people get hurt … can't make it home. Or wild animals …"

"Oh, don't. Please. Where was he? At the house?"

"I don't know. His outfit's parked by the garage, like he usually leaves it, and Shep is here. I'd driven up to Miles City with Tim. When we got home, Elton wasn't anywhere around. He'd made himself some lunch."

I try to figure out what *outfit* she was referring to, and then remembered that an outfit in that country meant a car or truck. I roll my eyes and sigh. "Had anyone else come?"

"I don't know. We couldn't see any fresh tracks in the driveway. I've called the sheriff and he came over. They won't start searching until tomorrow morning. I'm just so worried, what with the blizzard. If he's out there somewhere, hurt, there isn't much chance." Her voice breaks. Muffled sobs come over the line.

"What do want me to do, Aunt Roberta? I'm flying to Mexico tomorrow with my friends. Remember? I emailed you."

"Yes. I got your email, dear." There's a pause. The sound of blowing a nose comes through the line. "I ... hate to ask, but ... could you come? You being a cop and all, I thought you might think of something that we've missed. Just come. I ... I need you, Gina. I'm afraid. Elton's been hiding something from me and it worries me sick. I know it sounds corny, but there's something *evil* going on here."

"Do you have any idea of what he's hiding? Or what he might be involved in?"

"He's been meeting with some men. There are never any names. Sometimes I think I'm imagining things. It scares me. Will you come this weekend?"

My heart sinks to the soles of my Reeboks. My vacation had been booked for a year, the tickets purchased, clothes bought, time off from work secured. But how can I refuse her?

I draw a deep breath and sigh. "I'll see if I can. Call you tomorrow."

Chapter 6

Blizzard Winds

From Gina's Blog, April 27

I rub my gritty eyes and try to concentrate on the long, straight road ahead. Driving across Idaho and most of Montana has been no picnic. Now as I approach Baker, Montana, I watch the dark bank of clouds that are building over the prairie. I'd never experienced a blizzard before, and now I was driving into the teeth of one. I wonder if I have enough warm clothes.

Baker, the last town of any size in southeastern Montana, is built along the railroad tracks, a sleepy little burg that boasts of a wide Main Street, the Last Stand tavern, two drug stores, feed and hardware stores and grain elevators. At a dirty little gas station, the attendant eyes me speculatively and warns of the blizzard.

Already the wind is so strong I can hardly walk against it. Fine flakes of snow pelt my skin. South of Baker, the storm hits with a vengeance. I drive white-knuckled, my eyes locked on the road, muscles aching, exhaustion as heavy as the ten-ton semis I'd passed on the freeway crushing my senses. Clamping my jaws tightly, I turn up my music. Bulldog determination, which Dad said I'd inherited from the Lindsey clan, keeps me going. That, and the bitterly strong coffee I'd gotten in Baker.

Darkness edges the vault of the Montana sky and the wind pushes my bright green Toyota Corolla, which I'd named Georgie-girl, dangerously close to the drifted snow in the ditch. I turn on the headlights and crank up the heater. Bobbi had advised me to take Highway 7 south of Baker for about forty miles, turn left on the Mill Iron Road, then drive east thirty miles. The Lindsey ranch was near the Custer National Forest, only a few miles from the South Dakota border.

After I turn off the main highway, I fight to keep Georgie-girl on the gravel road. Swirls of snow, driven by the howling wind, mask the road. Time and again the tires slip on patches of ice, and the car swerves sideways. Every time it happens, I manage to correct the slide. At one point, it happens too fast, too hard. The car skids in a circle. "Oh, no. No, no!" I groan and cling to the steering wheel. And hit the brakes. Big mistake.

The car spins out of control. I take my foot from the brake, but the damage is done. The car careens toward the ditch. At the last moment, the tires grip gravel, whip the car in a complete circle and we stop. I pull back onto the road.

The snow lets up and the sky appears, grayish with purple edges, fringed with clouds. But I know it will close in again as suddenly as it cleared. Before it does, I need a rest. Just about anywhere is okay to stop as no one is behind me and there's nothing on the road.

A blast of wind whips the door from my hand when I open it and struggle to get out. The storm slices through my jacket, wildly grabs my hair and screams in my ears. The wide, empty spaces make my eyes ache. There are no houses, or old barns, or even telephone poles. Nothing, except the unending rolling fields, broken here and there with gullies where scraggly trees and a few bushes grow. To the southwest, a dark line of trees prick the horizon like a crew cut hair style -- that must be the Long Pines or maybe the Short Pines, one of the two state forests in the area.

A gnawing ache fills my heart and a dull fear sucks the breath from my spirit as the wind lashes my body. I feel naked and exposed. My cell phone reads, *No service.* I long for human contact – even a car passing, or a plane overhead! The wind wails like an evil beast over the rolling plains. *There's something evil in this country,* Aunt Roberta said. *Was the voice in the wind evil?* I shiver and tell myself to get a grip. What a quaint thought. Who talks about evil these days?

The heat inside the car is welcome. I'd programmed the GPS and even though it kept pointing east, I don't know if I can trust it out here. I check the map again. With no landmarks, I can't tell my location. I'd been driving for an hour -- had to be almost there.

A few miles later, I approach a crossroad and some abandoned buildings – what looks like an old white clapboard school and an empty gas station, leaning away from the wind. *Mill Iron*, the faded sign says. Incredible -- I was hoping for a Starbucks. My thoughts had turned to a warm supper and a hot bath when the headlights reveal a snowdrift completely blocking the road ahead. I can't swerve or brake in time to avoid it, so I slam down the gas pedal.

Snow flies over the Georgie-girl's hood. For an instant, it seems she'll break through the packed snow. She stops, her tires spinning futilely, her motor whining in frustration. I put it in reverse, back up and hit the gas pedal. We gain two inches. Again. Five inches. Over and over, I rock my poor little car, but it makes little headway. Finally we make none at all. I turn off the motor. Silence. Gusts of wind shake the car, bringing with it pelting snow. I zip my jacket, don my gloves and knitted hat, and try to open the door. It won't budge.

Scrambling across the seat, I try the other door. It's stuck, too. Stories that Uncle Elton used to tell about people being killed in cars buried in snowdrifts on the road haunt me. He said that the next driver coming through would often crash into the hidden vehicle. Still, Georgie's bright green. Surely the next car will see her. Yet what if she's covered with four feet of snow? I sigh heavily. If only I had some coffee.

Working the packed snow from around the door, I open it an inch. Progress. With freezing fingers I scoop more snow away until I can reach an arm outside. Awhile after that, I'm standing beside the car. In a sudden lull of the wind, I strain to hear the sound of another vehicle approaching.

Nothing. The front half of the car is buried in the drift, yet behind the car, the wind has swept the road bare. My hands and face are freezing; the cold seeps into my body like an insidious disease. I eye the road and think of walking. *No way.* Without Georgie, I might as well sign my death certificate.

The wind picks up again, and snow peppers my face like small shotgun pellets. I try to brush off the top of the car. It's no use. Snow covers it again in a heartbeat. *Is there something evil out there? Something that's determined not to let me through?* I hastily scramble back into the car. *Watch yourself, girl. Your imagination can get away from you out here.*

As darkness oozes in around me, a new fear strikes my heart. It's past eight in the evening. I haven't passed a single vehicle since I'd left the main road. I could be out here all night. Clamping my knees tightly to stop their trembling, I decide to wait until the cold is unbearable before I turn on the motor and flash the hazard lights.

In the meantime, I wrap myself in the afghan I brought from home, cocoon-like, and attempt to think warm thoughts. It doesn't work, even though the wool comforter gives me a sense of peace. It's the only thing I own of Mother's and I carry it with me wherever I go. I inhale slowly and exhale. A cloud of vaporized breath settles near the windshield.

So here I am, stranded in a snow bank and shivering with cold, when I could have been in warm, sunny Mexico. Unreal. I eat a few crackers and a piece of cheese, sipping water from a bottle. I eye the empty Starbucks coffee cup, as if I could will it into being full of the steaming, fragrant beverage. A grande-sized latte dances before my eyes.

When my fingers feel like frozen sausages and my toes ache, I turn on the motor and hazard lights and crank up the heater full blast. As the warm air hits my face, a thousand pins sting my skin. I ignore them and lean back against the seat. Tears well in my eyes, but I won't cry. I can hear Dad's voice saying, *"Be strong. Don't give in."* I snort and turn up the music. *Yeah, Dad. I'm glad you can't see me now. How stupid can you get?*

At least I can face it with the courage and dignity that he drilled into me, teaching me to fix my own problems, shoulder my responsibilities, refuse self-pity. And he practiced what he preached, especially after Mom left.

I can barely remember her cheerful face, laughing blue-green eyes, and a lilting, Irish voice. Everything else is gone; she left us when I was only four years old, and even though Dad suffered, he'd never once broken down in front of me. He never mentioned Mom again and he never cried. His voice still ringing in my ears, I turn down the heat and the music, lay my head back on the headrest and close my eyes.

Chapter 7

A Chancy Ordeal

Carter County, Montana

"What did you do about the leak in the dam?" The boss's voice came across the line with irritation rubbing it raw.

Butch sighed. "The leak in the dam is sealed. Problem solved."

There was a pause. Butch imagined the man lighting one of his expensive cigars. "You sure?"

"Yes, sir. Took care of it myself. No doubt. Dead as a doornail."

"Did you cover your tracks? You sure no one saw you?"

Butch jammed his cigarette into the ashtray and rolled up his window. The blizzard was bringing freezing temperatures and more snow than he'd thought it would. "It's a big country out here. You've been here, huntin'. Don't you remember? Nobody saw me, and nobody would care if they did. I can talk my way out of anything. Hell, I got the sheriff of two counties in my pocket. You can rest easy. No one suspects anything."

The man on the line let out his breath explosively. "Keep it that way, then. I want things tight over there until you plant. You got everything ready? The greenhouse okay?"

"Yes, sir." Butch wiped his forehead. How he hated reporting everything to this big time gangster! But he couldn't go back. He was in too deep. Besides, the crop was the most lucrative he'd ever grown, would put the ranch in the black by next fall, if all went well. And who would ever guess?

"Okay, cowboy. Just keep the goods coming my way and I'll be happy. We had a slight mishap over here, but I think we've got that covered."

Butch squirmed on the seat. He'd parked at the top of one of the highest buttes to get reception. Now he wondered if he could get down before the snow got too deep. "Oh, yeah? What happened?" He started the motor and turned up the heat.

"A couple of bright-eyed cops got a few of my guys. I'm sure they won't talk. One of the cops is headed your way. You can deal with her the same way you did the other problem."

"Her?"

"Yeah. Name's Gina Lindsey. She's on her way to find her uncle." He chuckled. "I'm sure you can deal with it, though. A nice, clean shot through the head and drop her down one of those convenient holes you have over there." He laughed.

Butch swallowed. He didn't like this business. "I ain't killing any more people, sir."

After a short pause, the man said, "I know where you live, Butch. I know who your wife is and where she works. I know where your son is. And where your daughter lives. I know where your grandkids go to school. You'll do what I say or they're dead meat. Do I make myself clear?"

Butch's eyes misted over and pain gripped his chest. It didn't take him long to come up with the answer. "Yes, sir."

"Well, I've got another call coming in. Talk to you later. Keep quiet."

"Yes, sir." He snapped shut his cell phone and drove down the narrow trail off the butte. Bucking through three-foot drifts, he wrestled the steering wheel and made it to the highway, turning toward home.

He wondered why he had ever been sucked into this whole deal. And what could he do to get out of it? Nothing. He was in. And he had to stay in or … He flipped on the radio. The consequences of disobedience were too much to even think. Yes, he would obey orders, and do the job thoroughly and well.

***

From Gina's Blog, April 27

Thump! Thump!

At first I think the sound is inside my head. After a bit, I realize it's coming from outside. I open my eyes and find I'm in an icy cocoon and I'm freezing. I turn the key, but there's no response. Out of gas. What *is* that pounding noise?

The door won't open. I yell and beat on the windows until my fist is bruised. Nothing. I scramble around frantically and push on every door. My frozen world remains intact. The pounding grows louder and stops suddenly. Silence. A gloved hand scrapes away the ice on the driver's side window, followed by a beam from a flashlight. I crawl to the driver's seat and bang on the window. The hand makes a fist with the thumbs-up gesture. Then it spreads out and up as if in question. Disappears. It returns, gripping a crowbar.

I huddle on the seat. At first I was elated that someone had found me and hadn't crashed into my car. But now, shivering uncontrollably, I wonder. Will Crowbar-man break the glass? Pry open the door? *Don't hurt my car. Please don't hurt my car!*

Crowbar motions for me to get back. *This is not good.* I crawl into the back seat and hold my breath. I would've prayed, but I remind myself sternly that there is no god. The crowbar crashes through the window. Glass flies everywhere. The gloved hand and a thick coat sleeve reach in. I grip the hand and shake it. Crowbar shows his face through the broken window. The hood of his heavy coat is pulled down so low I can only see his eyes, nose and frosted beard. His eyes are red-rimmed and watery.

He is not smiling. "I'm goin' to dig the snow away from the door." His breath comes in gasps. "You all right, miss?"

I nod, a wave of shame sweeping over me. That I had inconvenienced him, that I needed help, that I could not do it on my own, appalls me to the core. It's a few moments before I can answer him. "I'm fine. Just a little cold."

"Wrap up. This shouldn't take long."

Crowbar is a man of few words.

It seems to take forever. Shaking the glass from my afghan as best as I can, I wrap it around my body. My nose is cold. My feet are freezing. *Scrape, scrape, scrape.* His shovel sounds loud in the silence. At least the wind has died down.

Finally he pulls the door open. It creaks eerily, as if unwilling to allow me out of my prison. I grab my purse and scoot out. When Crowbar man tries to help me to my feet, I pull away and stand. For some crazy reason, I look up. Millions of stars spangle the dark expanse, stars so alive and beautiful they take my breath. I'd never seen anything like it. I stare at the night sky, mesmerized.

"You got what you need?"

I bring myself back to Crowbar and clutch my jacket tighter around my chest. "Yeah. For now. Thanks, mister. I might have been stranded all night if you hadn't come by. What will happen to my car? I don't want – "

"Your *car*, lady, will have to wait." He manages to impregnate extreme frustration into those few words as he leads the way to his truck.

I wonder about him. Will Crowbar take me to his cave and do what he wants with me? His rusted old pickup with its dented fender and broken windshield don't inspire confidence. I feel some reply is called for. "Well, I know I'll have to wait to get my car out. I don't suppose you have any coffee?"

He motions to the pickup. "Git in. Should be a ranch down this here road aways. I'll take you to git help, then I got stuff to do."

I wade through the snow, climb in the pickup and roll up the window. "You have a heater in this thing?"

He slams the door and starts the motor. "Sure." He turns it up. "Oh, just a sec." Leaping out, he rummages in the back and retrieves something that he carries to my car and sets on its roof. A yellow caution light blinks like a yellow eye in the night.

Crowbar gets in without looking at me. "Shore glad I spotted your car. Somethin' wasn't right about that drift. I think I caught a glimmer of your back windshield."

A long speech for him.

He reverses his truck about twenty feet, shifts, then accelerates, aiming straight for the snowdrift – and Georgie-girl. I think I scream. Just in time, he swerves to the left and bounces through the drift, missing my car.

The air escapes my lungs. "Well, Mr. Cowboy, or whoever you are … " The roar of the motor drowns out my words. I raise my voice to a yell. "I'm sorry I delayed you. I can pay for your time and gas, and any further expenses you might incur."

"That's okay, ma'am. Didn't cost me nothin'." He keeps his eyes on the road. "Where you from?"

"Spokane, but I'm originally from New York." The heat isn't doing much, only my toes are tingling. The rest of my body feels like an ice cube.

Crowbar is not talkative, but I don't care. I don't feel too chatty myself. Getting stuck in a drift, rescued by a redneck ranch hand, caught in an ill-smelling, rusty old pickup had not been on my agenda.

After about ten minutes, he breaks the silence and glances at me. "You gotta name?"

My teeth chatter like castanets. "G…Gina L…Lindsey. I'm g…going to visit my aunt and uncle, E…Elton and B…Bobbi Lindsey."

"Lindsey, huh. Their place is along here somewheres. Was just there yesterday. I go by Chance, by the way. Pleased to meet you, Miss Lindsey." To my surprise, he holds out a gloved hand.

I shake it and see laughter twinkling in his blue eyes. I'm not amused. "Want to fill me in on the joke? I could use a good laugh about now."

"Nothing. Just the look on your face like you didn't think I could be polite." He slows and turns into the Lindsey's long driveway. Under the cold light of the stars, a butte stands outlined against the sky. Lone Butte. I remember it from when I visited here so long ago.

"What do you do, Chance? Besides rescue people from the city who are stuck?"

"Right at the time, I'm lookin' for work. Got my application in at a guest ranch south of here. Maybe git me a job with forestry this summer. Aim to run my trappin' line next winter. I'm stayin' at a Bible camp right now, helpin' with the horses."

"So where's your coonskin cap?" I hug myself. He hadn't rolled up his window.

He stops in front of a ramshackle double-wide trailer house. "Here we are, Miss Lindsey."

"Gina."

"I'm sorry I was so short with you, Gina," he says in a gentler tone. "I'm in a hurry, and to tell the truth, I didn't want to stop. I had to go to Baker and wanted to make it back before the storm hit. " He tips his hat and smiles. "I'm glad I stopped. Hope to see you again."

"Thanks, Chance." I hop out of the truck. "Good luck with finding a job."

Chance, alias Crowbar, laughs, turns around and drives off.

I stand in the wind and watch his headlights disappear down the drive. As I approach the house, I realize it's dark, shrouded with trees and tall bushes. A gate leads through the hedge. Only one light shines dimly in the living room window.

Why isn't Aunt Roberta out here to greet me? Is she asleep?

For the second time that night, I feel the chill of a lonely, forsaken ghost sweeping through my soul. I open the creaky gate and start up the walk. Maybe I shouldn't have come. *And to think, I could have been in Mexico!*

Chapter 8

A Slammed Door

From Gina's Blog, April 27

Mounting the steps, I make my way across the deck, avoiding the gaps in the boards, and knock on the door. No response. Try the knob. It's unlocked. The entryway smells of dog and cow manure and mold. I hang my jacket over top of old ranch coats and enter the living room. "Aunt Roberta? Tim?" No answer. A clock is ticking loudly. "Anyone?"

A board creaks somewhere in the house. I think maybe it's coming from the hall that leads to the bedrooms. I lay my purse on the old sagging sofa and rub my raw hands. How I wish that my aunt had supper and hot coffee waiting!

In the living room, a wood stove stands along one wall, empty and cold. The sofa has a tattered quilt flung over it. It looks like the dog makes its bed there. Stacks of old magazines, newspapers and books fill every empty space. A massive elk head, mounted above the stove, looks down upon me sternly. The walls are full of family pictures and western scenes. I move toward the kitchen, still hoping I'd see dinner -- or at least coffee. The dining room table is clean and decorated with a vase of irises. In the kitchen, the counter is covered with boxes of cold cereal, a bowl of apples, appliances, a radio, a drainer with clean dishes and containers of small utensils. A night light glows near the stove.

Memories of that summer long ago flood my mind as I look around. Bringing my attention back to the present, I wonder, *where is everyone?* Have they *all* disappeared?

I creep down the hall toward the bedrooms. Another squeak. If I remember right, the master bedroom and a bath are on the left and a small bedroom and office on the right. A doorway at the end of the hall leads to the addition they'd built. Bobbi told me about it in great detail via email. It houses another guest room, Bobbi's quilting room and a bathroom.

As I continue toward the closed door of the office, I'm wishing I had my revolver. Is someone in there? What if Uncle Elton was murdered? What if he had something someone wanted to destroy? Would the murderer come to the house to find it? I crouch at the door, listening, thinking I hear the rustle of papers, the quiet footpad of stealthy feet.

My breath rasps in my throat as I grip the door knob. Slowly I turn the knob and inch open the door.

***

Bobbi shooed the last of the sheep into the pen, then turned. "C'mon, Tim. Let's get up to the house. Gina might have got here."

Tim shook back his blond hair and glared at her, his blue eyes rimmed with red as if he'd been crying. "I can't see why you called Gina. We can take care of things. What d'ya think she's goin' to do, anyhow?"

Bobbi straightened and closed the gate. All the sheep were inside, out of the blizzard. She sighed heavily and shook her head. "She's a *cop*. Maybe she can think of something we can't. I'm going up to the house. The sheep are safe. Are you coming?"

He shrugged and turned his back. "In a few minutes. Just gotta see if that one with the broken leg is okay."

The wind howled around the metal shed; its timbers creaked. Bobbi wished again that they'd found Elton, but of course they hadn't. Sheriff Crosby said he'd called all the hospitals and checked with the police as far away as Rapid City.

Rapid City. Desiree. The woman's face appeared before her like a nightmare from the past. Should she give the sheriff her name? But wouldn't that stir up a lot of talk in town? It seemed like it had just settled down.

She shook her head as she bent to the wind. No, some things were best left alone, and Desiree Pledger was one of them.

***

From Gina's Blog, April 27

Someone's in the room. I can feel them; hear the startled intake of breath. A sliver of light flickers from a pencil flashlight. I am just about to open the door wider when heavy footsteps thud across the carpet. A flurry of motion.

The door slams shut, catching my fingers. I yell, kick the door open and grasp my poor mangled appendages. Pain streaks up my arm and bends me double. My stomach churns. I'm suddenly dizzy. A window screeches open.

Fight past the pain! I burst into the room, flip on the light. The room's empty. The wind swooshes in, flinging the curtains aside. Someone swears just outside the window. I dash over to it, and peer into the darkness. A form is disappearing through the swirling white. Climbing onto the window sash, I jump out into the snow. Fall to my knees. Catch myself with my hand and reawaken the pain in my fingers. I follow the man, but he's getting away.

"Stop! This is the police!" The wind shoves the words down my throat. Besides, what can I do? My gun's in the car.

I run in the general direction of his flight, fighting through calf-high drifts. Snow falls sideways in great sheets of white. A few moments later, I hear a motor rev to life, then slowly fade away. *Darn!*

Turning back to the house, I hug myself, struggling against the wind that slices through my thin sweater, clear to my soul. *Failed! Again! What kind of a cop are you, anyway?*

Back in the house, I flip on lights as I return to the office. There I find papers scattered on the desk, the floor. The computer is turned on, the screen lit. Drawers are pulled out, their contents rifled, spilled. Boxes of computer equipment are dumped in heaps – floppy discs, flash drives, cords, cleaners, ink cartridges.

The front door slams. I jump and whirl around.

"Who's there?" It's a woman's voice.

Footsteps approach. I burst into the hall, barreling right into my aunt. "Oh, Aunt Roberta! It's you!"

"Gina! Why are you … I didn't see …" Bobbi flings her arms around me and gives me a hug. "You're here! What happened?" She peers over my shoulder and catches sight of the room. She lets her arms fall.

I hurry to explain. "Someone broke in, searched the office. Don't touch anything, Aunt Roberta! It was … an intruder. A thief."

"A thief?" Bobbi lifts her eyebrows and steps back. "But … we've never been broken into before. I've only known once when something was stolen around here. You say an intruder? I can't believe it."

I rub my arms. My fingers throb. "Well, it's the truth." I'm beginning to feel exasperated at having to explain myself. "I'm … so cold. I got stuck in a drift on the way here and I tried to stop that guy and he slammed my fingers in the door and … well …" To my shame, tears flood my eyes and roll down my cheeks.

Instantly Bobbi throws her arm around my shoulders. "Oh, honey! I'm so sorry! I ... I was thrown by the idea of a thief here, in this house. Come into the kitchen. I've got coffee and dinner's in the warming oven. We'll eat and you can tell me all about it."

"Wait. We have to call the sheriff. I'm not getting service on my cell. Can you call him, Aunt Roberta?"

"Just call me Bobbi, Gina," she says in her abrupt manner, her blue-green eyes snapping impatiently. "My land, Roberta makes me sound eighty years old. Yes, I'll phone Mike. Sit down." Her short salt-and-pepper hair sticks out from her head in every direction, and she's wearing a shirt and jeans that are rumpled as if she'd slept in them and a baggy, faded sweater that hangs lifelessly on her thin shoulders.

I sit at the breakfast bar and gratefully accept the cup she pours for me. While Bobbi makes the call, the front door opens again with a windy *swoosh!* Someone stomps snow from boots, then thuds into the kitchen. It's Tim.

"Hi!" I stand and greet my cousin with a half-smile.

He casts me a hurried glance and turns away. "Hi, Gina. Who's Mom calling?" His slouching posture and indifferent manner don't hide the panic that I see in his eyes.

"The sheriff. Someone broke into the house and searched the office." I reinstall myself at the breakfast bar and sip my coffee, carefully keeping my voice neutral. I'm a pro at the game of cool indifference. Tim isn't even in my league.

He wheels and heads down the hall.

I leap to my feet. "Don't go in the office! You can't touch anything." But he'd already disappeared through the door. I follow on his heels. "Don't touch anything," I repeat. "It's a crime scene."

"I know. I watch TV, too." He shoots me an angry glare from his strange pale eyes and paces the room. "He got out the window, huh. Couldn't a big time cop from New York stop him?" Sarcasm drips from his tone as he glances out the window. The wind lifts his long blond hair from his shoulders.

"I didn't exactly have time." I come up behind him and change my tone, suddenly weary of playing his games. "I'm sorry, Tim. He got away. Notice anything that's missing?"

"No." He slams the window shut. Whirling, he elbows past me. "I don't know why you came. It's just stupid."

I return to the kitchen and my coffee. Tim had always been weird, with his almost albino coloring and asthma problems. Well, he doesn't want me around, obviously. I grin. He can teach *me* a thing or two about outright rudeness.

Bobbi hangs up. "Mike said he couldn't get through the storm. It's worse in by Ekalaka. He'll come out first thing in the morning. Now, Gina. Tell us your story. Where's your car? What happened?"

"I got stuck in a drift about five miles away. Some guy found me and brought me here. When I came inside, no one was around. I thought …"

"I'm goin' home, Mom." Without looking at Bobbi, Tim snatches a cookie from the jar and turns away. At the door, he shrugs into his coat and pulls on his boots.

Bobbi brings a pan of lasagna from the oven. "You don't want any supper? It's your favorite." It's almost as if she is pleading for something from him … attention? respect? love? But she wasn't going to get it. Tim's too much into himself.

"I'll get some later." He slams the door on his way out.

Bobbi sets the pan carefully down on two knitted hot pads and shakes her head. "I'm sorry, Gina. He's so upset about his dad."

"Have you heard anything?"

"No. Yesterday we had a crew searching out here. With dogs and everything." She sits down on another stool as if her legs won't hold her up any longer. Her face sags with weariness, grief and shock and her eyes are red-rimmed and dull.

"We've gone over every square inch of the immediate area around the house and barns. Even went down to where he'd been fixing fence the day he disappeared. Not a trace. Like he just … vanished. Maybe he was raptured." She attempts a smile. "But if that happened, I hope I would go, too."

It takes me a little while to sort out what *raptured* means. Then it comes to me -- Bobbi and Elton, who are devout Christians, believe that Jesus is coming in the air to take them to heaven alive. I help myself to the lasagna and resist saying what I think of *that* particular teaching.

Bobbi says a prayer, and we begin eating. Between bites, I finish the recital of my adventures. When I mention my rescuer, Chance, she nods.

"New fella around here, but he's really nice. Staying over at the Bible camp. He came and worked all day. It's sure a good thing he saw you before he plowed into that drift. We would've had another funeral."

I try to laugh it off. "Me and funerals don't mix, Bobbi. I don't do them and don't want one when I go. Would hardly even go to Dad's …" My throat constricts. Gosh, I wish my body didn't betray me like this! I carry my plate and cup to the sink.

She follows me. "I'm sorry, Gina. I guess I'm being morose. Been thinking about a … memorial service for Elton if …" She puts the casserole in the refrigerator. Suddenly she turns to me and impales me with a direct stare. "I wish we could've come for your Dad's funeral." She sighs. "I'm sure you know how hard it is to get help in the winter.

And … well, New York's so far away. Anyway, I want you to know that we've prayed for you. Your dad's in heaven. I know that."

A cold hand of bitterness squeezes my heart. "Yeah, right." I hear sarcasm in my voice. It rivals Tim's. Avoiding her eyes, I run hot water into the sink and squirt dish soap into it. *How can she know that Dad's in heaven?*

Dad went to a Billy Graham evangelistic crusade when I was thirteen and said he accepted Christ into his heart. I didn't know what that meant and didn't really care, just so long as he left me alone. Being thirteen was a full time occupation -- all I wanted was to escape in my room and listen to my music. We went to School School for awhile, yet when I was older, I quit going.

In college, I'd learned the truth – that faith is foolishness at best and a crutch at worst. I decided that God was either impotent or wicked, for even though I'd prayed earnestly for Mom to return to us, she never did. So if God didn't need me, I surely didn't need Him. If there *was* a god.

I rinse the dishes and place them on the rack. "Is there a tow truck in Ekalaka? I'd like to get my car out of that drift, if it's not too much bother." The words are hard, yet I don't mean them to be cruel.

Bobbi's hands shake as she hangs up the dish towel on the oven door handle. "They probably can't make it, either. I'll fire up the truck. We have a plow on the front. Do you want to go? There's not much you can do."

"I'll come." I empty the sink and dry my hands. "Just let me get a couple more sweaters and my mittens. I'm not used to this weather, you know." I touch Bobbi's arm and smile into her eyes. It's the closest thing to an apology that I can muster.

Bobbi laughs. "I've got a heavy coat with a hood you can borrow. And some boots. Are your fingers okay? Do you want an ice pack?"

"Maybe later."

"Right. I'll call Tim and fire up the outfit. You stay inside and keep warm until we're ready to go."

Getting the car home turns out to be easier than I had thought it would be. Tim's sullen attitude disappears when he drives the truck. He pulls my car from its bed of snow, puts some gas in the tank, and follows me home. When I thank him, he shrugs and offers to take it into town when the weather clears to get the window fixed.

By the time I get my suitcases to the guest room in the addition, an ice pack on my aching fingers and a pain reliever in my system, I'm ready to crash. I want to sleep, tell myself I *must* sleep, but my mind whirls like the wind outside. I climb out of bed, get a drink of water and tiptoe to the office.

There I turn on the light and examine everything in the room, looking for a clue. To my disappointment, the customary snubbed out cigarette, the stub of a theater ticket or a shred of paper on which was written an important telephone number is missing.

As I return to my room and pull the covers up to my chin, a lingering sense of guilt dogs my consciousness, as if Elton's ghost walks the halls and taps on the bedroom door, begging me to try harder.

What kind of a cop are you, anyway?

With Dad's words rolling around in my mind like the lyrics of a stupid song, I turn over and finally drift off to an uneasy slumber.

Chapter 9

A Cold, Lonely Landscape

From Gina's Blog, April 30

On Saturday, Sheriff Mike Crosby arrives at the front door with an affable grin on his ruddy face. His eyes twinkle as he holds out a massive hand when Bobbi introduces us, saying he was from Alabama and moved to Carter County twenty years ago. I shake his hand, feeling dwarfed by his size. He's tall, broad-shouldered and has muscles on muscles.

Bobbi leads the way to the office.

I follow, impressed by his thorough manner as he proceeds at the scene. Despite his country ways and slow drawl, the sheriff possesses a fine procedural mind and an effective style in detective work. It doesn't take him long to dust for fingerprints on a few key locations. When everything comes up clean, he shoots me a glance that says *a professional job.*

"What do you make of it?" Bobbi leads the way to the kitchen. She pours coffee for him and serves a plate of her famous caramel rolls.

His eyes light up when he see the rolls. "Thank you, ma'am. Can't say yet what it means. I find it curious that they'd break in here lookin' for somethin'. Did you say Elton was actin' strange recently?" He bites into a roll and sighs contentedly.

She shrugs. "Well, I can't rightly say. He met with some men over to the Long Horn at Buffalo a time or two and wouldn't say what they talked about. I wouldn't go so far as sayin' it was *strange.*" She turns her back to him, and busies herself making more coffee.

He nods. "Fair enough. Wal, since nothin' seems to be missin', I'll write this up as a break and enter, although we can't even do that strictly speakin' unless the door was locked and I believe Gina said it was open."

I bend my head. "I did."

Bobbi glares at him. "We never lock our doors! You know that."

Mike holds up his hand. "Whoa. I don't mean nothin', Bobbi. Just sayin' that even if we caught the culprit, we might have trouble gettin' a conviction. Wal, I better be shovin' off. I'm shore glad the wind stopped blowin' that snow around. Good day, Gina. Nice to meet you. Cap'n Jed Matthews called when you was on your way. Said you was a plum smart agent."

"I bet he said smart *ass* agent." I grin, and he returns it with a smile. I like this guy. "Nice to meet you, too, sheriff. Keep me informed on the case. I can do some investigating from Spokane. The internet is a wonderful tool to link with other police departments. Here's my card. Let me know if you have anything you want checked out."

"Wal, we're gettin' into the twenty-first century around here, too. I'll let you know." He tucks the card in his front shirt pocket.

After he leaves, Tim comes over from his trailer. Together we straighten the office. "What about your dad's desk, Tim? His papers. Have you checked those?"

Tim nods. He looks and sounds tired -- I wonder what keeps him up all hours of the night, for I'd seen his light burning late. "We've been through every blasted thing. Even his truck." He rubs his forehead. "He kept most of his records in a little notebook. I'd transfer the figures onto the computer. I've gone through all his notebooks. There's nothing."

The despair in his tone melts my heart. I want to put my arm around his drooping shoulders and reassure him of my concern, yet I know he won't appreciate it. Not yet.

"Let me know if you find anything."

I watch him trudge back to his trailer. Throwing on a coat, I pull on some boots and pick up a pair of mittens. Outside, the cold wind burns my cheeks. I yank the hood up and head for the equipment shed. I want to get a feel for Elton again – how he was thinking, where he might have gone.

Inside the metal building, I step over motor parts and old tires and tangled hoses. A water truck stands in one bay and in another, the green combine towers to the ceiling. I climb the steps up into the cab of the combine and sit in the driver's seat, breathing the dusty grain smells.

Elton had taken me out harvesting when I was here that summer. I remembered saying, "Let me steer." And he had. Tears spring to my eyes. I wipe them away impatiently. If Elton's alive, he doesn't need tears. He needs clear thinking and sharp detective work.

I find no inspiration, though, as to his present location. *Is he still alive? If it's foul play, why would someone murder him?*

On the way back to the house, I pause to admire the view. The sky is pale blue and painted with purple and pink streaks above a bank of low clouds on the western horizon. I inhale the crisp, clean air and scrunch through the snow. I love the piles of drifted, molded snow -- it looks like mounds of meringue or ice sculptures, glazed with sugar, tinted with the colors of the sunset. I grab my camera and snap some pictures.

Bobbi makes my favorite dinner that evening – chicken enchiladas. As I enter the kitchen, ravenously hungry, I sniff the air appreciatively. "Bobbi, you shouldn't have."

She laughs. "Your last night here, dear. Sit down."

Tim joins us that evening. When the food is on the table, they bow their heads, join hands, and Bobbi says grace. Then she says, "I checked on the computer and it looks like the storm is clearing out."

I help myself to the food, passing by the cheese biscuits that look and smell delicious. It would mean a ten-mile run if I ate one. "I wish I had a better coat. The jacket I brought isn't warm enough if I get stuck again."

A ghost of a smile wavers on her lips. "Oh, honey, we have lots of coats. Elton has one that's really warm. I'll get it for you after we eat."

"I can mail it back to you."

"No, you can *bring* it back." Bobbi smiles, the first real smile I'd seen. "I want you to come and help us out this summer. Tim and I will be busy with the ranch work and we'll need someone to run errands and cook. Please come."

I set down my glass and suppress my excitement. Bobbi's given me the perfect reason to return. "I'll see what I can do. I might be able to manage a few weeks off, maybe even a month."

After we clean up, I follow her to the master bedroom where she opens the closet and selects a heavy sheepskin jacket. "Here. You can use this one." She glances down at the disarray of boots and shoes on the closet floor.

"Elton's very neat, except for how he keeps his shoes. No matter how many times I remind him, he brings his muddy boots into the house."

I pick up one of the boots. "I'd like to clean these. May I?"

"By all means, dear. Do what you want."

I carry his shoes and two pairs of boots to the garage. Bobbi provides me with leather cleaner and soft rags. After she leaves, I find pint-sized baggies in the kitchen. As I clean each shoe, I scrape a bit of dried mud into the baggie and label it with a felt tip pen. The dirt samples will go to the crime lab in Pierre, South Dakota, for testing. After I get the report, I'll notify Mike. I don't know what I'm hoping to find, but anything's better than doing nothing. Besides, I have to learn the truth about Elton.

Early the next morning, I carry my bags to the front porch. "Thanks for everything, Bobbi." I hug her close.

"Thank *you* for coming. You can't know how much your being here has helped. I'll pray for a safe journey home."

"I'll keep working on Elton's case, every spare moment I have. He's alive; I feel it. He'll come back. Hang onto that hope."

Bobbi's face loses color and she sways. I steady her, and she pushes me away with a weary hand and a weak smile. "I'm okay. Just feeling a little dizzy, dear. Bye."

"Get some rest." I climb in the car and start the motor.

Bobbi lifts her arm in farewell and smiles.

Tears sting my eyes and blur my vision. I return the wave and drive down the lane between the sculpted drifts of glistening snow. *I will find Uncle Elton, if I die doing it. For Bobbi's sake. For my own peace of mind.* I exhale slowly. *I'll show them what kind of a cop I am.*

Chapter 10

Grow Patch

Short Pines, South Dakota, May 15

Chance McNeil eased his sorrel mare, Cyndi, from the horse trailer. He tossed the saddle on her and tightened the cinch. She nickered and looked about, her nostrils wide. He chuckled. "No, girl. We're not roundin' up the dogies today."

He'd brought her to Montana this spring and was glad he'd done it. She was a Morab, which meant a combination of spirit, speed, staying power and good looks. He could depend on her to get him where he was going and back safely.

Today he was exploring the Short Pines, a national forest that spanned the state line between South Dakota and Montana. It was his day off at the ranch where he was employed. Since early April, ever since the snow melted, he'd been exploring the national forests, starting first in the Long Pines and then working south. The forestry map he'd gotten from the office in Camp Crook was creased and torn, but still readable.

He'd thought often about the red-headed girl from Spokane he rescued in the drift last month and wondered what she was doing. Once in a while he stopped by the Lindsey Ranch and offered his help. Bobbi was grateful for an extra hand, especially when it came to shearing the sheep or fixing fence. Chance heard that neighbors had pitched in to help on all aspects of ranch work. If Elton was found, he'd come home and find his spread running successfully.

He rubbed Cyndi's head and studied the sky. Thunderheads piled up on the horizon, and the air was thick, humid. Mounting, he gathered the reins and settled into the saddle. "Let's go, girl. We've got lots of trails to cover today and the weather could turn mean."

She settled into a comfortable gallop as they followed the narrow road down Grandma Schang Draw. Halting at the top of JK Butte, he pulled out his glasses as Cyndi blew. There was a ranch in the valley – the map said it was the Holcombe place. He moved the glasses up and down the valley and studied the layout of the land.

Once off the butte, he aimed north on an old logging road. Brush and fireweed, now blooming with a purple pink flower, grew among trees blackened by a fire that had raged through here several years ago. It was the kind of country bears and mountain lions loved.

A little over an hour later, he pulled the horse to a halt. A barbed wire fence cut across the road. He shoved back his hat and brought out his map from his shirt pocket. This area was marked forestry land – nobody should be fencing it off. He dismounted and led Cyndi off the old road and tied her to a small sapling. "I'll be right back, girl. Now don't whinny, okay?"

He crept to the fence and studied it for some time. Eight feet high, chain link. Right and left, it led off into the forest, topped with a roll of electric wire. There were probably cameras hidden along it, too. Prickles descended his back. Carefully picking his way, watching carefully for guard platforms built into the trees, he followed the fence right, up a steep, brushy hill. Then down again.

There. A guard tower. It was built high, maybe twenty feet off the ground. He watched it, but no one was around. The sun was directly overhead. Sweat soaked his shirt. He wished he'd brought his water flask.

With his back against a tree stump, he breathed deeply the resinous scent of pine and fir. A crow cawed raucously overhead and the wind soughed through the trees. Sheer rock cliffs lined a hidden valley. Just the kind of place he'd been looking for, yet it seemed abandoned.

He continued following the fence, his senses alert, his hand ready to the revolver he carried in a shoulder holster. He'd heard there were caves along here. Someday he'd come back and explore them. A wind storm had leveled one of the towering Ponderosa pines that stood sentinel on top of the cliffs. It crashed across the fence just twenty feet ahead. Praying there weren't any cameras along here, he mounted the tree and worked his way down it and across the fence.

When he jumped to the ground, he stood on the brink of the canyon. Following a deer trail, he descended to the bottom. Yellow rock walls closed in from both sides, sprouting bushes that bristled like an old man's eyebrows. A rustling sound in the bushes startled him, and he scanned the tops of the cliffs. Was it a cougar? He froze. No. Nothing.

A little further down, the canyon widened into a small valley, containing maybe five acres. In its center, a creek meandered lazily through high weeds and dragonflies flitted among the cattails. Following a rough road, he discovered soggy ground where the creek flowed silently through limpid, mossy pools.

He stopped. A large cultivated plot spread on each side of the creek. Yes, just as he suspected. A grow patch -- an old one that had lain dormant all winter. No one had been here to till the ground for a new crop. The area was strewn with the wintered-over remains of plants and the imprint of irrigation pipes that must have run from the creek. He picked up a dried leaf, squashed it in his fingers, and sniffed. *Marijuana!*

Bringing a small digital camera from his pocket, he snapped several shots. The patch was big enough for maybe a couple thousand plants. Quickly multiplying in his head, he whistled. The crop would be worth a couple million dollars, maybe more.

When he returned the camera to his pocket, something buzzed past his head. The explosion of a gun echoed off the canyon walls. *A bullet!* He ducked and looked around for the gunman. Another bullet zinged close to his cheek. He scrunched down, dashed to a boulder, rolled and threw himself behind it. Craning his neck, he tried to determine the direction of the shots. In the canyon it was impossible to tell.

He waited, listening. Crows squawked and flapped away, yet no sound came from the trees across the valley. Hunched over, he sprinted to a cover of rocks where he paused to wipe sweat from his forehead and catch his breath.

After a steep ascent up the bank, he squatted behind a bush. The crows returned to their nest. A squirrel scolded from the top of a box elder tree. A large black beetle whirred past. There were no more shots, no motors, no footsteps. Wait. There by the big pine on the other side of the valley. Movement. A cowboy hat. Chance glanced around. This brush gave him no protection at all from another bullet.

Where could he go? Up the cliff, further into the trees? But he'd have to crawl, exposed, for twenty feet. He'd never make it. Looking again across the canyon, he glimpsed the man circling the top of the rocks, moving into a position for a clear shot.

He knows where I am! I've gotta move! Trusting that the assailant would be busy traversing the trail and not be ready for a shot, Chance scooted downhill toward another outcropping of rocks and boulders that lay strewn on the lip of the canyon. *From there I can* –another bullet sliced the air, followed by the report of the high powered rifle. Something tore into his leg.

Darn! He scrambled the last ten feet and lay panting, gripping his pant leg where already a flow of bright red blood stained his torn jeans. He whipped out his kerchief and wrapped it around his calf, wincing from the pain. Thank God it was just a flesh wound and hadn't broken the bone.

His assailant was cautious and kept to a high ridge where trees and brush shielded his movements. Chance heard the snap of twigs. The man was getting closer. He had to move. Feeling exposed, like a bullet would rip through his chest any moment, he scuttled on hands and knees back up the slope. Just as he found shelter behind a big fir, another bullet thudded heavily into the trunk.

He didn't stay behind the tree. Couldn't. He thought of exchanging gun fire, but his little revolver wouldn't do much good unless the man was close and he had a clear shot. Wouldn't happen. If he kept this game up, he was going to get killed. Probably buried in the grow patch below. Use him for fertilizer.

It would serve him right. What a fool he was to come up here like a crazy tourist! What was he thinking? He knew the cartels had sophisticated surveillance equipment, gun power and man power. They could buy whatever they wanted – computer systems, submarines, jets. Heck, they could buy *governments* with the money they raked in. How could he have thought his efforts would bring them down?

His negative thoughts were not helping his desperate situation and he prayed that the man with the rifle didn't have friends down on the road where he'd left Cyndi. Blood soaked his pants leg. He couldn't wait until he had lost so much blood that he couldn't function. With a hurried prayer for help, he limped to the next tree, and the next. He made a dash to a jumble of boulders and on to a fringe of thick bushes.

Keep moving! His leg hurt more than he wanted to admit, but he shoved the pain aside and concentrated. Sweat ran into his eyes. He brushed his hand across his forehead and descended the last few feet to where Cyndi was tied. The horse tossed her head and nickered when she saw him.

He patted her neck. "It's okay, girl," he said in a low voice. "We're gitten outta here."

He mounted and kicked Cyndi to a fast lope down the road. To his relief, there were no other gunmen and no outfits parked on the road. When he arrived at his pickup, he trailered the horse as fast as he could and hoped they wouldn't get a plane in the air before he could get out. He glanced at his leg and decided against tending to it now.

He had to keep his cover or he might as well keep driving all the way to Washington. He was dead meat once the cartel found out who he was. What should he do now? Should he report this to the sheriff? What if the local cops were bought off? Or there was a mole in the sheriff's office? Whom could he trust? Not a single soul.

Settling his hat on his head, he put the truck into gear and hightailed it back to the ranch.

Chapter 11

Planting Trouble

Carter County, June 5

Maegan Peters settled into her desk chair and sighed. It was Monday. She sorted through the mail and checked her computer. Read her email. Sipped her coffee.

The big double doors opened, and a shaft of sunlight penetrated the gloom of the front lobby. It was made to look like the waiting room of a Jiffy Lube – hard plastic chairs along the wall, a TV set, coffee and magazines on a low table in the center. A visitor wouldn't know that the TV hid a security camera and a guard with a semi-automatic rifle sat on the other side of the wall. And he did not doze or flip through magazines. He meant business.

Two men entered the room. Both wore wide-brimmed straw hats, soiled white shirts and patched jeans. But there the similarities ended. Manuel Sancho, or Manny as he was called, was tall and thin and had a perpetual frown on his lean face. He headed straight to the inside door, pushed in key code numbers, and after a buzz, entered.

Jesus, pronounced *Yasus*, Manteo was shorter and chubbier. He lolled into the office and grinned at Maegan. *"Buenos dias, senorita.* How are you to-day?"* His English was precise and correct, yet his words held an accent. He perched on the edge of the desk and casually rolled a cigarette. He always had a funny story to tell about his two youngest children, Jilly and Roberto.

Maegan glanced at him, then returned her gaze to the monitor. "Yasus, the boss is in a hurry, so no fooling around today. If you don't get the job done today, he will be unhappy. And we don't want to make him unhappy, do we?"

He groaned. "No. Grumpy boss makes grumpy wife. Then we do no fun to-night." He managed a chuckle, but when she didn't even bless his attempt at humor with a smile, he shrugged and turned away. "Aw, right. Aw, right. I go. If I die from heat, send my body to Me-hi-co."

"The boss will do something worse than that to your soul if you fool around anymore. I swear! You'd try the patience of a saint!"

The man slouched through the door without a second look.

A few minutes later, Butch flung open the outside door and hurried to the desk, uncoiling and snapping a long whip he carried. "Are the plants boxed? We have to go! Now!"

She couldn't help but cringe away from him, yet she didn't want to show the fear that crawled up her throat. She shoved back her chair and gave him a level gaze, slowly shaking her head. "Why don't you have some coffee, boss? Take a load off your feet. You know you can't hurry these people. They do the best they can, and ..."

"I don't want to hear it! I've been hasselin' them every day this week. The trucks are here. We're ready to load. Why don't they have the plants boxed?"

She stood slowly and finished her coffee. Her flesh crawled at the sight of him. How could she have thought she was in love with this man who stood red-faced before her, this personification of evil? This man who had no more morality than a dog?

Once she'd thought he was handsome. And in a way, he was. He'd picked her up off the street in Rapid City when she was at the end of her rope. She'd believed his lies about helping her make a new start in life. He was impressed that she spoke Spanish like a native. Maegan rinsed out her cup at the small sink and shook her head. *New start. Buy that, baby, and I'll sell you a bridge.*

Yet now she had the upper hand. The man, she discovered, was married. With kids. And he cared about his reputation in this miserable corner of Montana. *Ah, ha.* One could profit with knowledge such as that. To stay alive, you had to be smart, you had to be fast, and you had to know how to defend yourself. She carried a revolver on her belt and a can of Mace in her backpack. She said it was for varmints. And it was – the two-legged kind.

Another worry surfaced. She knew he smoked the weed they grew, but lately he'd been edgy and violent. Had he started using something stronger? Heroin? That would explain his mood swings.

"Give us a couple of hours, okay? I've got everyone in there. Even little Roberto."

Butch punched in the code numbers on the door. "What's he doin' in there? I've told you I don't want those brats in with my plants! If he …" He disappeared through the door and with a sigh, she followed him.

The room she entered was humid and warm. The smell of damp soil, chemicals and tender new plants filled the air. Long aisles of rough wooden tables stretched the length of the immense building. They were crowded with baby marijuana plants, nearly two feet high. Long rows of fluorescent lights hung over each table. These could be raised as the seedlings grew. Water was brought along the ceiling in pipes that descended to the table tops and provided moisture in a fine mist. A generator hummed outside, night and day, providing the power for the giant greenhouse.

They'd already set aside five hundred male plants. These would stay in the greenhouse and die in about two weeks. When their pods were full, they would be harvested for seeds. The other sturdy plants, females, would be set out in the ground carefully prepared for them. It was all ready, except for boxing up the plants in the cardboard cartons that were placed at the end of each table.

Manny and his family, along with Yasus and his, plus the old woman, Angelina, five adults and ten children in all, had boxed about a third of the plants yesterday. Laughter erupted from the two youngest children, Jilly and Roberto, when a pipe burst and a fountain of water descended on Yasus' head. They were holding plants, ready to hand to their mother.

Butch loped down the aisle, infuriated. "What're the kids doing in here? Get 'em out! Now!" He snapped the whip. "And get that pipe fixed! I ain't wastin' water!" He brought the whip down again, right in front of the people who stared at him with wide, frightened eyes.

Startled, both Jilly and Roberto jumped. The plants they were holding flew through the air and landed in a dirty heap at Butch's feet.

He leaped over the mess and descended on the children. Jilly was closest and took the full brunt of the whip over her shoulders. It cut her shirt open and a red welt appeared. Screaming in terror and pain, she cringed on the floor.

"There! Take that, you stinkin' brat! And this!" Butch raised the whip to strike again, his face mottled red and eyes bulging.

Jilly's mother, Rosa, wailed aloud and yelled something in Spanish. The whip descended, but it never reached Jilly's tender skin. Yasus stepped forward and grasped Butch's arm. His flow of Spanish was interspersed with English swear words and his anger rivaled the boss's. Jilly was his pride and joy; he gloried in her golden hair, her quick mind and happy smile.

Butch broke free from the restraining hand, kicked Yasus in the stomach and when the man bent over, applied the whip to his back. Manny, who was working two aisles over, yelped loudly and leaped to the fray. The teenagers, Maria, Juanita, and Ramone threw themselves toward Yasus as if to protect him. Ramone raised a trowel threateningly toward Butch. Even Elberto, who was only ten, clenched his fists and hammered on the boss' leg.

Maegan darted forward. She had to divert Butch's attention and that wasn't easy when he mad. She grabbed his shirt and pulled him around. She prided herself that she was as strong, maybe stronger, than most men. His head jerked. He focused suddenly on her and she saw that at least she'd diverted his attention to herself. "Boss! You can't do this!"

"Who're you to tell me what I can and can't do?" His words were the slurred snarl of a wild animal. He glared at her with the look she knew so well – that of a bull about to charge.

"You ... you can't, boss! It'll destroy more plants!" She didn't release her hold and led him down the aisle, away from the Mexicans. "I'll clean up the mess. Repot the plants. There were only two that spilled."

He shook his head and glanced back. "You'd better. I'll ... I'll kill every one of those wetbacks ... if they give me ... more trouble."

"Just calm down. Come into the office. I'll fix things. I promise." She relaxed her fingers and led the way to the office. Once there, she gently nudged him to sit in the chair and poured him a cup of coffee. "Now. We'll get the plants boxed in no time. There's already a truckload ready. Why don't you start with those? When you get back, we'll have another load ready to go. I'll help, that way it'll go faster."

He sighed and wiped his face. "I'll take it out of your pay if there's any damage."

"Yes, sir. Now go see about the truck and I'll get to work. Okay?"

"Get in there, then." He stood. "You deal with those ... fools. It's beyond me." Grumbling, he left the building.

She reentered the greenhouse. Already Marguerita Sancho had repotted the plants. The others resumed their work silently with flying hands and closed faces. Little Jilly was sobbing. Juanita held her and stroked her hair. Maegan made a mental note to bring the little girl a gift. A soccer ball. She'd been wanting one lately.

When they saw her coming, smiles broke out on their faces. *Gracias, Senorita*, several of them said quietly.

She shrugged. "*De nada. Como esta la hija?*"

Yasus looked up. "*Si.* She is better."

As she bent to help them, she had to admit she liked these people. They were illegal aliens, unable to get work elsewhere, shipped in from Mexico by the cartel. Yet they were good people. They loved their children, had a sense of humor and endured the shame of slavery with a kind of noble dignity that went straight to her heart.

Carefully she lifted a female marijuana plant from the table, swathed it in a sheath of plastic, and set it in the box. Slavery. Wasn't she a slave, too? Yes, she had to admit it. She was as bound to this operation as any of the Mexicans. More so, for she knew too much. Her life would not last very long if she escaped.

How she wanted to leave! It was an ache that filled her days and nights. Yet there was no hope for her. No rainbow over her sky. No silver lined clouds. She might as well bury her dreams along with these plants. She'd sealed her doom when she came here in the first place.

And now she knew she would never escape.

Chapter 12

Hired Guns

From Gina's Blog, June 10

As I drive a dark blue Honda pickup into Ekalaka, Montana, I'm thinking about my last night in Spokane. Nick took me to our favorite place, Joe's Fiery Wings on North Division. After we ordered, he gave me an intense blue-eyed glare. "Hey, it might not be too smart to drive your car to Montana. Why don't you take my pickup?"

I knew it was a generous offer as he adored his Honda pickup. At first I demurred, but when he pressed the issue, I accepted. Gladly. It was four-wheel drive and who knows what kinds of roads I'd encounter? He said he'd bring my Toyota down in a couple of weeks.

"Don't blow my cover, Bailey."

He laughed, his eyes twinkling. "I can pose as your boyfriend."

"Yeah, I guess that'd work. But you couldn't stay at the house. Aunt Roberta isn't going to want you living there with me. They're rather conservative in Carter County."

"God forbid! D'ya think I want to *sleep* with you?" He grinned and tipped back his beer. "Conservative, huh. More so than in Spokane?"

"Oh, yes. Blue collar Republicans to the core. I think they all go to church. And they know everything about you. If you swat a fly, it's reported in the newspaper."

He mused on that for awhile. "Tell you what. I'll bring my tent. Camp out. Surely there's a park around there somewhere. Say I'm fishing. We can make it work. You know Cap doesn't want you to do this alone. Agents have a way of dying when they try to take down the cartels."

I took a swallow of beer and shrugged. "So you want to be the hero and die along with me?" I wiped my lips and sighed. "All right, darn it. Just give me a couple of weeks to get settled, okay? Nothing's going to happen in that length of time."

He leaned forward and touched my hand. I could smell his after shave and see concern in his eyes. "I'm not so sure about that. You have a way of stirring up trouble. C'mon, let's go. We have time for a movie."

Good ole Nick. I'm going to miss him.

Now I top a low hill and apply the brakes. Below me spreads the tiny town of Ekalaka. I haven't seen it since that summer I was a teenager, yet it seems the same, like time's stood still. Even the same large dog is asleep unconcernedly in the middle of the street.

A quaint little museum, built of beautiful slabs of rock from the area, stands solidly on the left of the wide main street and on the right I see a modern-looking bank. I pass what I suppose is a garage of some sort, made of yellow-painted brick, then the Guest House motel, only it's more like a hotel, sandwiched next to the Main Street market. Next is the Wagon Wheel café, and after that, the Old Stand Bar and Grill. Legend has it that the town grew up because a man who had a wagonload of beer broke down here.

Benches on the sidewalk provide a handy resting place for the old men who patronize the bar. Across the street from the bar is a large apartment building for senior citizens.

The two old men who lounge on the bench today watch curiously as I drive past. I lift a hand in greeting, remembering that everyone waves in this country. They nod. I know from what Aunt Roberta's told me that they will report to the sheriff about the strange outfit they'd seen in town, driven by a red-headed woman. Good. Now I won't have to give Mike a call.

I make a circle of the town and pass the Ekalaka Bible Church, tall steepled and built of rock, too. Obviously people in this country don't want things blowing away. I pass a small motel, drive around a pothole and then I run out of town and I'm driving again across the rolling plains.

This time there are no storms or snow drifts, just miles and miles of country, so green and beautiful that it takes my breath away.

Yellow clover lines the highway and among slender birches grows a tall purple flower that I have no name for.

A little ways out of town, I pass a sign advertising Living Waters Bible camp and I remember that fellow, what was his name? Oh, yeah. *Chance.* Is he still working there? I wonder if I'll see him and crane my neck when I spot a line of horses with young riders. Two cowboys shepherd the group, front and back, but I can't see if one of them is Chance. Probably not. He's more than likely long gone by now.

I glance in my rear view mirror. A little later I look again. Is someone following? Two men on motorcycles keep an even distance behind me as I turn onto Mill Iron road. The bikes look like Harleys. Their riders are in black from head to toe. Goosebumps tickle my skin. Why would someone follow me? If they wanted to find out about me, all they'd need to do is listen to the gossip in town.

For awhile the bumpy road keeps my mind occupied. I bounce over one of the many cattle guards (they're called *auto gates* here) and when I look again in the mirror, the cycles are gone. That unnerves me more than their presence. I pull over to the side of the road, shut off the motor and get out. Silence.

Slowly I turn a full circle while the ever-present wind whips my hair and clothes. Where have the two Harleys gone? There are no ranches, no homes. Nothing out here as far as you can see, except a herd of antelope near a creek. Behind me, the road dips into a gully. Are the bikers waiting down there? But why? I sigh and rub down the goose bumps, remembering Cap Matthews' last warning: *they know who you are; they know why you're there. Be careful, Lindsey.*

I get back into the pickup and start off again, watching the rear.

Five miles down the road, the cycles reappear suddenly and gain on me, even though I accelerate. The little Honda hasn't enough power to outrun them. On a straight stretch, they make their move. I hear the roar of the Harleys as they power up and pass. But they don't go by. They stay even.

The man on the lead bike looks over at me. Slowly he draws a revolver from his pocket and grins. I can't believe this is happening. Not in this country. I wish for the MG16 rifle I'd left in Spokane.

Well, I don't have it and I can't get it. As I look down the barrel of the gun that's leveled at my head, I know he means to kill me. Glancing ahead, I see we're going to cross a small bridge that spans a creek. Maybe I can delay them a bit.

I roll down my window and yell, "What do you want?" I hope he can hear me above the full throttled roar of the hog and the wind.

"Scared, lady?" The man laughs.

"No. Are you?" Instinctively I know we crossed the creek. As I make my move, I wonder if I'll roll Nick's pickup. I have no choice. I have to do it now or I'm dead meat. My hands are slick on the wheel as I accelerate. He keeps up with me, a smirk on his face.

The smirk disappears (and so does he) when I hit the service brake, hard, then ride the pickup in a semi-circle, gravel flying. I feel the vehicle tip on two wheels and hang on for all I'm worth, bouncing across a ditch. When I hit a barley field, the pickup thuds back to the ground.

I haven't a clue where the bikers are. I jam down on the gas pedal and spin out, leaving deep ruts in the barley, and regain the road in a shower of mud and gravel. The motor on the Honda whines like a sick cat. As I wheel onto the track, swerving sideways for a space, I see the two bikes on their sides in the middle of the road behind me.

I don't look back, don't even breathe deeply until I drive another ten miles and am sure the bikes are not on my tail. At Mill Iron, I pull behind the old school house. That's when the shakes begin. It's also when my stubborn determination to do this alone starts to crumble.

Maybe I can't do this. They'd already spotted me and sent someone to ice me. *Good gosh!* Maybe I should call Aunt Bobbi from someone's house and explain – explain what? That I couldn't come, after all? That my investigation's finished before it began? That I'd been threatened, nearly killed on the way? That I was here as an undercover DEA agent?

I shake my head slowly as reason takes over from my nerves. No, if the gang knows me, if they'd already gotten into Lindsey's house, they'd also have Bobbi's phone bugged. I can't call. I clench the steering wheel and swear under my breath. *No.* They aren't going to scare me off so easily. Cover or no cover, I'm going in.

Thirty-five minutes later, I pull into the long drive of the Lindsey Ranch. This time Bobbi's seen me coming and is standing on the front porch. I wave and climb out of the pickup. As she comes forward, I can hardly believe it's her. Her hair has whitened in a streak above her forehead and she carries herself stiffly as if her burden must be born with a straight back and wooden legs.

"Gina! You're here at last! Praise God!" She envelopes me in a hug that seems to last forever.

I laugh and when I can extricate myself, I step back. "Yes, I'm here. It was a good trip. Should I bring my things in now?"

Dark circles haunt her eyes. Her whole face seems to sag into haggard lines of worry. "No, no. Leave them. Come on in and rest." She glances at the pickup. "I see you brought a four-wheel drive outfit. Figure on gettin' stuck in another drift, dear?" She chuckles briefly and leads the way inside the house.

I chuckle, too, at the memory. "Not exactly. But I thought it might come in handy if I wanted to explore. I've taken up photography as a hobby and want to get some shots. The pickup's a loaner, actually, from a friend."

I allow her to take me to the kitchen, pour me a cup of freshly brewed coffee, and serve me a warm caramel roll. And who can resist one of Bobbi's caramel rolls? I promise myself a five-mile run as I bite into the delectable, gooey sweetness.

After we talk and I finish my coffee and the roll, we carry in my suitcases to the same room I'd occupied in April. After that, Bobbi feeds the bum lambs (lambs abandoned or orphaned), and I sit on the back deck and bring out the satphone I'd purchased on my own. I dial Cap's personal phone number and get him on the first ring.

"Lindsey? What's going on?"

"I had a little … encounter on my way out here, sir. Two guys on Harleys followed me out of Ekalaka. They cornered me on the road and pulled a gun. I think their intent was serious. I did a skidding turn and shook them off. I'll send you the full report."

"Did you get a license number?" I hear shock in his voice.

"No time, chief."

There is a long silence. Finally he says, "I'm tempted to call you in, Gina. The mud samples you sent in to Pierre came back today. Traces of marijuana on them. Your uncle must have walked in a patch. You sure you want to go on with this?"

I stroll off the deck onto the grass. "Yes, sir. My aunt needs me and I have to know the truth, wherever that leads."

He sighs. "You're a good officer. Don't try any heroics. Just identify the gang, find their grow patch, and get out of there. You hear?"

I smile. "Yes, sir."

"Keep in touch, Lindsey! Did you check in with Mike Crosby?"

"He knows I'm here. I can't reveal that I'm investigating drugs, Cap. Sorry, sir, you know the cartels buy off the cops. How do I know whom to trust? In this country, you can't sneeze without everyone knowing about it. I'll be careful and when it looks like I've got it nailed down, I'll contact you."

"Is that a promise?"

"Yes, sir."

Later that evening, after dinner and the kitchen is clean, I sit on the wide front porch with my final cup of coffee. Bobbi is already in bed, or at least in her bedroom. I'm guessing she isn't asleep.

Night descends quietly over the ranch. From here I can see Tim's trailer -- his lights are still on. He'd come for dinner and seemed even more preoccupied and non-communicative than he'd been in April. Bobbi said he was struggling with his dad's disappearance. I know he resents my presence and the way Bobbi mothers me.

A mourning dove coos from the stand of pines near the barn. The cattle are gone from the ranch; both calving and branding's finished. Bobbi said they'd trucked them to the Long Pines for the summer. The sheep have been herded out to pasture, with the Great Pyrenees sheep dog, Bonnie, guarding them. The ranchers are already haying and the harvest of winter wheat will begin soon. Following that, in the fall, they will harvest the barley and oats and then the regular wheat.

Shep plunks down on the porch beside my feet with a sigh. I look at him, lying there with his head on his paws. *What do dogs have to sigh about? Does he miss his master?*

I zip my windbreaker, for the night air's cool, and think of my conversation with Cap Matthews. Could he hear past my positive, assured tone of voice? Does he know how scared I am? For the first time in my life, I wonder if I can do this. I know the fire power, the man power, the money that the Mexican cartels possess. They'd taken over the Columbian cartels and that was indicative that they are more ruthless, if it could be imagined, than their southern brothers. And I'd *seen* what they did to narcotics agents.

Out here, in the middle of nowhere, I feel lost, like a little kid again. I have no base of reference in this country, with these people. Raised in New York, I never imagined that anyone could live like this. I feel so vulnerable, almost naked. The big empty spaces seem to mock me. I shake my head and calculate how far I have to drive for Starbucks coffee -- four hours northwest to the little western burg of Billings, Montana, and five hours to Rapid City down in South Dakota. Loneliness is a huge empty ache inside my soul, and I'm not prepared to deal with it right now.

I sigh. Well, I'll just have to deal with my insecurities because I *have* to succeed on this case. I can't give up -- there's too much hanging in the balance. I've pledged myself to help Aunt Bobbi locate Elton. As a DEA agent, I'm committed to tracking and bring down the drug cartel that we believe has moved into this country. And beyond that, I have to prove to myself that I can do it, that I am competent and capable as a cop, as a person.

No, I can't give up. Something very serious is going on in Carter County, and it might end in a blood bath if somebody doesn't stop it. And that somebody seems to be me.

Chapter 13

Clueless in Montana

From Gina's Blog, June 16

Bobbi fries eggs and bacon for me the next morning, yet she doesn't eat more than a bite herself. She sits in an easy chair in the corner of the sunny dining room while I finish. On a small table beside her chair rests her coffee cup, her open Bible and her glasses.

"Can I ask you a question?" I rinse the breakfast dishes in the sink and put them in the dishwasher.

Her eyes had been on the birds at the feeders on the deck. She jerks around and glances at me. "Oh. Yes. Of course."

I pull a chair over by the window and sit down. "Well, I'm interested in your neighbors, Bobbi, and I was wondering if you could tell me something about the people here. Being from New York, I find this culture, the way you do things here, very interesting."

She gives me a steady stare. "What do you want to know?"

I turn to gaze out the window and watch as two male finches fight for a place on the feeder. "Would you consider the ranchers around here prosperous? Wealthy?"

She doesn't answer right away, and from the frown that darkens her features, I know it's the wrong question. I sip my coffee and wait.

She says, "Well, that depends. None of us are what you'd call wealthy. Not by New York standards, that is. We work hard and sometimes we have good crops. Other times we just barely get by. You see the fields and the cattle and all and think maybe we're rich, but there's all sorts of things you don't see. Like the years we get hailed out. Or the times sickness runs through the herd. Or the equipment breaks down." She sighs. "It's always such a struggle." She shifts uneasily and lifts her Bible to her lap.

Normally I would decamp in a hurry when she starts reading her Bible, but now I settle back in the chair and allow silence to fill the room. Outside the birds twitter at the feeder and I hear the tractor fire up down at the barn. Tim's going out to do something.

"I know that you struggle, Bobbi. I was just wondering if ..." I pause, wondering how I can wring out of her the answers I need. "Is there a rancher around here who was really hard up, like he was going under, and all of a sudden he's doing quite well? Buying more land? And stock? And equipment?"

Again she doesn't reply at once. She starts to speak, then checks herself. She fidgets with the markers in her Bible, glances at the birds, tucks a stray hair behind her ear. She looks at me with the faintest expression of reproof in her eyes.

"Well, dear, I can't rightly say. There's plenty of ranchers who're about to go under, what with the economy and gas prices and all. The ranchers who are doing the best, they have more land and more money set aside. They're the ones who own the land and aren't still payin' on it. I know one or two from up by Baker way who've been bought out by a big corporation. Then there are the folks who have oil on their land. They're doin' all right, I hear."

I avoid looking directly at her and study a large aerial photo of the ranch that hangs on the wall. I keep my tone neutral. "Who are they?"

"I don't rightly know, dear." She lays aside her Bible and gets to her feet. "It's time to feed the bum lambs. You want to help?"

No, I don't. But how can I say that? If I want information from Bobbi, I have to cooperate. I sigh and load my arms with bottles. This is going to be harder than I thought!

***

"Why didn't you get her?" The voice on the line went up an octave and a string of cuss words erupted from the cell phone.

Butch held it away from his ear and grimaced. When the man was finished, he brought it back. "Well, boss, it's complicated. I'll get her. We got time. She don't know nothin'."

"But she will. It won't take her long. I want this leak sealed, Butch. Now."

Butch sighed. "You gotta wire me some money, then. I ain't payin' for her elimination outta *my* pocket. You send the money and I'll see to it."

"Don't hire those idiots from Rapid City again, y'hear? They botched this last deal, looking like fools on their big Harleys. Just get a shot to her head and it'll be done. I don't want to hear any more reports about a failure."

"Yes, sir." Butch wiped the sweat from his forehead. He didn't need to be told what the penalty for failure was. The boss knew what college his kid was attending. He knew the address of his daughter and her family in Billings. He knew where the grandkids went to school. Heck, the guy knew when his wife went to the bathroom!

"Tonight?" Anticipation laced the boss' voice.

"Not tonight. I gotta get my ducks in a row. That'll take a couple of days. I'll call when it's done."

"Make it nice and clean like you did the last time, okay, my friend?" The boss laughed. "And if you do this job for me, maybe your little family will live."

The line went dead.

Butch sat in his truck at the top of the butte and rolled a joint. He needed a pick-me-up. He needed his weed. But he wanted the other stuff. The white powder. His mind raced with the details of the hit on Miss Fancy Pants. He'd have to make some phone calls. Get the guys down here. Make sure the body was never found.

Well, he could do that. They'd never found Elton's body. He'd thought of returning to the cave and burying it somewhere. Surely the cougars and other wild animals had taken care of it. No, it was safer to stay away.

He started his outfit and drove off the butte.

***

Carter County, June 16

Chance knew the probability of getting into the grow patch again was slim to none, but he had to try. If he could get a picture of the actual plants, and maybe one or two shots of the workers, he'd have concrete proof of a large scale operation.

After he scoped out the general location from high points in the vicinity and poured over forestry maps, he decided on a backyard approach, coming in from the north, driving as close as he could get, then hiking the rest of the way. It would be tricky. The canyon was narrow that led into the valley, and he could miss it and a miss was as good as a mile, as they said. Yet even if he made it to the rim, he could get a picture.

It was a warm day, full of buzzing insects and the chirp of birds. After about an hour, he stopped to eat a sandwich and a couple of cookies he carried in his backpack. Afterward, he started off again in what he figured was the right direction, following a deer path that petered out in a circle of dense bushes. The sun went under a cloud and a faint rumble of thunder muttered in the distance. A storm was brewing somewhere nearby. He studied the sky. A low bank of clouds formed above the western fringe of trees. He'd better get back to the pickup.

Still, he hesitated. He was nearly at his destination -- he knew it, could feel it. Moving carefully, he crept ahead, keeping his eyes on the trees. He spotted the fence first, and after that, the guard tower, cleverly hidden amongst the branches of a big fir. He squatted and waited. Slender against the dark sky protruded an antenna. Radio? Satellite internet? This place would probably have all the latest equipment -- and the best. Highly sensitive radar equipment, police scanners, cameras, movement sensors. They'd know before a surveillance plane got in the air and have plenty of time to cover the crop.

He saw movement -- someone's cap and another person's shoulder. A low murmur of voices reached him. Prickles descended his back. *Gotcha!*

After taking a couple of pictures of the guard tower and the fence, he crawled to the left, following the fence line. Along here somewhere was that place where the tree had fallen and smashed it.

A few hundred yards farther, he saw the downed tree – or the stump of it, rather, and large chunks of sawn wood. The fence had been repaired. It was also hot. Were there cameras, too? You'd better bet your bottom britches there were. Well, he wouldn't be getting into the valley that way again.

As he drew a deep breath, a clap of thunder rolled overhead. The wind brushed his face and moaned in the treetops. The first drops of rain pattered on the bushes. Circling the valley, he discovered they'd been smart when they planned the fence. From no vantage point could he see down into the canyon. He heard a motor and figured it was a gas generator, probably for the irrigation system. There was a guard tower on the southern end. Working his way back to the point on the northern rim where he'd begun the circuit, he shook his head. No doubt about it. This was big and they had plants down there.

About that time, the storm hit. He crouched under the overhang of a rock and waited while rain fell in sheets and lightning lit the air, followed by claps of thunder. Up there in the guard shack, they'd be hunched down and maybe drinking coffee or beer.

He crept closer to the tower. Just below him, on the canyon floor, he spotted a large roll of material that spanned the northern end. *Camouflage netting!* The roll was like what people used to cover swimming pools, only much larger. He figured it was powered. With just a push of a button, the netting would stretch out over the plants. From the air, you'd never know a grow patch was here. Clever. He took several more pictures and pocketed his camera. As he was turning to go, a man shouted.

He'd been spotted! Like a fool, he'd ventured into a bare patch of ground. Guns blazed and bullets whined around his head. He hit the ground and rolled, sheltering behind a rock. The shots were coming uncomfortably close.

Sweat ran into his eyes. He didn't have long – only a few moments to make his move and get out of there. Could he do it? He squinted through the rain, his jaw clenched, trying to decide which way to go.

Chapter 14

On the Run

From Gina's Blog, June 16

I'm washing the dishes from supper when Bobbi hits me with a declaration. Not a question, mind you. A statement of fact.

"Oh, I forgot to tell you. Tomorrow we're going over to Mill Iron for their potluck."

"*We?* Who's the *we?*" I scrub a dirty pot so vigorously suds creep up the side of the sink and threaten to overflow. Taking my irritation out on it seems much better than on her.

She zips around behind me, sweeping the floor energetically. "You and I, dear. I go every Wednesday. People from the community put it on, and we have such a lovely time. I told them you were coming and that you'd say a few words about your work. You wouldn't mind doing that, would you? I mean, it's nothing formal. Just tell a couple of stories about your police work in New York. Easy as pie."

I finish the pot and rinse it. "Aunt Bobbi, I don't particularly want a lot of people to know I'm a cop. They tend to clam up when police officers are around. Why did you tell them?"

"Oh, I'm sorry. They've known for a long time. Every time I get a letter from you, I share it around. We all pray for you. And love you."

"Huh." I school myself to patience. Where does Bobbi get it that she can pass my letters around? Thank the gods I hadn't sent very many! I take a deep breath. "I'm not speaking about police work. I'm not speaking, period. My brain is fried and I'm not comfortable in front of people. Besides, I'm not a cop. I don't work for the city police any more. I stopped that when I moved to Spokane."

"It's the same, dear." Bobbi dries the pots and pans I'd stacked in the drainer. "You work for a federal agency, right? Is it the FBI? Can't you talk about that?"

"Afraid not. I'd have to kill them if I did." I laugh when I see Bobbi's shocked face. "Just kidding. I don't work for the FBI. I'll come with you, but I'm not speaking." I drain the water from the sink and scrub the stove. I'm determined that before I go home, the stains will be gone from the undersides of the burners and the oven will be spotless.

Bobbi leaves the room without a word.

I sigh and wipe off the counters. At least the potluck will be a way to meet some of the neighbors and get information. So far I haven't turned up one single clue.

That evening I help Bobbi organize some clothes she no longer wants. Elton's things hang in ordered rows in the walk-in closet, and there are some stacked at the bottom.

"Get that pile, would you?" Bobbi dumps her pile on the bed and starts folding them into the boxes that sit on the floor. "That one outfit, the jeans and blouse, was what I was wearing the day he … disappeared. I just can't force myself to wear them again."

I shake out the offending pair of jeans. "These are cute. Too bad you can't wear them." As is my habit with clothes to be given away, I explore the pockets. My fingers touch a paper in the rear pocket. "Hey, what's this? A note?" I draw it out and without unfolding it, hand it to Bobbi.

She sweeps strands of long gray hair behind her ears and gingerly takes the paper. "Oh, my. It *is* a note. The one Elton left me on the table that day. I'd forgotten all about it!" She unfolds it and reads silently, her face turning the color of putty.

I can't stand the suspense and step closer. "What does it say? It might … be important to our investigation. Although you might not want me to …"

"Nonsense. Here. Read it. It doesn't say much, but if it leads somewhere …"

I take the note and read out loud. "Bobbi, I'm going out for awhile. Butch came by in his new pickup and wants to take me for a spin. See you later. Elton." I glance up. "Who's Butch?"

Bobbi shrugs and turns to the stacks of clothes, busying herself with her chore. Yet I notice that her hands are shaking. There's silence, then she says in a low voice, "I wasn't born here. I've lived here for thirty years and I know everyone. Yet I don't know who Butch is, I swear. Oh! Wait a sec."

She stares into middle space, lost in thought. Then she straightens and shakes her head. "Something jogged my memory ... something Elton told me once about his friends in school. They all had nicknames. I think he said his was Bubba." She laughs. "No, it's gone now. Yet I wonder ..."

"What?" I stare at her, willing her memory to be jogged again. Why is she being so secretive? Who's she trying to protect? Is it Tim? Does Tim have a friend nicknamed Butch?

"Don't pay attention to me, dear. I'm scattered-brained these days. No, I don't know any Butch."

I have the uncomfortable impression that she knows, and the knowledge rocks her deeper than she wants to show. I fold the jeans and put them in the box. "If we're going to find out what happened to Elton, I have to be aware of what's going on. At this point, I don't have *anything*. If you know something, it could be dangerous."

"Dangerous? What do you mean?"

"I mean just that. I'd like it a whole lot if you locked the doors at night."

Bobbi chuckles. "We never lock doors. Who'd want to break in here?"

***

Carter County, June 16

Chance reached a cover of rocks. He heard the splat of bullets on the ground, the big booms of the guns. *How many guns do they have up there?* Sounded like an army.

Flinging himself sideways, he managed to get to the shelter of a big pine, then to some more rocks. The bullets sought him out and splintered pieces into his face, blinding him. Something hit his shoulder. He felt no pain but knew he'd taken a shot. *Great.* He was just getting over the wound in his leg!

The scrub junipers and elder bushes gave little shelter from the blazing gunfire that came from the tower. *Got to keep moving.* He scrambled to another tree. Panting, he felt his shoulder. Blood oozed through his shirt. Now it hurt like the dickens. He rubbed away the stinging shards of rock from his eyes and looked around.

Can't stay here. They'd be on the ground in a few minutes, hunting him. Even now he heard them descending the rope ladder. If they found the truck before he got back to it, he was as good as dead. He pulled himself to his feet and started off. Their voices echoed through the trees behind him.

The ground was wet, muddy in some spots. He had to pay attention, or he'd lose his way. Keeping to the cover of bushes and trees, he loped through the forest. His pursuers closed the distance swiftly. Forcing himself to ignore the pain in his shoulder, he kept moving. In one place, he had to dash across a small meadow. They spotted him and got off a couple of shots. The bullets went wide. He arrived at the pickup, panting, fumbling for his key. *Where is the stupid key? C'mon, c'mon!*

Looking back up the old logging road, he saw two men appear, sprinting down the hill, approaching fast. He pulled his rifle from the back of the cab -- maybe he'd give them some of their own medicine. Carefully he aimed and got off a shot. The first man reared back, yelled. The other man knelt down, leveled his gun and took aim.

Chance thought he'd better get out before they shot out his tires. *The key!* He still couldn't find it. *God! Help me!* A bullet brushed past his head, shattered the rear pickup window. He searched his front pockets, his back pockets. His jacket. He ducked as another bullet smashed into the vehicle. The man leaped up and ran toward him, then knelt down, took aim again. This one wouldn't miss.

Chance's fingers closed around the metal key ring in his jacket. It had slipped through a torn place into the lining. Jumping into the cab, he turned the ignition and put it in gear. He roared away, sending mud flying, tires spinning. After sliding in the mud for a few feet, the tires caught and in a few seconds, he'd swung around the first bend and was bouncing down the road. He knew he wasn't out of danger yet. At least he'd brought the ranch's pickup, a beat-up 1987 Chevy. If they'd seen the license plate, it wouldn't lead to him.

Out on the main road, he kept a wary eye on the rearview mirror. Any moment he expected to find he was followed. They wouldn't let him get away. The guys in the tower would radio for help. He floored the accelerator and the old motor whined. It wouldn't last long at this speed. Something was bound to break – it was held together with baling wire and duck tape.

At last he turned into the long drive of the ranch where he worked. Decorated with a cow's skull, the sign read the *Stevens Family Ranch*. At the equipment shed, he piled out of the pickup and headed over to the modest white farm house where he pounded on the door.

No one answered. Then he remembered. They'd gone to Rapid City to pick up their son who was flying home from college. He loped over to the old trailer where he bunked and scrawled a note. *I am quitting as an emergency came up. Thanks for the job. Sorry about the window on the pickup. Take it out of the pay you owe me. Chance McNeil.* He paused and added, *Lock your doors at night. I stirred up a hornet's nest.*

He ran back to the house and left the note on the kitchen table. After he bandaged his shoulder, which turned out to be only a scratch, he threw his belongings into suitcases and boxes. Cyndi was near the barn. He loaded her. It didn't take more than thirty minutes to collect his gear from the tack room, connect the trailer to the truck, and make tracks – this time in his white Chevy Silverado.

He lifted his index finger to the outfits that he passed on his way to Ekalaka and watched the road behind him. No one followed and he saw nothing suspicious. Where should he go? Where could he lay low for a couple of days? As if in answer to his questions, he spotted a sign beside the road. *Living Waters Bible Camp*. He drove into the camp and after leaving his truck and trailer by the barn, walked up to the office.

Camp was in session. Groups of kids followed their counselors around and others played ball on the grassy meadow. In the office, he was greeted by a young woman whose name he forgot.

She looked up with a smile. "Ah, Chance McNeil, the cowboy. What can we do for you today?" She was pleased to see him – he could tell by the way her eyes brightened. It somehow warmed his heart.

He grinned and removed his hat, glancing at her desk where a cup sat -- it was printed with the words, *Connie's Cup, steal at your own risk*. "Hi there, Connie. Got an extra bunk I could use for a spell? I plum ran out of work and need a place to lay my head. I'll help with the horses, or do whatever you need me to do. Just don't give me a cabin full of kids."

She laughed, her brown eyes twinkling. Shoving back her chair, she stood. "That would be cruel and unusual punishment, right?" She was almost as tall as he, heavy set, dark hair pulled back in a pony tail, no make-up whatsoever. "Are you all right?" She was looking at his shoulder where blood had seeped through the make-shift bandage he'd placed there.

"Oh, yeah. Just a scratch."

She nodded. "Mr. Fairchild's in the log cabin over there. Why don't you go talk to him? I'm sure we can use help with trail rides. Come to think of it, Mr. Fairchild said we had to get a ferrier to shoe some of the horses. And here you are."

"Yes, ma'am." He tipped his head. "I'm willin' to work for my grub. Thank you. You just saved my life." She couldn't know how much he meant that!

She chuckled and walked with him to the door. Her proximity did funny things to his heart. She was pleasant, down to earth and a lot of fun. Besides that, she was a Christian. She shook her head. "You say the funniest things, like out of a Louis L'Amour book. Hey, what are the *chances* I'll see you around?"

He chuckled. "Fair to middlin', I'd say. Oh, and one more thing."

"Yes?" She smiled at him coyly.

"Uh, if anyone comes askin' for me, I'd appreciate it if you said I wasn't here."

"Well … that'd sorta be like a lie, wouldn't it?" She brushed a mosquito from her arm.

"Yeah, I guess it would. Maybe you could say that you can't give out information. Then I'd appreciate knowin' about it. Would that work?"

She nodded. "Sure. Hey, what's going on? You in trouble?"

"Me? Heck, trouble's my middle name. Catch you later, Connie."

Life suddenly looked a whole lot better than it had a few hours ago, yet he wondered if he should endanger these people. Sooner or later, probably more like *sooner*, the drug dealers were going to find him and when they did, they wouldn't care who got caught in the crossfire. He'd heard stories where they bombed a whole apartment building to get one guy and shot up whole towns for revenge.

Well, he had to deal with that as it came. For now, he had to find shelter somewhere. After his talk with Mr. Fairchild, he unloaded Cyndi and settled into a small trailer the camp used for temporary staff. He promised himself he would only stay until … until when?

Time was running out. He had to wrap this up before the unthinkable happened.

Chapter 15

A Cowboy Named Jesse

From Gina's blog, June 17:

The community hall is a long white clapboard building sitting forlornly on the hill like a lonely old man. Cars and pickups circle it. After Bobbi parks, she gathers her covered dish and I grab the salad, dreading what lay ahead. Why does she have to haul me around to meet people like I'm some kind of trophy? Yet common sense tells me that I *have* to get to know these ranchers. How else can I crack this case?

The interior of the building is as plain and unadorned as the outside. Long tables covered with white paper fill the center of the room. At the far end, ladies in the kitchen bustle busily with the food, while their men stand in tight knots drinking coffee. As Bobbi joins the women, I get a cup of coffee and inspect a large handmade quilt that hangs prominently on one wall. A plaque is mounted below it. *Quilted by Rebecca Anderson and donated to Mill Iron Community, December 5, 1989. Won First Place in the State Fair.*

I wander the large room aimlessly and listen to the men. Their conversation is all about weather, crops, cows, sheep, and winter wheat prices. I smile.

Finally a man calls us to attention and asks someone to say the blessing. I think that's strange, but I bow my head as all the men remove their hats. The man who prays, maybe it's the pastor, ends his prayer *in Jesus' name*, totally politically incorrect. Yet I realize it's the norm in this society. Not only the norm, it's expected.

Bobbi comes over to me and directs me to the back of the line. I must say, these ladies know how to cook. I'd never seen such an extravagant display of food in all my life and my resolution to stick to my diet flies out of my head.

We sit at one of the paper-covered tables and begin to eat. An older man and wife sit across from us. He's wearing a long-sleeved, collared checkered shirt and denim coveralls, and she's dressed in a cotton dress and white tennis shoes. I almost expect her to don a hat and pull the netting over her face.

Bobbi introduces them as Chuck and MaryLou Winthrop. After we greet one another, Bobbi turns to another lady on her left and becomes involved in a deep conversation with her – something about a new recipe for peach jam. Then they proceed to the high prices of chicks that year. Chicks, as in baby chickens, not girls, I gather. *That* relieves my mind!

The two people across from me do not look up from their plates.

I set my cup down and clear my throat. "Did I hear my aunt to say that your nickname is Butch?" I study the man. Could he be a drug grower? He has rough hands, a weather-beaten face and scraggly gray hair. His forehead has a hat line – sunburn below, white skin above. He takes so long in answering, I wonder if he heard me.

He scrunches up his eyes and looks at his wife as if for inspiration. "Don't have a nickname, ma'am. Folks just call me Chuck, like I was named. It's good enough for me."

"Do you know of someone they call Butch around here? I was … trying to find an old friend from college. I heard he'd settled here. That's the only name I know him by."

The rancher shifts uneasily. He doesn't like this talk and shoots more than once glance over his shoulder to the door as if he wants to escape. "Wal, I don't know …," he says in an agonizingly slow drawl. "Some kid was called that when I was in school. MaryLou, do you know someone called Butch?"

"Butch?" She arches her eyebrows and glances at me with a look that says volumes about what she thinks of city folks and their strange ways. "No. Can't help you."

I straighten on the hard wooden bench, gazing around the room that buzzes with talk. Most of the people who gather at the community center for lunch are older. I suppose the younger ones would be working this time of day.

Bobbi introduces me to several other ladies as we eat. I study each one – the heavy set matron who wears a chiffon scarf and a shawl. Then there's a tall, spare lady with hair in a bun, who looks like her face would crack if she smiled. One or two of the women are maybe in their early forties. They're wearing jeans, t-shirts and short hair styles. Their body language fairly shouts a no-nonsense attitude toward life, yet they laugh more than the other women. I find myself thinking I'd like to be their friend. Their husbands place cowboy hats on the shelf above the coat rack and dust off their jeans before they sit to chow down.

I'm just finishing my meal when the door opens and two men enter. I set down my fork and dab at my mouth with a paper napkin. The first man is in his fifties, a typical rancher with sunburned face and eyes that crinkle along the edges like he'd looked into the distance all his life. The second man has to be his son. He removes his hat and smiles at the lady who invites them to the food table.

I tap Bobbi's shoulder, pulling her from an incredibly fascinating conversation about the best way to make pickles. "Who's that?" I tip my head in the direction of the newcomers.

"Oh. That's Bryce Anderson and his son, Jesse. Bryce lost his wife a couple a years ago. She won the blue ribbon every year for her strawberry jam. Now some of the rest of us have a chance. I think they come cuz he can't cook. But he's the nicest neighbor I got. He's come over to the house a dozen times t'help me out. Come on, I'll introduce you."

She yanks me upright and drags me in front of the two men who are sitting down with their plates. From this vantage point, I fully appreciate Jesse's good looks. Brown eyes, dark wavy hair, wide shoulders, darkly tanned skin and dimples that flash with his charming smile. *Wow.* I draw a breath, speechless.

He stands and takes my hand. "My day is definitely lookin' up, Miss Gina Lindsey. I'm mighty pleased to meet you. Would you like to sit here for a bit? You do the talkin' and dad and me'ill do the eatin'. I'm famished." He sits.

Bobbi giggles. "He's the rodeo champion in these parts, Gina. For three years. Goin' big time now, Jesse? I hear you're headin' for the Calgary Stampede."

His eyes twinkle. "Yes, ma'am."

"Well, I'll let you two get acquainted. You want some more coffee, Gina?"

"Please." My knees give way and I drop down on the hard bench across from Jesse. Mindlessly I accept the coffee. "Do you own a ranch around here?" *Now isn't that just the cleverest thing to say? He'll think I'm an idiot. Pull yourself together, Lindsey.*

"Yup." Jesse pauses long enough from his meal to smile proudly. "We own a ranch *and* a business."

"Oh?"

"Yeah, we bottle water. Montana Mountain Springs Water. Best water in the world. We've even had studies done that's proved it's helpful for some kinds of cancer and other sicknesses. Excuse me a minute. Gotta git some more grub." He returns to the food table and loads his plate.

In his absence, I turn to Bryce. "I imagine your ranch work and the water business keeps you busy." *Gosh. Another inane comment. I'm just full of them today!*

He grunts and wipes his mouth with a napkin. "Yes, ma'am. You should come over some time. We'll give you a tour of the plant and a free sample." His smile erases the sour look on his face and I think he's a pleasant enough fellow, considering he's a red-neck and probably a Republican.

I return his smile. "Thanks. I think I will."

"And bring your aunt. She needs to git out more."

I glance over at Bobbi and nod. "Will do that." When Jesse sits down again, I wonder if Bryce is making a move on Bobbi. Is he planning to annex the ranch?

"You ride?" Jesse asks around a mouthful of fried chicken.

"Some. I moved out to Spokane a couple of years ago and went riding with some friends. I really liked it, so I bought a mare. An Arabian."

He grunts. "Not much of a breed. You'll have to come ridin' with me. I'll put you on somethin' that's real horse. You say you moved to Spokane? Where'd you live before then?"

"New York." I brace myself. Most people look at me like I just admitted to being released from prison when I tell them I'm from New York. It's almost as bad as saying you're from California.

But he merely nods and finishes off his biscuit. "Not many New Yorkers out this way. What'dya think of the west?"

"I … I like it. Of course, it takes some getting used to. Look, Jesse. I know you want to eat and it looks like my aunt's getting ready to leave." I stand. "It was nice meeting you, Bryce. And you, too, Jesse."

Bryce doesn't smile. His eyes, piercing blue, are hard and cold.

Jesse gets to his feet and comes around the table to my side. He leans closer. "I apologize for my dad. He's not been himself since Mom died. Doesn't do small talk. But wouldn't harm a fly. C'mon, I'll see you to your car. Food's not as important as a pretty lady."

I laugh. "I don't need help to the car. Now you sit down and enjoy your meal."

"Can I call you?"

His presence staggers me, and here I thought I was impervious to male charms. "Sure. Or come over to Lindsey's. I'm there most of the day. I'm the accountant, go-fer girl and cook."

He nods solemnly. "I'm sorry about … what happened to Elton." He squeezes my arm and smiles. "See you later, then, gopher girl."

I try hard to look nonchalant. "Sure."

Bobbi isn't anywhere near ready to leave. I say I have a headache, so we gather our food dishes and go to the car.

That evening, I do a wash, send off some emails and call Nick. I only get his answering service. Funny. He usually answers, but maybe he didn't recognize the ring since I'm calling from the land line.

As evening settles over the prairie (I always think of it as a *prairie* but the folks out here say it isn't a prairie; it's a high plateau), I lounge on the back porch with my last cup of coffee and stare out into space. From this vantage point, I can see the barns, the corrals, the equipment shed, Tim's trailer, and Lone Butte standing solidly against the violet sky. The wind that had been blowing tumbleweeds across the fields and stacking them up by the fences has now died to a soft murmur. The birds twitter sleepily from the branches of the firs around the house.

Shep lies down with a thump beside me and groans.

I rub my forehead, thinking I haven't gotten very far on either finding Elton or the drugs. Where should I start? Maybe I should contact Sheriff Crosby and see about an aerial surveillance flight. No, I can't do that -- if it got around that I was searching for a grow patch, I'd be dead in the water, finished before I'd begun.

No, I have to play this carefully. I'd already learned that while Bobbi and her friends are eager to talk, they aren't going to converse about certain things, like money or people's dark secrets. Especially to strangers. Would they rat on a neighbor they suspected was growing marijuana? Probably not. Maybe I'd find out something from Jesse.

Um. Jesse. He was a surprise. Who'd have thought that someone who looked like Matt Damon would be in this place? I fold up the laptop and return to the house. Bobbi's already in her bedroom. I rinse out my cup and set it in the sink.

Bobbi appears in the hall in her bathrobe. "How's your headache, dear?"

"Oh, it's a lot better. Thanks. I think I'll go to bed."

"Did … did Jesse ask you out?" Her eyes glint in the dim light.

I chuckle. "Oh, Bobbi. You're a match-maker to the core. There's nothing going on, though. I don't have time for boyfriends." I turn to go, then glance back and see Bobbi's disappointed look. I relent. "He said he'd call or come over. There, does that satisfy you?"

She grins. "He's a nice boy -- not that I want you to fall in love with him. But he might convince you to stay a little longer." She fidgets with the belt on her robe. "Gina, there's something I think you'd better see. I found it tonight."

"What?"

"Just come."

In her bedroom, I notice a plastic bag from the cleaners on the bed.

Bobbi pulls a suit coat from the closet. "I remembered I had this cleaned … oh, way back, before Elton … disappeared. I hadn't ever picked it up, and when I heard that my friend was going up to Baker, I asked her get it for me. She dropped it off while we were out. I was hanging it up and saw this note pinned on it." She handed the note to me. Stapled to it was another piece of paper.

I read the top note. *We found this in the pocket. R&B Cleaners.* I lift it up and see the second note. Rough handwriting is scrawled across a yellowed piece of paper. *Tomorrow, JK logging road.1500. S Pines.* "Is this Elton's handwriting?"

Bobbi shakes her head. "I don't know who wrote it." She looks away.

I catch a funny look on her face, and when she turns away, I know she hasn't told the truth. I'm trained to read body language and I've honed the skill considerably over the last ten years as a cop and detective. Usually I'm pretty accurate. Yet why would Bobbi fib? Didn't she *want* me to find Elton? Is she hiding something, protecting someone? "When was the last time he wore this jacket?"

"Let me think. It must've been at Wylie Herkum's funeral. Elton spilled coffee all over himself during lunch after the service. We took it up to Baker a few days later."

"What was the date of the funeral?" I grip her arm.

Bobbi shoves my hand away. "Gracious, girl, is this how you interrogate your suspects?"

I relax. "Sorry. Dad always said I was too intense for my own good, that I was a workaholic. He was forever telling me I needed to lighten up, that relationships are more important than the job." I grin. "Can't you just hear him saying that? Of course he never took his own advice."

"Oh, yes," she says, then draws a sharp breath. "I can certainly hear *Elton* sayin' that, and they're brothers." She rubs her arm. "I never talked to your Dad much, just once or twice on the phone." She turns away abruptly and I get the impression she's lying. Again I'm confused. Why would she lie about that?

"Now, about the date of Wylie's funeral. I'm tryin' to think. These days I get things jumbled up. We might find it on the calendar." She leads me to the office and lifts a calendar off its nail. She pages through it backwards, running her finger over each line. "May, April. Here it is on April 12th. W. H.'s funeral."

"Thanks." Just before Elton's disappearance! Hope surges in my heart. Maybe there *is* something to investigate, after all.

"There's something else, too." She gets up and shoves her hair behind her ears. I know she's gathering courage to say something that's hard for her to get out.

"I ... I didn't want you to know, but now that you've seen the note, I'd better tell you." She draws a deep breath as if she's about to plunge into cold water. "A while back, Elton had an affair with a woman named Desiree Pledger. After I found out, and confronted him on it, he said he'd end it and I believed him. I ... think that note sounds like he was meeting with her."

It takes me a bit to realize how deep Bobbi's pain is over her husband's affair. Don't most people have them from time to time? I remind myself that these people are different – they have old-fashioned ideas. It's hard for her to even *admit* that their marriage has problems.

I pat her shoulder. "It's okay, Bobbi. These things happen. Besides, I think Elton kept his promise to you. Look at the note again." I hold it so she can read it. "A logging road. Does that sound like a place for a secret meeting with a lover? And the hour, *1500*. How many women write assignation notes using military time?"

A smile tugs at her lips. "Not very many."

"And S. Pines. Short Pines, right?"

"Yes."

I nod, sure of myself now. "My guess is that this note is from someone from the forest service. Maybe they had business about your grazing rights down there. I'll check it out in the morning. I don't think you need to worry about him breaking his promise to you."

She wipes her eyes with a tissue and blows her nose. "Thank you, dear. But I still don't know. It's all such a muddle."

I tuck the note in my pocket. "That's why I'm here, Bobbi. To unmuddle things. Just remember I'm not your enemy. If you work with me, we'll find Elton. I know he's alive."

"If he's alive, why hasn't he contacted me?" A tear slides down her cheek. She wipes it away impatiently.

I shrug. "There's such a thing as amnesia. We have missing persons reports all the time. People wander off because they can't remember who they are." I start down the hall, then turn back. "Could I have Desiree's address or phone number?"

Bobbi stares at me. "Why?"

"I have to follow up on all the leads. That's all."

She nods and rummages in her desk for a time. "I got it in here somewheres. Oh, here it is." She pulls a crumpled piece of paper and hands it to me. "We kept in contact with her for several years. Her boy needed work. He'd come summers and help us. We haven't called her for … well, for a long time."

"Okay. I just need information. *Someone* knows something. *Someone* saw something that day. They had to. People know everything in this country. How could a man just disappear?"

She sighs. "I've asked myself that many's a time. Well, good night."

"Did you lock the doors?"

"No, dear. If it makes you feel better, go lock them."

Chapter 16

A Secret to Die For

Camp Crook, South Dakota

Sabrina Philips parked in front of the Forest Service building in Camp Crook and slid her computer case off the seat of her black CRV. It was quiet tonight. A big rig lumbered up the highway to Buffalo and a few stars dotted the evening sky. Not far away a door screeched and a man called his dog. Goosebumps tickled her arms. *Someone's walking on my grave.*

She shoved her jitters aside, stepping carefully over the cracks on the sidewalk. Smokey the Bear pointed to *low*, indicating the fire hazard for the day. Beyond the office were the homes the Forest Service provided for the three department supervisors and behind them were the two large apartment buildings that housed the summer fire crews. A few of the guys lived there year around; she cleaned for one of them.

The main office was small. She sighed as she set her things on the counter. She hated working evenings, but she had to live while her photography business got going. Some day, she promised herself, she'd be working from home and cleaning offices would only be a bad memory. From the cleaning closet she got the mop, broom, garbage bags and dusting cloth. She filled the mop bucket with water and had just started on the hallway floor when the toilet flushed upstairs. Who was here? Usually the building was vacant by the time she arrived.

Footsteps thudded down the stairs. She heard a low, off-key whistle. Randy Whittier, the District Ranger Director, swung into the office and shrugged into his jacket. He ran his fingers through his light colored hair and studied a memo on the secretary's desk. When she clanked the bucket, he swung to face her. "Oh, hi, Sabrina. Be sure you get my office clean this time, or I might have to come after you." He flipped through some memos on the desk and dug his keys from his pocket.

She swished her mop in his direction. "I always empty your trash, which is no picnic after you eat apples and bananas all day. Still on the diet?"

He moved to the door. "Yeah. See you around." He paused. "Want me to lock you in? So the *crooks* don't get you?"

It was their little pun about the town's name. "No, thanks. If they *camp* out here, I'll put 'em to work. Take care."

The door shut on his mumbled answer.

She finished the hall and started on the BLM's office. This job would take about two hours. After that, she could go online to check her mail and browse the web. Randy didn't care if she used internet service here as long as the offices were spotless on Monday morning.

As she worked, she snooped at the papers in the wastebaskets, a harmless habit, she reasoned. If people didn't want others to see their trash, they should shred it. She smoothed a torn, crumpled note from the trash. "Meet me at … " The rest was torn off. Interesting. A lover's meeting? Was Randy having an affair? She giggled. What would Susan say if he was?

She threw it away and went on with her job. Two hours later, she stowed the supplies neatly in the closet and straightened her aching back with a sigh.

It was dark by now. She peered out the big office windows. In the light from the quarter moon, she saw the trees swaying in the wind. A storm was coming. Were they going to get more rain? She hoped not. Driving home over those roads in a rainstorm was not something she enjoyed.

She grabbed a can of Pepsi from the staff refrigerator, returned to the front desk and turned on her laptop. After checking mail and surfing the web, she remembered the pictures she'd taken the other day of the beautiful yellow trees in the secluded valley. She opened the file and began looking through the pictures.

Yes, these were definitely good. Oh, darn. There was that stupid red pickup! She was tempted to edit the picture right then, but decided to wait. It would take time and she wanted to get home and watch her favorite show on TV. After she edited them, she'd send them to Snapfish and have them developed. They'd come next week and maybe she'd select some to mail to a postcard company she'd called the other day. Wait. She should back these up. She had a flash drive somewhere … she pawed through her purse and found it.

It didn't take long to download the whole file onto the flash drive. When it was done, she pulled out the flash drive and laid it on the desk, then went onto the Snapfish site and leaned back in the chair, watching the pictures as they uploaded.

"Hi, Sabrina."

Startled, she looked up. "Oh, it's you. You about scared the livin' daylights out of me."

"I remembered I wanted to ask if you would do a cleanin' job for me. Saw the lights on, so I came over. Would you do it? On Thursday? I'm having some guests over. Hey, nice photos. Who took them?"

Sabrina smiled, glowing inside. She always loved to hear praises of her pictures. "Thanks. See this one? I'm going to take that dratted pickup out. I was so mad at that man who parked there! He must've been hunting or something. He carried a gun."

"Anyone you know?" His tone held a kind of suppressed excitement. He edged closer. She could smell his after shave lotion and caught a whiff of cigarette smoke.

She shrugged. "No."

"Those are nice shots. Where's your camera?"

"Why?" She glanced up at him. He stood just behind her, hunched, studying the pictures.

He straightened and smiled. Yet his smile was forced, awkward. Sabrina wondered at it, thinking he might want a copy of one of her pictures. "Oh, no reason. Just curious. Well, I gotta go. So can you come next Thursday?"

"Sure. I'll come over about four. I get off my other job at three."

"Okay. See you then." He left quietly.

She'd gone back to the yellow tree picture and was getting ready to edit it when the door banged open again and the man reappeared.

"Hey, could you give me a hand? My outfit won't start. Could you give me a jump? I've got the cables." He held the door open and ground out his cigarette in the dirt outside. "Sorry to bother you."

"Oh, it's no bother." She stood. What was wrong with him tonight? She thought she knew him but he was acting like a stranger. Deftly she slid the flash drive into her purse and shoved the purse under the desk. She could retrieve it when she came back and if he stole her computer or pictures, she'd have that, anyway.

She left the building and climbed into her CVR. She started it, then jockeyed around until the front bumpers of their two vehicles nearly touched.

He connected the jumper cables and climbed in his truck. "Rev your motor a little. I'll try to turn her over."

She nodded and pressed the accelerator. His motor roar to life. He got out and unclamped the cables. She shut off her car and climbed out.

"Thanks so much." His voice was strained and his smile was stiff.

"It was nothing." Turning, she stepped onto the sidewalk. "See you later." She took two steps up the sidewalk, thinking only of finishing her pictures and getting home.

Suddenly she heard the scrape of a heel on the sidewalk. She turned to look. In that moment, something heavy crashed onto the back of her head. Pain such as she'd never known and would ever know again shrieked through her brain. She fell. Before she hit the sidewalk, she was dead.

***

The man swore softly at the crumpled body. It would be a chore to get her into his outfit. And pray God someone didn't come along. Of course, he could always say he found her like this.

After several minutes of heavy lifting, he got the body stowed in the cab of the truck and covered with an old blanket. He fished his flashlight from the jockey box and shone it over her car. He hadn't touched it, so he didn't need to wipe off any fingerprints. He studied the ground for blood and found only a little puddle. He scooped it into an old box from the back of his truck and smoothed the dirt over the spot.

Returning to the office, he collected Sabrina's computer and found her purse under the desk. Carefully he wiped the door handle inside and out and checked the floor for tracks. It was clean. With a sigh, he returned to the truck. That had been close. Too close. Good thing he'd seen her car and had gone in to ask her about the cleaning job. His luck was holding.

Now if he could only find her camera!

***

From Gina's Blog, June 18, Thursday

Even though I didn't mean to take special pains with my appearance this morning, I change clothes three times and it takes me thirty minutes to put on my make-up and arrange my hair. Now what to wear? I settle on a pair of jeans, a green t-shirt and a cowboy-cut vest. With my new riding boots, I think I look the part. Yes, I can play the cowgirl. What really bothers me, though, is the lack of technology here -- no cell phone, very little internet. I feel like I'm cut off from the rest of the world. Oh, well. I'll be back in Spokane soon.

The drive to the Anderson ranch takes me a little over an hour. My GPS tells me to turn into their driveway. I obey and begin the journey down the two-mile gravel road to the ranch house. It's a nice place. Newly mown hay lay in neat rows across the fields, drying in the warm sunshine.

The house is a modest affair – a white two-story farmhouse that has been remodeled and added onto, like many in the area. A wide front porch looks out over rolling acres of farmland. In the back, corrals surround a large red barn and several other buildings.

The area between the house and the barn looks like a sale lot for equipment – I count three trucks, three pickups, two combines, a water tanker, sprayers, a tractor and several other farm vehicles I can't name. Among them are two good-sized stock trailers.

Jesse greets me on the front porch with his wide smile. "Howdy, Miss Lindsey."

"Please. Call me Gina." I follow him into the house, expecting to find chaos and disorder – the norm for most bachelors. But the front entryway is clean and sweet smelling and the rest of the house follows suit. Cookies are cooling on the counter in the kitchen and I smell a roast in the slow cooker.

"C'mon in. Dad's out hayin', and I should be out there, too, but he said I could show you around for a couple of hours. Would you like some coffee? A cookie?" He pours coffee into a mug and hands me a cookie – not on a platter, as a woman would. I resist a smile.

"Thanks." I bite into it. "Yum. Did you make these before you mopped the floor and vacuumed the carpet and did the dishes?"

"Sure. My cookin' and cleanin' skills are known all over the county." He laughs and shakes his head ruefully. "I have to be honest, I suppose, especially as you'll probably find out on your own. My Aunt Myrtle, Dad's sister, comes and does the house for us. She lives in Ekalaka. She's a tyrant. Keeps us on our toes."

"I can see that. I'm sorry you have to suffer so much." When I finish the coffee, Jesse takes me to the corral. Five horses are milling around – all quarter horses of various colors.

"I'll let you ride the black one. We call him Reverend. You'll like him. He's got a smooth gait. Mine's Charlie, the buckskin. Wanta come in the tack room and help?"

"Wouldn't miss it for the world." I hope my tone isn't too dry. There's nothing missing from the charm he'd displayed yesterday – if anything, he seems more expansive and friendly.

I brush Reverend and allow Jesse to saddle him. He's a large, friendly gelding who noses my hand for more treats after I give him a carrot. I rub his forehead and bridle him.

Jesse could have matched any tour guide in New York as we ride out across the prairie, stopping now and then to open a gate. We trot past a bubbling creek, wind our way through a patch of woods, and climb to the top of a butte. From there he points out the Rimrocks to the north, Highway 12 winding its way to Alzada, and the markers for their place.

"Where's the water bottling plant your Dad told me about?" I dismount stiffly, trying my hardest not to show my sore muscles. A cool, fresh breeze lifts my hair from my shoulders. I face into it and gaze out across the prairie.

"Behind the barn." He stands near my shoulder. "It's closed right now. We ran out of supplies, so we gave the workers some time off." He grins dismissively. "We're not like the big time producers, I'm afraid. A little more laid back."

"That's funny. Your dad invited me to see it and even offered me a free sample." I cock my head, watching him. Is he lying? Doesn't he want me to go inside the bottling plant?

His face is all innocence and he doesn't drop his eyes or turn away. "I'm gettin' a little worried about him. Ever since Mom died, he's been on medication for depression. Things don't stick in his mind. I told him we had to close shop for a spell." He paces to the brow of the hill.

"Do you run the plant?"

"I help with it, but he's the boss." He shrugs. "Gives him somethin' to do, I suppose, when we're not workin' the ranch." He steps closer to me and puts a light hand on my shoulder – not an intimate gesture, just friendly. "So what do you think of the west now, Miss Gopher Girl?"

I make the mistake of looking into his eyes. They are the deepest brown I'd ever seen. "Not bad." I laugh a little awkwardly and bend to pick a purple flower, managing to evade his hand. "Beats Central park by a mile. How many people do you employ at the plant?"

"Five or six. Why are you so interested? Do you want a job? I could probably manage that … then I'd see you a lot more." He circles my waist with his arm. Slowly he exerts gentle pressure to draw me closer.

"No!" I step away from him again. "I mean, no … I don't want a job. It just seems strange to me that you have … an industry like that in a rural area."

He pulls Charlie's head from a clump of grass. "It's not strange when you think of it. With the economy the way it is, lots of ranchers supplement their income with other things. Like ol' Billy over to Camp Crook. He has his own lumber mill and sells to the Japanese. And Randy Whittier, the head honcho at Forestry, he and his wife have a little nursery business, besides runnin' their spread. I can think of several others, too. Heck, even your uncle's got a processing plant. He makes liquid organic fertilizer."

"He does?" I meet his eyes to see if he's joking.

"No lie. You ask your aunt. Hey, let's get back. I want to show you the horse barn and the rodeo grounds. We've hosted some big events at our ranch."

I climb in the saddle, dreading the ride back to the ranch. I hate to point out to Jesse that Reverend's gait is as rough as sandpaper compared to my Arabian mare. He settles his hat firmly on his head and leads the way off the butte.

Back at the barn, we dismount and unsaddle both horses, watching as they trot out to pasture. He invites me to see the arena and barn. From this vantage point, I can see the large pole building that Jesse says houses the water bottling plant. There's no sign or indication of its purpose -- just a long metal building with weeds encircling it.

I decline a cold beer at the house, even though I would have liked one. I know his time is precious. Thunderclouds are building along the horizon and the forecast called for more storms tonight. He mentioned several times that they were sorely pressed to get as much hay baled as they could before it rained.

I make my way to the Honda and open the door. "I better get going. Tim and Evelyn are out haying, too, and I should be fixing them dinner."

"Wait a sec. Be right back." To my surprise, he lopes off to the house and returns several minutes later carrying something with both hands.

"Wha—" I stare as he plunks down a case of bottled water on the passenger seat.

A grin splits his face and his eyes twinkle. "Just so you know we really *do* bottle water." He shuts the door and comes around, standing very close to me, yet not touching.

I smile up at him. "I never doubted you bottled it. Whatever made you think I did?"

"Where'd you get that red hair? You know it shines in the sun like a copper penny?" He touches it almost reverently. "And those sea-green eyes that snap and sparkle like so many fireworks. Are you an Irish sprite or somethin'?"

"My Mom's Irish. Dad was English and Irish. Even though I'm not a sprite, you better watch yourself because I have a temper to match my hair."

A silly grin plays on his lips as he nods. "I can imagine. About the temper, that is."

I hope he can't hear the acrobatics my heart's performing in my chest, or see the way his touch sends my mind reeling and my perception of things softening. I know it sounds crazy, but it's like something is melting in my heart. *Is this love?* Right then a little voice speaks clearly in my mind. *Focus, Lindsey. You're not on a vacation.* It sounds like Dad.

"Thanks for the ride, cowboy. And the water." I hold out my hand to him. I don't know why. Do I expect him to kiss it like knights of old?

He squeezes my hand, leaning so close I smell his after shave. His lips brush my cheek and his tone is tender. "I enjoyed it, too, Gina. You have definitely brightened up the landscape around here! Can I ... see you again?"

I climb in the cab and turn on the ignition. "Definitely, Jesse. Anytime." I put the pickup in gear and glance at him as he removes his hand from the window. *Have I been too abrupt? Too formal?* I brake. "What's there to do around here, anyway?"

He grins, his dimples flashing. "Movie in Baker. Dance once in a while at the community hall. Or I could take you up flying. What would you like?"

"I'd love to fly with you." I say it sincerely. "When do you want to go?"

"I have to finish the haying, but we're about done. How about Sunday?"

"Sounds good."

"Come on over around ten. We can fly up to Medora and have lunch there."

"Medora?"

"Yeah. In North Dakota near the badlands. See you then, darlin'."

"Okay. Bye." I wave and head down the drive. Had he been a little too eager? Or is he as love-struck as he appears? It doesn't matter, I tell myself firmly. Maybe I could even persuade him to fly over the Long Pines and Short Pines. I nod, satisfied. Yes, this has possibilities. I begin to smile and as I pull onto the main road, the smile gets bigger.

At last, I'm getting somewhere. Not much but maybe enough.

Virginia Ann Work

Chapter 17

Slim Chances

From Gina's Blog, June 18, Thursday

I pass the entrance to Living Waters Bible Camp and spot a line of horses just entering the riding corral near the barn. The last rider is a man who looks familiar. I apply the brakes and turn into the driveway. It's the guy who'd helped me out of the snow drift in April. Chance. I wonder what his last name is. Slowly I drive past the corral, watching the kids dismount. Chance and another wrangler assist them.

I drive to the parking lot and wait as campers, counselors and maintenance staff file past. Drumming my fingernails on the steering wheel, I watch until I see him striding up the hill. Just as he passes my car, I climb out and catch his eye.

"Do my eyes deceive me, or is it truly Mr. Chance? Do you remember me? The woman you rescued last spring from a snow drift?"

"Gina Lindsey!" He strides over and shakes my hand heartily. "Chance McNeil, your friendly pick-up guy, at your service." He laughs at the double meaning, his face reddening. "Are you here to stay or just visitin'?"

"I'm working for my aunt on the ranch for a couple of months. I was driving by and thought I'd stop in. Have you been here all this time?"

I like the direct way he looks at me. He's built tall and slender and has long blond hair that is pulled back in a pony tail. His chin is covered with a two-day-old growth. He's wearing a dilapidated cowboy hat, worn jeans and a checkered long-sleeved shirt. His eyes are like blue ice chips except when he's smiling.

He swipes off his hat. "I've worked around. Ran out of a job just recently and came back. Been helpin' with the horses. Let's go up to the dining hall. I think they have coffee in there." He leads the way to the long, low building where the campers are already queuing up for lunch.

Inside, the big room is busy and loud. He glances in the door. "Just about time for lunch. Hey, why don't we grab something in town? I heard the Wagon Wheel has mighty fine hamburgers and milk shakes. What do you say?"

"Sure. I think my aunt's out in the hay field, so she won't worry if I'm late. You want to ride in my pickup?"

"No. Let's take my outfit. I gotta pick up some feed for the horses in town anyways."

He leads the way to his truck – a white Chevy Silverado. I'm surprised. It looks almost brand new. He opens the passenger door for me and I climb in.

"This isn't the pickup you were driving last April. Did you get a new one? Nice leather seats." I run my hand over the seat appreciatively and fasten the belt.

He chuckles. While he isn't charming like Jesse, his smile is genuine and when he laughs, his eyes light up, like the laughter's bubbling up from some deep fountain within. "Oh, the old thing I was drivin' that night belongs to the camp. I'd borrowed it. This one's mine."

He drives slowly by the meadow where the horses are feeding on lush grass. "See the sorrel mare over there? That's my horse. I have more in Washington but I favor that one. She's a Morab."

"In Washington? Where do you live?"

"North of Spokane is where I hang my hat mostly, yet I take jobs all over. I like to travel, see the country. I take jobs all over. I know you told me last spring where you're from, but I forgot."

"I'm from Spokane, too. Isn't that a coincidence?" I glance at him. He makes no response. "I keep my horse at a ranch outside of town. I used to live in New York."

He nods. "So I take it they haven't found your uncle yet?"

"No. That's why I'm here, I'm looking into it. I haven't found out much. These people are kind of closed to outsiders. Have you found that to be true?"

He shifts down as we enter Ekalaka. "These folks watch out for their own. They're friendly enough, salt of the earth by my reckonin', but they ain't goin' to open up to strangers. And you're a stranger for a long, long time in these parts."

As we eat hamburgers and fries in the small, home-town café, Chance fends off my questions and asks some of his own. I feel like we're dueling. I tell him I work for law enforcement and he doesn't ask which branch. He says his mother died when he was in high school and after that, his dad took a job in the U.S. Consulate in Columbia.

He shuts up when I ask him about his life in Columbia. He has me baffled. While he's friendly and talkative, I sense he's covering his true thoughts and intents. I long to pierce his barricade, to find out who he really is and what he's about. There's a lot he isn't saying and I wonder why. I steal a glance at his profile. *Chance McNeil!* It isn't his true name; I'd bet a month's wage on that.

I study the locals as I chew the thick, juicy hamburger thoughtfully and wash it down with a Diet Pepsi. A group of men fill one table, nursing cups of coffee and talking about fixing an old tractor; some women sit at another table, talking about gardens, grandkids and their aches and pains. They are as Chance said -- downright good people. I compare them with the crowd at the coffee shop I frequented in Manhattan and smile. I have to admit -- I'd rather be here.

When we finish and he's paid the bill, we get in the truck. "Wal, I gotta get that feed. After I do, would you like to run up to see Medicine Rocks? It's not far. Did you see them on the way down?"

I nod. "Yeah, I saw them. When I was here before, Uncle Elton and Aunt Bobbi took me to see them. I wouldn't mind driving up with you, if we don't take too long. Aunt Bobbi probably wants me to fix supper." Even though I really don't want to go to the state park with Chance, I think he'll open up more and tell me about himself. This bit about Columbia has me intrigued. *He knows something; I swear he knows a lot, and I'm determined to break through his defenses.*

Call me calloused for accepting his invitation to get what I want out of him, yet I've learned to be that way. You can't witness some of the things I'd seen without a certain hardening of the arteries or, as in my case, the heart.

"Great." He backs up. "I hope that storm doesn't hit before we get there. Or while we're there." He drives over to the feed store and loads up.

On our way north, I study the vast expanse of sky. Black clouds are rolling in over the prairie and the wind's picking up. "I bet everyone who's haying is praying like mad that the storm will hold off." I laugh. "Slim chance *that* it will do them any good."

"You don't believe in prayer?"

"I don't believe in anything except hard work and determination." Even though I don't want to sound hard, I believe it's best to let people know right off where you stand on issues. "I strongly support the pro-choice movement. After all, a woman should have the prerogative over her own body. And ..."

He holds up his hand. "Hey, get off your soapbox, Gina. I'm not much into arguing. You can believe what you want. Period. End of discussion."

I stare out the window, feeling like a ten-year-old kid that had just been slapped down.

He looks over at me and smiles. "Friends?" His eyes are light colored now, more gray than blue. They seem to change with his mood, as I'd noticed when we talked. When he mentioned his Mom dying they were dark, almost black. I have to admit he has a certain kind of good looks, if only he'd clean up.

I smile. "Yeah, okay."

Huge sandstone rocks appear on the horizon, their pock-marked sides looming white in the rays of sunshine that escape the cloudbank. "Why are they called Medicine Rocks?"

"This was a sacred meeting place for the Sioux in the region." He grins. "I picked up a brochure in the library." He pulls onto a narrow dirt road which winds through the park. "They gathered here to sing and dance for health, for good success in their wars and to have lots of kids." We pass the first of the standing monoliths. "Maybe some of their spirits still live here. Eerie place, huh."

"I like it. It's kind of austere and lonely, but I don't believe in ghosts."

"No, I don't suppose you do. Miss Practical always, aren't we?" He tempers the words with another smile and I let the comment slide away.

As we continue down the road, I can't take my eyes off the rocks that are scattered across a wide valley like children's toys littering a playroom. They are solid giants on the gentle hills, carved by the wind and rain into fantastic shapes, some tall and narrow, others squat and fat, all with footholds, worn by climbers through the centuries, marking the sides. Stately pines, standing guard over the quiet meadows, sway in the wind.

Other than a black CRV that's parked in one of the picnic places, we seem to have the place to ourselves.

Chance shifts down. "Hey, do you want to hike around some?"

"Sure. See that big rock? I remember it. There's a cave inside, isn't there?"

Chance opens his door and comes around to hold mine. "Looks like it. I've only been here once. You'll have to show me around."

I lead the way through knee-high grass. The wind moans in the trees. "I guess we'd better hurry. That storm's almost here. Let's get over to that rock and inside the cave."

I can't help but compare him to Jesse. Chance is rough-hewn, angular, with a sharp jawbone and a scar that traces its way down his cheek. At times his eyes search mine unnervingly and his manner is just shy of brusque. While I'm not afraid of him, I wonder why he won't talk of his past. Of his family. Why does he hold his jaw tense and his back straight? Why does he wear a shoulder holster and a gun?

The sun appears suddenly from behind the clouds, warming my back, and the wind brings the fresh smells of sage and pine and sweet clover. I inhale deeply. "It doesn't get much better than this."

He helps me up a steep incline to a massive rock and into the cave that's carpeted with sand. It's nothing more than a narrow fissure that widens toward the bottom, but there's a feeling here as if we're not alone. The floor's littered with bird droppings and feathers. In the very center, underneath an opening in the rock at the top, a black spot marks the remains of a campfire. The sides of the cave twist like molten metal.

I gaze at the sky through the hole. "Oh, yeah. Now I remember why I liked to come here."

Chance peers out an opening in the rock on far side. "I don't think you can get down over here."

I follow him and look. The rock slopes down about ten feet, indentations for feet and hands marking the way. "Sure I can, on my butt. You go first and catch me if I slide too fast."

He scoots down first, leaping the last five feet to the sandy soil, then turns and holds out his arms. "Don't come too fast. I can't hold that much weight."

"Why, you …" I descend carefully, grabbing onto the handholds, using my feet as brakes. Bumping to the ground, I stand and dust off the seat of my jeans. "See? I can do it. Let's go."

We look into several other holes, startle nesting birds that fly away with a flurry of wings and loud protests, and admire the purple and white wild flowers that bloom in clumps as if someone had planted them. I take pictures of everything – the rocks and the prairie with the storm clouds rolling in over a blue sky. I even snap several of Chance, even though he keeps his head bent and his face in the shadow of his hat.

As we circle around on the track, he points to a secluded glen. "You wanta rest awhile? I've got a blanket in the truck. Be back in a jiffy."

The words are on my lips to call him back, yet something stops me. Is it the funny way he looks at me, as if he's bewitched by my beauty? I chuckle. *Yeah, right.* The idea of a blanket makes me a little uncomfortable. What did he mean by that? I climb a slight incline and enter a circle of small boulders. Maybe it was in a place like this where the Indians danced. The wind gusts among the pines and the sky darkens. Off in the distance thunder rumbles.

Chance trots into the circle and spreads out the blanket. I sit on it cross-legged and he lounges nearby on his side, his eyes on the far horizon. We watch the storm approach over the prairie and more than once I feel his gaze on my face. He hasn't broken into a long speech about his checkered past. If it was checkered. Why won't he talk?

Like I was thinking aloud, I say suddenly, breaking the long silence, "What's your *real* name?" It catches him off guard, for he'd settled back on one elbow and removed his hat. I know he's startled because he lets out a muffled grunt.

Yet he only cocks an eyebrow and gives me a quizzical glance. "I'll tell you, if you'll tell me what you're really doin' here, Miss Lindsey."

I laugh. "So it's back to Miss Lindsey, huh? I'm investigating the disappearance of my uncle and trying to help my aunt with the ranch. Now, don't you think we'd better head home? That storm's getting closer." I lift my palm. "Rain."

He studies the sky and puts on his hat. I can *feel* him throwing up walls, and wish I hadn't said that about his name. "Just a little squall. I guess ..."

What he guessed I will never find out, for just then a bolt of lightning splits the sky just above our heads and on its heels, a clap of thunder. The smell of sulfur fills the air, the sky is indigo and the wind howls in the trees like demons on the loose. Or maybe it's the ghosts of enraged Indians. The bare-faced rocks loom over me like hollow skulls, leering menacingly.

We leap to our feet. I grab the blanket. He stalks off toward the truck with his head bent. I wish he'd waited for me, asked if I needed help, taken my arm, *something*.

"Hey, Chance! Wait up!" My words are flung back on the wind.

Then the rain comes – solid sheets of it, so much so I can hardly see. He pauses and looks back. I'm drenched by the time I reach him. He grabs my arm with a fierce grip, and suddenly I'm more afraid of him than the storm. He points ahead. "There's an overhanging rock over there! C'mon!"

He pulls me through the rain. At one point, I fall and he yanks me up. Another bolt of lightning lands not twenty feet away and gathers into a ball of rolling fire. I scream.

His face is pale in the flickering light. "Hurry!" He casts about as if getting his bearings. "Follow me."

I stumble after him, but I can't keep up. He ducks into a shallow hole underneath an overhanging ledge, and I arrive several seconds later, huddling against the sandstone as the storm rages. Pulling my knees to my chest, I try to keep from screaming every time a bolt lands close. Slowly the storm recedes like an angry dog, its mutterings and grumblings echoing among the standing rocks.

In the dim light, Chance's face is shiny with sweat, his lips compressed in a thin, white line.

I stretch my legs. "Whew! That was a show I hadn't counted on. Let's get back to the truck. I'm soaked." I crawl out onto the wet grass. Yellow sky appears from under the ragged edges of the skirts of the storm and the wind shrieks across the prairie.

He stands beside me. "Yeah. It looks like it's about over. Let's go."

"Which way?" I try to wring water from the sodden mess of my hair.

He nods to the right. "Let's go that way, around by the road. It'll be easier walking."

I follow his lead, yet heavy dread fills my heart. It seems a long way around, if my sense of direction is correct. Why is he going this way? My feet feel like there are leaden weights on them. I glance at Chance to see if he feels like anything's amiss, but I can tell nothing from his stern countenance. Is he mad at me? Is he afraid?

The light returns and yet clouds still block the sunshine. I shiver in the cold wind. "I think we're heading wrong. We should be going that way." I point in the opposite direction.

"Wait." He holds up a hand. "I thought I heard something."

"Where?" All I hear is the heavy thumping of my heart.

He stops and swings his head right and left, his eyes searching the undergrowth. "Over there. Might be an animal."

"Let's get out of here!"

"What's that?" He points to a lump of something lying near a rock.

I shrug, just barely glancing at it. "Just some clothes." We walk forward. It appears to be a sodden mass of clothes, or is it …? It's lying still, too still. A deadly chill sweeps through me.

"Stay back!" He moves forward cautiously.

"What is it?" Without waiting for an answer, I stride to where he stands five feet away from the object. But it's not an object. It's a person.

A woman lies at the base of the rock, her legs twisted underneath her, her head gashed and crusted with blood, her mouth open, her hair a tangle of short, blonde curls. Blood stains her white t-shirt. Her jeans and tennis shoes are smeared with mud.

My training kicks in. I step forward and feel the neck. No pulse. "She's dead." I stand. "Stay away, Chance. Don't touch anything. We need to call the sheriff. Do you have your phone? Do you get service here?"

"It's at the truck." His ashen face is inscrutable. He clenches and unclenches his fists. "I know… knew her. It's Sabrina. I don't know her last name. She worked at Forestry, cleaning. She cleaned the house at the ranch where I worked, too. That's how I knew her." He swallows hard. "Must have come here and … climbed up … then fell."

"We don't know what happened. We only know she's dead. We have to call the police. Go get your cell phone. I'll stay here. Hurry!"

I watch him lope toward the truck and disappear around one of the sandstone rocks.

A few minutes later, he returns. "Crosby's on his way. He's also the coroner." He takes off his jacket and drops it over my shoulders. I find a semi-dry place near the rock and lean my head back, weary beyond telling, wondering how I can make it through the next few hours.

He squats beside me. I almost expect him to roll a cigarette, but he doesn't.

A wondering sort of fear fills my being – I always feel like this when confronted with death. The wind soughs through the trees and they sway gracefully. Now the formations shine wetly in the dim light, inviting me to climb them. Funny how a few moments ago they were objects of terror and danger. Rays of sunshine escape the clouds and warm my back. A crow caws raucously from a tree overhead.

He takes a deep breath. "What branch of law enforcement are you with, Gina?" He doesn't look at me. His tone indicates something … I didn't know what … concern? No, more like the fact that he wants our relationship to go deeper. He wants to know about me. It's the first crack I've sensed in his defenses.

But how can I tell him I'm an undercover DEA agent? What if he's one of … them? The drug cartel? *Fall back on your story and make it sound convincing.*

"I was an officer with the NYPD, street detective, and got caught in a firefight. My Dad died and I was put on probation. After that, I got more training and worked for two years as a detective. I wasn't happy … couldn't be happy … in New York, so I put in for a transfer and came to Spokane. You know why I'm here. Looking for my uncle. Maybe investigating his murder. Now how about you, Mr. McNeil? Care to share a little with me about yourself?"

He studies the sky. "I was raised in Colorado on a ranch. When my mom died of cancer, my dad took a job with the U.S. Consulate in Bogota, Columbia, like I told you. My older brother, Stan, died there." He pauses, his jaw working. "I came back and went to UCLA. Studied law. Worked for time as a private investigator for a guy. Then Dad moved to Seattle. He's a state senator. We got ourselves a little ranch north of Spokane."

"How come you're here?"

He grins and casts me a sharp glance. "Just knew you'd ask that. Wal, it's like this …"

"Here they come." I see lights out on the highway and stand up. "Yes? You were saying?"

"I got the wanderin' itch, I suppose you'd say. Heard a lot about this country from a friend of mine and wanted to see it. When I get tired of it, I'll mosey on home."

We're sparring again. I'm getting tired of the game. "You don't have to pour that western accent on me, Mr. Cowboy, or you're going to mosey right out of my life." I turn away, but not before I catch a twinkle in his eyes.

The squad car drives up and the sheriff steps out.

Chance waves as Mike Crosby glances around. "Over here. Howdy, sir. I'm Chance McNeil. And this lady here is Gina Lindsey."

Mike shakes Chance's hand and smiles at me. "Howdy, Chance. Miss Lindsey. We meet again. What do you have here?"

I answer in a low voice. "A woman's dead, sir. I'll show you."

Chapter 18

Harding County Sheriff

From Gina's Blog, June 18, Thursday evening

I lead Sheriff Mike Crosby to the body.

"You haven't touched anything, have you?" He kneels in the damp sand and feels the woman's neck.

"No, sir. Do you want me to call an ambulance?" My voice is terse, professional.

Mike straightens. "Nothing they can do for her. Her body position indicates she fell. I ain't assumin' nothin', though." He studies the rock face. "No sharp protrusions sticking out, no little ledges, nothing."

He examines the ground carefully around the body. "She shouldn't be dead. At that height, a broken leg, yes. It's not high enough to be lethal. I think she's been here overnight. Did you see her hiking around? Hear anything? A call? A scream?"

I wipe my eyes. I'm not crying, just tearing from the wind. "No, sir. We didn't hike much. We went south of here, around those rocks and back up over there. The storm came and we huddled under an overhang. I think she's been dead awhile."

He rubs his chin. "Maybe. Can either of you identify her?"

Chance nods. "Uh, yeah. But only her first name. Sabrina. She cleaned houses around here. There's a black CRV over by the entrance, and I think it's hers. I didn't think much of it when we drove in."

"You'll both be expected to give a deposition in my office. If you can think of anything that would shed light on this ... "

Another squad car pulls in. Mike groans and rolls his eyes. A sheriff and a deputy get out and walk over. I wonder who it is and why they came. Had Mike called in back-up? The other sheriff puffs, short of breath, as he forces his short, fat legs across the grass, his belly protruding from his waistline. A day-old scruff of a beard covers his lower face and part of his breakfast, egg, I note as he draws close, decorates his shirt.

He holds out his hand to Mike. "Good afternoon, Sheriff Crosby."

Mike shakes it. "Howdy, Dugal. Sheriff Dugal, this is Chance McNeil and Gina Lindsey. Chance and Gina, this is Pierce Dugal, sheriff of Harding County over to Buffalo, South Dakota. This is his deputy, Waldo Clayton. Dugal, just to let you know, Miss Lindsey is a police officer from Spokane, Washington, and she's assistin' me with this case."

Dugal wears a revolver on his belt and carries a 30.06 rifle. When I shake his hand and look into his small piggy eyes, I recoil. His face holds the look of an ill-tempered bulldog and his eyes are icy, staring at me like he would rather fill me full of holes than shake my hand.

Waldo, the deputy, is a pleasant relief from his boss. He grins at me appreciatively and tips his hat. He's young, of slender build, red hair and greenish eyes.

"Whatcha got here, sheriff?" Dugal blows out his cheeks and glances around.

Mike clears his throat. "Ain't you leavin' your county under-manned, Dugal? I didn't request back-up. I think Miss Lindsey and I can take care of this."

Dugal loops his thumbs in his belt and rocks back on his heels, giving Mike a belligerent grin. "Heard it on my scanner and since I was in the area, thought I'd check to see if you needed help. Someone fall from the rock here? Is she dead? Who is it?"

I catch Chance's eyes and shake my head. *What an idiot! Like someone out of Dukes of Hazard.* Of course the woman's dead, about as dead as they come.

Mike shifts his feet. "Chance identified her as Sabrina. She cleans houses, it seems."

"Sabrina, huh? Wonder what she was doing here?" He feels for a pulse, examines the body and turns it over, trampling the ground with his clumsy feet.

Mike clenches his fists. "I haven't finished with my investigation yet. I'd appreciate it you'd let me do my job."

"Wal, excuse me. You'd better git busy, then, Sheriff." Dugal steps back.

Mike turns to me. "Could you get my notebook from the seat of my car and the camera? And the caution tape."

"Sure." I'm glad to get out of Dugal's presence, even for a few moments. When I return, the Harding County sheriff is still hovering. He watches as Mike and I string out the caution tape and tie it to two slender pines.

Dugal frowns. "Why're you doin' that? This ain't no crime scene. It's an accident scene. You're the coroner. You just need to take the body away, that's all."

Mike kneels beside the dead woman. "All we know is that she died. And as Carter County's sheriff and coroner, I decide when to take the body. I suggest that you and your deputy search a wider area for anything she may have dropped, any kind of clue as to why she was here. Check to see if someone was with her. And try not to get lost."

Mike pushes back the woman's hair after they had gone. "Look at this, Gina. A sharp blow to the back of the head. If she fell, wouldn't she have hit the front of her head? Head wounds bleed a lot, but I don't see much blood. I'm guessing she was killed somewhere else and transported here to make it look like an accident. Give me the camera. I'll take a few pictures. You go ahead and draw the scene for me. I hate doin' those sketches."

While he took pictures, I examine the sand. Had the woman dropped something? I find nothing. Chance stands nearby, his hands jammed in his pockets.

I spare him a quick look. "Cold?"

"I'm okay. Would you mind if I wait in the outfit? In fact, I can drive it over here."

"Sure. I won't be long." I begin sketching the crime scene. It's something I enjoy doing and I'm glad I can assist the sheriff.

Mike comes over and studies my drawing. "Nice work. Now add in the dimensions and we'll call it a day." He searches through the grass.

"What's the name of Dugal's deputy?"

"Waldo Clayton. A good cop, even though he's made some big enemies here. Jesse Anderson, for one."

"Why?"

"Rivalry for the ladies, I'm thinking. They're both good looking, in case you didn't notice. There's something else, though. An old grudge, maybe."

I motion to the top of the rock. "Are you going to climb up there?"

"Yeah. You don't have to hang around, though. I think I can wrap this up. You're cold. Why don't you go on home?" He takes the notebook from me. "Thanks for helpin' me out."

"Any time, sheriff." I *am* chilled and it isn't just from the rain.

I can't keep my teeth from chattering. I feel funny, too. Sort of wobbly and dizzy. *What's going on?* Why does finding a body bother me like this? I'd seen countless bodies. Scraped them off the pavement, pieced them together to find cause of death, gagged over them, examined them, dreamed them. Then I think of Uncle Elton and shudder. Maybe it's his death … disappearance … that bothers me. Is this how he died? Did someone drop him down a hole or off a cliff?

Mike lifts his hat and scratches his head as he watches Dugal and his deputy scrounge under the trees. "What are those two bozos doing? I hope they don't get their mitts on the victim's car. Might ruin a lot of prints." He sighs and puts his hat on. "After the undertaker removes the body, I think I'll call it a night and come back tomorrow."

"Aren't you supposed to post an officer here to make sure no one disturbs the scene?" I hand him the caution tape.

He shrugs. "Supposed to, but we don't follow the rules here in Carter County. Who's goin' to come and mess things up? Dugal already did a pretty good job of that, didn't he?"

I want to remind him that if this truly was a murder, the killer might come and change things for his advantage. After telling Mike good-bye, I climb into Chance's truck. He has the heater going and it feels good. Neither of us talk much on the way back to the camp. Chance seems pre-occupied and moody.

I push back my hair and sigh. "I suppose we ought to go give our depositions tomorrow. You wanta ride in with me?" He looks over and I see something behind his eyes – is it worry? Fear?

"No, I have some things to do in town. I'll go on my own. Thanks, anyway."

He drives into the parking lot at camp. I open my door. "Thanks for the lunch, Chance, and for taking me out to the park. I had a good time."

He grunts and comes to hold the door while I get out in an old-fashioned gallantry kind of way. I like it. "Sorry it had to end like it did. But one good thing – I got to see you in action. I believe you're a fine cop."

I grin at him, pleased at his praise. "Thanks. See you around."

Climbing in my (or rather Nick's) blue pickup, I wave to him as I drive away. He stands in the center of the parking lot, a lost and forlorn expression on his face. I wish I could confide in him. Yet there are many things that still puzzle me about him.

Why had he suggested we drive out to Medicine Rocks? Why had he taken the longer way to his truck? Was it so I would find the body? Did he know it was there? I shake my head. No, until I know a lot more about Chance McNeil, or whatever his name is, I'm not going to spill my guts to him. I don't care *how* forlorn he looks!

The wind whips my hair and rolls a tumble weed across the drive as I step out of the pickup at the Lindsey Ranch. I mount the rickety steps and enter the house. Tim and Bobbi are out in the hay fields. I take a shower, do some wash, and send a report to Cap Matthews.

After putting a casserole in the oven and setting the table, I pour myself a cup of coffee. In the rocking chair on the front deck, I watch the sunset fade over Lone Butte. It's so quiet here! Peace settles over my soul, as if the gentle wind and the soft colors of the sunset and the sound of crickets by the creek are for my benefit alone.

Wait. I see a glimmer of light up on the top of the butte. I stand to see better, but can't locate it again. Running to the pickup, I fetch my binoculars and scan the area. Still nothing. I have the eerie feeling that someone's on top of the butte, spying on the ranch. Not a nice feeling. I settle again on the chair, rubbing down the gooseflesh on my arms. It isn't long before I see headlights bouncing home from the fields.

The peace is gone, and a strange kind of terror replaces it, as if someone lurks in the shadows of the bushes, waiting to kill me. Maybe I'm not far from wrong. I find myself clenching the arms of the chair, fighting against sheer panic.

I've got to stop this madness. I have to solve this case and get back to Spokane.

As I finish preparations for dinner and as Tim and Bobbi come stumping up to the house, I resolve to get going on the case. Time is wasting and the delay is playing into the hands of the criminals.

Chapter 19

A Good Deed Never Goes Unpunished

Carter County, Montana, July 19, Friday morning

Chance squinted at his laptop's small screen. The cursor blinked annoyingly at the end of his half-finished sentence in the email to his older sister, Emily. Why couldn't he concentrate this morning? Why did Gina Lindsey's face keep intruding on his thoughts? He pushed back from the desk and glanced around cabin, searching for inspiration.

He was sorry his encounter with Gina had ended so disastrously. He'd watched her drive away and wanted to call her back. Wanted to confide in her. Wanted to see those lips turn up in a smile. A real smile. Why did she have that haunted look in her eyes, as if she'd seen things no one should see or fought personal battles that have no end?

He stood and stretched. He was glad he'd moved from the small trailer to this cabin farther from the center of the camp. It was furnished with a double-sized bed against the far wall, a love seat that had seen better days and a desk. A bathroom the size of a small closet took up one corner, a kitchenette the other. A small, wobbly table served as his dining room. His 30.06 rifle hung on hooks above the door.

Well, he'd better get this letter finished to Emily. He plunked down on the hard chair and finished his reply. After sending it, he pushed back, got another cup of coffee, his mind still on Gina.

Why was he so intrigued by her? She was so different than any other girl he'd ever known. Her hair was like a reddish gold halo. In the rain, it lay thick and curly around her small face, framing eyes that mocked and challenged him. She brought to mind an elf, a mischievous elf, who would nab your best silverware and your virtue at the same time.

He paced to the table and picked up the pictures he had printed the other day in Baker – photos of the empty grow patch he'd taken last April, then the ones of the fence and the patch he'd taken a few days ago. Not much to go on, but something. They'd come out crisp and clear. He tapped the desk and wondered where the operation was based. It must be at a ranch or farm around here somewhere.

And who should he show the pictures to? Sheriff Crosby? The Short Pines wasn't his jurisdiction. How about Randy Whittier, the supervisor over at the Custer National Forestry office in Camp Crook? He'd met him when he applied for work and had taken an instant liking to him. How about Sheriff Dugal? No. He wouldn't go to Dugal with a lost cat report. Well, he had to contact someone.

The growers were getting bolder. He had no doubt that the woman whose body they'd found at Medicine Rocks had died at the hands of the drug cartel. If they'd killed Gina's uncle, this made two deaths. More would come. It was inevitable. With that much money, people were going to die.

He rose. First he'd make a phone call to his contact with the FBI, Agent Alan Costain, in Rapid City. For three years now, he and Alan had tracked the flow of illegal drugs in and out of the country, especially from Mexico. For two years he'd worked as an undercover agent and after that, he decided to cut ties with the FBI and go it alone. Maybe that wasn't such a good idea.

He tucked the pictures into his shirt pocket and pulled on his boots. At the camp office, he asked Connie if he could make a phone call. "I need a little privacy. Is there somewhere ..."

"Go over to Mr. Fairchild's office. He isn't in right now. In fact, I don't think anyone's there. You can use the phone. Just punch zero for an outside line."

"Thanks, Connie."

"Who was the redhead? A girlfriend?"

He was more than a little surprised that she'd noticed. "No. Just a ... friend. I should have brought her up and introduced her, but I thought you were busy."

Connie grinned knowingly. "That's okay. Next time, though, I want to meet her."

He made his call and agreed to meet with Alan the next day in Buffalo. In the meantime, the FBI agent suggested he talk to Randy Whittier and try to get a location on the grow patch. Even though Chance agreed to his suggestion, something at the back of his mind sent off a warning signal. The more people who knew about this, the more danger he was in, and he was reluctant to talk to anyone. Yet he needed help. Needed it desperately.

He hung up and jumped in his truck. Glancing at his watch, he accelerated, for it was nearly lunchtime. Hopefully Randy would be in his office. The muddy road was slippery and tedious, but he made it to Camp Crook and the Forestry office without mishap. The bell dinged and the secretary looked up. "I'm Chance McNeil, ma'am. May I see Mr. Whittier?"

She gave him a thorough, if swift, once-over, then punched a button on the inter-office phone. When she hung up, she said, "You can go on in, Mr. McNeil. He said he'd see you right away."

Randy was on the phone when he entered. He waved Chance to a chair. His sandy colored hair stood out stiffly from his head, as if he'd combed his hands through it all day. He smiled pleasantly at Chance, his grey eyes twinkling. His green uniform was rumpled and coffee stained.

Forestry maps covered the walls, dotted with pins. Untidy stacks of papers covered the desk. A half-eaten apple kept company with a Hershey's bar and a cup of coffee. Despite the clutter, Randy directed a vast portion of land in the Custer National Forest that included both South Dakota and eastern Montana with admirable efficiency. He had a no-nonsense approach to his job and a forthright manner that Chance liked.

Randy ended his call, uncoiled his large body from behind the desk, and held out his hand. "Good afternoon, Chance. Thanks for coming in. Your application's been approved for the summer." He tapped a file folder and smiled. "I sure can use you."

"Thanks." Chance shifted uneasily, still uncertain if he should confide in him. "I got something to show you, sir. Can we go somewhere private?"

"Yeah. I'm finished for this morning." Randy rearranged a pile of papers, finished his coffee, and put on his hat. "Let's grab a bite at the cafe first, and then I'll show you what we've been doing up in the Pines."

After a quick lunch, Randy drove south out of town toward Capitol, then turned west toward Wickum Gulch. Half an hour later, he drove onto a dirt road. He motioned to a charred patch on the hillside. "We've been doing some controlled burning up there."

He pulled to a stop and shut off the motor. After silence filled cab for a few minutes, he said, "What did you want to show me, Chance?"

Chance brought out the pictures. Without a word, he handed them over. Randy opened the envelope and flipped through them.

He wiped his forehead. "What am I looking at, Chance? Is this what I think it is?"

Chance nodded. "I found a grow patch right here in the South Pines. A big one. Last spring I happened onto it and went back just a few days ago. That's when I got these. They have a camouflage net that I imagine they spread over the plants. Couldn't see down into the canyon but I got these of their guard towers. I also got a souvenir in my shoulder."

"Have you talked to the sheriff about this?" Randy handed the pictures back and lit a cigarette. His florid face was illuminated for a second with the match.

"No, sir. Don't know who to trust."

"Can you find this place again? You say it was in the Short Pines?"

Chance tucked the pictures back into his pocket. "Yes, sir."

"Then I suppose we'd better go in and talk to Crosby. Although the Short Pines are in Dugal's jurisdiction."

"I know. Can you do an aerial surveillance of the area?" Chance stared out the side window, weariness pulling at his muscles, his soul. He longed to be finished with this business. Four years was too long to spend seeking revenge. *Seeking justice*, he reminded himself. It was time he figured out what else God had for his life. He couldn't stop now, though -- he was in it, up to his neck.

"We can try, but if they have camouflage netting, I don't know what we'd see."

Silence descended while Randy finished his smoke, his hand shaking as he ground it out in the ashtray. He turned to Chance. "I need help, too. This is ... sorta confidential."

"What's up?"

Randy stared out the mud-splattered windshield. "Elton and I had our differences. The man had a temper. The last time he came in, we had words, and he left in a huff. Never spoke to me again."

"Was he upset about the leasing agreements for summer pasture up in the Pines?"

"Naw. That was a smoke screen, I think. 'Course old Elton was always mad at everyone who didn't give him what he wanted. This was something different." He paused.

Chance shifted, wishing he'd get to the point.

"The day before Elton disappeared, I was in the restroom at the Buckhorn, in the stall, and two men came in. It was Elton and Sheriff Dugal. Elton said he had to talk, right aways. He sounded nervous or scared. Dugal said not in here, idiot, come to my office tomorrow. Elton didn't sound too happy, but he said okay."

"You got any idea what he had on his mind?"

Randy shook his head. "Not a clue. I didn't think of it again until after Elton disappeared, and I got to thinking. What if he was onto something and got himself killed for it? I'd be to blame, wouldn't I? I talked to Mike about it, but I still feel there's somethin' else I ought to do."

Chance let out his breath, slow and easy. "You're not to blame, Randy. Did you hear any names?"

Randy shook his head. "No, come to think of it, I didn't.

"What'd Mike say?"

"Said he'd check it out." He sighed. "You know Mike. It takes him a while to sink his teeth into something. That's why I'm askin' you. You're all around the country and you can find out all sorts of things. I can't do nothin' until I have proof."

"Well, I'll go talk to Mike." Chance straightened his legs.

Randy turned the truck around. "You'll keep this under your hat, won't you?"

"Bet your boots. And I'll keep my ears open, too."

They drove back to the Forestry office in silence. After Chance told Randy goodbye, he climbed into his pickup and drove over to Buffalo, South Dakota. After parking at the new town building, he walked into the sheriff's office.

Sheriff Dugal was busy and barely gave Chance a nod when the secretary told him to go in.

Chance waited a decent time and cleared his throat. "Hello, sheriff."

Dugal lifted his head. "Howdy. What can I do for you?"

"What would you do if I told you I found a big grow patch in the Short Pines? Marijuana."

"Have you found such a place, son?"

"Not very likely, is it, sir. Just wondering what I should do about it. Whose jurisdiction would it be under?"

Dugal lifted himself from his chair, pulled down his jacket and glared at Chance. "Listen, son. I don't have time to talk in riddles and what ifs. I'm a busy man. You come in here with proof, and I'll take a look into it. It's my jurisdiction, yes, but you're barking up the wrong tree. There ain't no grow patch in this here whole dang county. Or in Carter County, neither."

Chance nodded. "Thank you, sir. Just curious."

Dugal shot him a glance, returning to his computer.

Back in his truck, Chance sighed and turned the key. Well, so much for that. He had been interested to see Dugal's reaction and he'd gotten his answer. Yes, sir. Dugal wasn't about to get involved. Not even if he had proof.

He ordered a hamburger in the Oasis Cafe in Buffalo, and by the time he finished, it was getting dark. The trip from Buffalo to Camp Crook was uneventful, and he drove out of Camp Crook in the swiftly falling darkness.

A few miles later, he saw a car tilted crazily in the ditch. A young woman stood beside it, picking her way carefully through the mud. He stopped and lowered the window. "You all right, miss? Need some help?"

She nodded, wringing her hands, her dark hair flying in the wind. "Oh, thank you for stopping. Yes, I need help. Do you think you could pull me out? Or call someone?" Her voice wobbled. Tears streaked her cheeks.

"I'll try, but I don't know how much I can do."

The car was an old Ford with a dented fender and a broken tail light. He squished through the mud and leaned down to see where he could attach the chain. It was while he was in this awkward position that he heard heavy footsteps coming around the car and he knew he was in trouble.

Two men wearing ski masks appeared. One held a sawed-off shotgun, the other a baseball bat. Chance reacted immediately. He dove in low, choosing to tackle the one who held the bat, grabbed his legs, twisting his head to avoid the bat as it swished menacingly through the air. It hit his back as he connected.

Pain seared through his body, blinding him in its intensity. They fell together, rolling in the mud. He landed a punch on the man's chin, then pushed away and scrambled to his feet, hoping the guy holding the shotgun wouldn't get a good sight on him. Not a nice way to die, a shotgun blast in your stomach.

The man with the bat regained his feet and swung again. Chance dodged the blow and kicked, connecting with the man's groin. The assailant doubled over, dropped the bat, groaning.

The second man, casting aside the shotgun, rushed Chance and pulled back to deliver a blow aimed for his stomach. Chance danced away, then came charging back to land a fist on the man's chin. He dropped. By now the other guy had recovered and grabbed the bat again. He swung. Chance ducked away and kicked upward, hoping to get him in the groin. Suddenly, from behind the car, a third man appeared. *Great.*

They threw him to the ground, tied his hands in front and pulled a ski mask over his head. "Get him out of here before someone comes."

Chance didn't recognize the voice. Someone fished his keys from his pocket. He was thrown onto the back seat of the car. It lurched forward. Dimly he heard his own truck start up; the headlights burned through the mask. His heart sank as he realized they weren't leaving it on the road. This was going to be serious.

He felt each bone-jarring bounce on the short journey. The car stopped, and they yanked him out. He smelled the damp wetness of a creek, heard the men's grunts and muttered comments. His mask slid sideways and through the eye openings, he glimpsed a decrepit trailer house and an old barn. Box elders bent their branches to the wind. A door creaked open and they dragged him into the barn. Rotted hay and mold assaulted his senses.

Someone jammed the mask down tighter over his eyes while two pairs of hands patted him down and searched his pockets, removing everything, including the pictures.

A deep voice barked in his ear. "Who're you working for?"

"Living Waters Bible Camp." His voice was scratchy, his throat dry. He wished he sounded tough. And brave.

"Have some fun with him, fellas," the boss said.

Chance lifted his arms to protect his head, but he couldn't shield his body from their kicks and blows. One man hit him with the bat; it felt like a train slamming into him.

"Not the bat, you fool!" The ring-leader's deep voice boomed in a sudden stillness. "Just your fists and feet!"

Kidneys, back, buttocks, knees, the blows were placed wickedly and skillfully. Finally their leader called them off. Through a fog of pain, Chance groaned and tried to hold onto consciousness. The men panted with exertion.

The boss leaned down, very close to Chance's ear. "Listen well, my friend, because I will only say this once. If I were you, I'd saddle that little sorrel of mine and hightail it out of this country. You don't know who you're tangling with. This is the big time, my friend. And we know how to deal with small fry like you. Just for a reminder, I'm gonna let my boys go to work on you again. Next time I won't stop them from killing you. That's what we do to narc agents. You hear?" The man moved away. "Okay, boys."

Chance braced himself, wondering if he could survive another deluge of blows. It already felt like they'd broken his ribs, crushed his kidneys, smashed his knees, and split open his skull. *God, keep me from crying out. Please.*

They started again, and he lost consciousness.

When he came to, he heard low moans and realized they were his own. The boss's gravelly voice said, "That's enough for now." Heavy breathing. Shuffling feet. "You don't get another warning, my friend. Tomorrow morning, early, you will be heading out. Am I right?"

Chance lay still. Footsteps thudded away. He tore the mask from his head. The barn was empty. A motor roared to life and rumbled away. Raindrops pattered on the roof. He tried to rise, but everything hurt, especially his ribs and knees. *Please help me, God.* Slowly he rolled to his side and sat up. He was dizzy, nauseated. He waited for his head to clear, praying, hoping for a miracle. It came in the form of a jagged edge of an old can. Through a mist of pain, he sawed the thin rope that bound his hands.

Rain from a hole in the roof washed his face, revived his soul, as if God's hand touched him. He got to his feet, fighting the pain. His knees gave out. He fell heavily into the dirt with a cry. Crawling to the doorway, he pulled himself to a sitting position. The rain intensified.

A vehicle approached and headlights washed the barn through a heavy curtain of rain. He rose and clung to the doorframe, ready to run. Had the men returned to finish him off? But these headlights were low to the ground. It was a car, yes, but not *their* car.

His arm wouldn't obey when he tried to lift it. The driver of the car shifted down, seemed to hesitate. The car swung in a wide circle, its lights hitting him square in the face. When he tried to raise his arm the second time, it cooperated.

The vehicle stopped. A man stepped out. He carried a rifle under his arm. Suddenly Chance recognized him. *Tim Lindsey!* "Hey, Tim! It's me. Chance … McNeil. Hey, I need … help." Darkness swooped over his mind and he knew no more.

Chapter 20

Seven Hundred Pounds of Death

From Gina's Blog, June 20, Saturday morning:

I didn't do much on Friday except things around the house. I caught up on my emails and Facebook entries, sent a message to Nick, and washed my clothes.

On Saturday morning, I get a call from the sheriff. I'm surprised he's working. He says the dead woman was identified as Sabrina Philips, that she had no close relatives and lived in town in a small rented house.

He adds, "She kept to herself and cleaned houses and the Forestry office over in Camp Crook. We've purty well decided she was murdered on Wednesday night. Randy Whittier, the supervisor over there, saw her as he was leavin' for home. He's the last one to see her alive. Her computer's missin', and everything else that's personal. Didn't find anything of interest in her house. Randy said she has a sister livin' in Denver, but we haven't been able to track her down yet. You comin' in to give your report?"

"Today? Are you going to be in the office?"

Mike chuckles. "Shore. I'll be here. See you."

I set the phone in its cradle. I'm about to get my shower when Jesse calls and asks if I'm coming over tomorrow as we'd planned.

"I'm looking forward to it." I hear his soft laughter coming across the line.

I fold laundry from the washing machine as I talk. I have Bobbi's wireless phone propped between my shoulder and ear. "Hey, while you're on, could I ask you something? Would you mind repeating what you told me about small businesses in the area? I do some photo journalism as a hobby, and thought a story along those lines would be great for a magazine I contribute to." I scurry to the desk and grab a scrap of paper and pen.

"Uh." There's a longish pause. "Can't remember what you're talking about ... oh, yeah. Small businesses around here. Okay. We have the water plant and I think I mentioned a specialty lumber mill. That's a guy who lives over to Camp Crook. Billy Palmer. His place is north of Crook on the road to Marmouth. On the right about five miles out. Then there's ... uh, the guest ranch, Buffalo Ridge. That's down by the Short Pines. Owned by Charlie Pickens. Then there's Randy and Susan's nursery. Randy Whittier's the director of Forestry. They live in South Dakota, just over the line."

I write them all down. "Thanks, Jesse. Just wondering."

"Wal, wonder no longer, Gopher-girl. See you later."

I set down the receiver and stare off into space. Had he been a mite touchy when I'd asked about businesses? Is he annoyed? Busy? Or is he deliberately hiding something? I still want to get inside his water bottling plant. What will I find if I do?

An hour later, I park in front of the Carter County courthouse and admire the vine-covered arbor that arches over a wide sidewalk. Beyond it stands the quaint, white clapboard building with a tall bell tower. I feel like I'm back in time a hundred years. I get out of the car, straighten my blouse, and start up the walk. A man emerges from the double doors and holds it for me. I thank him and step inside.

The interior of the building is in pristine condition. The woodwork, stained dark and varnished to a shine, looks original. Antelope and deer heads are on the walls. I whistle at the wide, wooden stairs leading to the second story and turn in a slow circle, taking in the floor to ceiling cabinets and the solid wooden desks. What a magnificent piece of history is preserved here! I almost expect to see Wyatt Earp come striding out of one of the doors.

"Good mornin', Gina." Mike Crosby ambles out to the foyer. "You found my stompin' grounds. 'Bout time I showed you the lay of the land." He shakes my hand. "Can I get you some coffee?"

"That sounds great. Thanks." I follow along behind him and enter his office where he introduces me to a young man who is working on a computer. "This is Ty Rhoades, Carter County deputy sheriff. Ty, this is Gina Lindsey. Ty is Jesse Anderson's cousin."

Ty rises and shakes my hand, his round face serious. "Nice to meet you, Gina. Sorry about your uncle. Sure wish we could solve that case." He has a nice smile.

I look into his earnest brown eyes and say quietly, "That's what we all hope, Ty."

Mike holds a chair for me. "Sit down, please. I need a minute or two to get everything ready."

I settle onto the chair and accept a cup of coffee from Ty. I study his face, but see no resemblance to Jesse there. "I've met your cousin. He took me riding yesterday. I didn't know he had a relative in law enforcement."

Mike opens and shuts several drawers, then gets to his knees and paws through the bottom one. "Didn't Bobbi warn you that everybody around here's related to everybody else? You gotta watch what you say about people in these parts, or you'll insult somebody's grandma and before you know it, all hell will break loose. Kinda like the Hatfields and the McCoys."

"Nice thought."

Mike lifts a stack of papers from a drawer. "Now, where'd I put that durned tape recorder? Oh, there it is." He yanks it out and regains his feet. "I think I got everything now."

He plugs the recorder in, sticks a cassette tape into it and sits opposite me with a yellow legal pad on his knee. "Ty, bring us two a'them cinnamon rolls Sylvia sent round from the café this morning."

"Yes, sir." He leaves in search of the rolls.

"You ready?" Mike eyes me. When I nod, he pushes the button. "What happened Saturday night at Medicine Rocks?"

I describe everything from when Chance and I first entered the park to when Mike arrived on the scene. Now and then, he interrupts with a question. The rest of the time, his eyes move from my face to my hands. I know he's studying my body language, but I'm not going to tell him anything that way. I accept the sweet roll from Ty and keep my hands and feet steady. I meet Mike's eyes squarely each time he asks a question.

When he's run out of questions, he switches off the machine. "That about covers it. Anything you want me to help you with?"

I drink the coffee and bite into the sweet roll. After awhile, I manage to answer. "No, sir. I sent Matthews a report, not that I have anything to report. Haven't learned anything about … my uncle's disappearance." I don't mention my investigation of drugs. I hope that if he knows, he'll keep quiet about it. No telling how many ears are listening nearby.

He shakes his head. "Wal, anytime you need anything, anything at all, give me a whistle."

"Sure thing. Has Chance McNeil been in to give his deposition?"

He doesn't answer and moves to the door. I set my cup on his desk, pick up my purse and follow him. He takes my elbow and steers me through the double doors and outside.

On the lawn, he leans closer and lowers his voice. "He called me late last night. He's had a little … accident. Said he's clearin' out of the country, the game got a little … too rough." He gazes at the sky and sighs.

"He's gone?" I feel ambivalent between sad and bewildered. Chance is hurt, how bad I don't know, and Mike won't tell me why or where he went.

He nods. "Yup. Got clean away. I say more power to him, if you catch my drift."

I do. What I *don't* understand is Chance himself. What part is he playing in this? Why was he attacked? Is it the same as what happened to Uncle Elton? Will someone find Chance's body … *No. I can't think like that!* Despite the cool, professional front I allow the sheriff to see, I'm quaking inside.

"Who is he, Mike? What's he doing here?" I'm getting a little tired of Mystery Man. "Is there something I should know about him?"

Mike shrugs. We get to my car and he opens the door for me. "Just be careful. Chance isn't who he pretends to be. I'll let him tell you about it." He shuts my door. I start the motor and lower the window. "Do you have any leads at all, officer? About the drugs?"

I nod. "Four."

He raises his brows.

I continue, "I figured there's got to be a home base for the drugs. A cover business. I asked Jesse Anderson and he told me about four of them. One of them is his dad's water bottling plant. I intend to investigate all of them."

"Can you give me the list?"

"Sure. I'll email them to you. Watch for it and erase it as soon as you can. There's a mole in the system somewhere. How else could they know about me?"

"Don't worry. I'll be careful. Keep in touch. I don't want you to be the next victim."

It feels like someone's slammed a fist into my gut. I lift my chin and manage a smile. "Okay, sheriff. I'll call."

I grab a bite of lunch at the café, enduring the stares and whispers of the locals, and mail some letters. As I drive home, I mull over what had happened. Where had Chance gone? Will he contact me? There's no reason whatsoever that he should, but deep down, I hope he does.

***

June 19, Friday night

"Hey. Don't die on me now."

Chance roused himself enough to acknowledge the statement and nod half-heartedly. Through puffy lips, he said, "Just … get me … to truck." He nodded toward where his truck was parked. Tim's 2005 Mustang roared beside it. Tim supported him as he staggered to the truck. "Now, if you'd be so kind … help me get in."

"You're not going to drive, are you?" Tim cast Chance a dubious glance.

"Can't see … why not." He pulled himself upright. Pain shrieked across his back. With Tim's aid, he got into his truck and turned it on. He rolled down the window. "Thanks, Tim."

"I'm followin' you, man. Where you goin'?"

"Bible camp. 'Preciate it." Chance rolled up the window and started out.

There were times during that hour drive when he almost drove into the ditch, but he doggedly kept at it, fighting the overwhelming pain. When he got to the camp driveway, he signaled and pulled in. His cabin looked a welcome sight when the headlights lit it.

Tim parked beside him and hopped out. "You need help gettin' in? I should've taken you to Baker to the emergency hospital. You want me to call the doctor?"

"Just help me into … cabin." Chance slowly swung his legs out. When he tried to put weight on them, his knees collapsed and Tim grabbed him. With Tim on his left, Chance hobbled up the steps and into the cabin. He switched on the light.

Clothes, blankets, pot and pans, everything lay scattered across the floor. He groaned. "Oh, no. Someone … went through my … stuff. Here. Help me … sit."

He lowered himself to the chair and took stock of his injuries. His hands were raw and bleeding, but he could still move his fingers. No teeth knocked out. Broken jaw; maybe a couple of ribs, too. Knees damaged, definitely. He moved his legs tentatively and sighed when he discovered he could use them. His head wound still bled. The worst was his shoulder blade and his ribs.

Tim picked up a few items of clothing and heaped them on the bed. "What do you want me to do?" He sat down and lit a cigarette.

"There's some wash cloths in the bathroom. Could you get them wet and bring them? I'll try to clean up the worst places. After that, I'll get you to help me bind up my ribs. Do you mind helping me take a shower? Feel in the need of one."

Tim rolled up his sleeves. "Sure. Who did this? And why?" His hands shook as he helped Chance out of his outer clothes and sponged off most of the blood.

Chance shook his head. "I wish I knew. Have an idea of the *why*. I'm not sayin', though. Not to you."

"Why not? I have an idea myself. Same people who did away with my dad." Tim's face was poker still; he kept his emotions shrink-wrapped inside and only occasionally did he allow anything to show.

Chance shook his head. "It's drugs, you know. Big time. I've been on their trail for four years. Landed me up here. Guess I'm finished, though. They've got me figured out and I can't endanger the camp anymore. Called me small fry. I guess that's what I am." He took four pain relievers and wiped his mouth. "Don't know what I was thinking, that I could take them down by myself. I found the grow patch. Took some pictures, but they got them. Knew I had them."

Tim sat back on his heels. "Who'd you show them to?"

"Randy Whittier over at Camp Crook. I mentioned them to Sheriff Crosby, too, and hinted to Sheriff Dugal at Buffalo that I knew something." He took a drink of the water Tim had brought. "Hey, you wouldn't mind makin' some coffee, would you? Pot's over there. Coffee's in that cupboard."

He leaned back and closed his eyes. "Maybe someone overheard my conversation when I phoned from the office here. Or my contact with the FBI is bought off. Or Crosby told his deputy. It could be that Dugal's on the take, or someone in his office overheard our conversation. There are a dozen possibilities for leaks. The bottom line is that they know me, they know Gina, and they're taking care of problems. Systematically. Thoroughly."

"Maybe it's Randy Whittier."

Chance nodded. "Yup. Could be. I showed him the pictures. He seemed as concerned as I am. Lost, sort of, like he didn't know what to do. Or maybe scared." He watched as Tim picked up more of his belongings and stacked them carefully on the table. Good thing he kept his laptop and evidence in his truck!

Tim made the coffee.

Chance knew he couldn't let his guard down too much with Tim. He sensed that the young man was hiding something, that he knew more than he was saying. When the coffee was brewed, they drank it. It soothed Chance's nerves. He was starting to get drowsy. "I have to leave the country. Or make it *appear* that I've left."

Tim rubbed his jaw. "How're you goin' to manage that?"

"If you'll help me, I can do it. Thing is, they're watchin' your ranch, they're keepin' an eye on the camp and my truck." He took measure of the young man across from him. They were approximately the same height and build. Tim was shorter and more slender but from a distance, no one would know. He leaned forward, fighting the urge to lie down and go to sleep. He couldn't do that. Not yet.

"Tell you what. We'll change clothes. I'll drive the Mustang back to your place and cool my heels there for a couple of days. You got a couch or an extra bed?"

Tim nodded, his eyes lighting. "Extra room and bed. What do you want me to do?"

"Put some of my clothes on. Load my horse. The sorrel Morab mare with a white snippet on her nose. We'll pack my things. Throw it all in the truck. Then you will drive out of here tomorrow morning."

"Where should I go?" He reached for another cigarette but stopped himself and finished off his coffee.

"Do you have a relative or friend in ... say, Miles City or Rapid?"

"I've got an uncle who owns a ranch outside of Rapid."

Chance nodded. "Great. Give him a call and see if you can keep a horse there for awhile. Park the truck and trailer at his place. Do they have an outfit you could borrow?"

"I suppose so. They have lots of rigs. Okay. Should I drive home tomorrow? Or do you want me to stay away for awhile?"

"No. Come on back tomorrow. They won't be watchin' too closely if they see me drive away." He stretched, forgetting his wounds. "Ouch! Can't do that." He groaned and slowly stood, hanging onto the chair back. "Let's get this show on the road."

Chance started packing up his belongings while Tim went into the bathroom and changed. Most everything he'd leave, but he'd take enough to make the gang think he'd fled for his life. Fighting pain with every move, he got into the Mustang and nodded to Tim who stood on the porch.

"See you tomorrow. Take care with Cyndi. I'd be pretty upset if anything happened to her." He held his hand out the window. "Thanks, my friend. I'll be prayin' for you."

Tim shook his hand. When he answered, his voice was low. He struggled to get the words out. "Just … take care. We'll get these guys. I know we will."

Chance attempted a smile and knew it was only a grimace. He met Tim's eyes and his heart lifted. "Sure thing. Be careful." He backed the Mustang away from the cabin and drove slowly down the road, every bump sending shivers of pain throughout his body.

Oh, God. I hope he's right, yet I'm getting tired of this. Help me, Lord. Please help me!

***

From Gina's Blog, June 20, Saturday

It's around three in the afternoon when I arrive back at the house. I get out of the car and glance over at Tim's trailer. His Mustang's parked out front, but it isn't where he usually parks it. Beside it is another vehicle – a white truck, an older model with a dented fender and a cracked windshield. *Chance?* No, the pickup's too old. Strange. Tim must have a friend visiting.

I shrug off that little mystery and mount the steps to the front porch, thinking that if I have the time, I'll sand and repaint the deck this summer. I'd helped Dad with our deck in New York one time, so I feel confident I can do it.

In the kitchen, I find a note Bobbi had written. "Gina, there's some hamburger in the fridge and leftover potato salad. If it's not too much trouble, could you bring dinner out to Tim and me? We're in the hay field to the south of the house. You can drive the four-wheeler. The key is in it. Bring some ice water, too. There's a jug in the utility room. Thanks. Aunt Bobbi."

After I change clothes, I wash my hands and peer into the refrigerator. A package of thawed hamburger, wrapped in white butcher's paper, sits on top of a casserole dish while the remains of several weeks' worth of food crowd alongside it. On every shelf, little containers of leftover food are stacked, residual dinners scraped from serving dishes and put aside to be eaten later. I smile. *Bobbi's got her own chemical plant right here.*

I find a frying pan and begin molding the patties. Trying to locate all the necessary items to create a meal in Bobbi's kitchen is like a search for the treasure game. At last I have hamburgers, potato salad, chips, two apples and a half dozen cookies packaged and ready to go. I find a red thermos water jug and fill it with ice water.

Then I search for my shoes – *oh, darn.* I remember that my tennis shoes are upstairs and I don't want to take the time to go fetch them. I'd worn my new riding boots that day and still had them on, even though most everyone took their shoes off at the door in this country.

The four-wheeler is parked behind the barn. I stow the lunch on the back and turn the key. Driving straight ahead, down the rutted dirt lane alongside the fence, I try to stay focused, for I hadn't slept well last night and my eyes are bleary.

I spot the tractor out in the hay field and press my thumb on the accelerator. Ahead, I see a pile of rocks blocking the lane and I turn the handle-bars to avoid them. *Nothing happens!* Horrified, I twist and turn frantically – all to no avail. The rocks loom closer. I apply the brakes, both on the handlebars and the foot pedal, but they don't take hold.

"Ah!" I scream, and at the very last second, I yank sideways and pull up with all my strength, thinking maybe the vehicle would jump the rocks.

It doesn't.

With a bone-jarring crunch, it hits the first rock, swerving sideways because of the wrench I give the handle-bars. I'm lifted up and for an instant think I can clear the boulders. The machine falls backwards. I know a moment of sheer panic, for it's coming down on top of me, and I'd heard stories of people being killed this way.

There's no time. My world goes black.

Gas. I smell gas. I slowly climb out of a dark, deep pit of unconsciousness to reality. Harsh reality. My first impression is that I've been buried alive, for a large and bulky object hovers over me. My leg's trapped by it. I must've hit the ground pretty hard, because my head hurts and everything else seems numb. At least the motor's shut off. I can't imagine having to hear it pounding in my ears on top of everything else.

I flex my fingers, arms, toes. Everything seems to be in working order. What really gets my attention, though, is the pain shooting up my left leg. My mind clears. I take a deep breath and gag on the gas. Yet I'm not dead. Moving my head a fraction of an inch, I see why. The front of the machine landed on the rocks and its weight is not crushing me to death. I suppose Aunt Bobbi will say it's a miracle.

The knowledge that a seven hundred pound machine teeters over me on a hair's breadth brings little comfort to my soul. What if it slides off the rocks? I will die. Carefully I move a fraction of an inch, trying to get out from under it. But my leg – no, it's my ankle – sends frantic signals to my brain that it doesn't want me to move. Not even a little.

I groan and manage to get my right hand to my face. The heat from the motor scorches my skin and beads of sweat roll off my face. How long can I stay under this thing before I suffocate? I don't want to know the answer to that question.

And how long before anyone finds me? A tear slides down my face and into my ear. Another one follows. I steel myself to endure the pain and heat. And I won't pray. With my jaws set, I close my eyes and try to think good thoughts. Positive thoughts. Thoughts that would calm my spirit and ease my body.

It doesn't work.

Chapter 21

Jilly

From Gina's Blog, June 20, Saturday

The rumble of a tractor's motor begins on the edges of my conscious thought and grows louder. I try to see, but can't, and every time I move my head, I'm assailed with sharp, stabbing pains. I take a deep breath and tell myself to hang on a little while longer.

The tractor draws near. Stops. Feet approach. A face appears in the small space between the ground and the four-wheeler – a very pale, sweat-streaked face – Bobbi's. I can't hear what she says, but I manage a weak wave.

Bobbi straightens, yells something. The motor dies. Her face appears again. "Gina! Are you okay?"

"So far," I manage to mumble. "Get this thing off me, can you? I feel … like I'm … dying under here … can't get my breath."

"Anything hurt? Are you bleeding?"

"Not so as I can tell. My ankle hurts like the dickens. And my head. Can you get it off?"

"Your head?" Bobbi attempts a chuckle. "Oh. You mean the four-wheeler. Well, we'll give it a try. Hang on." Bobbi's face disappears. She yells at Tim like the general of an army. If you want to get something nearly impossible done, you should ask Bobbi. If someone suggests she can't do it – that really gets her going.

"C'mon, Tim. Let's see if we can budge this. You grab it over there. Watch that hot exhaust pipe! Now, what we're going to do is lift it straight up about two inches, then swivel it in your direction. Use your knees, not your back and lever it around. We won't go far. Just enough to get her out."

I hear Tim mumble something and see his feet braced under the vehicle.

"Oh, Lord, help us, please!" Bobbi murmurs as she grasps the machine. "Okay. On the count of three. One! Two! Three!"

The four-wheeler moves! She counts again. It moves some more. A clear patch of blue sky appears above my head. Not much, but enough. With a *clunk!* they drop the vehicle two inches from my leg.

"Don't move." Bobbi comes to my head, panting from the exertion. "Well, if that doesn't make you a believin' person, I don't know what will. That was a God-thing, Gina. A God-thing."

I smile. My skin feels scorched and stiff. "Okay. I get the picture. I'd call it adrenalin." I wipe moisture from my face. "Thanks."

Bobbi pats my shoulder, characteristically brusque, but I see streaks of tears on her cheeks. "That's okay, dear. You'll come around in time. Tim, there's some water and rags in the tractor. Get 'em, please."

He lopes back to the tractor and returns with his burden, then kneels beside me. "You okay?" His face is the color of bleached mud.

"Sure. I've only just about killed myself … injured my ankle … hit my head. Other than that, yeah. I'm okay."

"You don't have to be sarcastic." He stands and looks at the four-wheeler, as if to assess the damage.

"Oh. That's your specialty, huh." I try to laugh and can't even manage a chuckle. Bad joke.

Bobbi offers me water. I take the bottle and manage to drink. She ties up the worst of my wounds – the one on my head and one on my right arm where the handle of the four-wheeler gashed it. "Well, if you can stand, we'll get the tractor over here and make a run to the clinic."

I allow them to heft me upright, gasping from the pain in my ankle when I move it. The world spins a bit. After a few seconds, I hobble to the tractor that Tim brings up close. I perch on the back. Bobbi sits beside me and puts an arm around my waist.

At the house, she helps me into the Subaru. "I really don't have to see a doctor. I'm feeling much better. I think my ankle's just sprained." I look at my foot and groan. My brand new riding boot is ripped open, ruined! Bobbi helps me take it off. Already my ankle's swelling.

Bobbi shakes her head and purses her lips. "I want to have that x-rayed, dear. Tim can get the four-wheeler back into the barn. Whatever happened? I saw you comin' and figured you'd drive around those rocks. Didn't you see them?" She holds out a wet wash cloth.

I push back my hair and scrub my face. When I finish, I give her a stern look. "I'd like you to have a mechanic take a look at that four-wheeler. Something went wrong with the steering. It didn't respond when I tried to turn and the brakes didn't work, either. I had plenty of time to stop. I think someone tampered with it."

"Who would do that?" Bobbi jumps into the Subaru and starts it. "I mean, how could anyone know that you'd be driving it?"

"I don't know, Aunt Bobbi. We should have it checked out, is all I'm saying." I don't mention that maybe it's *Tim* who was the target. Bobbi has enough to worry about without adding that. Who would want him dead? Or had someone come in the house, seen the note and tampered with the four-wheeler, knowing I'd be driving it?

After we arrive at the hospital, Bobbi helps me into the emergency room. A nurse directs us to one of the beds. I notice two other unoccupied gurneys in the same room. The nurse takes my blood pressure, temperature and pulse. She jots down my medical information and leaves.

Bobbi hovers nearby. "I think I'll run over to the grocery, if that's okay with you, dear. Is there something you'd like?"

"A diet Coke, please."

"Anything else?"

"No, I'm okay." After she leaves, I study the ceiling tiles and school myself to patience as I wait for them to take me to the x-ray room. I suppose that will be next. Before the nurse returns, a woman enters the room, carrying a young girl. The nurse helps her settle the girl on one of the beds.

I glance over, for they hadn't pulled the curtain. The girl's red-rimmed eyes reveal that she's been crying. Her skin is dark and her hair, which is honey blond, is braided. Her large, brown eyes take in the room and equipment with solemn wonder. She cradles her left arm, which is bound up in a dirty rag. The woman holds her other hand.

The girl sniffs and glances over at me. "Mae-gan, *senora enfermo?*"

"*Si,* Jilly. Be *quieto.* Okay?" Still the woman doesn't look at me. She wears jeans, a man's long-sleeved work shirt and heavy boots. What I find interesting is the pistol and two-way radio on her belt. The bill of her baseball cap shadows her face. I can see enough of it to tell that she's experienced a lot of the wrong side of life. The streets of New York are littered with those kinds of faces, yet it's surprising to see it here in southeastern Montana.

Maegan. Her name is Maegan. For some reason, I think it's important to remember. Jilly squirms around and asks repeatedly when they would fix her arm. I find her interesting -- a Mexican girl with blond hair. The nurses arrive and prepare to wheel me from the room. On the way out, I say, "I'd rather wait, if you're short-handed. That little girl needs attention. She's in quite a bit of pain."

They exchange a look, like I'm not supposed to say anything. The one whose name tag reads Patty Jo nods. "The doctor's on the way. He's ordered something for pain. We'll take care of it. Don't worry."

There's quiet reproof in her voice. Maegan casts me a grateful glance. When I return from the x-ray room, they're preparing Jilly for departure to the same room. Maegan walks beside the gurney and gives me a shy smile.

"Thank you," she whispers.

Half an hour later, Bobbi comes in with six cans of pop, both Coke and Sprite, and a bag of chips. We eat and chat until the doctor arrives with the x-rays in hand.

"You have a sprained ankle, Gina," he says with a hint of a smile. His blue eyes twinkle. "You should be mighty grateful to be alive. Stay off that foot for the next couple of days, okay? Ice and heat alternately. I'll prescribe some pain medication. The nurse will come and wrap it. I want to see you in five days. Come in tomorrow and they'll fix you up with an orthopedic boot. You'd better get your driver's license for a four-wheeler, though." He gives me a wink. "Those things can be dangerous."

I attempt a chuckle. "Yes, I know, doctor."

"And another thing." The doctor pauses. "You better be grateful that you were wearing your boots. Whatever hit your ankle could have severed it clear off if you hadn't."

"Oh, my ..." I'm prepared to say *God*, but after a quick look at Bobbi, I say, "... gosh." Prickles descend my spine. "It was a fluke that I was wearing them."

Bobbi shakes her head slowly. "No fluke, Gina. It was God."

The doctor glares fiercely. "See you in five days. Remember to stay off it." He tips his head with a friendly grin and leaves.

I perch on the gurney while the nurse wraps my ankle. Bobbi goes to get the car. Before the bandaging is finished, Jilly is wheeled into the room.

I smile at her. "How are you doing?"

She nods sleepily and murmurs, "Okay."

Maegan stops beside me. "Her arm's broken."

"How did it happen?"

"Accident on a bike." The taciturn response is barely audible.

I lean toward the little girl. "Would you like some pop? Look. I have diet Coke or Sprite. My aunt brought me some. Would you like some Sprite, honey?"

Jilly regards me with solemn eyes and glances at Maegan, who shakes her head.

"She don't need anything."

Stubborn words. They smite my heart. She's erected a fierce barrier against the world.

"Jilly? Here." I open a can of Sprite and hand it over. I'm gratified to see appreciation in her eyes. I smile at Maegan. "I'd like to bring her a gift while she's recuperating. Where do you live?"

"Uh, well, um ... I can't ..." Maegan shifts uneasily. Fear widens her eyes. I can't miss the pleading in them as she speaks just above a whisper. "I can't tell you. I'm ... it's not what you might think. I'm not free to ... in fact, I shouldn't have brought her here, except that I figured her arm was broke. I might get in trouble. The best thing you can do is to forget me and ..."

"Wait a minute." I fumble in my purse and bring out a card. "My name's Gina Lindsey. I understand what you're saying but I *can* help you. Here's my card, and ..." I withdraw a pen and hurriedly write a number on the back of the card. "This is my unlisted number. Call me if you need help. Believe me when I say I'm your friend. Please don't let anyone see this, okay?"

Maegan nods and accepts the card. She shoves it in her back jean's pocket.

"Ready to go?" Bobbi reappears and helps me off the gurney.

At that moment, the doctor arrives with the little girl's x-rays. "Looks like a break, Jilly. We'll have to put a cast on your arm, honey. And guess what. You get to choose the color! The nurses will take you to another room. I'll be with you in a moment."

Maegan shoots me a glance and follows the nurse from the room, tucking the prescription she'd received from the doctor for Jilly's pain medication into her shirt pocket.

Bobbi collects our things and takes my arm. "So you made a friend, huh? Cute little girl."

I nod. In the hallway, I see a scrap of paper lying on the floor and think how untidy it looks. On an impulse, I pick it up, but don't see any garbage can handy, so I stick it in my pocket. Limping my way to the car, I'm wishing I could've helped the little girl more. *Where does Maegan live? What's she doing? Why does she say she isn't free? Is she a slave? Yet this is America -- the land of the free. There's a lot of slavery even here, though.* I shake my head. *But what about the drug traffickers? Is she involved with them?*

And most importantly, how can I find out? As I settle into the car, I sigh. I have the feeling I'd just missed a good lead. If only I had a chance to question Maegan more. Now I can't do any investigating -- at least not for a couple of days. By then I might have lost the lead altogether.

I clench the arm rest as Bobbi drives out of the parking lot. I will *not* let this get by me. I can't forget the pleading in Maegan's eyes, or the little girl she called Jilly.

Chapter 22

Wild Rose Lane

Carter County, June 20, Saturday

Maegan readjusted her cap and tucked a stray hair behind her ear.
They'd just finished casting Jilly's arm. Usually they wouldn't cast it
until the swelling was down, but she told the nurse that it was hard
for her to get into town and the doctor had agreed to go and ahead do
it.

Jilly was a good little trooper throughout the whole operation and
the nurses joked with her. The quiet jesting brought an occasional
smile to her lips. Maegan's heart went out to her. What future did she
have? How could she possibly take her back to the ranch … and to
her slavery?

But the little girl didn't know about all that. She only knew about
her family. More than once she'd inquired about them and Maegan
could see the longing in her big brown eyes. Once a tear slid from
under her closed lids and she said very softly, "I *esperar Madre's
esta bien.*"

"*Si*, your mother is fine, *Yilly*." But Maegan knew what she
meant. When the accident happened, Rosa Manteo had screamed for
help. The men were busy in the field, haying, and Maegan was
working in the office. She ran outside and saw the blood, saw the
crushed limb lying twisted under the girl and knew it was serious.

She knelt in the dust and assessed the damage. The blood was
from scrapes on her leg; the real injury was her arm. "I'll take her to
en casa," she said to Rosa. "And get someone to take care of her."
Just as she picked her up, Butch emerged from the building, his face
red.

"What's going on here? Get back to your work, woman, or I'll
…"

"She hurt her arm, boss. Can't you see? I'm taking her over to my house, and I'm calling the doctor. I think it's broken."

Butch descended on her like a mad bear. "You're doin' nothin' of the sort!" He grabbed her arm and jostled the girl. She started screaming. "Put her down! That's an order!"

Maegan gently transferred Jilly to her mother's arms and whirled to march into the office. Butch followed her.

"And I don't want you goin' over there to check on her. She's fine. It's just a scratch."

"Yes, sir." Maegan did not sit down. She prowled to the desk and felt the gun at her belt. *For rattlesnakes*, she told people. *Or worse things. Like Butch. Someday, God help me, I'm going to use it on him!*

After Butch finished his tirade, she calmly turned and walked out. She went over to her house and got a drink of water. After a short while, she checked to see where Butch had gone. He'd leaped on one of the four-wheelers and roared off down the road. Out the main gate. *Good.*

It didn't take her long to get over to the Manteo's shack. Rosa met her at the door and pled for help. Jilly lay on an old, dilapidated couch, crying softly. Maegan glanced around and weighed her chances. With any luck at all, or perhaps with the help of the Virgin Mother, to whom Rosa was praying, she could pull this off.

She nodded. "Bring her. I will go in my *carro*. *Venir, rapido!* We have only a few *momentos*." Without looking back, she made straight for the Land Rover that was parked behind her trailer. Rosa followed, carrying the girl, her face as white as the lace around her throat, murmuring softly to Jilly. Tears seeped from behind the girl's closed eyelids and she moaned in pain.

After Maegan helped Rosa arrange Jilly on the back seat, she pulled the keys from her pocket. "I will take her. You stay here and *orar*." Rosa kissed Jilly one last time.

Maegan hopped in the driver's seat and with her heart in her throat, drove through the open gate. Why no one had shut it after Butch had driven out was a mystery she didn't want to investigate.

She stomped on the gas and kept going down the long drive, thinking any moment she'd be stopped. But the road remained empty.

Now she thanked the doctor and the nurses and promised she'd bring Jilly back in a week for a check-up. *Yeah, right.* You couldn't expect the gods to perform that many miracles. One had got them there. She'd need another to get safely home.

After helping Jilly into the car, she treated the girl to a hamburger at the café. *Might as well make this an occasion. Don't think we'll get another.* As they returned to the car, she realized with a sinking heart that she would pay for this. Pay big.

At the ranch, the rules were set in concrete and a person did not disobey. *You may not leave the property without written consent from Mr. B.* The date, time of departure and ETA was noted carefully. Also on the form was the warning: *Do not speak to any person beyond what is necessary when you are off the property. Do your business and return to the ranch. Failure to comply with these directives will be dealt with decisively and firmly.*

She gritted her teeth and started off down the road toward the ranch. As she drove closer, the terror in her heart exploded into panic. She gripped the steering wheel and tried to keep tears from blurring her vision. She was cold. Freezing! She turned off the AC and rolled down the window. Jilly slept beside her, her head lolling onto the arm rest. She was beautiful.

What would they do to her? To Jilly? To the Manteos?

She determined that she would first deliver the girl to her parents. They wouldn't punish Jilly, surely. No, she would bear the brunt of Butch's rage. Would he let his henchmen have their way with her? She'd seen what they did to punish others who'd tried to escape or disobeyed the rules. Could she endure it? She didn't think so.

She put on the brakes and pulled into a driveway. Made a u-turn. "What am I doing? I can't escape. *I can't,*" she whispered. *Where can I go?* Now sweat beaded her forehead and her hands shook. Her stomach felt like someone had balled it into a hard knot. She glanced at the gas gauge. Nearly full. It would take her to Rapid. Maybe Miles City. No farther. *How much money do I have? Enough for a couple of days. But what, then? Who will help me? How can I hide?*

She brought death to whoever held out a helping hand. Even before she'd left the clinic, she ripped the card the woman had given her and thrown it away. But she remembered the name. Gina Lindsey. Lindsey. Wasn't there a ranch she'd passed with that name over the driveway? She shrugged. She couldn't endanger another woman's life. She'd have to find her own way.

Jilly awoke. Straightened. "*Como? Donde*, Maegan? Why we *parar?* I want go *casa*." Her face screwed up funny like she was about to cry.

Maegan patted her leg. "That's okay, honey. We stopped because I'm … I'm trying to decide what to do." She'd been teaching the children English and could see that Jilly understood.

"*Yo querer casa*. My arm hurts. *Yo querer Madre! Yo querer Madre!*" Her voice rose to a wail and tears descended.

"Hush, *bebe*. I know you want to go home and see your mama. I'll take you home, but first I have to see someone. Can you wait? Just trust me, okay, honey?" She knew Jilly didn't understand, couldn't know what she meant.

Maegan fished a candy bar from the glove compartment and offered it to Jilly. The girl swatted it away and stared out the passenger window. Maegan turned onto the paved highway that led into Ekalaka and sighed. What was she going to do? Running and hiding was one thing when she was alone; she wouldn't make it far with Jilly. Butch would call the police and they would stop her before she got out of Carter County on a kidnapping charge.

Well, she had to do it.

She brushed away the tears that stung her eyes as she headed into town. There was only one place she could go. Even there, her chances of escaping Butch were almost nil. She clenched the wheel and hoped Jilly would fall asleep again. Yet the little girl stayed wide awake as they reentered Ekalaka and drove down the wide Main Street into town.

***

From Gina's Blog, June 21 Sunday morning

I survive Bobbi's ministrations and coddling and spend a restless night, beleaguered with pain despite the medication I took. Bobbi went off to church. After she left, I got a shower and sent off some emails. The day is nice and my foot isn't bothering me too much, so I get in the pickup and drive over to the Bible camp.

Living Waters Bible Camp, the sign says. I'm slightly surprised that it's as nice as I find it -- immaculately kept lawns, neat stone-lined walkways, buildings all in good repair, flowers everywhere. I pull into the parking lot, noting that a lot of people seem to be arriving and leaving and kids are running around with their counselors.

Must be the day to leave off kids. I see parents telling their children good-bye as college-aged men and women corral the kids and take them to activities. The zip line is a busy place, as is the riding corral, the swimming pool, the sports arena, the big swing, the low and high ropes course.

I hobble up to the office on the crutch that Bobbi found for me. It's a busy place, filled with parents and children. Two women sit at a desk and are taking registrations. A man sits near the door and glances up at me from his clipboard. He wears a t-shirt and cap with the camp logo on it, along with a name tag on a string around his neck that declares his name is Isaac.

"May I help you, ma'am?"

I nod. "Yes. I'm here to look over the camp. I'm from Rapid City, and ... well, we have a kid's club sort of thing and we're thinking about bringing them to the camp. I'd like to check out the facilities and speak with your director, if I may."

He smiles. "Oh. Well, as you can see, we're a busy. Can you come back a little later?"

"No, I'm afraid not. I'm on my way to Baker and just decided to stop in."

He rubs his chin in thought. "Well, I can take you to Mr. Fairchild. I'm sure he'll give you a tour. Come this way, please." He looks back at me as I grasp that pesky crutch and try to follow him. "Or better yet, you stay here, and he'll come down."

He installs me at one of the picnic tables outside on the lawn and soon Mr. Fairchild appears, a big smile creasing his face. He's an older gentleman with white hair and bright blue eyes. His smile is genuine. He greets me with an affable handshake as I repeat my cover story, and I find myself liking him.

He has the feel of a man on a mission, a man totally dedicated to his work. I see no duplicity or craftiness in his manner or looks. If he *is* the drug grower, he sure hides it cleverly. He brings up a golf cart and after I'm in it, he takes me on a tour of the place, talking non-stop about the camp and the ministry to young people's lives. We end up at the dining hall. He introduces me to his wife who is in the kitchen up to her elbows in a potato salad. She's as openhearted and authentic as her husband. They invite me to stay for dinner.

I can't resist. Down home fried chicken, potato salad, a whole salad bar of fresh veggies, homemade biscuits and pie. I feel like a guest in a large happy family as I converse with all my new friends. I can't remember all their names, but I remember their faces as I leave -- hearty, friendly, loving faces. I'd never met anyone like that before.

As I drive home, I'm tempted to tick off the Bible camp as a possible place for the drugs. Yet there's a question hanging unanswered in my mind. Mr. Fairchild said the camp owns two hundred acres of prime forest land. What does a camp need that much land for? And what is on that land behind the camp? Surely enough room for a drug operation! And what better cover than a Bible camp?

When I get home, I call Jesse and apologize for not going over there for our flying date. He says it's no problem, and promises he'll take me up another time. Yet he's not his normal cheerful self. What's going on? It might be that he's busy, or that he's mad at me for breaking the date. He ends the conversation with a cool, "See ya later, babe," and disconnects abruptly.

Monday morning Bobbi drives me to town and I get the orthopedic walking boot fitted to my foot. Even though it's easier to walk now, they say to stay off it. *Yeah, sure.*

Later that day, I put some clothes in the washer and go through my pockets to remove any tissues. I feel a piece of paper in my front jeans pocket and pull it out, puzzled. Where did this come from? In a flash, it comes back to me – the emergency room, the scrap of paper on the floor. It's an envelope, torn jaggedly in half. Typed across the middle is an address: 584 W. Wild Rose Lane, Ekalaka. The name is gone. Who dropped it?

My heart leaps. Was it – could it have been Maegan? Wild Rose Lane. Is that her address or where she works? I limp painfully to my computer and Google the address. The little bubble on Map Quest appears somewhere between Camp Crook and Ekalaka. I zoom in closer, but can't find the lane.

My foot aches. I hobble to the chair in the living room and lift it to the footrest, feeling a little guilty because I'm not putting ice and heat on it like the doctor ordered. How else can I find that lane? Ask Bobbi? Ask at the post office? I decide to do both when I can.

About that time, a pickup arrives. It's Tom Fruit from town. Bobbi's outside, so I use the crutches to hobble to the door and open it. I tell him the four-wheeler is in the barn. He leaves and awhile later knocks on the door. This time Bobbi answers it.

"Come on in. Want a cup of coffee?"

"Sorry, I can't stay," he says. I can hear his voice from where I'm sitting. He explains that both the steering cable and the brake cable were broken. "Can't rightly say how, Bobbi," he says nervously. "They just broke. Strange it happened at the same time."

"Thanks, Tom." Bobbi presses some money into his hand. "We were just curious."

After he left, I ask Bobbi about the address and show her the torn envelope. "I think that woman, Maegan, dropped it. I'd sure like to find out where they live and take Jilly something."

She tells me that there's been some new developments opening up south of Ekalaka and that some of the roads into those are named like that. I ask her exactly where they are and get a map of the area on the computer. She points them out to me -- just south of the camp, in the valley below the Rimrocks.

"Now don't you get into your head anything about heading over there," she says. "You're staying right here until that ankle heals a bit."

I shake my head, turning back to the computer. It's hard to deal with her bossy manner, like she owns me or something. Yet I allow her to bring out an ice pack for my ankle. Awhile later, Tim pokes his head in the living room and asks how I'm doing. He has a funny look on his face, like he's hiding something.

He started acting strangely when he disappeared Friday night and didn't show up for dinner on Saturday. Bobbi said he'd driven to Rapid City to help a friend and returned in someone else's truck. Yet his Mustang is there, parked in front of his trailer. How had he gotten to Rapid?

"He won't tell me where he's been or why he drove that truck home. He just says he helped a friend. I can't figure him out. Would you talk to him, Gina?"

When he comes in for dinner, he looks tired. I ask him about it. He shrugs. "Been busy, that's all." I notice something at the back of his eyes, a furtive look. I wonder about it, but again, what can I say? He tells Bobbi that he has a bad headache. She gives him some pain pills she had left over from her shoulder surgery.

That evening, as I get ready for bed, a strange sense of unease creeps up the back of my neck. Has Bobbi locked the doors? I doubt it. I'm too tired to go check, so after I make sure my revolver is near my pillow and I've finished a chapter of Sue Grafton, I turn off the light.

On Tuesday, I arm myself with a pen, notebook, map, water, binoculars, munchies and my revolver shoved deep inside my bag, climb in the Honda pickup, and set off for Camp Crook. I'm glad I injured my left foot, not the right, and am also grateful the Honda's an automatic.

I have trouble finding Billy Palmer's specialty lumber mill and when I find it at last, he's not home. Just my luck. I nose around the place, swearing at my dumb boot. I peer into a sweet-smelling lumber barn, take some pictures of the mill, and bless the gods he doesn't have a dog.

There are sheds – pole barns, I think they call them – a ways from the house. I scan the place with my binoculars and discover one building is encircled with a chain link fence. It looks like it has ventilation and electricity. Probably heat, too. A shop building? Why would he have something like that so far from the house? Interesting.

I want to hobble back there and check it out, but I *don't* want a trespassing charge and a night in jail. Or a rear end full of buckshot, if Mr. Palmer is up there on that butte, watching the place.

Next I visit Susan Whittier on their ranch. She's a pleasant woman, in her middle forties. Her brown hair is pulled back in a jaunty pony tail and her blue eyes are direct and friendly. I introduce myself and explain my mission. She wipes flour from her hands and invites me to come in. She's wearing jean shorts, a tank top and flip flops.

The house is a nice double-wide trailer, painted green with white trim, with a neat yard and flower beds around the front. She has it fixed up pretty nice inside, too, with a leather couch and loveseat around a gas fireplace in the living room, a solid oak table and chairs in the dining room, plants growing everywhere, and a spotless kitchen.

I sit at the breakfast bar while she pours me coffee. She tells me the ranch has been in her family for nearly a hundred years. I gawk at all the family photographs. She serves me a piece of rhubarb-strawberry pie with ice cream.

A sense of doom falls over me as I eat the pie, because I know if I stay here much longer with these wonderful ranch women, I'll have to buy a whole new wardrobe and Nick will hoot with laughter at my rolls of fat. I vow to never eat anything sweet again if only I could have another piece of that pie. Of course I don't ask for one.

Susan tells me all about their nursery as we walk down a gravel road to the greenhouses. I admire the hanging baskets of petunias and fuchsia and take pictures of her with the front of the nursery as a background. Inside, I see tables full of flowers and vegetables, all watered from overhead pipes. The smell of growing things, of soil and fragrant blooms fills the air. I find myself relaxing and feel a little foolish for my suspicions. Will I always be like this, or will I someday see someone like Susan Whittier as a friend?

There seems to be nothing covert or even remotely secretive about the nursery. Is there a building I don't see? I notice a butte nearby and a road that leads over to it. On top of the butte is a tower. Nothing unusual with that, I tell myself, maybe it's a water tower. She gives me a hanging basket of petunias for Bobbi and as we walk up to the house, a man drives a pickup down the lane toward the nursery. She stops and introduces me to him.

"Gina, this is my husband, Randy."

I step forward and shake his hand. "Nice to meet you, Randy," I say in a muted tone. He's wearing his Forestry uniform with a cowboy hat. I look into his hazel eyes and see approval there -- the kind I see in most men's eyes.

"How do you do?" His smile doesn't reach his eyes. "Any word on Elton?" His body fills up most of the seat of the pickup. He's probably in his middle forties, has a ruddy complexion and high forehead. His hair is brown streaked with gray and his manner seems just short of brusque. I put that down to a busy schedule.

"Not yet."

He tips his hat and glances briefly at Susan. "See you later." He drives off.

Susan chuckles at his abrupt departure. "Sorry about that, Gina. He's got so much on his mind. The season's just beginning for the forest and he's trying to line up his crews, plus run the ranch." She sighs. "It's a lot to do for one man."

I thank her for the plant and drive back to the ranch, lost in thought. Someone in this country is growing drugs on a big scale. Someone probably killed my uncle. Someone sabotaged the four-wheeler and is trying his best to kill me. Who can it be? I'd met a number of the ranchers, but I can't pinpoint the kind of personality who would be capable of doing such things. Is it Bryce Anderson, Mike Crosby, Sheriff Dugal, Randy Whittier, Chance McNeil or someone I hadn't met? How about the people at the Bible camp? Mr. Fairchild? Or someone else on staff?

When I arrive home, I eye Lone Butte behind the Lindsey ranch, wondering if I can drive up there and investigate that light I'd seen. No, not today. My foot's bothering me more than I care to admit. I plunk down on the couch as a sense of desperation and loneliness sweep over my heart. I long to give up the hunt. After mulling things over for a bit, I try to call Cap Matthews in Spokane. He doesn't pick up.

Limping down the hall to my room, I look again at the torn envelope. After writing down the address in my book, I stick it in an envelope and seal it, dating it and signing it. After that, I put it with my other clues in the briefcase. About that time, a thought occurs to me: what if someone dropped something out by the four-wheeler when they disabled it? Oh, surely not. No one's that stupid. Well, it's worth a look.

I hobble out to the barn with a flashlight and go to the back, where the four-wheeler's parked. The light's fading. I search in the rubble on the ground, moving straw and hay and dirt carefully. My search proves fruitless and I straighten with a hand on my aching back. That's when I spot it -- something silvery glinting in the light from my flashlight. It's farther away than the circle where I'd been probing. I pick it up and dust if off. A silver cigarette lighter.

Back at the house, I examine it closely. It's inscribed, *To MP Love RW.* On the reverse side is a company logo of some sort, mostly worn away; I can make out a red ram's head and the faint letters WAPL Association around it. I draw a deep breath and pocket the lighter. A clue at last!

While Bobbi's fixing dinner, I find a phone book and look up the RW names. Lots of them. I note down the RWs in the Ekalaka area: Richard Wilmont, Rex Williamson, Rock Wilcox. I show my list to Bobbi and she says she knows some of them. Their addresses are in the book, too. I look up the MP names and find Mike Phillips, Martin Petersen, Matthew Paulie, Mason Phylon. This is too confusing. I decide to concentrate on the RW names first.

Something's bothering Bobbi – I figure she's worrying about Tim because he said he didn't want to come over, that he had things to do. While we eat the delicious tacos she's made, I see a shadow of sorrow in her eyes and try to cheer her. She smiles at my poor attempt at jokes, but nothing alleviates her pain.

"It's almost like I've lost Tim, too," she murmurs as she rises to get dessert.

I know what she means: he's withdrawn so much she hardly ever talks to him, can't connect with him on any level. Over ice cream, I bring out my list and show her. Maybe this will take her mind off her troubles.

"Aunt Bobbi, are there others with the initials RW that you know, people around here? Or MP? Some people aren't listed in the phone book if they use cell phones."

Her shoulders droop and she has that lackluster look in her face, as if she's given up hope. She glances at my list and sighs. "I don't know. Why are you asking?"

"I'm just curious. Humor me." I'm exhausted, too. For once she could cooperate -- after all, I'm trying to find her husband.

She rolls her eyes, gets her glasses and picks up my list. "Well, I don't know of any other names with the MP initials. I do know some women with RW, though."

I'm jolted. I'd been thinking that RW was a man; of course it could be either.

She's speaking in a low tone, "Rebecca Anderson's maiden name was Waters, so that would make her a W. Then there's a Rachel Wangle and ... let's see ... Ruth Worander." She removes her glasses and gives me a ghost of a smile. "I guess I'm one, too. Roberta White. My maiden name was White."

We laugh about that. I realize I hadn't known what her maiden name was. "Oh. Well, I was asking because I found this out where the four-wheeler was parked." Casually I bring out the lighter. "Have you ever seen something this? Did Elton own this?"

It lies on the palm of my hand, shining in the light from the chandelier.

She draws in her breath sharply. I look at her, surprised.

Covering her emotion smoothly, she rises and turns away from me. "It's pretty, isn't it? Silver. No, dear, Elton never owned anything like that."

I hear dismissal in her tone and see it on her face as she begins cleaning up the dishes. Her walls are up. I know further questioning will get me nowhere. Yet her eyes and her gasp gave her away; she'd seen the lighter, or one like it, and knows someone who owned it.

My ankle's hurting again. After taking a pain reliever, I get ready for bed and propping my foot on a pillow, I immerse myself in Sue Grafton's *L is for Lawless*. When my eyelids get heavy, I turn out the light. For awhile I stare at the full moon and listen to the coyotes on the prairie. Is my imagination going wild, or can I hear someone opening a door? *No.* I'm sure of it.

A board creaks just outside my bedroom door. I get up slowly and grasp my gun.

Chapter 23

Buffalo Ridge

"It's okay, boss, I have it sewed up." Butch eased his body into his pickup and swiped at his forehead. He'd been dreading this call and now it had come at the worst possible moment. If only, for once, he could give a good report. He couldn't lie about this. Sooner or later the boss would find out about Maegan's disappearance with the little girl, so he might as well tell him now.

"*What's* sewed up, you idiot! You better tell me that your cop friend is dead."

Butch swallowed hard. "I've got that started. I'll do it soon. I had to take care of some other details, boss. These things don't happen overnight, y'know."

"I know that if you don't follow through on this, buster-boy, we're finished. And you know what that means. I want some forward movement before tomorrow night or I'm going to take care of it myself. My boys will make a little call at your spread. No sign of our cowboy? We scared him off?"

"Yessir." Butch had grave doubts on that score, too, yet he wasn't about to share that with the man. "I got another problem, though. My secretary's disappeared. One of the little girls here got injured and she took her to the doc in town. They never came back. I called the sheriff and they're watchin' for her. Probably will catch her on her way outta the county if she's runnin'. I told him she'd kidnapped the girl." He chuckled nervously because the boss had been too quiet for too long. "Boss? You there?"

Something like a low growl erupted from the phone. "I'm finished with your bungling, Butch. This time I mean it."

***

From Gina's Blog, June 23, Tuesday

153

I search the house, feeling uncommonly stupid as I'm in my nightie and bare feet, boot and all, but I don't find anything amiss. When I return to my room, I lay my gun on the nightstand, crawl into bed and fall asleep.

The next morning I drive south of Camp Crook, toward the Short Pines and find Buffalo Ridge Guest Ranch. I shake my head with a chuckle when I see a faded sign hanging beneath a bovine skull. *I bet they've never even seen a buffalo here.* It sounds romantic, I guess, although bison are about the least romantic animal I can imagine. And they don't have wings, no matter what the barbeque places say.

The guest ranch is a dingy little place with maybe ten cottages, a run-down barn, a large log cabin that I suppose serves as a lodge, and several equipment sheds. The house itself is an old two-story farmhouse in desperate need of repair and paint. There's a white picket fence around an unkempt yard and a large dog. The dog begins barking ferociously when I pull up. I can't stand aggressive dogs, especially Rottweilers, like this one.

I cautiously open the pickup door and slam it shut, for he's unrestrained and comes at my vehicle with bared teeth and low growls. This dog has been trained to attack. I eye the front door, hoping the owner will call his dog off. No one appears. The dog circles the pickup and finally shuts up. It takes a position only three feet away and doesn't lie down. Every once in a while, if I move or cough, it throws itself into another apoplexy fit of barking. My head's beginning to ring when I see a tractor approaching down the dirt road from the corrals.

It seems to take forever, but finally a man descends from the tractor and calls the dog down. Without a glance at me, he drags it into the house and slams the door. Then he stalks out to me in a foul temper, wiping his hands on his worn coveralls.

Gravel crunches as I gingerly alight from the pickup with a smile pasted on my face. "Hello, Mr. Pickens. I'm Gina Lindsey. I live not far from here ...," I wave vaguely toward the west, "... and I'm looking for a place to have a family reunion. Someone mentioned you had cabins for rent. Would I be interrupting your day too much to see them?"

When he looks up and I see his face for the first time, I almost yelp. I know this face. One of my less appealing characteristics, or gifts, however you want to look at it, is a photogenic memory. Regularly I scan the photos of convicted felons that come on the DEA's secured internet site for the use of its agents. I can't say how long ago I'd seen this man's face, but I know he'd been convicted of dealing drugs in … now where was it? *Ah.* Wyoming.

It isn't uncommon for a felon to recommit after a light sentence of, say, five years. They usually move to another state and resume business. My pulses thud heavily in my ears as I attempt to keep a calm façade. Deep in my soul, I know I've found my target. This man, probably in league with bigger fish outside the county, is the person who's growing and selling marijuana.

He hadn't moved an inch since I'd spoken and the long silence doesn't seem to threaten him. His reddened face is covered with a scrubby gray beard. Hostility gleams from his deep-set eyes and his shaggy eyebrows stick out like a bristling porcupine. His gray hair, when he removes his baseball cap, is damp, plastered to his balding head.

"So how about it, Mr. Pickens?" I hope by asking, I can prod him into some sort of response.

When my explanation sinks in, he shifts, spits and nods, dredging up a smile. "Wal, now, that's a diff'rent story, miss. Thought you was one of them danged government survey people." His grin reveals yellowed tobacco teeth and a large gap. I wish he'd remained surly. "Shore. I'll show you 'round. Got a bum foot, miss? Shore you can keep up w'me?" He chuckles and I wonder if he laughs at the thought of a city woman falling into a pile of manure.

"You lead the way, Mr. Pickens. I can keep up, I assure you. Is it okay if I take a few pictures?" I draw out my Nikon D80 Digital camera. "To show the others in my family."

I say the last because he stares at the camera as if he'd never seen one before.

He grunts permission and stumps across the driveway toward the cottages. I follow, wishing I'd saved this little jaunt for later. My foot's hurting more than I'm willing to admit, and I'm too proud to lag behind him. He walks rapidly to the first cottage and opens the door. It isn't locked.

After I snap a few shots of the outside of the cabin, I hobble forward and step inside. Primitive doesn't even begin to describe it. The best thing about the living room is a small gas fireplace. A tattered brown carpet covers most of the floor, limp green curtains hang at the window, and a couch and two easy chairs sit alongside the wall; both of them had seen better days in the '50's. An eating area holds a formica-topped table and four rickety chairs. The sink in the kitchen is stained. The smell of mold and something else – like rotten eggs – assails my nose. Is it the water? I inspect two small bedrooms with queen-sized beds and a pocket-sized bathroom that desperately needs cleaning.

"There's another cabin with three bedrooms," he says, lurking in the doorway. "It holds twelve people and has two bathrooms. We ain't cleaned it since the last party left. They was hunters. Do ya want to see it?"

I hurry out of the cabin, restraining myself from holding my nose. "No thank you. Let me get a few more pictures of the whole place and I'll think about it. Do you have a brochure?" He looks blank. "Literature? Like a pamphlet that tells about your place?"

"Oh! Oh, that. Yeah, come on over t'the house. The misses works in Buffalo. Should be home any time now." He has a peculiar body odor – I'm guessing it's a mixture of grease, sweat and smoke. Mostly sweat.

"Do you mind if I walk around a little and get a few more shots?"

He shrugs. "Do what you like. I'll put Henry in his kennel. Damned dog. My grandkid's supposed to see he's tied, but he must've forgot. C'mon over. I'll git some coffee going."

Coffee was the last thing I want from Charlie Pickens. He'd probably lace it with dope. I thank him and watch as he saunters back to the house. Slowly I make my way around the back side of the cabins, wondering where he grows the marijuana. It will probably be a pole barn in the back somewhere. As I gaze around, I realize this is actually a perfect set-up.

The guest ranch is located in a small valley and the buildings back up against the timbered hills of the Short Pines. It wouldn't be difficult to throw up a metal equipment shed, pipe water and heat into it, and use it to grow drugs. Transporting the grown plants to the forest would be a cinch, too.

In my present condition, I can't tromp around the guest ranch and investigate. By the time I make it back to the farmhouse, I know I shouldn't have attempted even the little walking I'd done. My ankle and leg are on fire. I meet Charlie at the door and decline his coffee as graciously as I can. He hands me a creased leaflet and I tell him good-bye.

I have a good reason to return if I want to, and I definitely want to. Hopefully Mr. Pickens and his henchmen won't be aware of my second visit.

Back home I take a shower, eat dinner, swallow some pain relievers and after sending a report to Cap, flop into bed. It's strange that I hadn't heard back from Cap. Why hasn't he returned my calls or emails?

As I'm staring at the ceiling, I remember I hadn't locked the doors like I usually did. Groaning, I flip back the covers and without the aid of my boot, hop down the hall to the main part of the house. A bar of light gleams under Bobbi's door. I bump into a small table.

"Gina? Is that you?" Her voice sounds like a child's.

"Yeah. I'm just locking the doors. Sorry to have bothered you."

She appears in the doorway and gives me a reproving look. "Out here in the dark and you don't have your boot on." She shakes her head. "Come in here for a minute. I want you to see something."

I follow her into the room. She retrieves a piece of paper from a drawer in her desk and without a word, hands it to me. It's torn from a legal pad of paper. The writing's scrawled, the letters uneven and poorly formed, like a child's hand. Taking it, I focus on the words. "Another note? You keep finding these." My voice holds the skepticism I'm feeling. Has she written this herself just to get attention?

This one seems more ambiguous than the others. *Be careful, Bobbi. They are close on your tail and they watch the house. Don't trust anyone. Especially your neighbors.*

***

Wednesday, June 24

Chance pulled himself from the couch and trudged to the kitchen. Today was the first day he'd felt like a human being again. Yet his side still hurt if he moved wrong and he couldn't put much weight on his right knee. He dumped out his coffee cup and glanced out the window. From here, he could see the ranch house.

Gina's pickup was still parked in front. Good. He'd been concerned when Tim reported that she was almost killed on the four-wheeler and was now driving all over the countryside, taking pictures. What was she up to? Was she after the drug dealers? If she connected Elton's disappearance with the drug dealers, she might be.

The bad thing was that sooner or later the drug cartel was going to figure out what she was doing. And they played rough, as he could testify.

Silly girl. Why didn't she call in backup? Yet he understood her stubbornness and determination to solve the case. Hadn't the same kind of thing driven him? Personal revenge and the quest for justice are powerful motivators. What drove Gina? What did she know that would be useful for his own investigation?

As he stared out the window, Tim appeared on the porch. He'd gone over for breakfast and would probably bring something back for him. At least Chance had eaten well – he couldn't complain about that. Yet now that his body was healing, he felt restless, anxious to be at the job again, to have it finished so he could pick up the pieces of his shattered life.

Who would've thought he'd spend four years like this?

When Tim walked in, he was sitting at the table with another cup of coffee.

"Mornin', cowboy," Tim said, depositing a plate of coffee cake on the table. He seemed ill at ease and strode to his bedroom at the other end of the trailer. When he emerged a couple of minutes later, he headed for the door. "Gotta run. See you in a bit."

"Sure." Chance wondered where he was going in such a hurry and why he wouldn't stay to talk. Was he getting pressure from someone to divulge his knowledge? Did someone know about his presence there? Who? He'd been careful not to talk above a whisper and not to allow his shadow to fall on a window.

Chance helped himself to the cake, finished off the coffee and cleaned up the kitchen. When he looked again to the house, Gina's pickup was gone. Shucks. He'd have to wait until she came home. He watched TV and played games on Tim's computer. It felt strange to be so isolated from the world, from the action.

Although he'd written down his clues and conjectures, nothing led him forward. He had only a few pictures as hard proof. His list of possible culprits included his contact in Rapid City, Alan Costain; Sheriff Mike Crosby and his deputy Ty Rhoades; Bryce and Jesse Anderson; Randy Whittier. He studied the list, then wrote down, *Someone at the Bible camp, maybe Mr. Fairchild, possibly Connie.* He looked at that and crossed off her name. Then he wrote one more name with a firm hand: Tim Lindsey.

It was likely that Elton had been involved in a drug deal, been propositioned by the gang, or at least knew something important that led to his capture and death, and that Tim knew something about it, too. If it was Tim, though, why would he patch him up? Was he playing both sides of the game? If he was, he'd learn in a hurry it wasn't a game.

Chance studied his list again and his eyes lighted on *the Bible camp*. The camp! It was located on a little over one hundred acres of pristine forest and meadow land. Could it be that the white-haired gentleman, Mr. Fairchild, was the mastermind of the gang, that somewhere on that land was a grow shed? And worker's houses?

He shoved back and ruffled his hair. Naw. Couldn't be. Maybe Mr. Fairchild rented some of his land to the gang. For extra money. He'd heard how the camp was in need of money. Maybe Fairchild didn't *know* what they did with the land they rented. Had someone been in the back room when he made that call?

Chance felt cold. He got up and paced up and down the length of the trailer, glancing out the windows. Maybe it wouldn't be a bad idea to fetch Cyndi from Rapid City and do a little exploring. *No, not today*. He had to find a way to talk to Gina.

He stared out the window, fighting down the urge to dash out and do something. Time was running out. What if they learned from Tim that he was here? Would he get another unfriendly visit?

***

From Gina's Blog, Thursday, June 25

This morning when I get up, I find my foot isn't quite as swollen or sore. After a simple breakfast of cold cereal, a banana and coffee, I throw my stuff on the front seat of the pickup and turn the key.

Bobbi appears at the driver's window. I roll it down. "Surely you're not going again," she says. "You look tired. You better stay home and rest."

"Thanks," I retort. "You're looking lovely, too." Her face falls. I relent. "Sorry, Bobbi, but I have to do this. I'm really having a good time. I'll be home early, I promise. Be careful out in the hay field today." We'd doubled our precautions on the equipment and vehicles and so far nothing else had happened.

She grins. "Bryce is coming over to help. We should finish. See you later." With a jaunty wave, she heads to the equipment shed. They were picking up bales and stacking them in the hay barn today.

I'd saved the Anderson's water bottling plant to the last. No one is home when I drive into the ranch and park by the house. I'm glad to be alone. I grab my bag and set off, limping with my orthopedic boot, across the yard toward the so-called water plant. *Water plant, my eye*. Now, if my luck holds, I'd be able to peer in a window and find the answer.

I can't reach them. The windows are high off the ground and so dirty that even if I could have climbed up, I wouldn't see anything. I tromp through the weeds around the metal building, getting thistles in my socks and tripping over a half-buried pipe. Sitting on an old tire, I hold my ankle and moan for five minutes. *That* wasn't the smartest thing I'd ever done.

Maybe this whole thing is a wild duck chase. Or is it goose? *Duck, duck, goose.* I smile, remembering the game I'd played as a kid. No one liked to play with me because I always had to win. I rubbed my ankle again. Hadn't I learned anything in twenty-six years? Am I still on a dead-end chase to find the illusive golden pot at the end of the rainbow? For me it was always measuring up to Dad's standards. I can never do it, but I keep trying.

I sigh and regain my feet, glancing around. *Hey.* If I can drag a couple of those old tires below the window, I might be able to see in. I slap the dirt from my rear end and manage to get one tire on top of the other. They are dirty. Mounting them, I balance carefully on my good foot.

"I told you. We're closed!"

The deep masculine voice sounds right in my ear. I jump, lose my balance and sprawl in the dust. From that ungainly position, I look up into Jesse's taunting smile.

I struggle to a sitting position. "Oh, hi! Fancy meeting you here!" Trying to look as nonchalant as possible, I attempt to stand and finally have to take his hand.

He's laughing. "How's the foot, Hopalong? I didn't expect you'd be on it so soon." When he tries to draw me close to his body, I push away and dust off my clothes.

"Oh, my foot's okay. This is actually the new fashion look this summer. Didn't you know?" I manage a grin. "You didn't seem to be home, so I … I thought I'd look around on my own. I'm surprised you didn't get the dogs after me for trespassing."

"Oh. The dogs." He snaps his fingers. "I knew I'd forgotten something." He stays at my side as I gimp to the car.

"I'm glad you came. Did you see everything you wanted to see?" His tone's playful, yet I hear an undertone of anger.

"Yeah. It's just a water bottling plant, after all. I thought you were making counterfeit money in there."

He yelps a laugh and takes off his cowboy hat. "You didn't get a beer the day you came for a ride and I have time now." He raises his brows and smiles charmingly. "We have a lovely back yard."

"Okay, but I can't stay long. I promised Bobbi I'd be back early."

"You've had a busy schedule, even with an injured foot."

I laugh. "I've been exploring the countryside, taking pictures and meeting people."

He helps me up a series of shallow steps and through the garden gate. He hadn't lied. They have a lovely back yard, complete with a water feature, beds of petunias, marigolds, hydrangeas, asters and geraniums, and an immaculately kept lawn. Bird feeders. Stepping stones. A swing. Padded lawn chairs. I'm impressed and allow him to install me on one of the chairs, lift my foot to a stool, and dash off to fetch the beer.

"Now what?" I drink the beer and watch hummingbirds at their feeder. "Don't you want to know why I was trying to see into your plant? Or are you tanking me up with alcohol so you can drag me off to your private prison?"

He laughs long and loud, throwing his head back in genuine amusement. When he regains his composure, he wipes his eyes and says, "Oh, Gina. I didn't think you were the kind to have an imagination. Have you ever considered being a comedian?"

I don't think it's *that* funny. "You know, that hasn't ever occurred to me. I'll have to consider it. Maybe it's just your influence." I set my glass on the marble-topped table between us. "You haven't answered my question."

"Oh, yeah. It's kind of fun playing with your mind, especially when you're so serious most of the time. The water bottling plant is a joke around here. I'm supposed to be in charge but I don't spend much time on it during our busy season. We employ some kids, mostly high school kids, and run it in the winter months. It brings in a bit of cash. Would you like to see inside of the building? Or is your curiosity satisfied by my explanation?" He raises his glass in an exaggerated gesture of knightly courtesy. "More beer?"

"No. I've had enough." I don't mean to sound so abrupt, but his attempt at humor at my expense is wearing thin. I get to my feet without his help. "Thanks, Jesse. I better get home and see how Bobbi's doing. Since my accident, we've been a little edgy and I worry about her."

He follows me to the car and leans against the door, peering in at me. "I hope you're not offended by my jokes. When do you want to go on our flying date?"

"Oh. I suppose tomorrow would be okay. Ten o'clock. I won't wear my detective hat. I promise."

He moves away as I start the motor. "I'm relieved to hear that," he says with a sideways smile. "Who knows what horrible secret you'd pry out of me if you did?"

He displays a devil-may-care façade yet behind his eyes, I see something else. They are cold and hard, glinting with … what? Fear? Anger? A warning? It sends shivers down my spine, and I sense that Jesse Anderson could be a formidable foe if he chose.

As I drive away, I realize I still hadn't seen the insides of that building. *Darn!*

Chapter 24

Evil in the Air

Thursday evening, June 25

Chance finished his supper of canned chili and bread. As he washed the dishes, he peered out the small kitchen window. A few minutes later, Tim's Mustang roared up to the trailer. He parked and hopped out, bouncing up the steps and in the front door.

"Hi there, Chancey-boy. Busy doing the housework?" He laughed breezily and shrugged out of his coat. His manner was light, talkative, expansive. He was so different than what he'd been the last couple of days that Chance wondered what he'd been doing. Or taking.

"Just cleaning up from supper. What're you up to?"

"Nothing much." He sat down at his computer, like he did most evenings.

Chance went to his room and tucked his revolver into his shoulder holster. He was nervous about staying here much longer. If Tim was into drugs, could he expect another visit from the cartel's police force? Another demonstration of what they do to people who get too nosey? When he re-emerged into the tiny living room, he asked Tim if he'd take Gina a note.

Tim shot him a quizzical glance -- yet he ran it over to the house. Chance watched as she emerged, then ducked out of the trailer's rear door and met her in the barn.

"Well, this is a surprise," she said as she came limping down the wide center aisle. She was smiling and as she got closer, he saw warmth and appreciation in her eyes. Without any hesitation at all, she enclosed him in a brief hug. She stepped back to give him a once-over. "And here I thought you'd vamoosed. Isn't that what they say in the westerns?" She laughed. "So what's up?"

He removed his hat and plunked down on a bale of hay. His knee still wasn't up to holding his weight for long. "Well, three guys took a strong dislike to my looks and determined to rearrange my body parts. Tim found me after they was through. Don't know why he drove by that farmhouse, but I shore appreciated his help. He took me back to the camp and we exchanged places. He drove my rig and horse trailer down to Rapid Friday mornin'. I've been keepin' a low profile ever since in his trailer."

She nodded. "That's why he wanted pain pills and heating pads and extra food. I was curious about that. Was going to investigate, but got too busy."

"Busy gettin' hurt." He grunted. "How's the ankle, by the way? I see you're still wearin' that cute little boot."

She grimaced. "I'm all right."

"My episode should clue you into the fact that you're outclassed here, Gina. Why don't you call in backup? I'm a little surprised your boss let you come alone, knowin' the drug cartels' penchant for eliminatin' pesky cops." It was a wild shot and he was gratified to see it went home.

She whirled, paced down the aisle, and when she returned, her face was red. He didn't know if she was angry or embarrassed. Or both. Her voice was low. "I think that's my business, Chance." Slight inflection of her tone when she said his name.

He smiled. Dang it all, she was pretty when she was mad. "Fair enough. I want you to consider, though, that this case may be too big for one of us. We might have a chance at it if we work together."

"Are you FBI?"

He shook his head. "I'm a maverick. Like to work alone."

"I'm supposed to believe that?" She stared at him with her big green eyes, a challenging look. "And see what it got you." She had the grace to grin at her own remark, for it was as incriminatory of her actions as it was his. "What's your real name?"

"Blaine McPherson." He dredged up an alias and cover story from the past. "Okay. Now we've met, proper like and all. Tell me what you know, where you've been, and where you're goin' with this."

Indecision flitted across her face. She turned away.

He snorted. "For proof of my allegiance, I proudly wear the marks of the drug cartel's displeasure on my body. Isn't that enough for you, Miss Lindsey? Or do I have to die before you believe me?"

She whirled back to him. "I'm ... I've just learned to be cautious, Blaine." She pierced him with one of her rapier looks. "That's not it, is it." It was not a question. "You're not Blaine McPherson any more than I'm Oprah Winfrey."

He laughed. She had him. How did she do it? "You got me. I confess. But the reason I keep my true name to myself has nothing to do with you or with this case. 'Nuff said?"

She nodded. "I'm going to call you Chance because that's what I take every time I talk to you." She sat down on an adjoining bale and sighed. "Okay. I'll tell you. I have to hurry, though. Bobbi thought I was going out to pull weeds and if she doesn't see me, she'll panic."

"She keeps a pretty close eye on you, doesn't she?"

"Yeah. Okay, it's like this."

He watched her face as she began to tell her story, marveling in the beauty of her eyes, her clear skin, her golden-red hair.

"I met a woman in the clinic," she said as she twisted her hair between her fingers, "when I injured my ankle. She had a little girl with her who'd broken her arm. The woman's name was Maegan, and the little girl was Mexican. I wanted to go visit her, but Maegan cut me off. She was terrified of something. Or someone. She wouldn't tell me where she lived. I've thought about it a lot and I bet the drug growers keep Mexicans as workers. Illegal aliens, so they won't run."

"Have you got a line on where the plant is?"

She shook her head. "No. I think ..." Suddenly her phone rang. She straightened and stood, withdrawing the satphone from her belt. She looked at the number. "Sorry, Chance. I gotta take this. It's my boss."

She walked down the aisle, speaking in a low voice while Chance watched the shadows lengthen. Again he was cold – chilled clear through to the bone. Something was going to happen; he could feel it, sense it. *Danger! There's something out there.* He eased his revolver from the holster.

She finished her conversation and returned, stumping toward him, using her foot more than she should have. It was as if she'd forgotten about her pain. She stared at him from a face that had suddenly turned the color of old cheese, her lips compressed into a thin line with white around them, her nose flared.

"That was my boss, Cap Matthews. They found ... " Her voice broke and she looked away. He glimpsed tears in her eyes. She took a breath and regained her composure. "They found my partner's body in the river. He'd been ... shot. Nick. *Nick is dead.*"

He waited, trying to swallow the lump in his throat. "Are you going back to Spokane?"

She shook her head. "They don't know why he was ... no, he didn't say. They're sending backup. Another officer. I can't believe it."

She took another breath and clipped her phone onto her belt. Her eyes glinted. "I'm going to get these guys, Chance. I know it's the drug cartel. He must have found out something. Cap said he wanted to tell me something, that he couldn't trust a phone or email. He was going to come." She stifled a sob and stared up into the rafters. "There's a mole. Somebody's passing information on to the cartel. I wonder who it is."

He stood slowly, feeling eighty years old. "I don't know. I'm real sorry to hear about your partner, Gina. You've gotta be careful. They're gunning for you. Do you want me to walk you back to the house?"

She glared at him. "And hold my hand? I don't think so, Chance. We'll have that talk later. I'm going on the warpath." She whirled and stomped away, her back straight, her hair flying about her head.

He stood in the darkening barn and listened to the creak of the old timbers, to the yapping of coyotes on the butte, to the wind in the box elders. The feeling he'd had earlier intensified. Something was out there. Something that smelled like a dead skunk.

***

From Gina's Blog, June 25, Thursday

My eyes burn and my mouth's dry as I hurry along the rutted dirt road from the barn to the house. I can't stop thinking of Nick's dead body, floating in the Spokane River. Where will all this killing end? I grit my teeth, berating myself for my failed attempts to bring the drug cartel down. *I haven't accomplished anything. It's true -- I'm a failure just like Dad said, and because of me, Nick is dead. I'm a washed-up cop and a disappointment of a daughter.*

The warning Chance gave me echoes in my brain, yet I can't focus, can't think beyond the fact that Nick is gone. I'm almost running now and my breath comes hard and labored. The sky's red, or is it the rage that's building inside? *I'll get my gun; I'll set out tonight and find the gang. I'll show them. I'll kill them all.* I'm out of breath. Can't ... run ... have to ... stop.

Stop it, Gina! You can't do it!

I fall to my knees, remembering Dad's voice from long ago. It was when I was going to try for the high jump in track. I'd injured my knee and he was being practical, as always. Now I know he was concerned about me. I didn't listen to him -- I clenched my teeth and did it just to show him. Won the event, too, but was crippled for several months with an injured knee.

Now I see Dad's face from the pillow of his hospital room – his eyes are haggard with pain, his face is hollow and pale, his body is lying still beneath the white blanket. His lips move. I stop in the middle of the road and hold my breath, hoping I'll hear his last words.

I cover my face with my hands. *Please, Dad! Please! I have to know! I have to know what you said at the end!* As I reach out to grab the memory, it evades me and disappears like a wisp of smoke. I weep like a baby – for Nick, for Dad, for my lost Mom.

Suddenly I hear the click of metal against metal. It comes from the narrow band of trees that serves as a weather break for the house, some twenty yards away. *Funny how sound carries,* I think as I fling myself on the ground and roll. A volley of shots blast the air. Heavy footsteps behind me crunch on the gravel and I cringe smaller. Someone lands on top of me.

Chance. I know by his scent, by his grunt.

Over the roar of gunfire, he yells something I can't understand. I twist from underneath him. The *pinging* thud of bullets hit the dirt, just inches from my head, a steady rain of them, and I know we are only an instant from death. I react instinctively, rolling, twisting, my body doing contortions a side-show freak would be proud of; Chance is right behind me.

Thank goodness a tractor stands nearby. Scuttling like a lame crab, I maneuver behind it and sense more than see Chance scrambling in beside me as more shots split the air, bullets spewing around our heads like angry hornets and ricocheting off the tractor. The barn takes the brunt of them. I wish I had my rifle. My revolver's no good at long distances.

"Who … do you think …" I glance over at Chance who is holding his revolver with both hands. As I watch, he draws down and returns the fire carefully, choosing his target.

"Git to the house. I'll cover you."

Another round of bullets blast the tractor. A rifle booms from the house. *Bobbi!* "I'm going. There's a mole, Chance. A traitor. I wonder who it is." I tug on his jacket.

He ignores me and shoots. "For God's sake, Gina! Git to the house! Now! I'm goin' to run out of ammo! They're aimin' to kill us all!"

All of us except Tim. I note with cold detachment that the gunfire doesn't reach Tim's trailer, which is dark and silent. His Mustang's gone. Has he set us up? Is he the traitor?

The rifle roars again from the house, a series of shots, sweeping the band of trees.

"Okay … I'll go. When I was out there on the road, I saw Dad when he was dying. And I've got to remember what he was saying." I sniff and wipe my nose on my sleeve.

"Now! Go now!" He shoves me away. "I'll draw off their fire."

The shots from the trees stop; evidently the attackers are finding new locations away from Bobbi's rifle fire and are drawing closer to the house.

I get to my feet and glimpse Chance as he darts from the tractor in the direction of the barn. After that, I concentrate on a mad dash, wincing against the pain in my ankle, to the house with a pause behind my pickup, then again behind a clump of bushes near the gate leading into the front yard, which doesn't give a lot of cover. I hope the assassins haven't found good positions yet.

I'm wrong. Bullets seek me out -- crashing into the vehicles and the house, shattering glass and slamming heavily into the siding. I have to keep moving. Chance's revolver pops now and then, and the return gunfire from the men booms from the trees. I was right -- they'd moved in closer. As I scramble onto the porch and flee inside, I worry about Chance. What are his odds? Will I be the cause of another death?

Once inside, I don't hesitate a second, running to Elton's gun closet in the living room. It's unlocked; the glass doors stand open. I grab a 30.06 rifle, load it with shaking hands and bolt to Bobbi's quilting room in the new addition.

I find her sitting with her back against the wall, a rifle cradled on her lap, her face the color of white sand. The window's blown away; glass pebbles cover the carpet.

I crunch across it and kneel beside her. "You okay?"

She nods, her lips thin, her eyes wide. "Who would ...?"

The rifle fire starts again. She peers out the window. "I called the sheriff but he won't get here for awhile."

I hear desperation in her voice. I say, "Stay down! I'm going over to the office window. You watch this side. Shoot to kill." I impale her with a stern glance. "I mean it."

***

June 25, Thursday

Maegan stretched and padded to the window. There were no street lights back here on this narrow little street and a cloud cover muted the moon light. Voices drifted through the thin walls of the house. Lifting a corner of the curtain, she watched two girls, laughing and talking, as they jogged along the deserted street. She dropped the curtain and paced to the kitchen restlessly. Someone started a motor. She lifted the curtain on the front window again. The neighbor man and his wife were climbing into their big red truck. Were they going to the bar for drinks and dinner? She turned to the small living room and surveyed it with a sniff. Thankfully Jilly was asleep. It had been difficult to keep the little girl quiet and in the house.

After five days in this place, she had to get out. How could she do it? Her chances of escape were practically nil. Returning to the easy chair, she picked up her book, staring into middle space, remembering the day she decided to cut and run with Jilly.

After driving into Ekalaka, she loaded up with groceries and parked her Land Rover on a street behind the museum. With one hand holding the little girl's, she carried the plastic bags of food down the street. No one would be looking for her for a few hours, at least, and she had a good idea where to spend the next several days.

Good thing she'd befriended Betsy Schmidt, the woman who delivered the mail to the ranch. In one of their talks alongside the road, the woman had invited her to her house for a cup of coffee and a chat whenever she came to town. Although it was against the rules, she visited Betsy several times at her small cottage.

"Come anytime you want," Betsy said with a toothless grin. "If you need a bed for the night, I got an extra room."

So she aimed straight for Betsy's house that day and when the woman answered, she explained in an uneven voice what she needed. "My boyfriend's after me. I'm afraid I need some place to stay for a few days."

Betsy was more than happy to help her out. After she invited Maegan inside, she said, "I've been meanin' to go visit my sister down to Rapid. This gives me a chance to do it. I'd appreciate it if you'd feed my cats and bring in the mail."

Maegan's heart lifted. "How long are you planning to be gone?"

Betsy stuffed some clothing into a paper bag, grabbed her toothpaste and brush and headed for the door. "Don't know, dearie. If you have to leave, give Muffin and Tuffy extra food and water, would you? Thanks so much."

"Oh, uh, Betsy!" Maegan stopped her before she went out the door. "Please don't tell anyone about us staying here. Like I said about my boyfriend. He … threatened to kill me. That's why I have to keep low. Okay?"

Betsy nodded knowingly. Her pet peeve in life was men. Get her started, and you'd soon wish you could shut her up. "Shore thing. Thanks for your help."

Now Maegan wondered how she'd make it out of town. She was sure her car was watched. Maybe the whole town was watched. She'd been doing some observing herself, and knew that the neighbor across the street left every week-day morning at four and didn't return until five in the evening. When she got a call from Betsy who phoned to ask about the cats, the woman told her he worked in Miles City at the post office.

A plan formulated in her mind. It was risky, yet she figured it was the only way out of town unnoticed. She determined to try it tomorrow morning. First she had to feed the cats and bring in the mail. She always waited until it was dark to fetch it from the mailbox by the street. Tonight she donned her jacket, tied on her shoes, and quietly stepped from the house, closing the door behind her.

The Russian olive tree near the house swayed in the wind and down the street a dog barked. She heard someone's TV and the sound of a party two houses away. She drew in a breath. How she hated going down the cracked sidewalk, stepping through the gate and retrieving the mail! She felt like all the eyes in the town were fastened on her. And worse, spies from the ranch, Butch's henchmen, might be waiting behind that big lilac bush on the corner or lurking near the Ford pickup in the neighbor's drive.

Well, she'd do it once more, and after that, she'd make her escape from this place. Tomorrow morning, she'd get Jilly ready; they'd crawl into that man's car, hunker down in the back seat and cover themselves with a blanket. If she was quiet enough, and could keep Jilly still, they'd get a free ride to Miles City and hopefully a new life.

Just as she took a step away from the door, someone screamed. She jumped and froze, listening. Was it a woman? *No.* It was just an owl. *Okay, that was weird.* Tentatively she moved down the steps, every muscle tense, her jaw clenched, her fingers curled around the gun in her pocket. A yowl and sudden explosion from the hedge sent her scurrying back to the door.

A cat. She swiped the sweat from her forehead. The wind stirred the tree limbs above her head, a scritching noise that sounded like nails on a chalk board. Music erupted from the bar downtown. A pickup roared out of town. She took a deep breath and told herself to get a grip. This was stupid – running, scared all the time. Maybe she should just give up and drive back to the ranch.

No. She couldn't do that. If they got their hands on her, they'd make her talk. They had ways. Oh, yes, she'd tell them where she'd been and who she'd talked to. They might even threaten to kill Jilly in her presence. They'd done worse things. She extended her right arm, loosening up her fingers. If she had to draw her gun from her pocket, she'd do it fast and shoot without thinking. She'd practiced enough to know she could hit whatever she wanted.

She stepped out onto the walk and hurried to the gate. The latch was cold under her fingers and the wind sent shivers down her spine. The darned hook was stuck. She wrestled with it, swearing under her breath. With a shriek, it gave way. Her shirt was drenched with sweat. She darted to the mailbox, only five feet away.

Opening the box, she yanked out the mail. Turned. Fled back to the gate. Pulled it shut. Something darker than the shadows rustled the big bush by the door. She froze, horrified. A big black thing moved and stepped out into the dim light of the stars.

It was Butch and she caught the glint of a gun in his hand. He was not smiling.

"Take your hand from your pocket and don't try anything stupid. I don't want to mess up Betsy's front yard."

Chapter 25

Friendly Fire

June 25, Thursday

A cool breeze fanned Chance's face as he hunkered down behind a stack of old lumber. It felt good, yet it didn't stop the sweat from soaking his shirt and rolling down his face. He only had two bullets left in his revolver, and he had to make them count. Three men hid behind the barn, and he figured they knew where he was.

They'd been talking in low tones, probably making plans. Anytime now he expected they'd split up and surround him. He caught a flicker of movement to the right and one to the left. *Okay, boys. Let's get this show on the road.* One man, he figured it was the boss, remained sheltered by the building. He could see his shadow.

Leaning against a stack of firewood, he drew a deep breath, and wiped his hands on his pants. The rifles from the house had fallen silent. He'd heard two – a big fifty-aught caliber rifle and a lighter thirty-aught six. Gina must be firing that one. Good. She'd made it to the house.

Gravel crunched nearby under a booted foot. He ducked. The shot came from the right and just missed his head. *Okay, now I know where you are, buddy.* Chance heard the other gunman creeping in from the rear left. He counted silently. *One, two, three …* he rose, whirled and shot the man who was closing the distance from the right, who'd made the mistake of coming out from behind a truck.

The man crumpled to the ground without a sound. Got him. Assailant number two was approaching for a close shot. Chance crouched lower and waited. *Wait until you see the whites of their eyes.* He smiled grimly, remembering Custer's famous words. About that time, another gun boomed from the windbreak. The man behind him screamed. Chance half-stood and peered around the wood pile. The man lay on his back, his arms and legs spread wide. Chance glanced toward the trees. Someone was on their side – someone with heavy fire power. Could it be the sheriff?

He took a deep breath when the third man who hid behind the barn made a break for it, dashing across an open space, aiming for the garage. He heard the thirty-aught six bark from the house. The shot pinged off the metal equipment shed. *Gina!*

Taking aim on the running man, he led ahead and gently pulled the trigger. The man staggered, fell. He regained his feet. Now he wasn't trying for the garage or house – he headed back to the cover of trees and disappeared quickly.

Silence fell over the farm. Chance fought against the way his stomach twisted and threatened to eject his supper. Every time he shot a living human being, this happened. The gun in the windbreak was silent. He guessed the man had an outfit parked over there. Who was it? Why did he shoot? Hearing a step behind him, he turned.

Gina popped around the corner of the equipment shed and hurried toward him. "You okay?" Her face was pale; her nose and eyes were red, like she'd been crying.

"You see that guy behind me?"

She nodded. "He's dead. You got that last guy, winged him. He made it to the windbreak. I could've taken him out, but I let him go." She sighed and leaned against the wall. "I hope the sheriff gets here soon. Did you shoot that other one, the one over by the barn?"

"I don't think he's dead. We better go secure him. I think he was trying to find his gun. Who was firing from the trees?"

She looked at him, her eyes big in the dim light. "I don't know. You mean a friendly?"

He nodded and made his way to the wounded man. Blood flowed from a wound in his shoulder. He opened his eyes and groaned.

Gina covered him with her rifle. "Know him?"

Chance shook his head. "Nope. They must be recruitin' them from Rapid now. Looks like a Mexican." A siren wailed in the distance and rapidly drew closer. He lifted his head. It wasn't long before he spotted the revolving red light on top of the sheriff's patrol car glinting in the waning light.

Mike Crosby and his deputy, Ty Rhoades, hurried over to where Chance and Gina guarded their prisoner.

Chance nodded. "Howdy, sheriff."

Mike Crosby didn't appear surprised at seeing him. "Had a bit of a gunfight here, did you? One dead? How many others?"

Chance nodded. "Just one other man. He hightailed it back to the trees. It was pretty intense there for a bit. They had me surrounded. If it hadn't been for that guy in the windbreak…"

"What guy?"

Chance shifted his weight. "I dunno. Someone over there, friendly fire. Big gun. He's the one who shot the dead man. Shore wasn't my shot." He nodded to the body lying on the ground not far away and returned his revolver to the holster.

"Huh." After Mike glanced quickly at the trees, he prodded the prone man with his boot. "What's your name, son?"

The man glared at him and said nothing.

The sheriff grunted. "Okay. You want it the hard way. Gina, why don't you bind up that wound so he don't die of loss of blood before I git him to the hospital. Ty, when she's done, cuff him and cover the dead man. I got a tarp in my trunk. We'll be back to pick him up and in the morning, we'll comb them woods."

Gina limped to the house and returned with strips of cloth which she bound around the man's shoulder, oblivious of his moans and groans. Chance helped transfer him to the patrol car. Ty covered the body and washed his hands under the outside spigot.

Bobbi emerged from the house, still holding her rifle.

Mike wrinkled his brow. "Howdy, Bobbi. I'd shore appreciate it if yu'd go on into town tonight. You have folks in there, don't you?"

She shook her head stubbornly. Tears were streaking her cheeks, but her shoulders were thrown back and she stood with one hand on her hip, the other cradling the rifle.

"Nobody's drivin' me off the ranch, sheriff. They want to come again, I'll give 'em a taste of lead. I'm staying right here. It's what Elton would want." Her mouth was set in a grim line. Chance knew Mike would have a tussle if he tried to force her.

Mike grinned and shrugged, giving in easily. "It's your call, ma'am. Just a suggestion. I'll leave Ty here. At least for tonight. He and Chance can help patch up them windows until you can get some glass. We'll be back in a jiffy to clean up. See you later, Bobbi. Gina." He tipped his hat and drove away.

***

From Gina's blog, June 25, Thursday

I'm not particularly happy to see Mike drive off, as I'm thinking that if the man who'd gotten away finds some of his buddies and returns ... I don't want to think about it. I can't believe we all survived. That was close. Too close.

I study Chance as we troop into the house. His face is set, like he's hopping mad, and he isn't saying much. None of us are, for that matter. Ty and Chance find some plywood and nail it to the outside of the house over the gaping window while I help Bobbi round up some dinner. An hour later, the sheriff returns and picks up the body. No one goes outside while he's about it and he doesn't come in.

Tim arrives while we're eating. He stops suddenly in the doorway of the kitchen when he sees Chance and Ty at the table, chowing down hamburgers and potato chips.

"What's going on?" His voice is high, like he's under a lot of stress.

I watch him. He looks genuinely surprised. His glance shifts around the room as if trying to find a place to light, and he keeps his hands hidden, shoved deep in his pockets. He stands sideways, too, like he's aiming to get out of there as fast as he can.

Bobbi stands. "Oh, you've come back, have you." Her tone's accusing. "Where've you been?" Not *oh, my dear son, come and have dinner and let me fix your troubles.* She's angry and I don't blame her. Will he give her a straight answer?

I've studied body language and I know the signs of a lie. Or evasion. Tim's answer comes straight and has the ring of truth in it. He doesn't lower his eyes as he says, "I got a text, Mom. It was

Doug. He said he needed help. When I got there, he wasn't home. Nobody was home. So what's going on?" He takes a step farther into the kitchen and glares at Ty. "What's he doin' here?"

Bobbi pats Ty's shoulder. "We had an incident. Sit down and I'll get you some supper. Are you hungry?"

He shakes his head, crosses his arms over his chest and remains standing. Now he looks like his mother did when she refused to leave the ranch.

I sigh and get up. That pesky Lindsey pride is forever getting in the way of things. "For pity's sake, eat something, Tim. We aren't going to bite you." I make room for him and fetch another plate, glad to see he takes my advice. We tell him the story, and once I get the ball rolling, everyone chimes in with their version. Tim shakes his head repeatedly like he can hardly believe his ears. When he's finished, he shoves back his chair. His face is mottled white and red – mostly red.

"Goin' back to my house, Mom." He gets to his feet and strides out of the house. He doesn't slam the door. He's shook – real shook.

Chance excuses himself soon after. I follow him to the door.

"I gotta go get my horse, Gina. Me and some bad guys are goin' to have a show-down or my name ain't Chance."

I can't help but smile. It sounds so much like a Louis L'Amour book. "I don't think your name *is* Chance, but that's beside the point. How're you getting to Rapid?" Someone had retrieved the old pickup, so that wasn't available.

He shrugs. "Tim might take me."

I shake my head dubiously. "I don't think he wants anything to do with this business. He's had a shock. Maybe some of his friends were involved with …"

"Gina, you aren't leaving, are you?" Bobbi comes into the living room, wiping her hands.

My skin prickles at her tone. Yet I know she's been through a lot, and Tim isn't much support right now. "Just for a few hours." I turn and give her a weak smile. "Think you'll be all right? You've got Tim and Ty."

She glares at me, her jaw clenched and brows raised. "I'm fine, just thinking of you. You're still limping on that foot. You don't need to go roaring off again so soon."

I let that one go and swing back to Chance who's striding out to the front porch. I follow him. "Get your things. I'll take you down."

"Now?"

I sigh, exhaustion pulling on my body like ten-ton weights. "Yeah. Tonight. I want to see someone there and tonight's as good as any other time. See you in ten minutes."

***

June 25, Thursday

Maegan's throat constricted. She felt a scream coming and quickly throttled it. No one would help her, not here. Loathing and dread swept across her soul. She thought for a moment she would be sick. When the nausea passed, she was cold clear through, like someone dumped a bucket of ice water on her.

She could have easily shot the man who stood before her, the man she'd once been in love with. Now she saw him for what he was – a coward, a cheat, a liar – and worse, a murderer.

His eyes flicked across her body hungrily and he licked his lips. "Maegan, I'm not sayin' it again. Come along quietly. My outfit's parked over there." He waved the gun to the next street. He closed the distance, felt in her pocket, removed her revolver. "I wouldn't like to put bullet holes in your beautiful body, my dear."

His breath smelled of beer and his face was prickly with a beard. She held herself still, like she did when he demanded she give herself to him. She had to be careful. Her nerves tingled as she stepped down the cement walk and out the gate, his footsteps close behind her. He stayed a step or two back – he was clever, if somewhat stupid. He knew she could kick.

She wasn't about to tell him about Jilly, left alone in the house. Somehow she had to get free of him and back to her. It was unthinkable that she'd leave the little girl alone. The party suddenly erupted into the front yard. Maegan glanced that way. Some boys stumbled out of the house. There was a lot of shouting, taunting each other, circling.

Butch said in a low voice, "Easy now. Just keep walking. I don't want to hurt you."

She felt the gun barrel in her back and grunted. "Not until you get me to the ranch. Then you'll let your men hurt me. Right, boss?"

He didn't reply, and she wasn't going to risk a look at his face. She needed every faculty alert, ready for her chance. Her muscles were tight, even as she strolled ahead of him, swinging her arms as if she didn't have a care in the world. She reminded herself to breathe. And she prayed. *Oh, God! Help!*

It surprised her -- the prayer. She hadn't thought of God for a long time. Yet here she was, murmuring a desperate prayer. Was there a god? Would He hear her? She didn't know. Gravel crunched under her feet. Now she turned the corner and saw Butch's red truck.

There was one street light along here. She avoided the sidewalk, keeping to the street, hoping for a miracle. *Was* there a miracle for her? *Was* there any grace left in the universe? Half a block more and they would arrive at the truck. She heard Butch expel his breath like he thought they were home free.

She repressed a snort. Her miracle appeared in the form of a dented old-model pickup, driven carelessly by one of the boys at the party. She glimpsed his face as he two-wheeled it around the corner and almost smashed into the telephone pole. He was drunk. The truck careened straight toward her.

Butch swore and jumped back.

She held her ground, gritting her teeth, staring past the blinding headlights, timing her jump. *Now!* She poised and leaped, grabbing for the passenger door, managing to wrench it open, twisting her wrist in the process. She jumped in. Half in and half out. Butch fired a shot and missed. She saw his face as she whizzed by – startled, furious, confused.

The boy looked over at her. "Uh. What d'ya think ..."

She grabbed a wrench from the floor and wielded it over his head. "Keep up the speed. I don't want to hurt you. Get out of town. Drive out the Miles City cut-off road. Do you *understand*?"

He shook his head and almost took out a dog that had wandered into the street. She pulled on the steering wheel and they missed the dog. A truck approached behind them. *Butch!*

"Here! Turn here!" Again she grabbed the wheel and the vehicle screeched around the corner. The boy was almost too far gone to know what was going on. He'd crouched down by the driver's door, whimpering. She crawled over and almost sat on him, taking over the steering and the gas pedal.

They turned again. She glanced in the rear view mirror. The pickup behind hadn't reached the corner.

Slamming on the brake, she leaped out of the driver's door, ramming it shut. Leaning inside, she pulled the kid upright by his jacket and screeched in his face, "Keep going, kid! That guy behind you is aiming to kill you! Drive! Drive out of town!"

She jumped away from the truck and ducked behind a hedge of lilacs.

The kid must have understood and believed her. She heard him grind into gear; the roar of the motor filled the night air. Gravel flying, the tires dug out, sliding sideways and gained traction. In a matter of seconds, the pickup was flying down the road.

And a second after that, Butch's truck flew past.

As she stood behind the thick bush, somehow her heart was lighter. It seemed the sky was not as dark as before. The wind, blowing over the sweet grasses, smelled of the damp, green places under the box elder trees. She took a deep breath and trotted along the silent street, avoiding the pools of light cast by porch lights.

She wasn't free of him yet. She had to get back to the house and wake Jilly. Somehow she'd have to escape. Yet for this moment, a sense of freedom and joy flooded her heart. She looked up at the stars that glittered overhead. "Thanks, God. I didn't really think You were there."

Chapter 26

Desiree's Picture

From Gina's blog, June 25, Thursday

I get the address of Elton's brother's ranch from Bobbi and Google it to find a map. Uncle Herbert's place is located just outside Rapid City, to the southwest. With that in hand, I give Chance the keys and we set off in the Honda pickup. *Nick's* pickup, I remind myself.

From the very first, Chance makes it clear that he isn't in a talking mood. It makes me mad. I figure he has information I can use. Of course I'm not about to spill my gut to him, so why should he trust me? We're at an impasse. Yet it bugs me that he has the nerve to be stubborn when people are dying and so much is at stake!

I'm curious about the dead woman we'd found at Medicine Rocks. Strange Mike hadn't ever told me anything about that investigation. I clear my throat and say, "You mentioned you knew that woman, Sabrina, the one we found at Medicine Rocks the other day. What was she like?"

He shrugs. "I dunno. She kept to herself mostly. Didn't talk much."

"What did she do for … fun? For a hobby? Did she say?"

"Don't rightly know. Except that she liked to hike. And take pictures. She showed me a few once." He glances over at me, a shadow of a grin sliding across his face. "An album of them, actually. Some were purty good. She said she sells them."

I consider that for awhile. "Did Mike say if they'd found a computer or camera in her things?"

He shakes his head. "Mike hasn't talked to me since." He let silence fill the cab while he navigates past several big holes in the road. Then he says, "I saw her. About the time your uncle went missing."

I straighten and stare at him. "Where?"

"Up on the Rims. I'd gone up there, lookin' for a good trap line. Saw her on the hillside, making her way up a trail. I think she had her camera."

"So, let's say she saw something she wasn't supposed to see and had evidence in her camera. She doesn't know what she's seen. Someone else sees the pictures. And she has to die because of that."

He doesn't answer right away. A big stock truck passes and splatters the wind shield with mud. Finally he says, "You might be right. If I were you, I'd have a talk with Mike about it, though. He mighta found a camera. Or her computer."

"Yeah, I think I'll do that. Oh, by the way, I might've found the place where the drug dealers are growing their weed."

"Oh, yeah? Care to fill me in?"

I tell him how I'd driven all over the county, investigating home businesses and that my top suspect was Charlie Pickens and his guest ranch near the Short Pines.

"It has everything you'd expect to find," I conclude, "if a rancher wanted to grow drugs. Solitude, proximity to the forest, water, light and lots of land. He might have a whole village of Mexican workers back behind, in the woods. And to top it all off," I glance over at him, proud of my clever deductions, "he's served time in Wyoming for running drugs. I'm going back there, Chance."

He snorts, waving away my findings negligently as if I were a ten-year-old kid. "You can forget Charlie. It ain't him."

I stare at him. "Why not?"

"Cuz I worked there for three months. I had the same thought you had. Good reasonin', but that boat won't float. Though Charlie's done time for drugs, he's cleaner than a whistle now. I had plenty of opportunity to search the place. It's not him, Gina. Did you investigate anyone else?"

The way he says *investigate* makes my temper rise. "That's classified information." I clamp my mouth shut tight.

"Fine with me."

I slide down in the seat and pillow my head against the passenger door with my jacket. I guess I slept, because the next thing I know, we're pulling into the Flying W Ranch.

He parks at the house. "I guess I'll go tell them what I'm doin'. You comin' in?"

I shake my head and get out, glad there aren't any dogs. "No, I don't know them. Besides, I need to see someone in town. Are you going back tonight?"

"Guess so. I don't want to sleep here in my truck."

"By the way," I say as I grip the door handle. "Just so you know. I visited Billy Palmer's specialty lumber mill, the Whittier's nursery, and the Anderson's water plant. I didn't get in to see the water plant. You have any ideas?"

He grins at me in that infuriating way of his. "No, Gina. I'm kinda fresh out of ideas. Just wanta get me my gun and my horse and we're gonna make dust fly. If you catch my meanin'."

"Just where are you going to start?" A coyote yaps in the forest. I climb into the driver's seat.

He shrugs. "Heck, I don't know. There was a guy popping shots off from the trees and I swear it was friendly fire. In fact, I think he took that one guy down. You didn't hit him; the guy in the trees did."

"I know. What about it?"

"Wal, I aim to comb those trees. The sheriff said he would, but I'd like to have a look myself. I have a notion about ..." He glances over his shoulder. A dog begins to bark from inside the house. "I'd better go declare myself and git back."

"Well, be careful." I intend to give him a frown and find myself grinning. There's something so ... well, so innocent about him, it makes me smile. Yet the very thought of someone finding his body floating down the Yellowstone River is enough to give me the shakes. "They're playing for keeps."

"I know that, Gina Lindsey." He leans in the cab and takes my hand. "Thanks for the ride. I'll be praying for you."

I'm so surprised, I shake his hand like an idiot and watch him stride over to the house. "I don't need your prayers, mister cowboy,"

I mutter to myself as I turn the Honda around. "I'm going to do this on my own."

Driving into town, I locate the address I want and park in front of a dilapidated one-story house in a poor residential area. It needs a paint job and the lawn is brown and scraggly. There's a light on in the living room. Evidently she's home and awake.

I gather my purse and ring the doorbell. Pretty soon a woman opens the door a crack and peers out.

"Hello, my name is Gina Lindsey and you're … Desiree Pledger, right?"

She nods, not unlocking the chain, not changing her expression.

I take a deep breath. "I'm … Elton Lindsey's niece. You know he disappeared, right? I heard that you used to work for my aunt, cleaning. I'm a … detective from Spokane, and I'd like to ask you a few questions, if I may. I promise I won't take much of your time."

She thinks about that for a moment, then nods. She shuts the door, unlocks the chain and opens it. "I don't have much to do with them anymore, you know. I can't imagine why you'd want to question me, but heck, come on in. You wanta cup of coffee?" She pushes back her blond hair that has more gray in it than blond and gives me a shadow of a smile.

"Sure." I follow her into the living room where she gestures to a sagging sofa. She turns off the TV and leaves to get the coffee. The inside of the house is much like the outside – one window is cracked, there's a gap around the door, the carpet is stained and scuffed. It has the air of a house neglected, either by lack of money or the know-how to fix things, or both.

She returns with the coffee. "Cream? Sugar?"

"No thanks." I accept it gratefully and wait while she stirs both into her cup and leans back on the easy chair. Now I can see that behind her heavy make-up, she has the haggard look of a woman who works too long and too hard. She'd been pretty once, a long time ago, but now her figure is plump and the way she walks, stands and sits tells me she has little regard for herself.

"How long ago did you live in Ekalaka, Mrs. Pledger?"

"Please. Just call me Dez." She adjusts her sweats and crosses her legs – the top one pointing away from me. Distancing, protecting herself. "I lived there a few years back. Guess it was three, no, four years now. Time goes so fast, doesn't it? When you're havin' fun." Her attempt at a smile comes out more like a grimace.

"Sure does. I want you to know that this interview is not recorded, will not be used against you, and is ... well, just my own idea. I'm not here in my official capacity. Just as a person who loved my uncle and ... I'd like to find out what's happened to him."

She glances at me sharply and says nothing.

I continue. "We're hoping that it wasn't ... murder. Yet we're taking every possibility into consideration. What can you tell me about him? Did he often come to Rapid City? Where do you think he might have gone?"

She shrugs, picks up a pillow and holds it to her stomach. Protecting herself again – from me. I don't know what I can say that will reassure her.

"I don't know nothin', ma'am. I cleaned at their house, yes. I ain't seen them since ... well, not for a long time. He didn't come to Rapid much, from what I understand. Was the stay-at-home kind. Devoted to his family and the ranch. Sorry." She glances longingly at the TV, maybe figuring I'll catch the hint and leave.

"I'm sorry I've made you remember some unpleasant ..."

"Oh, no. There wasn't nothin' unpleasant about it, besides the fact that my husband, he died while we were there, and I had to start cleanin'. My boy, Conan, he liked it there swell."

I stand and stroll to a shelf on the wall that holds several family pictures. "This your son?" I point to a handsome young man who poses behind a deer he'd just killed.

"Yeah, he'd just gotten a prize buck. See those antlers? We still have 'em out in the garage."

"Nice looking kid. Where's he now?"

She lifts one shoulder and looks away. "Down in Colorado. Don't know for sure where. Calls once in a while."

I set my cup on the end table, growing restive. This isn't getting anywhere. I sense that the woman knows a lot more than she's willing to tell me, yet there's no way I will get it out of her unless I stay a couple of weeks. Even then, I doubt if she'd open up to me. Well, it was a gamble, and since I'm in Rapid, it didn't hurt to try.

I start to turn from the shelf when another picture catches my eye. I lean closer. It's of a group of people, both men and women, in front of a building – a barn. "This looks like a happy bunch of people," I say casually and touch the picture. "A family reunion?"

She laughs and gets up to stand beside me. She picks up the picture and dusts the frame, taking it to the lamp where there's better light. "No. It was … just some friends." She seems lost in a memory. A smile flits over her face.

"Was this in Ekalaka?" Something about the background seems familiar. I'd seen that hill formation before … but where?

"Yeah. Before Bill died. We helped build that barn for our friends." She sighs and is about to return the framed photo to the shelf. I hold out my hand for it.

"Would you mind telling me who they are? Some of them seem familiar to me. I can't remember most of them even though I visited Ekalaka when I was in junior high."

"Okay. That's me and Bill, there. Then Elton and Bobbi. And next to them is the people we built the barn for – Randy and Susan Whittier and their two kids. Next to them is Bryce Anderson and his wife, Rebecca. That little kid is their son, Jesse. They were going in on the business, too. In fact, they were the ones who …" She sighs. "My, we had a good time! The barn had water and heat and everything. They were so excited about it."

"So this is the Whittier's nursery?"

"Oh, no. This one's … somewhere else. You can't rightly see it unless …" Her voice trails off.

"Whose land is it on?"

She gives me another of her sharp-eyed glances and shrugs both shoulders, holding the pose for a moment longer than I think is normal. She's going to lie. I can see it forming in her eyes.

"Over to the camp. You know that Bible camp? Behind that place … in the woods." She returns her gaze to the photo. "We were so happy. That was before everything fell apart."

"You mean before your husband died?" I allow her to set the photo on the shelf. My nerves are tingling. I'd just seen or heard something significant, yet I can't sort it out right then.

"And other things. People change. Times change."

I stare at the picture again. "It doesn't look like it's in the forest."

"Oh, really?" She rubs her forehead and paces to the window. Several minutes tick by. I wait, easing from one foot to the other.

When she turns, she's composed her face and tries another smile. This one reaches her eyes. I can see why Elton was attracted to her. "Well, you can't live in the past, can you? Is there anything else? Would you like more coffee?"

Of course she speaks from politeness. She wants me to leave.

"Uh, no thanks. Is there anything else you can tell me about your time in Ekalaka? Did you make any friends? The sheriff is also investigating the murder of a young woman by the name of Sabrina Phillips."

She starts violently and spills her coffee. "Oh!"

"Do you ... know her?"

She nods, taken completely off her guard. "Yeah. We was friends, sort of, and we've kept in contact. We have lunch together once in a while when she comes to Rapid." She stops. "Or I should say, we did. We ... uh, she cleaned places and I met her at the Forestry office."

"She was working at Forestry the night she was killed. We were hoping to find some of her pictures. It might have a bearing on her murder." I'm talking at random, hoping to hit another nerve that will give me a clue. I don't expect her to throw her hand to her mouth and exclaim loudly.

"Oh, darn!"

"What?" I lean forward.

She whirls and disappears into a back room that I assume is her bedroom. When she reappears, she's holding an envelope.

"I think you might want this." She hands it to me.

I take it. It's an envelope addressed to Desiree Pledger. When I open it, I see something wrapped in a piece of paper. With thumping heart, I withdraw a photo card.

"She sent it to me and said to keep it safe in case somethin' happened to her. She sells her photos and didn't want 'em stolen, I guess. It's full of pictures, she said, and she didn't have nowhere to keep it." She wipes her eyes. "I guess she was smart to do that. I wonder what's on it."

"Did you look?"

She shook her head. "Not me. I ain't gettin' involved in that kinda stuff." She shifts and looks at the door. She wants me to leave. Desperately.

I drop the card in my purse. "Thanks so much, Desiree." I really mean it and shake her hand. "I appreciate how you've allowed me to barge in here like this, and for the coffee. And this letter. It may mean a lot."

"I'm just sorry I couldn't tell you more." She walks to the door with me. "If you ... find out what happened to Elton ... would you mind lettin' me know?"

"Oh, yes. Thank you again."

***

June 25, Thursday, midnight

When Chance pulled into the Lindsey ranch, a man, who'd been leaning against the big sign at the road, approached the pickup. It was Ty Rhoades, carrying a rifle.

Ty nodded as Chance rolled down the window. "Just keepin' watch."

"Seen anything interesting?"

"Nope. Quiet as a graveyard." Ty glanced at the horse trailer. "Got your horse?"

"Yup. I don't think Bobbi will mind if I keep her here for a short spell." He tipped his hat and drove down to the barn. Unloading Cyndi didn't take very long. He left the pickup sandwiched next to the combine and grain truck, hoping the gangsters wouldn't spot it right away. He walked to Tim's trailer and tapped on the door.

Tim opened it immediately. His face held a strained, uneasy look and fear was in his eyes. He gripped a rifle in his left hand. "Oh, it's you. C'mon in. I didn't know where you'd gone. Got your horse?"

Chance nodded and took off his hat. "I need a little sleep, if your guest room is unoccupied. Just for the rest of the night."

"Oh. Oh, that's fine." Tim fluttered around like a banty rooster. "Want a cup of coffee? Or somethin' to eat?"

"No, I'm fine." Chance removed his boots and settled on the couch. He looked at Tim and motioned to the easy chair. "Why don't you set yourself down? We need to chat."

Tim edged away, his eyes flitting over the trailer as if searching for an easy way out. "I ... uh, I need to get some work done on my computer." He started for desk.

Chance stood. Turning his body to face Tim directly, he rested his fists on his hips. "I said to *sit down*, and I mean it." There wasn't any way in God's green earth he could force the man opposite him to obey, but he hoped his lowered voice and body language would do the trick. It did.

Tim perched on the chair. "What d'ya want?"

"I want some accountin', my friend." Chance returned to the couch. Leaning forward menacingly, he stared at Tim. "I know you've been ... foolin' around, probably with drugs. Flirtin' with danger, huh? Gettin' a little extra cash? I need to know who you've seen and what you've told them." He drew a breath. "It was *you* who set me up at the barn, wasn't it? But you came back. I wonder why."

Tim's face hardened and he leaned back, crossing his legs. "I don't know what you're talkin' about."

Chance sighed. "You know, we can make this nice and easy, or we can make it hard. Your choice." He let that sink in. "Easy way – you come clean right now and join up with me to fight the men who probably killed your dad."

Tim jerked upright and placed both feet on the floor. Still he wouldn't talk. His lips formed a thin line, rimmed with white. He crossed his arms over his chest. "I don't know who think you are, bargin' in here like this. I've half a mind to call the sheriff – "

"Or we can do it the hard way. I used to be FBI. I know the agent in Rapid. I can arrest you and take you in tonight." He pulled his revolver from his shoulder harness and held it casually, opening the chamber, shutting it, polishing it a bit on his jeans. "That's the hard way. They have means to make you talk. So which is it, *amigo*?"

Tim's eyes slid to his rifle. After a moment, he relaxed against the chair. His shoulders rose high and he held them there, almost like a turtle sinking into its shell. "You ain't got nothin' on me." He let his shoulders sink down and gave Chance a sideways glance. "Okay, I'll come clean. I swear I never made a deal with them. Never! I did it mainly because I wanted to know about my dad." He sighed deeply.

"Who's *they*? Let's start there."

Chapter 27

Undercover

From Gina's Blog, June 25, Thursday evening

After driving about five miles out of Rapid City, I pull over and stop. *No! I'm not going back. I don't care. I'm not going to be the duck in their shooting gallery again. Not today. Not ever.* I make a u-turn and start back into the city. I'm clamping my jaw so tightly it hurts.

After a quick stop at WalMart, I check into a Motel 6. It's a dumpy little room that smells of mildew. Oh well, it's only for one night. After a long shower, I boot up my laptop. I'm glad the photo card I'd gotten from Desiree fits into my camera. I plug it in and wait impatiently for the pictures to load.

The thumbnails come popping up -- 286 of them! I scroll down and come to the last ones she'd taken -- nice shots of spring in the forest, close-ups of flowers, an interesting rock, several featuring the cliffs with an angry sky behind them. I stop at one that shows a red pickup, parked in what looks like a valley. Behind it is a huge tree all decked out in its spring finery.

This must be the picture! A red truck. I zoom the picture larger. But there's no mark, sign or anything on the truck to say whose it is. I go back to the thumbnail prints and look at the next picture. It's a close-up of the license plate! Wow. With this, the sheriff can make a positive ID on the owner. I file the photo card in an evidence envelope and stick it in my briefcase.

After that, I call Cap's private number, using the secure satphone. He answers on the first ring. "Where are you?"

It isn't what I expected he'd say. "I ... uh, I'm in Rapid City, sir. Had to come down here to follow up a lead. How's things there?"

He grunts. "Not so good. I've got state officials on my back, an inquiry into Nick's death. It seems they're doing a thorough investigation of the whole unit, and they're talking cuts, deep ones. Might mean your job, officer, so if I was you, I'd get back here. We got a meeting coming up with a bunch of high level guys all the way from Seattle. What's your progress?"

"Well, sir, I've had some problems. We got into a fire fight at the ranch this afternoon. Heavy. Some guys really wanted to take us out."

"Us?"

"Uh, yeah. There's this other guy here. I think he's undercover FBI. Anyway, they started shooting. I got to the house and helped Bobbi from inside."

"You okay?"

"I'd tell you if I wasn't, sir. Yeah, we're all okay. By the time the sheriff got there, the gunmen had left. We killed one and winged another. I'm hoping Mike can get something out of the one we got. Other than that, I've continued to work on the case."

There's a pause. "I want you to come in, Gina. We'll leave it to the FBI if they have an agent there."

I pace the small room. "Sir, I'm not sure he's FBI. He might be a guy with a chip on his shoulder. Anyway, I'm making some progress. Just got a solid lead tonight. A picture of a red truck at the place where I think Uncle Elton was killed and a close-up of the license plate. Please, sir. Give me a few more days. I promise if nothing breaks, I'll come back." I thought quickly. This is Thursday. "If I could have just until Monday, I know I can wrap this up."

Another pause. I hear the shuffle of paper. He sighs and says, "Very well. Monday. I've sent Officer Dennis Quaide your way."

My heart sinks. I'd worked with Quaide before, and we didn't get along. He's not a good detective in my opinion. I figured he'd only gotten promoted because he married Cap's daughter.

"What's his cover name?"

"Mark Smith. He's staying in the … (more papers rustling) Guest House in Ekalaka. Cover is an insurance salesman. First contact, tomorrow morning at ten at the … Wagon Wheel Cafe."

"I have some things to do. Can we make it two in the afternoon?"

"Sure. Call me, Gina. I don't like being in the dark, and I don't like you facing that kind of fire power."

"I'm fine, sir. Thank you."

***

June 25, Thursday evening

"I didn't ever see their faces. They're pretty clever that way, y'know." Tim stabbed bacon with a fork and plopped the pieces into a frying pan. In spite of the fact that Chance said he didn't want to eat, Tim said *he* was hungry and started preparing a quick meal, one more like breakfast than dinner.

Chance paced the tiny living room, peering out into the darkness. Could he believe Tim? He seemed contrite, yet he'd lied before and seemed to have no compunctions about it. "What I can't get is why you joined with them. Especially when you knew …"

"It started before Dad disappeared." Tim pulled off a sheet of paper towel. He fetched two plates from the cupboard and flipped the sizzling bacon. "I guess I needed … something to do. I've never liked ranch work, and Dad wouldn't listen to me. I wanted to work on computers, go to school and learn more and make my own company. But …" His voice trailed off as he poured coffee into two mugs. He lifted the bacon from the pan and broke some eggs into it. "I needed the challenge, the work. It seemed exciting to me, although that sounds stupid now."

Chance nodded and put two pieces of bread into the toaster. "Could you tell me their build … anything that would help me identify them?"

"Well, one was about as tall as me but had broader shoulders and weighed about fifty pounds more. He kept a kerchief over his face, and his eyes. He was in charge. I got the feeling he was taking orders from someone else, though. There were two other bozos, one tall and beefy, the other shorter than me and quick on his feet. I think I could recognize their voices. They mainly had me haulin' the stuff out for them, like when I went to a rodeo I'd take a couple of pounds and pass it off to their contact. Pretty easy money and, like I said, it had challenge and excitement. I felt … needed, I guess."

Chance pondered that as he buttered the toast and accepted the plate of scrambled eggs and bacon. Tim's descriptions led nowhere. How many tall, beefy men were there in this country? He could give testimony to that much from the encounter he'd had with the men in the barn.

They ate without much comment. As Chance cleaned up the kitchen, he said, "Well, we'd better get some rest. I have some things to do tomorrow mornin'."

Just as he was crawling into his sleeping bag, Tim appeared at his door.

"I … I just thought of somethin' else."

Chance turned on the lamp and nodded encouragingly.

"I don't know if it's important or not. One time I got in the boss-guy's pickup and there was a jacket on the seat. Before he pushed it off, I caught a glimpse of it." He paused and brushed a hand through his hair. "I saw … I think I saw an emblem of some sort… "

Chance kept his face calm despite the pounding in his ears. "Like … a police uniform? What color was it?"

Tim rubbed his forehead. "Man, that's hard to say. I'm color blind, you know. Let's see … I'd say brown but it might've been green. Or even blue. There was a patch on the sleeve. I couldn't see much; he shoved it aside so fast and stuffed it behind the seat. Yeah, it was like the sheriff's. Different, though. Maybe Forestry. Or maybe he belonged to some kind of a club, like a flying club. The Andersons host fly-ins once in a while." He shrugged. "I don't know."

"Don't worry about it, Tim. Thanks for telling me." He turned off the light and pulled up the sleeping bag, his mind awhirl. He had to think … to sort it all out … but sleep overtook him almost as soon as his head hit the pillow.

In the morning, as soon as it was light, Chance made his way to the windbreak, the narrow band of trees that sheltered the house and barns from the full onslaught of the wind. He searched the ground in the underbrush. It didn't take long to find evidence of a vehicle – no, two – that had been pulled into the trees. He found tracks where some guys stood and smoked, watching the house. A little further away, behind a screen of bushes, something shiny glinted in the first rays of the sun that slanted across from the butte. *Ah!* He leaned over and picked up a shell.

Not the kind that had been fired from the assassins. This was bigger, heavier. A Big Bore forty-five, or fifty-aught caliber hunting rifle, he was guessing. Evidently someone was here, hiding in the bushes, watching the watchers. Strange. The man waited until the three attackers broke cover before he made his play. Again – why?

Chance pocketed the shell and leaned closer to inspect the dim footprints. They wouldn't stand up for a cast. He made his way back to his truck, found an envelope, put the shell in it, labeled it and sealed it. This he hid in a compartment under the seat where all his evidence was kept. Four years of evidence.

Climbing in the pickup, he tapped his fingers on the steering wheel. Where should he go next? The Bible camp? Or Whittiers? Or Andersons? He'd wondered about the Andersons before and even shadowed them for awhile. Maybe he'd watch Pierce Dugal.

Dugal was one shady character, even though he wore a sheriff's uniform. Was his the jacket Tim had seen? No, Dugal wasn't tall. He was stout, with a big over-lopping stomach. Somehow he was involved, though, but how? He had too many questions and not enough answers. And time was running out.

The drug cartel people were getting edgy – and dangerous. What would they do next – wipe out a whole town, like they'd done in Mexico? Or maybe they'd get the kids and counselors at the camp and hold them hostage. The thought sent shivers down his back.

Should he ride back to the grow patch? No. He'd tried that twice and hadn't gotten anywhere, except lead in his shoulder. He sipped cold coffee from his travel mug. Okay. He had to eliminate the leads. Tick them off, one by one. Today he'd start with the camp. What better cover than that for the drug cartel?

He hooked up his trailer, loaded Cyndi and drove out of the ranch, tipping his hat to Ty who stood near the house with a mug in his hand. Even though he saw questions in Ty's eyes, he didn't stop to explain.

***

From Gina's Blog, June 26, Friday

The next morning, I grab a bite of breakfast at McDonald's and after that, locate a walk-in beauty parlor. There, to my anguish, I have my hair cut and dyed. Now it's black and cut so short I feel shaved. I run my fingers through my curly hair as I drive to a thrift store. There I purchase scruffy jeans, a flannel shirt, a jacket that's seen better days and work boots that fit fairly decently. After I change into the clothes, I drive to the airport where I rent a bright yellow Jeep Laredo 4x4.

I'm going in as Josie Robertson, a cover name I've used before. At least the change will put them off the scent for a little while; maybe long enough to give me bead on them. I drive toward Camp Crook, turning onto highway 323, which is a dirt road, and head east toward Ekalaka.

After about an hour, I spot a ranch sign on my left. The Whittier spread. I pull off the road. As I open the door and step out, I'm surprised by a gust of wind that almost blows me off my feet. I thought I was getting used to the wind. Black clouds are rolling over the prairie.

Bent almost double, I walk the mile into the ranch. Dang these long driveways! I teeter over a cattle guard (the metal bars across the driveway that keep cows in or out) and open an unlocked metal gate. A dog greets me, barking, as I approach the house. He's a border collie and his tail is wagging. He's friendly enough after he sees I'm alone and willing to give him a pat.

I ring the bell on the door. After waiting and no one comes, I circle the house and trot down the lane to the long building that's their nursery. The door's shut; not locked. I find it rather strange that no one is around -- you'd think at a nursery, someone would be there for customers. Maybe their season is over already.

I knock on the greenhouse door and stick my head inside. The long shelves are mostly empty of plants. "Hello? Anyone here?" There's a rustling toward the back and footsteps.

A Mexican woman emerges. She pushes back her dark hair and straightens her apron as she approaches. "*Si?* I am here. Can I help?" After a brief, friendly smile, she turns her head away from me.

I catch a glimpse of a blackened bruise on her left cheek. "I ... uh, I need help. My car ran out of gas. Can you sell me some?"

"Ah? Gas?" She nods and gets a two-way radio from her pocket. After speaking with someone in Spanish, she returns it to her apron. "My husband, he will help you. He is coming with can of gas. You can wait by house." She tips her head to the Whittier's house, then turns to go.

I let her walk away a couple of steps, then I say, "I met a little girl the other day in the hospital. She broke her arm. I promised I'd visit her. Do you know her? Her name's Jilly."

The woman freezes. She recovers quickly and glances my way. "Yilly? *Se.* I know no Yilly. It is a pretty name, *se?*"

"*Si. Gracias.*" I wait by the house, as she instructed me. I have enough time to look around. Behind the ranch is a small valley surrounded by rock cliffs. I can't tell from here if the formations are the same as what I'd seen in that picture. I tell myself I'd have to hike back there, maybe tomorrow. A man approaches in a Toyota pickup.

I climb in the cab. He smiles a welcome and nods. There's no point in asking him questions as I know he won't answer. At the car, he pours gas into my tank. When I offer money, he shakes his head and says, "*Se.*" I tell him *gracias* several times. He smiles his appreciation for my courtesy and drives away.

My pulses are racing as I climb back in the Jeep and head for Ekalaka. This is it! It must be the place. Randy Whittier. Who would've thought? But is it truly him? What do I have to go on? The hesitation of the lady in the nursery, a formation of the cliffs, Mexican workers, a greenhouse. There might be dozens of rock formations that resemble the one in Desiree's picture. And the woman -- she might have thought I said something else. Or ...

Maybe my imagination is running away from me. It could be I'm so intent on solving this crime that I've left behind my cool practical brain. I have to get proof. I determine to find out who employs Mexican help in the area. I should've done this already. I'm getting sloppy. Where's the focus I usually bring to my work? Why have I bungled the case so far? I shake my head. It's time to get on with it.

Spotting a small road leading up to one of the buttes, I drive up to the top. There I turn off the motor and pull out my satphone. I dial Bobbi's number. She isn't home, so I leave a message.

"Hi, this is Gina. I won't be able to get back today. Don't worry about me, I'm okay. Something's come up. And don't try to contact me. You won't get through. Talk to you later. Bye."

I sit in the Jeep as the wind shakes it, thinking. Suddenly I glance at my watch. Oh, gosh. *2:34!* I missed the appointment with Quaide in Ekalaka. I dial his number and he answers on the first ring.

"It's me. I can't make it on time. Change of plan. Meet me at Camp Needmore at ..." I look at my watch again, "Three-thirty. It's an old government camp out of Ekalaka. You can get directions. Okay?"

He grunts. "Gotcha." The line goes dead.

I drive off the butte and head for the Ekalaka. I'm tempted not to meet Quaide. He's always been bad luck, and I know there's a mole in the system somewhere. The drug dealers seem to know when I sneeze, and now that I've changed my appearance, do I want anyone to see me as Gina Lindsey? Yet I have to keep Cap happy, so I'd better keep the appointment.

I'd rather have Chance as back-up. Should I contact him? No, I have to do this alone, even though it's going against all protocol, all chain of command, all my training. You go in with a team. You always have backup. You never attempt to break a case alone. Never.

But this is different, I tell myself. This time I want to stay alive.

Chapter 28

Camping

Friday, 2:14pm

Maegan settled her cap on her head and helped Jilly from the car. She straightened the little girl's clothes and gazed around. She couldn't believe she was here -- at the Bible Camp. What had possessed her? She sighed.

Last night after she escaped from Butch, she dashed back to Betsy's house, packed up her few belongings and got Jilly out of bed. After she reclaimed her Land Rover, she started down the street. If she figured it right, she'd have a small window to escape while Butch and his cronies searched the Miles City cut-off road.

As she drove past the grocery store on main street, she gazed longingly at it, thinking she'd love some comfort food -- a cup of coffee and maybe a pack of beer or a package of chocolate bars. She continued on -- she knew that if she went in, it wouldn't be long before the whole town was aware of her description, the make of her car, what she bought and which way she'd left town. And someone was bound to call the sheriff.

She turned north on Highway 21, nervously checking her rearview mirror every few seconds to make sure someone wasn't following. About ten miles out of town, headlights appeared behind her. She had to get off the highway. As if in answer to an unspoken prayer, she saw the sign for Medicine Rocks State Park, and without hesitation, made a left turn onto the road. The vehicle behind her passed the park and continued north.

After she parked in a campsite, she made a bed for Jilly in the back, reclined her seat as far as it would go and spent an uncomfortable night trying to sleep. Jilly woke her several times with exclamations, cries of terror, sobbing.

When dawn streaked the sky with red, she washed her face from the outside spigot and brought out the food she'd taken from Betsy's larder -- bread, pepperoni sausage, cheese slices, two apples and a gallon of milk. They glugged the milk from the jug. She tried to make a joke about it, but Jilly didn't think it was funny.

The little girl was sullen and unresponsive. Maegan urged her to change into some jeans and a t-shirt she'd bought at the second hand store in Ekalaka when she was hiding at Betsy's. They washed their hands, filled their water jugs, and started out.

"Where we going?" Jilly's English had improved since they'd been away from her family.

"I ... don't know," Maegan responded, her heart sinking.

"I want to go *casa*. Find *Madre*." Jilly's voice rose up the scale. Maegan knew she was working up to one of her crying spells.

"Okay. Okay. Just calm down. We will go look." She glanced over at Jilly and saw she still had her face screwed up funny. Tears were forming in her eyes. "How would you like to go to a nice place where there are other children? And they play games and have fun. And you could maybe ride the horses."

Jilly's eyes widened and her tears stopped.

Maegan congratulated herself. The little girl loved horses. "What do you say? Shall we go?" She hesitated before turning on her blinker at the highway.

Jilly nodded. "*Si. Madre* there?"

"Maybe. Maybe we will find *Madre*." How she ever thought of going to the Bible camp, she never figured out -- but there it was, suddenly in her mind, the picture of the camp as she'd seen it so many times on her way to town. She always thought that weird people went there to pray and do strange stuff and she wanted nothing to do with it.

Now, in the parking lot below the building marked Office, she smoothed Jilly's hair and took her good hand. Inside the office, a woman sat behind a cluttered desk, talking on the phone. She lifted her eyes and smiled.

When she set the phone down, she said, "Yes? May I help you?"

"Hello. My name is Maegan and this is my daughter, Jilly. I was wondering if I could enroll her in your camp. How much is it?" She began to fish her wallet from her backpack.

The woman stood and came around the desk. She was young -- maybe younger even than Maegan -- and pretty with a nice smile and sparkling blue eyes.

She crouched down beside Jilly. "Hello, Jilly. My name's Connie. Did you hurt your arm? I'm so sorry." She straightened and snatched a sucker from a bowl on her desk. "Is it okay if I give her this?" She raised her eyes to Maegan.

Maegan nodded. "Sure."

"Here you go."

Maegan said, "Say *gracias* to the nice lady, Jilly."

Jilly murmured the word and went to sit on one of the metal chairs that lined the room.

Connie retreated behind her desk. "This is difficult, Maegan. Our camp starts on Sunday afternoon and ends on Saturday. You'd have to bring her back on Sunday. Also, we don't take children under the age of ten. How old is she?"

"Oh, uh ... she turned ten last month. She's just real small."

Connie nodded, leafing through a notebook. "I'm afraid to tell you that we're all booked up. Our camps fill up really quickly. Oh, wait. Here's an opening for the second week of August. Would you like me to pencil her in for that week?"

Maegan shifted. "Uh ... no, that wouldn't do no good." She fought back tears that stung her eyelids and sank down on the chair next to Jilly. "I ... uh, I need some help. I'm trying to get away from my boyfriend. He's threatened to kill me. I just need a place for a couple of nights. I can pay." She looked up hopefully. Usually the mention of payment opened doors.

"I see. Well, let me phone the director." Connie turned slightly and dialed the number. After she spoke into the phone in a quiet voice, she hung up and stood.

"He said you can stay for the weekend. You can use one of our guest houses and give a donation to the camp according to what you can afford for the room and meals. Come with me. I'll show you."

Maegan followed her down the hill, past the parking lot, and up into the trees on the opposite hillside. Inside an old trailer house, she sniffed. Mold. Rotting things. Mice. Yet she was glad for this place. Very glad.

"Use whatever you can find in here. There's some bedding in the utility room. And whatever else." Connie waved her hand generally around the trailer. "Dinner's at six. Mr. Fairchild wanted me to explain to you that while Jilly can participate in camp activities, as much as her arm will allow, we insist that you remain with her at all times. We can't be responsible for her. It's something to do with the insurance rules." She smiled. "If you need anything, please let me know."

"Okay. Thank you, Connie." Maegan could not express what this meant to her. All she could do was squeeze her new friend's hand and try to keep the tears from flooding her cheeks. Maybe there was something to this religion thing, after all.

***

From Gina's Blog: Friday, 3:12pm

I drive off the highway and pull onto the dirt road that leads to Camp Needmore. I have to get there and get situated before Quaide arrives. I'd been there before, so I know the lay of the land.

It's an old Civilian Conservation Corp camp, kept alive and in use through donations of the locals. Not a very attractive place, close to the Rims and right smack dab in the forest. If you want seclusion and quiet, Needmore would be a good choice. Don't expect very many fancy amenities, though. In fact, the camp offers none at all, except the wash house and showers, and a well equipped kitchen.

I drive to the camp. Beside the dining hall, I get out my satphone and call the Sheriff's office. "Hello. I'd like to speak to the sheriff," I say to the female voice who answers.

"Who may I say is calling?"

"Uh. Josie Robertson."

"Just a moment, please."

When Mike answers, I say, "Good afternoon, sheriff. Do you know who this is?"

There's a pause. "Yes. I'm not much up to playin' games, so what's goin' on?"

"I decided to go undercover, sheriff. In case you need to see me, I'm now a brunette. Short, curly hair. Wearing outdoorsy type clothes, driving a bright yellow Jeep Laredo."

"Not your best choice for stayin' under the radar," he comments dryly.

I chuckle. "Anyway, sir, my name's Josie Robertson. I ... I'd like you to come on out to Camp Needmore. I'm meeting my backup from Spokane. Come in rather quietly, if you know what I mean."

"Backup for a backup?" I hear a smile in his voice.

"Yes, sir. I'm convinced there's a mole in the system. I'd like to find it and eliminate it."

"I see. What else do you have?"

"The photo card from Sabrina Phillip's camera." I pause. This is my hole in one, my ace. He doesn't seem too impressed, only just grunts. "She sent it to Desiree Pledger. I visited Desiree last night. I guess they were friends. Anyway, I found a picture on it of a red Dodge Ram pickup, parked in the woods. I'm guessing it's up on the Rims and that it belongs to Elton's killer."

He hesitates. I can picture him writing the information down. He sighs. "Wal, we can't prove much by that. There are maybe a hundred red pickups in the county."

"But, sir, she also took a close-up of the license plate."

He draws in his breath sharply. "Did you write it down so I can look it up?"

"Uh ... no, sir. I was really tired. I've got it here with my evidence. I keep it with me all the time, under the seat of my car. I'll bring it over to you when I'm finished with Quaide."

"Okay." I hear papers shuffling. "You seen Chance?"

"Yes, sheriff. I drove him to Rapid last night, and he got his truck and horse. He's back on the job."

"Wal, that's good news, I guess. I gotta go. Be careful, would you? It's gettin' hot, and I'm mighty worried about what'll happen. All hell might break loose."

"Yes, sir. I'll give you another call and set up a place to meet after I'm done at Needmore."

"Okay. Take care."

I drive down the rutted dirt road about a mile. After ditching the yellow Jeep on a side road, I take my Glock and a pair of glasses and hike back. I find a position on the hillside above the camp and hide behind a clump of alder bushes. It's warm. A bee buzzes by. Ants crawl up my legs. I swat them off and move to a new position.

Now I'm directly behind the outhouse. It stinks. I don't move because I can watch the road, see both entrances to the dining hall, and get away quickly up the hill in dense ground cover in case things go horribly awry.

Quaide arrives on schedule and takes his time getting out of the car. He's nervous, I can tell that. He glances around, pats his shoulder holster, and runs a finger around his collar. The distance is only a little over fifty feet to the dining hall; there's no cover, which is probably why he's nervous. I scan the terrain around the camp, especially the woods that encircle it. A movement in the trees almost directly opposite my position catches my eye.

It was only a flicker. I crouch down, getting most of my body out of sight, and use my glasses. There, I catch it again, and this time I see him. A man is on the hillside, working his way down, keeping in line with Quaide. He's carrying a rifle.

***

June 26, Friday, 2:33pm

Chance unloaded Cyndi at the barn at the camp and parked the pickup and trailer in a small parking lot behind it. Without telling anyone he was there, he saddled Cyndi and rode out. He knew he couldn't cover the hundred or more acres that belonged to the camp, but he'd seen some smaller roads branching off from the main ones, and he was curious about them. If there was a barn or nursery, there would have to be roads into it.

He investigated old logging roads that meandered through meadows and petered out in swamps or on brushy hillsides. It felt good to be in the saddle again. After two hours, he returned to camp, having found nothing. Maybe the thing to do would be to hire a small plane to take him up. Up at the office, he startled Connie when he stepped in quietly. She had her back turned, was burrowing deep in a file drawer.

"Oh! It's you!" She laid her hand on her chest and shook her head. "I swear you'll scare the daylights out of me yet! What're you up to now? You disappeared like a ... phantom and now you pop in here like ..." Words failed her, and that was rare for Connie.

He grinned and removed his hat. "If you'd quit talking, I'd tell you. I had an ... accident and had to recuperate, which I did at a friend's house. Now I'm back, hungry as ever." He stepped farther into the office.

She rose and smiled. "It's good to see you. Are you staying around awhile this time? Or don't I get to know." She chuckled. "I thought you'd run off with that little redhead I saw you with the other day."

He laughed and led the way to a table and bench that sat outside the office on the lawn. "Nah. She dumped me." He plunked down on the table and turned to her. "Tell me, Connie. Does the camp own any buildings off in the woods?"

She stared at him, a surprised look in her eyes. "You say the funniest things. Buildings? What do you mean?"

"I don't know. Barns. Equipment sheds. Anything like that. There would have to be water and lights into them." He nodded to several of the counselors he'd met earlier as they trooped past with their small charges.

She shook her head. "I can't think of any. You might ask Mr. Fairchild." She brushed back her hair and adjusted her blouse. "There might be some old barns back in there somewhere. They bought this property from a rancher, you know. What're you driving at? Why the sudden interest in the camp property?"

He shrugged and stood. "Oh, just curious. Well, I'd better see if I can help out at the barn. See you later."

After he talked with some of the wranglers at the barn, he headed up to Mr. Fairchild's office which was behind the camp office -- a small log cabin they said was the original building on the site. This was where he'd made that call from the day he'd been attacked. Normally there was a secretary at the desk taking calls. He hoped she was at dinner.

Sure enough, no one was in the small receptionist area. After calling and getting no reply, he leafed through the papers on the desk. Nothing. He glanced through the nearest files. Again, nothing.

As he pulled out the bottom drawer, he came upon a file that contained maps of the camp property. Taking them out, he spread them on the desk. It was almost all forestland, yet here and there small squares were marked, what he supposed was a farmhouse or storage sheds. He noted them down, tracing the spidery lines of the roads back to the main road.

Yes, these might warrant another ride into the forest. Would they have water and lights? He didn't think so. Of course the drug dealers would have their own generators.

The door squeaked open. He glanced up, and froze.

"What are you doing?" It was Mr. Fairchild. He looked at Chance in surprise, then his face slowly turned red. "Chance?"

"Oh. Some of us wranglers were wondering if we could blaze a new riding trail." He folded the map and stuck it back in the file, then closed the drawer. "I ... no one was around and I didn't want to bother you."

Mr. Fairchild strode into the room, glancing about as if to ascertain that Chance hadn't stolen anything. "Next time come and talk to me before you go riffling through our files. Some of them are confidential." His voice was hard, his back stiff.

"Sure." Chance kept a calm face, not betraying the stab of guilt he felt. "Sorry." Chance backed out of the office. His neck burned as he made his way to the dining hall. He was genuinely sorry he had to snoop, yet a sense of urgency screamed in his mind. *Hurry! Lives are at stake!*

It had gone beyond seeking justice for his brother's death. Now he felt compelled to stop the drug dealers before they did something unthinkable in this little corner of Montana.

He entered the dining room and helped himself to the buffet, sitting at the table with the other wranglers. Tomorrow he'd ride out and check the places he'd noted. If he found nothing, he'd go over to the Anderson ranch. One by one he'd tick them off. Sooner or later he'd hit pay dirt -- and the way he was feeling, it had better be sooner.

Chapter 29

The Shooting Gallery Again

From Gina's Blog, Friday, 1:41 pm

The gunman on the hillside lifts his rifle and sights. He's aiming at Quaide who's taking an awfully long time to get across the open area to the shelter of the building. I grind my teeth in frustration. How can I warn him? There's probably no cell phone service here, and would he hear his phone? I can't hit the attacker from the hillside with my revolver, and to yell at Quaide would only make him stop and look around.

He'd be dead before he could hear what I was saying.

I shoot in the air. Like I figured, Quaide drops, yet there's no cover and he's not the most agile person in the world. He scoots along on his belly as fast as he can, looking like a crippled slug. The rifle booms from the cover of trees on the hill.

Quaide's hit, jerking upright and falling face first into the dust. He's not moving. I run from my position behind the outhouse to the ladies bathroom, shooting once into the trees, knowing I won't connect, but hoping to give the gunman pause for thought. He's faster on the uptake than I gave him credit for. A bullet whizzes past my head. I duck behind the ladies washroom, half falling, half spinning. So much for having my hair cut and going undercover. I'm still a duck in the shooting galley!

Quaide's up on his knees, moving quickly to the shelter of a large bush. Not good enough for the fire power coming out of the trees. Another shot booms from the rifle. Quaide's hit again! I see him fling backwards from the impact of the bullet and sprawl on the ground. He's taken two shots. If I don't do something quickly, he's not going to survive.

I dash from cover and make it to the far right corner of the dining room. From there I follow a gully and leap into the woods, scrunching down behind a scrubby bush. Between the branches, I see the gunman making his way toward the building. He wants to make sure Quaide's dead, and he didn't see my frantic dash. Good.

A little closer ... I hold my Glock with both hands, sighting down the barrel. A few more steps ... *now!* I gently squeeze the trigger. The shot hits him. *Yes!* I think I got him high on the right shoulder. He turns and glances in my direction, takes two steps toward my position and raises his rifle.

Another shot rings out. The gunman is hit again. He stumbles to his knees, then rises and crashes through the underbrush away from me. He's gone. I hold my breath, listening, and hear nothing. I tear back to the dining hall and around the corner. Quaide's lying flat on his back in a puddle of blood. His revolver is on the ground by his hand. He'd gotten that one shot off. The one that saved me. I rush over to him. "How're you doing? Shot bad?"

He shakes his head. "Don't know. But feeling a little ... groggy." He looks at me, puzzled. "Who are ..."

I smile. "It's me, Dennis. Gina."

"What's going on?"

"I thought they might be here. There's a mole in the system, Quaide, because no one except you and me and Sheriff Crosby knew about this meeting." I open his shirt. His upper arm and chest are a mess, but I don't think the two bullets hit any important organs. He'd be dead by now if they'd torn into his lungs or heart. I rip up his jacket, which is torn to shreds, to make bandages, and wrap his wounds to stop the bleeding.

After making him as stable as possible, I phone 911 on the satphone, and dash to the kitchen to find something better for bandages. A few minutes later, I'm back with dish towels and a basin of water. Layer after layer I wind the cloth around the wounds, sopping up the blood.

Quaide groans. His eyes are shut against the pain. I'd stopped some of the worst bleeding, but the wounds are large and he has a lot of tissue and tendon damage. "Gina! Help me! I'm ... I'm ... going."

"Hang in there, buddy," I say, bending over him, washing his face. "Stay with me. Help is on the way."

A pickup pulls in. I shout for help and two men pile out, come running to where Quaide lies. One of them is an EMT, he says as he approaches. He does his first responders assessment, elevates Quaide's feet, and tells the other man to bring the pickup closer to give the victim some shade.

The EMT doesn't touch the bandages I put on the wounds. I thought he'd do them better, but he says that he doesn't want to disturb it. The two men leave to wash their hands. I learned that they're archeologists on a dig for dinosaur bones. I sit back on my heels and rinse off my hands with the rest of the water.

Quaide opens his eyes. "Gina. Are you still here?"

"Yes, Dennis. Just hang on. I hear the ambulance now." It wasn't a lie -- I could hear a faint siren. He closes his eyes and I hold his hand.

When I see the first emergency vehicles approaching, I lean closer to him. "I've got to go, Dennis. I'll be in touch."

"You ... you said something about a mole. What do you mean?" He squints at me through his pain.

"Just what I said. Did you tell anyone about our meeting?"

"No. No one." He closes his eyes. "Oh, yeah. I called ... Cap."

"Cap? Cap knew?"

"Yeah. Hey, Gina. Don't leave me. I kinda like you as a brunette. Always did like them ... one in high school ... was too cute for words." He chuckles, then groans. He's wandering.

When I see that Dennis is getting good care by the ambulance personnel, and that he'll probably survive to bungle another assignment, I slip away before the sheriff and his deputy get out of the car.

***

Friday, 12:23pm

No, no, no! Chance crumpled the paper on which he'd written the directions and shoved it into his pocket. He'd found a barn on camp property, but it was just what it seemed to be -- a decrepit, unused shelter that held nothing but some mice and rotting hay. He'd wasted a lot of precious time on this. Now he had to start over again.

Reining Cyndi back toward the camp, he kicked her flanks. She responded with a little whinny. She loved to run and she liked her friends at the camp and the grain she got every night there. He groaned -- the jarring pace made his ribs hurt like the dickens.

As the wind whipped her mane into his face, he reviewed all the information he'd gathered. The very first clue from his contact in Spokane led him to Ekalaka. He investigated Buffalo Guest Ranch and several other spreads near the Short Pines. The grow patch was in the Short Pines, he knew that for sure, but where was the ranch? Where did they start the plants? On whose land was it? Who was the boss in charge of the operation?

It had to be around here somewhere. Tim had been involved -- that narrowed the circle. He wondered where Gina was going to investigate next. In his mind's eye, he reviewed the little he knew for sure: a brown or green uniform with a logo on the sleeve; a tallish, heavy set man; a voice like a meat grinder. He'd recognize the voice. There had to be *someone* with information.

He found himself at the end of his resources. He was tired, still aching from the beating he'd endured, and fresh out of ideas of where to go next. He felt cut off from everyone -- whom could he trust? How could he bring the drug cartels down by himself?

He arrived at the corral and dismounted. After brushing Cyndi and putting the tack in his trailer, he turned her loose in the meadow. Then he ate a quick lunch at the dining hall. Afterward he sat outside in the sunshine, allowing the noise of the campers to wash over him, totally oblivious to his surroundings.

This is too much to ask of anyone.

He cradled his head in his hands and stared at the dirt between his boots where two ants worked together, carrying a dead bug to their nest. *I don't care! It doesn't matter anymore!* He shuffled his feet, careful not to disturb the ants. The last ounce of determination seemed to drain from his tired body like grains of sand drifting through an hour glass.

He noticed the ants who struggled with their heavy load. They reached a rock. While it was just a little stone to him, to them it must have seemed a mountain. He expected that they'd detour around it, surely the easiest choice. To his surprise, they pushed and pulled their prize up the steep jagged side of the rock and without pause for breath, heaved it up and over, and down the other side. He watched as they dragged it slowly under a bush.

Lifting his head, he tried to remember the Bible verse he'd read a couple of days ago. *Ah.* He had it. In Philippians, the Apostle Paul wrote that we should forget what lay behind us and press on to the prize of the goal in Jesus Christ our Lord. *Press on.* Like those ants.

But I can't, Lord. It's too much.

Good. I'm glad you've finally admitted it. Now roll your burden on Me. I will give you the power to do what you cannot do alone. Like those ants.

He took a deep breath. *Okay, Lord. It's up to You because I'm at the end of my rope.* He looked around. Tears stung his eyes as new strength seemed to flow into his weary muscles. He stood and walked down to his pickup. Getting in, he glanced over at Cyndi who fed on the grass in the small meadow.

If they knew his horse, they'd know he was here. *They'd know this rig, too. Well, let them come.* Maybe he could smoke them out. This time he'd be a little more prepared for them than when they'd bushwacked him on the road. He just hoped he didn't bring trouble to the camp.

Driving out to the main highway, he turned right and headed into Ekalaka. The clues seemed to lead in that direction. Praying furiously and trusting his gut instincts, he thought of the long narrow valley that stretched behind Anderson's ranch below the Rims. Maybe he needed to do some spying there.

He turned off the main highway and drove the three miles to Camp Needmore, passed the camp, and continued down the rutted road to the top edge of the Rimrocks. After parking, he walked over to the cliffs. The clouds were still high, driven on a wind, promising more than a light summer's shower. Well, he'd been out in worse. Now and then as he hiked along the edge, he used his glasses on the valley below. Once he spotted an old farmstead. *No, that's not it.* He'd seen that place before.

About a mile further down, he stopped and trained his glasses on a butte across the valley. On the top he spotted a tower. *Ah!* He studied it for some time, and allowed his gaze to drop below the tower into a box canyon. Then he saw it. A fence. Chain link.

Chills chased up and down his spine. *Bingo!* He'd found it. As he continued to gaze across the valley, he wondered how he was going to get over there. There was a road that led off the highway, but it would be hard to find and harder to travel. Yet *they* had to get in and out. Or did they have an air strip at the top of the butte? Maybe that was the reason for the tower -- was it for air traffic and surveillance? Or a guard tower?

There was only one way to find out. He pocketed the glasses and turned back to the trail. Now was a lousy time to go nosing into some wooded fortress, yet he had to try. Storm or no, he was going in. He thought briefly of Gina and wondered where she was, what she was doing, if he should contact her. He shook his head. Long ago he'd decided he had to do this on his own.

He wished her well, said a prayer for her, and went back to his truck.

The wind was howling in the trees. This was a real blow -- he wondered what the velocity was. He got out his county map and spread it out on the seat, finding the road he wanted. It went right past Anderson's ranch and continued on down the valley. Wild Rose Lane, the map said. Must be some new housing development going in.

Folding the map, he grabbed a snack bar from the glove compartment and a warm Coke from the floor by the passenger seat, eating as he drove. This would have to do until he could get something better. He didn't stop at the camp, even though there was a crowd of people standing around in the parking lot, talking. He raised his brows when he saw the county sheriff's car and lifted his index finger to Mike Crosby. Whatever had happened seemed to be taken care of and time was steadily ticking away.

The long June evening was not calm or serene. By the time he pulled off the highway at the Anderson's driveway, the wind tore down off the buttes and battered its way through the valley. The box elders by the creek were bent nearly to the ground.

Guess they weren't joking about a storm coming. Tim said the weather forecast had storm warnings out with nearly hurricane speed winds, rain and possibly snow or hail. The light was fading rapidly; blue-black clouds rolled across the prairie; lightning strobed the sky, followed by peals of thunder. An eerie sense of impending doom set his nerves on edge, yet he clamped his jaw and continued on.

The Anderson's place seemed quiet. There were a few trucks parked by what they called their water bottling plant. No lights at all in the house. He drove by slowly, keeping to the left where the road veered around the corrals, following it along the floor of the valley.

After driving until he figured he was within walking distance to the box canyon he'd spotted, he found a nice little bunch of trees and scrub cedar where he hid the pickup. He got out and almost lost his hat. He zipped his jacket and settled his hat firmly on his head. At least it hadn't started raining yet.

A ridge of rocky cliffs reared their heights to the south. The long valley spread out before him -- rolling farmland with lush bottoms where creeks meandered their lazy way to the sea, where cattle fed in grasses up to their bellies, where mosquitoes and no-see-um flies bred like there was no tomorrow.

He wished he had his horse. Yet he started out doggedly toward the cliffs and the rock formations. He had his glasses, his gun, his flashlight and a small camera. He guessed that if he looked in the right place, he'd find what he was searching for. Preferably without getting killed.

Chapter 30

The Way Into Babylon

From Gina's Blog, Friday, 4:16pm

As I drive out of Camp Needmore, a wave of loneliness sweeps over me. *I can't call anyone -- not Bobbi or anyone from work.* Nick is dead; Quaide almost. What can I do? Where can I go? Without any direction or help from the police departments or the DEA, I feel like a stranded fish, gasping for air. Someone seems to know my every move. The mole. *Who's the mole?* Maybe a clerk or secretary who'd taken the call and listened in when I called Cap. Did he confide in someone? But wait. I'd also told Mike. Is it Mike? Or had he mentioned it to Ty?

Oh, darn. I remember I'd also told Mike about Chance still being around. So the information that he was back on the case was probably passed to the drug growers. And my cover was blown, because I'd told Mike what I looked like now and the vehicle I'm driving. I pound the steering wheel in frustration and anger.

I drive east and pass the Bible camp, thinking that maybe I can get a meal there, or a place to stay. Well, I'll come back if I run out of things to do. In the meantime, I'm heading for the Anderson's place. I want to get into that water bottling plant. What if the drug dealers have two places where they grow the plants? What if the Andersons and Whittier's are working together and they're making something more lethal than marijuana? Like heroin? Or meth?

I pull into the road leading to the Anderson ranch, and after a bumpy ride up their two-mile driveway, I park in front of the house. The place seems deserted, yet there's a lot of activity down by the bottling plant. I step into the wind and pull on my jacket, slinging my backpack on my shoulder. It's overcast and cold. Last night the weatherman said a big storm's coming. I just hope it holds off long enough for me to nail these guys. I head toward the plant, surprised that there's so much activity -- vehicles, people, noise -- coming from that direction.

"Can I help you?" A man accosts me as I approach, a large man with a graying beard and fierce eyes. He wears a plaid jacket and a billed cap, pulled low on his forehead. He doesn't smile or hold out his hand. In fact, he keeps both hands in his pockets. I wonder what he has in there.

I try on my best smile, yet I see it doesn't faze him. "Hi. I'm Josie Robertson. I'm looking for Jesse. Do you know where he is?"

"Oh. He's over at the hangar." He turns his back to me abruptly.

"So is the plant open today? Mind if I look around?"

He turns back and frowns. "Sorry, miss. This is a restricted area. If you want a tour, you'll have to speak to Mr. Anderson." He strides away.

I watch as he speaks briefly with two young men who wear blue uniforms and are standing at the double doors of the building. The first man disappears into the plant. The two guys take up a position on each side of the door. Their hands, too, are in their pockets.

Whoa. All my police training and instincts are blazing red hot. I want to see in that plant. But first I have to find Jesse; after that I'll do a clandestine investigation. I gaze around and locate the air strip and the hangar. It's at the far end of the corrals.

Leaning into the wind, I try to keep my feet under me as I make my way down a slight hill. Will Jesse fly today? Is he getting the plane ready to take out a load of drugs? I shake my head. It's terrible when you get so suspicious. That's the name of the game, though, especially when you get shot at regularly.

He's bent over, the top part of him swallowed in the bowels of the plane's motor. "Hi!" I call, my voice echoing off the metal quonset-shaped building. "Jesse?"

He straightens. When he sees me, he wipes a hand across his face. At first he doesn't recognize me -- not until I get closer. "Oh, it's you! What'd you do to your hair? And those clothes. It's not Halloween yet, is it?" He chuckles uneasily, like he's uncomfortable with the new me and is questioning my sanity. I'm beginning to question it, too.

"I ... I wanted a change. What're you doing? Takin' her up, or just doing a little messing around?" My face gets hot when I realize too late how that sounds.

He doesn't seem to notice. His hands are greasy and there's a streak on his face where he'd wiped it. "How do you like my Cessna Skyhawk? Got her last year. I'm doing some fine-tuning." He wipes his hands on a rag. "Hey, you wanta go up? We never did have that date. I gotta make a run to Baker to get some parts, but I'll take you for a sight-seeing tour first." He chuckles, like at some private joke. "Did you see the bottle plant's opening? They've run into a hitch and now *I'm* the gopher-boy."

"Isn't it too windy to fly?"

"Naw. This ain't nothing. I've flown in much worse. Hang on a second. I'll go clean up a bit." He tightens a few nuts on the engine, slams down the cover and throws his tools into a toolbox. Hitching up his jeans, he lopes off to the bathroom. While he's gone, I wander outside and admire the view of the Rimrocks from here.

A few minutes later, he returns, clean and combed. He gives me a huge smile. "All right! Let's get this show on the road. Or I should say in the air!"

After we wheel the plane out of the hanger, I climb into the cockpit, stow my backpack behind my knees and buckle the seat belt. He jumps in beside me and gives me a thumbs-up.

I glance over at him several times while he starts the motor and goes through his checks. There's something different in his manner. What is it? I don't know and it bothers me. While he's friendly like always, I see something behind his eyes, like he knows what I'm doing here, what I'm really all about. Has he found out I'm investigating drug dealers? Is he one of them? Has he been paid to bump me off? I take a deep breath and tell myself to get a grip. Yet I keep seeing unsavory pictures in my mind's eye.

What can I expect from him? A bullet or a pleasant flight? It's a little too late to get out of the plane. I fetch my camera out of my backpack and smile at him, hoping I'm not grinning at my murderer.

***

Friday, 5:34pm

"This is getting on my nerves." Bobbi rubbed her forehead and shoved back her chair. She and Tim had just finished dinner. "Gina's not coming home and I'm worried about her, with that storm coming on and all. Where's she staying? What's she eating? I hope *she* hasn't disappeared now."

Tim stood. "Gina's a big girl, Mom. She can take care of herself."

She began clearing off the dishes. "Well, I'm not so sure of that. It's like that night when Elton disappeared. I can't let it happen to Gina. I feel ... like I should do something."

"What?" He brought his plate to the sink and rinsed it off. "More than likely, you'll just complicate whatever she's got going. She knows what she's doing. She's a good cop."

Bobbi nodded absent-mindedly. "I know. By the way, I promised to take Bryce some rhubarb. I stewed some today. I think I'll take it over to him. You wanta come?"

"And bring my rifle?" He gave her an indulgent smile. "Sure, Mom. I'll drive my pickup in case we get into mud. Let me get my stuff. I'll be right back."

Bobbi didn't know what he meant by "stuff". She went blithely about packaging up the stewed rhubarb, adding some cookies to the package, even though she knew Bryce's sister baked for them. It didn't hurt to go over the top when you're trying to please. She wondered if she should confide in Bryce about her fears and doubts.

She shook her head. The note she'd found said not to trust your neighbors. Over and over again she'd thought about that note. *Don't trust anyone, even your neighbors.* What did it mean by neighbors? The Lindsey ranch was bordered by the Hoffstien's ranch on the west and White's spread on the east. Did the note use the word *neighbor* more generally than that? Like their friends? And acquaintances?

And what was really strange about the note was that she thought it looked like Elton's hand writing. How could that be? And if it was, and he was warning her, why didn't he show himself and come home? And that person shooting from the windbreak yesterday -- Gina called it *friendly fire*. Bobbi hadn't said anything, but she knew the sound of that gun. Elton had a rifle like that and it was missing from the gun cabinet. Still, if he was alive, why didn't he come home? Had someone stolen it?

She stifled a sob as she put on her shoes. Well, instead of hanging around the place with her head down, she was going to do something. She was going to look around. And the first place that came to mind was that little cabin behind Anderson's place, near the Rims. Someone could hide in there till kingdom comes and no one would find them.

It wouldn't take long to hike up there, and they could say they were going after mushrooms. Maybe they wouldn't have to say anything at all. She rose, her mouth set in a firm line. It was time. No. It was *past* time.

***

From Gina's Blog, June 26, Friday, 6:15pm

Jesse hands me a set of earphones and shows me how to adjust them. "It might be a little rough. Hang on, we'll make it." He grins infuriatingly and turns the plane into the wind.

"Okay." I place it on my head, wondering what I'm going to hang on to.

The wind shakes the small plane and the motor screams as we reach the end of the runway. I cling to the edge of the seat as I watch the trees get closer and closer. I think for sure we won't take off, that he'll have to abort and turn, but the plane grabs the wind just in time, soaring above the tops of the pine trees.

"Ha! I bet you didn't think I could do it." Jesse's voice booms over the headset.

"I have more confidence in you than that." I try to keep my voice calm. "Why don't you take those trees out? Do you like living dangerously?"

He laughs. "Sure. Don't you?"

I don't answer – I'm too busy looking out my window with my camera ready. I know if I'm going to catch a glimpse of any ranch buildings hidden on his place, now would be the time. Yet there's nothing below us except rolling meadows, creeks and trees as we gain altitude over the Rimrocks and in a few minutes fly over Ekakala. I don't even get to see the land around the Bible camp.

"Where do you want to go?"

"Can I see the area around the Bible camp? And the Rimrocks? Then I'd like to fly over Whittier's place out by Camp Crook."

He gives me a funny look. After circling Ekalaka, he heads back toward the forest and the camp. I snap a flurry of pictures. It's a bumpy flight and I don't know if any of them will turn out. He flies over his own place. I see some buildings in a small valley near the Rims and take some pictures.

"Just an old farmstead," he comments as he turns again, heading east. The plane bounces around like marbles in a little boy's pocket when we turn our tail to the wind. I notice he's having difficulty keeping it level.

"Why do you want to see Whittier's place? It's like any other."

Am I imagining it, or is there animosity in his tone? "I ... um, I was there a little while ago and wondered about some buildings I thought I saw in a valley behind their place." There's silence while an especially hard gust of wind keeps him busy. Then I say, "I saw a picture with you in it last night. You and your folks, the Whittiers, and several others. They'd built a barn. I was just trying to locate it. You remember when that was taken?"

I glance over at him. He's sweating. I think of the old joke about when a passenger asked the pilot what was the purpose of the propellers and he said they were like a fan -- that if they quit working, you'd really see the pilot sweat! Well, anyway, it doesn't give me much comfort to see beads of sweat forming on his forehead.

Finally we reach calmer air, and he says, "No, I don't remember that. Anyway, I don't remember lots of things from when I was a kid. Hey, look down. That's Whittier's place. See those buildings? Is that what you're looking for?"

"Oh, yeah." I click away happily at the long narrow buildings below me which are surrounded by smaller sheds -- some probably housing a generator, one a well, for sure, and other equipment sheds. There's no fence and the place looks deserted. I don't see what I wanted or expected to -- a hidden plant or barn near the buttes and the Short Pines -- a place where indication of much activity would be evident.

Jesse turns the plane in a wide circle, and we start back, not saying much, heading into the wind. After twenty minutes, we're over the Bible camp. I know the Rimrocks are not far to the south from here. The plane jerks and Jesse swears under his breath. I look at him in alarm. He glances down at the gauges.

"What? What's wrong?"

He doesn't say anything. Sweat is now running off his face in rivulets and his shirt is soaked. I smell his fear and mine. After pulling some levers, he says, "We're outta gas! I thought we had plenty. I filled 'er up before ..."

The motor coughs. And again. Frantically he tips the wings this way and that, like he's trying to get the last drops out of the tank.

"Can't you make it home? It's just over there." I point to the southeast. My fingers ache, I'm hanging on to the door handle so hard – for all the good *that* will do me.

He shakes his head. "Too far." Glancing out the side window, he swears again, softly, his face turning a coppery red. He noses the plane around in a sharp turn, so the tail is in the wind. "Hang on. I'm takin' her down. There's a meadow down there. Let's just hope it's level enough to land on!"

He works the levers again. "Get my radio. The two way. There. Beside me."

I find it.

He reaches over and turns it on, then speaks into it. "Long John calling Big Daddy. Come in, Big Daddy." Static. He calls again. This time someone answers.

***

Friday, 5:44pm

Chance's pulses were racing by the time he got halfway up one of the buttes about a mile from where he parked the pickup, and it wasn't entirely from the exertion. He was getting close -- this was it, he knew it. By now he could see lights down below, and as he crept nearer, he saw the dim outlines of buildings. He arrived at a ten foot chain link fence and stayed put, hiding behind a tree. They probably had cameras mounted on the fence.

With the approaching storm, it was getting darker by the moment and a sense of impending doom pressed heavily on his mind. He knew they had Mexican workers, even before Gina told him about the woman in the clinic, and he guessed those people were probably enslaved. As he crouched there, he scanned the place with his glasses. Yes, there were plenty of buildings -- enough to house the necessary people and equipment for an operation on the scale he'd seen in the South Pines. Yet he came back to the elementary question: *who is the boss?*

Bryce Anderson? But surely not. He seemed a decent sort of person. Maybe he'd started out small, thinking he could make a little money to help pay off his place. Maybe evil crept in with greed, born on the wings of urgency. Maybe the men who controlled him had something to blackmail him with -- or threatened that they'd kill his loved ones.

It might not be Bryce. Just because this place was close to the Anderson ranch didn't mean he was in control of it. It might be someone totally different. Randy Whittier? Gina's Uncle Elton? Dugal Pierce? But why would these men risk it? Anyway, all of them, with the exception of Dugal, he liked and couldn't picture them as cruel, evil or sold out for money. How about Mike Crosby? Excellent opportunities. Little pay. Maybe big debts. A memory hit him like a sledgehammer: the large man who was in charge of his beating that night in the barn. He fit Mike's description perfectly, and now that he thought of it, had he detected a slight southern twang? And he could be Gina's mole.

The wind howled over the top of the butte behind him. He strained his eyes to see any flicker of movement at the ranch. Did they have guards that patrolled with dogs? Or were they that nervous?

It was eerie -- the silence and the wind and that monstrous fence in front of him. The early darkness made it seem like he'd landed on another planet. Who would have ever thought they'd build such a place here? Washington or Oregon, yes. Even Idaho. They'd had drug raids in the corn fields of Washington; under tree farms in Oregon; camouflaged by sunflower plants in Idaho and Iowa. But here? In southeast Montana, Carter County, where everyone knew what you did and when you went to bed and what you had for dinner?

If he could get in there, he'd be able to collect some samples and get some pictures. He had to get in. Moving cautiously away from the tree, trying to stay in the brush, he groped his way along the fence. It took him further from the buildings. This was too tedious. He retraced his steps, trying not to crackle the underbrush or step on twigs.

Yet of course he did. At one point he stumbled, caught his balance. Crouching down, he expected dogs, sirens, guards with guns. Silence.

Continuing on, he passed the place where he first met the fence and against his better judgment, followed it, hoping to come to a corner. He wanted to see some of the other buildings. There had to be trailer houses or shacks for the Mexicans -- also barns, garages, and more than likely a house of some sort at the front. There would be quonset-shaped equipment sheds surrounded by corrals. Probably cattle. Maybe some sheep. You'd think there would be cars pulling in and out, lights on, maybe some music. Yet everything was shut down, dead still. The only light he saw was a glimmer coming from a window in the distance.

Arriving at a corner at last, he turned and followed the fence north, running out of shelter. After what seemed years of creeping through brush and tall grass, he halted at a three-strand barbed wire fence. The chain link fence ran along the pasture on his left. A couple of dark blobs under the distant trees must be some of the cattle -- probably bulls, as he knew most of the stock would be further out to pasture. He pulled the strands apart and crawled through, hoping the bulls were asleep.

He crossed a creek, cringing when he made a lot of noise sloshing through the water and came to another set of barbed wires and crawled through them. Turned another corner. Now he was close to the front entrance. A large house stood not over a hundred yards away. No lights. He hadn't found cover, yet he stood and stared at the house. It looked like a fancy lodge with a wrap-around deck, two stories and lots of really large windows. Had they created a dude ranch to launder the money? Was it a get-away retreat for the drug lord?

He shook his head and kept going. Now he was heading toward the driveway and the front gate, clear out of cover. He knew in the back of his mind that he had to stop. He had to go back. But he couldn't. Not yet. Was the main gate locked? Was it hot? He couldn't tell. Sheds stood in the rear, in the dark. Trucks and other vehicles were parked in the lot in front of the house.

He drew a deep breath. What should he do? How could he get in? He retraced his steps to the pasture with the bulls. At the creek, he stood staring at the water flowing under the fence. *Babylon! That's it!* It was a story recorded in the Bible in the book of Daniel. It told of the city of Babylon in the last days of the Assyrian reign under Beltshezzar. The Medes and Persians couldn't get into the city, so they dammed up the Euphrates River, drained it one night, and crawled underneath the walls to conquer the city and the entire kingdom.

Hm. Well, he couldn't drain the creek, yet he might be able to do the next best thing. He rubbed his chin. Yes, it just might work. Beside the creek, he went down on his knees. Taking a deep breath, he lowered himself into the creek, gasping at the cold water. Keeping his gun and camera just above his head, he worked his way steadily to the chain link fence and squirmed underneath it.

Out on the other side, he rose from the water, crawled up the bank and sat, wiping his face, dumping water from his boots, making sure his gun was dry. Once again he expected sirens, dogs and men with guns. None appeared. The wind covered any noises he might have made and now it was darker than the insides of a black bear.

He stood and looked around. He was sitting under a box elder tree. Not a hundred yards away was the back of a big barn. Bent over, he dashed to the cover of a large bush. From there he could find his way to those long buildings at the back. As he contemplated his next move, prickles of fear ran up his back. Was it a premonition that something had gone dreadfully wrong? Or was it the cold water? He didn't have time to think about it. Time was running out and he needed to get some samples.

He hitched up his soggy jeans and muffled a sneeze. Straightening, he headed toward the sheds. *Get the pictures. Get the samples. Then get out.*

***

Friday, 5:22pm

Bobbi wrestled the door of the Toyota truck shut and put her seat belt on. "Quite a wind we're gettin'."

Tim nodded and drove down the driveway where the wind hit the small pickup like a sledgehammer. He dodged rolling tumbleweeds and pulled out onto the main road. "If this keeps up, we're goin' to have downed trees and no power."

Bobbi shrugged. "We've had worse. Want me to drive?"

"No. I'm fine." He gripped the wheel tighter. "Good thing there's not much traffic. Of course, there never is, that I can tell. Not out here."

She slanted a glance at him and sighed. He'd spent six months in Seattle before he dropped out of college. That was enough for him and ever since, he'd stuck his nose up at country living, like he was such a city man now. She knew his heart was in the farm, yet he wanted more -- probably a degree in computer science along with one in animal husbandry. He was enrolled online for both, and she knew he could do it. If he didn't get distracted again.

If only Elton would come home. She wouldn't admit it to anyone, but her secret hope was what Gina had said -- that he was out there somewhere, maybe suffering from amnesia, and that he'd come back. Someday. And that things would be like they were before. No. Better than that.

They arrived at Anderson's ranch to find everything buttoned down like a go-to-meeting shirt. She parked by the house and rang the bell, feeling like Little Red Riding Hood. After pushing it twice, she started off the porch. But suddenly it opened. It was Bryce.

The surprise on his face was priceless. "Who ... oh, it's you. Come on in. Tell Tim to come in, too. You can't stand out there in this weather."

She called Tim, who ran over from the car. Stepping inside she said, "I can't stay, Bryce. Just wanted to bring you this." She held out her offerings. He took the plastic bag without saying much. She sensed that he was worried about something.

"What's wrong?"

"Oh, it's Jesse. He took off in the plane a while ago. Said he was goin' to Baker to get some parts. Should'a heard from him. I can't raise him on the cell phone or his radio. Got me a little concerned, what with the storm and all. It's supposed to bring rain and possibly snow."

She nodded and ran her fingers through her windblown hair. "I know. Gina hasn't come back, neither. She went down to Rapid and should've been back this mornin'. She left a message that something's held her up. I'm worried, too."

He took the bag to the kitchen. When he returned, she said, "I ... uh, I'd like to go up in the meadow by the Rims for a bit. Was lookin' for some mushrooms."

"Now?" His eyes widened. "In this?"

She nodded, not knowing how to explain her mission, remembering again the message in that note. "Yeah. Just for a bit. We'll be right back." She turned and grasped the door knob. "We better get goin' before the storm hits."

"It's hit already, Bobbi." He put his hand on her arm. "I can't let you go alone. I'll come."

She tried to laugh it off. "No, I'm in no danger. And I don't want you catchin' your death of cold out there. We're okay. Like I say, we'll be back. Those mushrooms are callin' to me and I know they'll be gone if they get a good wettin'." Of course *that* probably wasn't exactly the truth. It sounded good, anyway.

At that moment, Bryce's two-way radio buzzed. He ran to it, turned it up. "Big Daddy. What's going on, Long John?"

Bobbi heard a lot of crackling. A voice came over the wire sporadically. It was Jesse and he sounded like he was in trouble.

"Dad! We have to ... ditch plane ... over by ... we're ... Come ... Over."

"Jesse! Where are you? Repeat: *where are you*? Over."

"Rims, but not ... have to go ... Gina's ... Dad! Hurry! We're ..." Static.

Bryce called again and again, but there was no response. He carefully set the radio down and paced up and down the living room.

"Bryce! It sounds like Jesse needs help. Where did he say he was?"

He stopped in front of her, his face a twisted mask of terror. "I only heard one word. The Rims. I've got to go and check it out."

"I'm comin' with you." She zipped up her jacket and pulled up the hood. "I heard him say Gina's name. She must be with him, and they might need more help than you know. Gather up your first aid kit. Let's get over there! Now!"

Tim spoke up for the first time. "Did he say where? That's a lot of country over there."

Bryce shook his head and trotted off to get the medical supplies.

Bobbi eyed Tim. "I hope they're okay. What do you think?"

"I don't know, Mom. I'm mighty scared. I'm driving my outfit, though."

"Bryce will want to take his."

"We can follow him." He dashed to the pickup. Bobbi followed him. They waved to Bryce who hopped into his red truck and roared out of the drive. Bobbi prayed silently as they followed him through the wind and the night.

Chapter 31

The Rims

From Gina's Blog: Friday, 6:50pm

The ground approaches more rapidly than I thought it would. One minute we're over the trees, and the next they're brushing the underside of the plane. I scream as Jesse pulls up the stick in a valiant attempt to avoid the nose facing into the ground. It doesn't do much good, but a little spurt of wind right at that moment lifts us maybe ten feet. Then we're down.

The plane is dying. I hear it shrieking, tearing, splintering, crashing. Things are falling, hitting me. Glass. Something wet is on my face. I scream again and try to protect my head. Jesse yells something. Everything goes black.

When I awake, I'm sitting tilted crazily in the seat, held in it by my seat belt. Pain is shrieking up my legs from my knees. And something's jabbing my ribs. My head hurts when I move it. It's almost completely dark.

"Jesse?" Silence. I panic, reaching for him. He's below me somewhere in the darkness. "*Jesse!*" It's a shriek. The worst thing possible would be for him to be dead and me -- alone.

Movement. Sounds of splintered glass crackling together. He says, "Yes, what can I do for you?" Real calm and polite, like a store clerk.

I muffle my laughter. It's just so weird. "I ... I thought you were dead."

"Oh. Uh, you okay?"

"Yeah, if I can get out of this belt. You don't have a light, do you?" No reply.

"Jesse? Stay with me." Seems like I've been saying that quite often. *Stay with me.* Like who would want to stay with *me.* "You there? I need you, pal."

"Uh, yeah. Just ... can't stay awake. Blood. Too much blood."

I squirm around in my seat and find the buckle. I know if I unfasten it, I'll probably land in his lap. No good. Can't do that. I hang onto the top of the empty window, disregarding the shards of broken glass that are impaling my hand, and with the other hand, click open my belt, grabbing the window sash with both hands.

With an incredible effort, I lift my body, head first, out of the smashed plane, pulling my feet behind me. I drop to the ground. It's farther than I thought and I jar my injured knees. I fall to the soft, damp grass and lay there, moaning. When I pull myself up, I know I'm going to hurl, and I drag myself a few feet from the plane and find a convenient bush.

I can't feel sorry for myself too long, though. Jesse needs help. I pull myself to my feet and hobble around the nose of the plane which is buried in the ground. "Jesse?" It's so dark I can't see, can only feel along the fuselage for the door handle. Or is it my eyes? Am I blind? For a panicky moment, I think I am, then I see the moon as the clouds sail clear of it for a few minutes. *Whew!*

Now my eyes are adjusting to the darkness and I can see the window's gone and his head is slouching down on his chest. I feel his neck. He's got a pulse. When I try to open the cockpit door, the handle's jammed. I'm hurting all over, Jesse's gonna die, the darned plane might burst into flames any second, and now I can't get the stupid handle open.

"God? Are You there? Any help would be much appreciated right now." I can't believe I say the words, yet they come tumbling out of my swollen lips. Tears are wet on my cheeks; I imagine they're making rivers in the blood there. If I can't open the door, I'll have to haul him out the window and I'm not sure I have the strength for that.

I wrench on the handle. Again. Again. "Uhhh!" With all my strength, I twist it once more. It pops open. I can't believe it. And there, alone in the wind and the storm, with so much to do and pain dragging me down inch by inch, I lift hands to the sky and scream. I'm actually glad no one can see me when it's over and I regain my sanity. I wipe my face with my sleeve and mutter *thank you* to someone I can't see and to whom I don't think is there. Strange what extreme stress will do to a person!

I turn back to the plane and Jesse.

First I have to free him from the seat belt. Even that job takes more out of me than I thought I had, wrestling aside his body, climbing half into the cockpit, trying to squeeze the button on the belt. When I accomplish these small miracles, he flops over, almost into my arms. I ease him to the ground, wishing I had a protected place, wondering if there's any animals out there who'd like a nice easy meal. Like cougars. Not a good thought. I push it aside.

Wait. Maybe I can get under the plane. The tail is high in the air. I crawl underneath it, and pull him in with me, again easier said than done, but finally that, too, is accomplished. The grass is damp under here. I find a few rocks, which I chuck out, and decide that it's better than being out in the open, unprotected in the wind and rain.

I arrange him so he's lying neatly on his back. Returning to the cockpit, I rummage around in it, finding a flashlight that works, a first aid kit, our jackets, and my backpack. On my return, I assess his wounds, those that are visible. He's got a bad cut in his forehead, which was the source of the blood, multiple glass cuts on his face and his right hand is broken, crushed. His left foot is mangled. He groans when I gently remove his boot. I catch my breath at the sight of his foot.

It's not pretty. His knees and legs are cut and bruised, as I suspect mine are, too. There's a bad gash in his upper arm. Water. I need water and something to use for bandages. I struggle outside again and find two water bottles and a little packet of emergency food in the compartment underneath the seat. I snatch up a light blanket. I can use this for bandaging.

Yet there's something else in here.

It's a parcel wrapped in brown paper. Inside, I open a box, sort of like a cigar box. And inside that, I find plastic bags filled with white powder. *Oh, no.* My heart pounds in my ears so loudly I can hardly think. Opening one, I dip a finger into it and taste it.

Heroin.

***
Friday, 6:34pm

Chance crept as quietly as he could through the darkened yard of the ranch he'd infiltrated. Using a pen light, he entered one of the long buildings at the back, feeling like someone was peering over his shoulder and would jam a gun into his back at any moment.

The place was deserted. It was a nursery, empty except for long wooden tables. Shining his light on the floor, he found plenty of dried leaves and after picking some of them up, he smelled them. *Marijuana.* It didn't surprise him. After taking a couple of pictures, he folded the dried leaves into his pocket kerchief, wondering even as he did it how he'd get it through the water. Well, he'd worry about that later.

In the back of the building, in what seemed like a small kitchen, he found beakers and burners and the remnants of chemicals. He smelled it and jerked back. Codeine! Someone was stewing up something stronger than marijuana here! He took some pictures and scraped a sampling from one of the beakers. This he deposited in another fold of the white kerchief.

When he emerged from the building, there were still no lights visible. Anywhere. The wind was gaining velocity -- tree limbs crashed to the ground occasionally and the sound of splintering glass crashed through the night. Maybe no one was here. Maybe they'd vacated the place.

He moved forward and found an older model trailer house. It, too, was silent and dark. When he tapped on the door, no one answered. He moved to another shack and found the same thing. As he made his way toward the equipment shed and the main house, he gained more confidence. He'd investigate all of them and call the sheriff. After that, he'd hightail it out of there.

He inched open the equipment shed door and shone the light around, stepping cautiously inside. It was as he figured -- a place to store equipment, vehicles, tools, tires, spare parts. He was about to bring out his camera from his pocket and take some pictures when the door creaked shut behind him. He jerked back toward it, gun in hand.

Sudden bright lights pinned him to the spot. A voice said, "Drop the gun, Chance. Now."

He let it slide from his fingers, heard it clatter on the cement floor. His throat closed and his heart thudded heavily in his ears. Slowly he turned and tried to see the face of the man who was going to kill him.

***

From Gina's Blog, Friday, 7:11pm

With shaking fingers, I carefully replace the plastic bag into the cigar box and put the package underneath the seat like I'd found it. I take the blanket and food outside. It's starting to rain. I crawl under the plane and find him awake. Without saying anything, I hand him the water, and while he drinks, I tear the blanket into strips. Good thing it's old and worn thin.

"I've gotta bandage that wound on your head and your arm." I bind up his cuts as best as I can, even though he groans and kind of slumps down. He's out again. Good. Methodically I wrap his wounds and finish with his foot. Splashing a bit of the water on it, I bind it up as best as I can to stop the bleeding. Sitting back on my heels, I take a sip of water. Now what?

My own wounds need a little attention and I apply bandaids and strips of the blanket to them. My knees hurt the worst. I have a few cuts on my legs, and a cut on my chest, just below my right breast. I wind a bandage on that, lifting my shirt, and look up to see him eyeing me with a crooked grin on his face.

"How far you goin'?"

I pull my shirt down and zip up my jacket. "I didn't think you were awake."

He tries to sit up and I press him down. He winces. "Uh. Everything hurts. You okay?"

I nod. "Yeah." I pull my knees up to my chest and look out into the night. "It's a wild night. I suppose I should go get help."

"No, Gina. You're staying right here. I got through to Dad. He'll be along soon."

I shake my head, unconvinced. "There's a lot of country here. They won't find us until ... the storm's over. No, before it gets any worse, I'm out of here. I have a good idea which way to go, but I don't want to leave you."

He grunts. "I'll be all right. Take the revolver under the seat. And the water. You'll need it more than I do. Head north and east. Should take you out to the road. From there, you can get a ride."

I'm so exhausted, I honestly don't know how I'm going to crawl outside again and stand up. I sigh and pat his arm. "Okay. I'm leaving the revolver with you, though. There might be a cougar around here looking for an easy dinner." I grin at him.

He doesn't argue. His eyelids are fluttering shut. "Come ... back soon."

That's all I get out of him before he's gone again. I check his pulse. Strong. Climbing out into the storm, I find the revolver he has hidden. Making sure the gun, food packet and the water are close to his hand, I back out from under the plane and stand up.

The wind's still howling and rain comes in solid sheets. I put up my hood and find myself drenched to the skin almost immediately. I shake my head. I'm tired to the bone and hurting all over. Yet somehow I have to find help -- Jesse's not going to make it if I don't.

"Bye, Jesse," I say to him, bending over, just in case he can hear me. "Stay dry."

I try to orient myself. There's no land marks. Nothing. He said to go northeast. Wish I had a compass. Let me think. We turned our tail to the wind just before we crashed and he said it was coming from the south. So north must be ... that way.

I start off through the trees, trying to keep the direction in mind, but the wind blows me off course before I get to the edge of the meadow. Great. Now I'm going to wander around in the forest, lost. Maybe I should stay with the plane. Does it have one of those tracker things on it? I glance back at it. The mist and darkness veil it from my view.

Well, I'll do the best I can and go until I can't go anymore. With that grim thought in the back of my mind, I start off again, glad for my own revolver and my backpack. Jesse hadn't known about my Glock, tucked safely in my pack. Or had he? I have water, a flashlight, an energy bar and an apple. Remembering the satphone I'd left in the car, I shake my head. How could I have been so stupid? At least I have my cell phone, for all the good it will do me in this country.

I stumble through the darkness and rain for what feels like ten miles. By now I feel I should be coming out to a road. Or to someone's house. My legs feel like logs and my head hurts so bad I have to clamp my jaws shut tight against the pain to keep from crying. No house. No road, only more and more forest.

I glance at my watch. *8:32pm.* I'd been walking for about an hour. Should have come out to something by now! Suddenly I do. In fact, I almost fall down a rocky cliff. I catch myself at the last moment and jerk backward, landing on a prickly bush. Getting to my feet, I pull out the flashlight and peer over the edge.

The truth pierces my consciousness like a knife. I'm at the *Rimrocks!* I've made a big circle around and now I'm going in the opposite direction than what I wanted. I sit down on a rock and fight tears. *What am I doing here? Why am I doing it?*

I don't have the answer to the questions that buzz around in my head like angry bees. I rest my head in my hands and the next thing I know, I'm weeping. As the tears mingle with the rain on my cheeks, I silently review my sorry past up to this last moment and I know I'm finished. What a joke I've become!

I can't even find my way out of the woods. Dad's angry words sear my consciousness like a hot iron: *you're a failure as a cop, Gina. Give it up.*

Yeah, Dad, maybe I should. He'd said something else just before he'd died. *What did he say? Why can't I remember it? Why is it so important?*

The darkness and rain give way to a hospital room, to antiseptic smell, the squeak of nurse's shoes, the silent *beep, beep* of the heart monitor, the hissing breath of the man on the bed.

Dad! His eyes are closed, his mouth slack. I want to button his shirt, wipe the dribble off his chin, see his smile, watch as his eyes light up with joy when he sees me. *Just once more. Please, God. Once more.* But God didn't answer -- He seemed as removed from that room as life from death.

I take a deep shuddering breath, pulling my jacket closer. *Wait. Now I remember.* I was turning from him, and he *did* open his eyes. He *had* said something. I returned to his side and grasped his hand. His eyelids fluttered and he tried to say something. I leaned forward, my heart in my throat. His mouth moved. *Gina. You must listen to me ... I ...*

But it's gone. Just like that.

Back again on a bumpy rock and a rain-swept cliff, I rub my forehead. A coyote howls not far away, a lonely sound that raises the hairs on my neck. Slowly I stand, thinking that maybe I should just throw myself off the rocks and end it all. I step to the very edge and wipe the water from my face. I can see nothing below my feet. I know it drops a long ways to the bottom. There wouldn't be much left of me.

No. The resolve grows in my mind like a swelling tide. If I end it here, then I *am* a coward. The worst kind of coward there is, bringing pain and suffering to my loved ones for as long as they live. Besides, I remember the way the handle popped open on the plane when I muttered that desperate prayer. Maybe there *is* a God.

I blow my nose on a sopping wet hankie. Well, I'll give it a try. If God's real, I'll find Him. And if I can't, I'll reassess my life. What's the worst that could happen to me? That others will sneer and call me a fool? Does it really matter what others think?

I sit down again, staring off into the turbulent darkness, trying to sort out my jumbled thoughts. I'd always lived my life to please others, to find significance. I'd thrown away a lot of meaningful relationships for my job because I'd always believed that I could find what I needed through my career. I thought about how I'd lost my mother. My dad. Uncle Elton. Nick. Would I lose Bobbi, too, and Tim? While I hadn't had a hand in my mother leaving, I wrestled with the fact that I hadn't known Dad very well or taken an interest in his life. I might as well face it: I hadn't ever truly invested myself in *anyone's* life. It had all been about Gina Lindsay.

What hogwash I'd swallowed -- *find meaning to life in my job!*

Life is meaningless without God. The thought is like a bolt of lightning reverberating through my being. Where'd that come from? Had Bobbi said it? It sounded like her. Maybe my morbid thoughts here on the edge of the cliff brought it back to me. Whatever did, I'm grateful. Because now I see that even if I don't find any other person to give me significance, if I find God, I'm okay.

I lift my head. A warm breeze seems to fan my cheeks. I feel cocooned, like someone's arms are around me. *I love you!* The thought invades my mind. It's sweet, almost painful, like a forgotten melody, like a lover's gentle touch, like the brush of angel's wings. Before I can hardly understand it, it's gone and I wonder if I imagined it. *No, it was real.*

It is my answer.

I stand and gaze into the night around me. *Now where should I go?* I shine the flashlight on the cliff. At my feet I see a dim path descending through the scrub bushes and rocks. *Down. Go down.* Starting out, I wonder where the path will lead. And what I will find at the end of it.

***

Friday, 7:35pm

Chance turned. Powerful flashlights shone on his face, so he shielded his eyes from the glare. He wanted desperately to identify the man behind the flashlight, the one who stood aloof of the others, but all he could see was the man's work boots and jeans. It could be anyone.

The weapon he held was a machine gun, a Micro Uzi, Israeli made. That's when Chance started to sweat despite the chill that was

Deadlocked

creeping over his body from his wet clothes. Those assault rifles could cut a man to shreds in seconds.

He stilled his breathing and looked up. "Hello, sir. I got lost up on the hill and I was tryin' to find my way back. Got under the fence and was comin' up to the house to see if I could use the phone."

There was a chuckle behind the rifle. The man's voice was a low growl. Chance couldn't place it, even though he knew he'd heard it before. "I'm not buying it, son. State your name and business. Then we're going to take a little walk."

Chance swallowed. "Name's Chance McNeil. I told you my business. Sorry you don't believe me."

"Boys, tie him up and bring him along. I'll call the boss, but I'm thinking we'll want to hang onto this prize. This fellow's trouble and he's put his nose in where it doesn't belong." He glanced up as they grabbed Chance's arms roughly. "Don't damage him."

Chance's heart sank. So this fellow knew who he was. This was going to be a lot more complicated than he thought. He pulled his camera from his pocket as he turned away from the light and held it in the palm of his hand. They bound his hands in front and didn't see the camera.

He winced as the ropes bit into his flesh, yet he didn't cry out. Leading him along with the rope, they took him across the windswept yard, past the pole barn, corrals and the vehicles parked side by side. As he passed a good sized bush on the verge of the lawn, he tossed the camera into it, holding his breath. Good. They hadn't seen. Now he hoped the rain would let up so it wouldn't be damaged.

They trudged through the back yard of the house, across the wide deck, through the back door and entered a dimly lit kitchen. In one glance Chance knew he was in a place where no expense was spared -- marble countertops, glistening black appliances, oak cabinets. Someone had recently cooked a meal in here -- he smelled greasy hamburgers. They'd cleaned up, too, not a sign of dirty dishes or littered floor. His stomach rumbled. It'd been awhile since he'd had a good meal, yet he reminded himself to focus. There might come a moment when he could escape.

They prodded him down a hall. He glimpsed other rooms off the hall -- a mini theater, a gym, two bedrooms, an office. The windows were covered with black paper. So that's why he didn't see lights. Where were the Mexicans? They had to be around somewhere.

He came to a doorway. When they opened it, he saw a stairwell leading down. They pushed him down these, and at the bottom he came to a large room that looked like an office for a prison. A metal desk sat along one wall. Another wall was covered with files. There were three monitors for surveillance cameras and a desk and chairs for guards. No wonder he'd been caught. They'd spotted him and merely waited for him to snoop in the equipment shed.

They searched him thoroughly, even having him take off his socks and shoes, and relieved him of his gun and wallet. They didn't take his kerchief from his pocket. Were they looking for explosives in his shoes? Knives up his pant legs? Did they think he was James Bond?

They shoved him through a metal door on the far wall and slammed it shut. He was in total darkness and shivering from the chill air. The cold wasn't the first thing he noticed about the room, though. The first thing that caught his attention was that he wasn't alone.

Chapter 32

Old Blood

Friday, 6:14pm

The road turned to mud. Tim had trouble driving through some of the lower places. He gunned the motor and spun through the mud holes, following the taillights of the truck ahead, wondering where Bryce would stop. How could he know where to look? Shouldn't they call the sheriff and get some people and dogs out here? Why search this whole country with three people? It could be weeks before they'd find anyone.

Finally Bryce stopped. Tim pulled up behind the truck and got out, yanking his hood over his head and reaching for his rifle. "For critters," he said when he saw Bryce's sharp glance. They stood in the rain by the vehicles and listened for the sound of a shot, for voices, for anything. It was silent except for the wind screaming in the trees.

Tim brushed a hand across his face, eager to get on with it and return to the warmth of the house. "So. Let's get going."

Bryce zipped up his jacket. "I don't know if they have a gun or not. Fire your rifle every so often, and if they do, they'll return the shot. Stop now and then to listen."

Tim didn't look at Bryce. His words were dry, just short of sarcastic. "I know. I've been on searches before."

"Yes. You have." Bryce fetched his rifle from the truck. "Let's go."

Tim was about to reply sharply when Bobbi joggled his elbow, and gave him a look with a shake of her head.

She took a step forward. "I'd rather we all stayed together. In this storm, it would be easy to get lost."

"We won't cover nearly enough territory if we stay together." Bryce's tone was patient like he was explaining something to a child.

"I'll go down that draw by the Rims. Bobbi, you and Tim take a swing over that way on the other side of the road. Meet back here in about an hour."

Tim glanced at his watch, still prickly over Anderson's domineering attitude. "Okay. I still think we should call the sheriff and get a search party up here."

Bryce shook his head like an old bull about to charge. "No. We'll do this search first. If we don't find 'em by morning, we'll call Mike. Not before."

Tim wanted to say a lot of things, but he shut his mouth tight when he saw his mom's face. She strode ahead, not minding the rain or wind, and he followed. When he looked back, Bryce was gone. He was surprised.

How had the man disappeared so fast? True, it was nearly dark, but one minute he was standing by the truck, the next he was gone. Did he know where the plane was? Did he point them in the opposite direction so that he would find the plane first? What was going on?

Why did Bryce Anderson want to be the one who found Jesse and Gina?

***

From Gina's Blog, Friday, 8:33pm

The path disappears and I'm not even halfway down the cliff. I pause and shine the light, searching for another trail. Below me is a stretch of sheer rock, glistening in the rain. Can't go that way. I move two feet forward and stop. Not much room to maneuver here. Scrub cedars and other bushes grow close by the edge.

I step out, searching for a way down, moving forward maybe a foot. Suddenly the rock crumbles under my feet. I'm falling ... arms flailing, a scream forming in my throat. Bushes smack me in the face, I try to grab them, but they slide out of my grasp. Soil and debris fall with me. With a *thump!* I land.

It takes me a couple of seconds to get my breath and rise to my knees. *Ow!* I try to move the left knee and almost pass out. *Oh, great.*

I don't need this. I grope around in the darkness to find my flashlight. It's gone! I'm desperate, frantic. I enlarge the search and my fingers come in contact with it. Relief washes through me when I turn it on and see the beam of light. Funny how such a small thing can bring such big comfort.

Slowly I get to my feet, hobbling on one leg to protect my knee, and discover that I'm on a ledge. Behind me is the opening of a cave in the hillside. Gimping along painfully, I explore it. It's sandy-floored, dry and large enough to stand up in.

I shine the light around. It's what you would expect: leaves and dry bones of an animal on the floor, bird poop scattered around, dry rock walls that slope toward the back. It doesn't seem to go anywhere. It's not much in the way of accommodations, yet for me at that moment, it's the *Palace Royale*. I pull off my backpack and gather some dry wood from a dead tree that grows beside the cave mouth. Lowering myself to the sand, still protecting my knees, I gather the dead leaves into a pile and search in my pack for a lighter.

Ah, ha! I pull it out and hope it still has fluid in it. I flick it. *Yes!* A small flame appears. But small or not, it's all I need at the moment. *Like small faith.* I pause just before I light the leaves and twigs. *Where do these things keep coming from?* The leaves ignite with a crackling sound. Carefully I add more dried twigs and a pine cone. Settling down in the sand, I pull out my water bottle and the energy bar and have a little supper in front of my fire, as pleased with myself as if I was dining in the nicest restaurant in the world.

I tell myself I can't sleep ... that I need to get help for Jesse. That's when I think of my cell phone. *Oh, gosh.* Why hadn't I tried it? I pull it out and turn it on. No service. Slowly I get to my feet and hobble out on the ledge in front of the cave. I try it again and am surprised when I see one bar.

I have service! I dial 911, careful to hold the phone still so I won't lose the signal. A woman answers. I tell her my plight and position. She says to hang on, she's going to call the sheriff. I say, "Wait, I ..." She's gone. I hold on the line for awhile but my battery dies.

When I return to my fire, I wonder if Mike will get the information, if he will come and get me. Will dispatch call Mike? I'd assumed she would. What if she calls Dugal? Now that's not a pleasant thought! Maybe the mole will get the information first. *That's* a worse thought.

I put some more fuel on the fire and lean back on the cave wall, telling myself I'll close my eyes for just a minute. My last waking thought is of Dad. He had faith. Not a lot, but enough.

***

7:40pm

"Anyone have a light?" Chance's voice sounded hollow and thin, even to his own ears.

A man's guttural tone answered. "Who ... who are you?"

Chance cleared his throat and lowered himself to the floor. "Chance McNeil, *amigo*, at your service. Do you have a light?"

There was a bit of movement, clothes rubbing, a cough. A small pen light illuminated the darkness. Chance reached for it and shone it around. Oddly shaped bundles covered the cement floor – a dark head poked from one. *The Mexicans!* He flashed his light on the walls. Another door across the room. Getting up, he stepped over the bundles and tried the door. It was locked, of course. What was on the other side? A tunnel leading to the airstrip? Or to the nursery in the back? So they could shuttle people and goods back and forth without being seen? If they closed this operation down, were they going to smuggle the people out this way?

He directed the light at the people and saw a woman's face.

"What do ... you do here?" Her eyes were distended, her face pale.

He knelt beside her. "Don't be afraid. I'm here to help." He glanced around, counting fifteen others who huddled in the darkness, some of them mere children. Two men and three women. Must be families.

He sat back on his heels. From the conversation he'd heard as he walked with the men to the house, he knew they didn't have much time. They were going to take the people out by plane, and with the storm coming, their window of opportunity was closing mighty fast.

He realized the people didn't fear him -- they were terrified of what was going to happen to them. Now they fastened eager eyes on him. He knew they expected nothing short of a miracle. He prowled the room. No windows. Two locked doors. A small bathroom. No way out. *Oh, God. Give me a plan.*

He turned off the light, squatted down by the wall and closed his eyes. He was chilled to the bone from his wet clothes. His old wounds from the beating flared up -- the headache, the sharp pain in his ribs, the dull ache in his hands. Exhaustion pulled at him like a thousand ton boulder. He told himself he had to stay awake. He had to come up with a plan. Yet in a few moments, he fell into an uneasy slumber.

***

Friday, 9:34pm

Tim was wet and tired by the time he and Bobbi arrived back in the clearing where they'd left the vehicles. He stopped abruptly as he drew closer to where they were parked. Bobbi bumped into him.

"What the --" She took a step around him and stared.

"Bryce is gone." Tim could hardly get the words from his mouth. With long angry steps he strode forward and using his flashlight saw where the man had driven through the grass in a wide circle, then rejoined the road.

"Well, I'll be ..." Bobbie didn't say what she'd be, but her tone matched Tim's disgust. "Why'd you think left?"

He shrugged and climbed into the pickup. He got the thermos out and poured himself a cup and handed her the thermos. The coffee smelled good. "He must've found the plane and was able to get them to his truck. Why didn't he shoot or something to let us know?"

"Maybe we didn't hear him." She gave him a look that said she didn't believe her own words.

He put the pickup in gear and swung it a circle. "Well, all we can do is go home. I guess he'll call."

"He better." Her mouth was a stern line and her brow was puckered. "I don't like bein' left out in the cold like a stranded calf. It'd be nice if Gina would let us know what's goin' on." Her tone was hard. She glared straight ahead and didn't even think to drink the coffee.

He shook his head. "I doubt if she will. Maybe she can't." He glanced over at her. "You have to let her go, Mom."

She snorted and looked out the side window.

He turned on the windshield wipers and concentrated on driving, wondering if somewhere out there in the dark and the night, Gina really did need help.

***

From Gina's Blog, Saturday, 2:32am

All night I run through a dark forest. A woman screams in the trees above me. No, a woman couldn't climb so high. It must be a cougar. I train my gun on the tree and fire. The big cat snaps branches as it falls to the ground. When I reach the spot where it landed, I find Maegan's body, broken and bleeding.

Life is seeping from her eyes as she searches my face. "I thought you said you would help me."

Tears flood my cheeks. I cling to her hand. Suddenly someone touches my shoulder. I jump. "Time's up, Gina. You can't help her now."

"Chance?" I untwine my fingers from Maegan's and stand. "Is it you?" I can't see his face. Others are near; I hear their footsteps. "Cap, is that you? Jesse? Nick?" Footsteps fade and the hopeless words float away on the night breeze. *You can't help her now.*

I jerk awake. It's still dark. Grabbing my flashlight, I look at my watch. *2:32 am*

Where am I? I try to clear my head, still remembering the dream. *Oh. The cave.* My little fluttering flame is gone. The hopelessness from my dream lingers in my mind like the echo of a tortured soul. I explore my body parts where I'd been injured; flex my knees, feel my ankle and ribs. Things seem to be in working order, not too painful. Of course I haven't tried to walk yet. My hair is crusty with dried blood. I'm glad I don't have a mirror -- I must look a sight.

The cave is narrow and deep; its sandy floor dotted with bird droppings. Pain shudders through my body as I slowly stand and steady myself, one hand against the wall. My stomach heaves but with gritted teeth, I bring it back into order. As the pain subsides, I move toward the entrance, dragging my pack with me.

The rock wall is cool, worn smooth by wind and water. A few feet from the mouth of the cave, my hand scrapes against a jagged spot. I flash my light on it and touch it -- it's a narrow channel, maybe five inches long, scoured into the rock. A bullet did this, and from the looks of the newly exposed rock, it hadn't been there for long.

Carefully I study the cave walls and the sand. Near the back I find a place that is dark red. Just a tiny spot. I lean closer, barely breathing. It looks like very old blood. I let out my breath and examine the sand at my feet, brushing it lightly to reveal the next layer down.

Yes! My fingers encounter something soft, like cloth. Gently, I pull it to the light. It's a bit of a shirt. Red plaid. Now my pulses are pounding so hard I can hardly hear. I go on to explore the rest of the area but find nothing. No shell casings. No bones. No more blood. Wrapping the scrap of plaid material into a tissue, I stow it in my pack.

Outside on the ledge, I gaze at the cave, trying to memorize its position, yet it's so dark, I can't see much. The wind and rain are as strong as ever. Now I'm sure I've found the place where Uncle Elton was killed. I'm sure of it. All that I need to do now is find his killers.

Outside, carrying my pack on my back, I move along the ledge and find a narrow path that leads to a road. I lean down. Old tire tracks. They're so faint I'm sure no one would be able to take a cast or a picture of them. Orienting myself to where I suppose the valley is, I continue down the road, knowing where it will end. At Anderson's ranch. Strange how everything leads back there.

An hour later, I'm working my way down through the trees and getting pretty close to the valley floor. I'm soaking wet again. I comfort myself with the thought that it won't take long to get to Anderson's. Once I'm there, I can get into something dry. Pausing, I sit on a rock and drink from my water bottle, glad I'd saved some.

I heave myself to my feet and set off in the direction of the lights I see twinkling in the valley. I have to get help for Jesse. Dawn's beginning to grow in the east and now I can make out the shapes of rocks and trees. About that time, I see someone below me. I freeze. He's wearing a dark hat, dark clothes. He's hunched behind a bush, studying the valley. There's something furtive about his movements like he's tracking or searching for someone. I inch forward, my hand on my revolver. *Who is he? Is he a friend or foe?*

As I move, I keep my eyes on him. A twig snaps loudly beneath my foot and he whirls, a rifle in his hands. He lifts it and brings it to his shoulder to fire. It's aimed right at my heart. I don't wait for a bullet to come tearing through my chest. With a cry of despair, I throw myself behind a bush, hearing the blast of the rifle and the impact of the bullet.

My head hits something hard. It feels like my skull's been split open. Lying there under that bush with my whole body crying out in pain, I try with all my strength to hold onto consciousness, because I know he's coming; he's coming to finish me off.

Blackness swoops down upon me before I can move. The last thing I hear is his crunching footsteps.

Chapter 33

Between A Rock and A Hard Place

Saturday, 3:43am

Worry characterized Maegan's days and nights at Living Waters Bible Camp as she took care of Jilly, attended the religious meetings, ate in the dining hall, chatted with a few of the other young women her age and even rode the zip line. Jilly's arm stopped bothering her, yet the cast hindered her from trying the climbing wall, riding the horses, or taking part in the numerous activities the camp offered.

Maegan appreciated the friendliness of the staff, the good food and sense of safety, yet she knew it wouldn't last. Nothing this good ever lasted for her. She found herself jumping at the sound of a hurried footstep on the path behind her, or a sudden shout, or when branches scratched against the windows of the old trailer.

The nights were the worst. Because Jilly often talked about her family and the Sancho family, Maegan thought about them a lot and wondered what would happen to them. If the law discovered the drug operation, the big boss might close the place down, order the deaths of the Mexicans and bring in some new people. The Sanchos and Manteos might even be sold as slaves.

Butch was often under a lot of pressure to grow marijuana and make heroin in his lab. At first he wasn't so bad to work for, but in the last few years, he'd picked up mean, nasty habits and a careless way of thinking about people -- like they weren't really people -- just things to forward his goals. He'd allowed bitterness and a heavy financial burden to mold him into the kind of man who would do anything the boss ordered.

Friday night, after Maegan put Jilly down to bed, she climbed into her own bunk, tossing and turning, unable to sleep. It was due partly to the wind that tore through the trees, partly to her own fears. She heard branches crashing to the ground, and maybe even small trees. She finally rose and made a pot of coffee. She drank it, sitting at the rickety formica-topped kitchen table, her mind whirling like the blades on a helicopter.

As she stared off into middle space, she remembered the people -- Rosa and Yasus Manteo and their children, along with Angelina, the grandmother who worked alongside them despite her age; and the Sancho family -- Manny and Marguerita. They were sweet, handsome people. How could she turn her back on them?

Rinsing her cup, she went to Jilly and shook her awake. The girl sat up with a cry, her eyes large in her small face. "Wha--!" She stared at Maegan. "Mae-gan. What you doing?"

"*Yilly,*" Maegan, said, kneeling beside the bed. "I want you to do something *valiente* for me."

The girl's eyes increased in size. "*Valiente?*" She pulled the covers up to her chin as if to protect herself. "What? Why?"

Maegan smiled. She knew those two words in English, at any rate. "I am going to go find your family, *Yilly.* You must stay here. In the morning, when you wake, get washed and dressed and go down to the big room where we eat. *Escribe?* You must tell them that I am sick. I cannot get up. I will give you a note. Okay?"

"And what after that, Mae-gan?" Jilly gulped. "I no want to stay alone. Take me with you."

"I cannot take you. You must stay here where you are safe. I will come back and bring your *madre.* Okay?"

Jilly nodded, still unconvinced. "You bring Madre? I will stay if you bring Madre, Mae-gan."

Maegan smoothed her hair. "Okay. I leave you a note on the table. Take it with you."

Jilly nodded. Her eyes drooped shut. Maegan kissed her forehead. She wrote the note, leaving it on the table. After that, she dressed in jeans, a t-shirt, and pulled on a warm sweatshirt she'd found. Over that she donned her own jacket and zipped it up.

Taking a flashlight, she stepped outside. It was snowing! She couldn't believe it -- not in June! She got into the Land Rover outside the trailer and turned it on. Good. It didn't even hiccup. Now if she could only get out of the camp without being seen. She turned on the heat and the headlights and drove down the hill, past the office and the playing field. Putting on her turn signal, she turned left on the highway. No cars were on the road -- not a soul was moving.

It looked like she was going to make it. Suddenly she saw headlights behind her, approaching fast. She tromped on the gas, skidding on a patch of wet pavement. She drove as fast as she could on the slick highway. At one point, she hit a patch of ice and the back tires slid. She was heading for the ditch, but she didn't hit the brakes. After swerving for a bit, she gunned the motor and drove back onto the road. *Darn!* They'd gained on her. It was a truck -- a big black one. She poured on the gas.

Ten miles out of town, she noted that she'd gained enough on her pursuers that she could get off the highway. There was a corner up ahead and she knew of a dirt road that led off to the right. She pulled off onto it and bounced along for about a mile, checking her rear view mirror often. No headlights. Driving off the road into the woods, she hid the car in a clump of bushes. Getting out, she listened -- silence. Yet would they see her tracks and follow?

It would be best to get out of here as soon as she could. She placed a flashlight in her pocket and got her rifle from the rack on the back window, making sure it was loaded. Light was beginning to seep through the black clouds overhead. In a few hours, it would be morning.

By that time she should be at the ranch.

She aimed to hike down the valley, keeping to the shelter of the trees on the hillside. What she would do after she arrived was still a big question in her mind. Hoping for an inspiration to hit her as she made her way there, she settled the rifle in the crook of her arm and started out.

***

From Gina's Blog, Saturday, 5:10am

I swim through a murky pool and surface. It's cold. *I must not be dead – hell is hot. Hurry, girl! Get moving!* I roll almost reflexively and hear another shot. Blood is running down my face. I wipe it away with a shaking hand. How can it be that I've survived? I crawl to a rock and hunch down. Maybe I can get back up the cliffs. As my senses clear, I hear the wind whipping through the trees. The rain is still pelting down and now I feel something hard in it -- is it hail? Will it snow?

I hear someone behind me. Men shout in the woods. How many, I wonder dully, as I huddle behind the rock, knowing that I'm not safe here for long. How many did they send to kill me? And how do they know I'm here? I think about the phone call I'd made and silently curse my stupidity. *The mole, you idiot! The mole is in the sheriff's office. He has to be!*

Leaning on the boulder, I pull myself up, wiping blood from my face, then I hobble down the cliff, aiming for a thick tangle of elder bushes.

"Over here!" A man shouts. I recognize the voice. Sheriff Dugal! So he's in this ... I should've known. Had he overheard something on Mike's radio? Is he the mole?

I search for an escape route. The trees are thick on the left but to the right, a rift in the terrain slopes into a small meadow. A bullet whines overhead. There are at least two guys out there ... maybe three. I know I can't outrun them. Yet the darkness might be an ally.

Making my way forward carefully, avoiding sticks and leaves, I come to a jumble of rocks at the base of the cliff. The men trail along behind me. Now the light is growing. I can see one of the other men and recognize him as Waldo Clayton, Dugal's deputy. *Oh darn.* Dugal's got his whole police force up here after me! There's someone else, too, who's keeping to the shadows. A big man. They're closing in, forcing me down. Are they herding me to a cave? A cliff? Will my death look like an accident?

I get my gun from the pack, making sure it's loaded. I know I have to wait until they're close. Really close. Dugal comes barreling around the gap in the rocks. I aim and pull the trigger, but something spooks him. He's already in motion when I shoot, leaping aside to a tree, more agile than I thought possible. The bullet must have parted his hair.

Now I've betrayed my position and am in danger from the unknown man above me. The man fires. Doesn't hit me. I dodge to a tree, and from that, to a circle of rocks. Hiding behind a massive boulder, I try to get my breath. Keeping track of three men isn't fun. I know Waldo's down below to the right and Dugal's to my left. Where's the other one?

The wind's gaining velocity. Branches crash to the ground and once in a while I can hear the crack and splinter of a tree falling. A person could get killed from one of those. It begins to snow, swirling around me, taunting me, chilling me to the bone, piling up in little drifts all over the place. I take several shots at the men as I see them flitting to positions, but I don't connect. Now I'm starting to sweat. I'm almost out of ammunition and I don't have Chance at my back this time. I'm hoping that they'll be running low of ammo, too.

Dugal pops around the rock. He's only about five feet away. He points his big Carbine Henry Repeating rifle at me. I'm outclassed and overpowered. His face is red, his eyes bleary, his stomach protruding from his belt. He's panting. I'm hoping he'll have a heart attack. "Drop it, Gina," he says.

I drop my gun, figuring I might as well try to bluster my way out. "Oh, it's you, sheriff. Thank goodness! There's these guys up there in the woods, and I think they're trying to kill me. I ... was in a plane wreck with Jesse Anderson and got this far. I *have* to get help for him. What's going on?" I step forward.

"Just stay where you are and put your hands up!" He barks out the command and wipes his forehead with a kerchief. The mention of Jesse's name flusters him. He must not have known I'd been flying with him.

Stepping out from behind the rocks, the large man reveals himself. His face is covered with a ski mask. There's something about his build and the way he walks that I know. I'm sure I've seen him before, but I can't concentrate on it while I'm trying to think of a way out of this.

I grin at them. "What ... is to be, gentlemen? A bashed head ... or a bullet in my heart? Are you going to bring me in alive or is it to be murder again?" Turning slowly, I beckon with both hands.

"C'mon, let's see what you can do. You can't be afraid of a *girl*." I'm pretty sure now they intend to capture me or else I'd be dead already. The assurance brings me hope -- at least I have a window of opportunity now.

Dugal's chest heaves -- he's still having trouble breathing. Is he the soft target? I'm watching his eyes. He lowers his rifle. "No use standing out here in the – "

A tree cracks and he glances over his shoulder. I leap in the air and aim a kick to the side of his head. My foot connects. He falls. Waldo, who's kept to the shadows, leaps toward me and drops into a karate stance, his hands out. The big man raises his gun like a club.

I'm not going to fight. Not like that. My knee won't take it. I turn and flee. Bursting through the ring of stones, I stagger across the uneven terrain, still thinking that maybe I can climb the cliff and get back to Jesse. *Like that would be a good idea. He's a drug runner, remember?*

They follow close behind me, swearing. Dugal can't keep up. Waldo's close enough at one point to grab my jacket. I slap his hand off it, he pushes me, tries to knock me down. I kick, connect and fall. The ground is slippery with the snow. When I get to my feet, both men lunge at me. Dugal arrives and pulls out a knife.

Waldo draws his pistol. "Okay, let's finish this," he snarls and brings up his weapon. I can't let that happen. I spring and kick it out of his hand, whirl and kick again at Ski Mask, connecting with his *solar plexis*, right where I wanted. Both men drop. I've still got Dugal to contend with. He growls like an angry bear and leaps at me.

I decide to run again. My injuries and the snow hamper my movements. I plunge forward, take three steps, then fall, my knees taking the brunt of the fall. I scream. Rolling reflexively, I dodge Dugal's stumbling attack. Ski Mask is on his feet. He leaps at me, too. Again, I'm puzzling over where I've seen him. Is he the local boss?

I jump to my feet and dash off. Well, maybe not *dash* -- *scurry* is a better word. Dugal's played out: he's sitting on a log, panting heavily. I run down the hill, sideways across it, seeking some sort of cover. It seems I've lost Waldo. Maybe he's circling around, trying to cut me off. Now it's Ski Mask who continues the attack. He's fast and agile, and he's seen where I've gone. I glance back to gauge the distance I've gained. Not much.

"All right! Let's get 'er! Kill her! Now!" It's like he's rallying the troops. I notice it's no longer *capture* but *kill*.

He's almost on top of me and I can't get away from him. I fall again and regain my feet. Ski Mask is right behind me, grunting like a pig in heat, a knife gripped in his hands. His eyes are red; he's hot for the kill. I can hear his low muttered cursing. It seems I've caused him a lot of trouble. A gleam of triumph shines from the narrow slits of his eyes as the knife descends.

I don't try to get away, which is what he's expecting. Instead, I lunge toward him and throw myself at his legs, wrapping my arms around them and yanking hard. He falls, almost on top of me. I roll -- and keep rolling -- to a depression behind a rock. Sick with pain, I disentangle myself from him, rise and stumble, limping and whimpering, down the hill toward a small camping area I'd spotted. Maybe I can hide down there.

Ski Mask regains his feet and now he's really mad. He yells as I stagger downhill through the trees. A huge stone, like those at Medicine Rocks, looms ahead. I get there and huddle behind a low bush, the rock at my back, trying to catch my breath.

Dugal appears over a rise, a rifle in his left hand, a tree limb in his right. "Hey, Boss! Over here! I think she went this way!"

I crouch low and stay still. *My last stand. I'll die here, I suppose.* Only I don't want it to be like this. A phrase from a hymn Dad used to sing comes to mind: *Rock of Ages, cleft for me, let me hide myself in Thee.* I shake my head. What a stupid thing to think of now. But is it stupid?

"She was by that rock a minute ago," Dugal calls.

"Where?" I see Ski Mask, only now he's removed the mask. It's almost daylight. The storm's bringing low clouds overhead and it feels more like late afternoon. All at once, I see his face. It takes me a couple of seconds, but suddenly I remember a big man in a Forestry truck that day at the Whittier ranch.

Randy Whittier! My stomach twists. I should have known. Sabrina Philips worked at Forestry. The big red truck. The Mexican workers at the nursery. The *RW* initials on the cigarette lighter. Clues were all over the place and I couldn't put them together. *What kind of a cop are you, Gina? You're a big flop, a failure.*

I'm sick over how stupid I've been, but I know I don't dare show my feelings now. I have to bluster my way out of this, or I'll not live to see another morning. And suddenly I want to live. Desperately.

Whittier bends like a dog to the scent to see my tracks in the snow. He straightens and looks about. Sees me. "Oh. There are you are. Cornered like a treed coon." He lifts his rifle and sights. As he's standing only about twenty feet away, I figure my chances of survival are slim to none.

Trapped between the rock and the two men, I slowly stand. I'm in an indentation of the rock, almost like a cave. If only I had my gun, I'd take out a couple of them before they got me. "Well, hello, Mr. Whittier. It took you long enough." The wind dies down and my voice is sharp and clear in the quiet. "Did you bring your dog along?"

I glance up as Dugal arrives. "Well, not your dog, but the sheriff will do. Hello, sheriff. So we meet again. Are you going to bash in my head and say a tree fell on me?" I try to chuckle. It comes out like a cough.

Dugal's eyes slide to Whittier and back to me. "You come out of there, nice and easy, girl. Ya hear?" He pulls out a pair of handcuffs. "I'm goin' to arrest you for the murder of Sabrina Philips. And then Deputy Waldo's gonna take you to the jail in Sturgis."

Waldo appears. "Come on out, Gina. You heard the sheriff, and his word's the law in this country."

I stare at him. "Montana isn't his jurisdiction, deputy. Sheriff Dugal thinks he's the boss. I wonder how Mr. Whittier feels about that." I glance at him and see anger flashing across his face. He raises his rifle like he's going to hit me with it. I hold myself firm, meeting his eyes squarely. "It's strange to think you really aren't in control, right, Mr. Whittier?"

That stops him. He shakes his large head and grunts like a bear. He takes a step closer to me.

Dugal stops him. "That's far enough, Whittier. I'm the law here, when there ain't no other sheriff around. She's comin' with me. Back off and let her come out." He turns to me. "No fancy tricks, now Miss Lindsey."

"Of course not, sheriff. I'm just glad you're finally shaking free from Whittier's money and influence. He can only buy so much; he can't buy a man's soul."

My words have the desired effect. Dugal scowls at Randy. "Soon's this is done, I'm cuttin' away from your bunch."

"Cut away, Dugal. It's your funeral."

I hold my breath. If only I can get Dugal to come a couple of steps closer and move in front of Whittier's rifle that he has trained on my gut, I can get away.

I turn to the sheriff and smile like we're old friends. "You don't have to handcuff me, sheriff. I'll come with you. Anything to get out of this storm. I bet your car's warm and I'll be able to sit in your office. Maybe you'll give me some coffee?"

He nods, his flabby neck wobbling, his skin beet red from the cold. "I think we can manage that." He steps toward me.

"I'm tired of waiting." Whittier looks down his sights again. "This is long overdue. I've got to take care of her now." He glances at Dugal. "You take a step closer, sheriff, and I'll blow you away, too."

I can't believe he's going to kill me in cold blood, although my blood seems pretty hot at this moment. I think of the cave above me, and the blood I'd found on the walls of it. Is this how he shot and killed Uncle Elton? I hold myself stiff against the blast of the bullet that will tear into my flesh. Bitterness sours my mouth. I've failed. *My God, how thoroughly I have failed!*

Maegan and Jilly, Bobbi and Nick, Tim, even Chance. I tick them off mentally as he pulls the rifle tighter into his shoulder and his finger curls against the trigger. A tidal wave of despondency presses me down. I can't breathe. Can't cry. Can't even pray. So what's there left to live for? If I get out of this wretched place, will anyone hire a cop who'd blown an op like this? I stare at Whittier and fight back the tears stinging my eyes.

But suddenly a bird chirps. I glance up. Weird. A bird singing in this storm? A small flame. A song from the past. A tiny bird's song in the storm.

I know I can't let them win. I promised to help Maegan. And Bobbi. Anger swells within me and sweeps away despair. I've got to keep trying. But I can't do it on my own.

God, if You're out there, now would be a darned good time to show up.

Chapter 34

The Code

5:32am, Saturday

Chance awoke, disoriented. His mouth felt like cotton and the room smelled of dirty socks and mold. He sat up slowly. It all came back to him like a bad dream – his search of the ranch, his capture, the room with the workers. He stood, stretched and used the pen light to see his watch. *5:32am.*

He shone the light around and saw the faces of two men and three women in the tiny beam. Several children huddled under the bedding. Gritting his teeth against the waves of anger that swept over him, he tried to clear his brain and think. He had to get out of here. He had to get the evidence to the police. He had to help Gina.

Yet he couldn't ignore the plight of these people; they were like slaves. Would they be killed if the boss didn't need them anymore? Did they know too much?

He smiled at one of the men, the older one. "Hello. My name is Chance McNeil. And you are ..."

The man returned his smile. "Yasus Manteo."

Chance nodded. "Great. Do they ... feed you here?"

The man nodded. "Food and water." He looked at his watch. "They will come soon."

Chance nodded and went to the door. It did not fit tightly. There was a narrow band of light along the side, and by putting his ear to the crack, he could hear what was being said in the outer room.

A chair scraped back and someone cleared a throat. "Man, I'm tired of this waiting game. The boss said we gotta move them out *today,* but the damned wind ain't lettin' up. If the storm brings as much snow as they're sayin', we won't get out for a week. I think we should take 'em out by van."

A deeper voice answered. "I just talked to the boss and he said we'll wait. He said the van's too risky between the storm and the cops. They're watchin' the roads. Somehow they been tipped off. Probably that snoopy girl cop. Whittier and Dugal's taking care of her right now. We got word she was below the Rims, comin' down into the valley. Waldo's up there, too. They'll do the job."

Chance swallowed. His hands were ice and his mouth dry. So it was Whittier all along! He could kick himself as he ticked off the clues he'd missed -- the green jacket with a logo; Sabrina worked in the Forestry office; and *he* went and confided in Randy just before he was attacked! Dugal was deep in this, too. He wasn't surprised at that! Yet the news that Gina was nearby and was being hunted by these goons sent his pulses racing. He leaned closer to the door.

"You think we should go help 'em?"

"Don't think it'll take that many. If she gets back here, I'll take her out. That won't be no problem. I'll take her out *after* I've had my way with her." There was laughter. "Guess it's about time to get some food to those jerks in there. C'mon, you gotta help. They ain't goin' nowhere." Footsteps faded away.

Chance turned to Yasus who stood nearby. "We have to escape. Now, here's my plan." He spoke urgently to the man, outlining what he should do. He ended with, "First I have to get these ropes off my wrists."

Yasus smiled and drew out a tiny blade from his pocket. "They did not find this in my wife's hair knot. She always keep one there ... for safety. Will it work?"

Chance nearly kissed him. After the ropes were cut off, Chance reviewed what they should do. Yasus explained it carefully to the others in Spanish. There was quite a lot of discussion, which Chance interrupted by saying, "We have to hurry. They may come any moment."

Yasus nodded. "*Si, senor.*"

Chance went to the bathroom. It was small -- a shower, a toilet and a sink with barely enough room to stand between them. He found a plunger behind the toilet and picked it up. Not much of a weapon. He grimaced and prayed it would do the trick. Stepping behind the door, he waited, wondering how long before the men returned with the food.

Ten minutes later, the lock on the outer door rattled. Peeking out, Chance saw a man enter with containers. He set down the bins and glanced around. "Where is the man we brought in last night?" The people looked puzzled. "The tall *gringo*. Where is he?"

They all chattered, pointing this way and that, while the man stormed around the room, tossing the children aside and dumping out the sleeping bags. The children began crying. "Oh, shut up, you brats!" He shoved Jaunita to the floor. She screamed as he barged past them to the bathroom and opened the door.

Chance brought the plunger down on his head. With a cry, the man fell and twisted, clutching Chance's shirt as he slumped to the floor. Chance yanked free, and landed a solid blow on the man's chin. It didn't seem to faze him, but it sent shock waves of pain up Chance's hand.

Desperate to end this quickly, Chance grabbed the man by his shirt and pounded his head against the sink. The man collapsed and lay still on the tiled floor, blood seeping from a wound on his head. Chance stepped out and Yasus and Manuel entered, holding strips of cloth the women had torn from the bedding. After binding the man's hands and feet, they gagged him so he couldn't cry out.

"Let him breathe," Chance said. "We don't want to kill him." They shoved him into the shower and Chance went to stand behind the door to the main room.

A few minutes later, another man appeared -- the other guard. He was a black man as large as a linebacker. Chance shook his head. *Oh, great. Just my luck to get a big guy when I have a broken hand!*

"Jim? Hey, bud. What the hell're you doing?" He waved his rifle from side to side, his voice tight.

"He's in bathroom," Yasus said.

"Well, he'd better hurry. We don't have all day." Minutes ticked by. Chance crouched behind the door, his insides squeezing together like sardines in a can. Pain radiated from his hand. He prayed that he could do what he needed to do and not pass out or get sick.

"Hey. Something's goin' on, and I don't like it!" Linebacker strode into the room.

Chance sprang behind him, pulled the gun from his arm and cracked him on the head with the butt. The man crumpled to the floor. One of the girls shut the door.

"Okay. You ladies turn your eyes away. Yasus, help me undress this bozo." Even as he talked, he started stripping down. He figured the man he'd just knocked out was about his height. He'd have to cinch in the belt, but the other clothes would fit. He quickly got into the man's clothes, zipped up the plaid jacket, and put the baseball cap on his head.

They wrapped him as they had the first man, bandaging his head. He was too large to cram into the bathroom so Manuel lifted a pile of bedding that was stacked by the wall. "Here. Under here."

They dragged the body into a corner and covered it with the mats and blankets.

Chance picked up the rifle. He also retrieved a revolver from the man's shoulder holster and handed it to Yasus. "Keep them both quiet with this, okay? I'll be back with help. I won't let them take you away."

The man's eyes lit when he received the gun. "Thank you, Mr. Chance."

The others echoed his words.

Chance nodded. He laid a hand on Yasus' shoulder. "Keep everyone calm. I'll be back."

He mounted the steps two at a time, expecting to find another guard in the hall. It was empty. He tiptoed down the corridor and stopped at what he figured was the office. Through the door, he heard low voices, so he hurried out to the kitchen. He felt the presence of others -- maybe many others -- and kept to the shadows, easing out the back door.

Ah! He took a deep breath and glanced up.

Great, black clouds rolled in on the wind. Leaping off the porch, he circled the house, crouching to avoid the surveillance camera's eyes. When he left the shelter of the building, the wind slammed into him. Snowflakes stung his face as darkness fell, shrouding the landscape. He shivered.

No wonder they hadn't taken the people out. The weather gave him a breather – but not much. The first calm moment and patch of clear sky would be enough to get a plane in the air. And they still might try to get them out by van. His watch read 5:49.

He retrieved the camera he'd dropped into the bush by the back yard and crept from building to building, knowing they were probably watching the TV screens. He hoped the camera was undamaged, even though it was wet. Maybe the photo card inside was okay.

That they were closing down the operation was clear -- what wasn't clear was how they intended to save the crop over in the Short Pines and what they were going to do with the Mexicans. And where was Gina?

He heard a distant boom of rifle fire. She must still be alive. She was being shot at right now. Should he go and help her? Or should he stay here and try to save the people in the basement? It was raining again. He leaned back against a metal shed and shuddered. Closing his eyes, he prayed for Gina and for himself.

He straightened. The shooting in the hills had stopped. She was either dead or had escaped. Either way, he knew he had to get to his pickup. To call in help. To get something to eat and to warm up a bit. But how could he get out without detection?

The snow changed to a chilling sleet, drenching him to the skin. Should he go under the fence again? No. They'd have that hole sealed up by now. He edged around the big house, keeping in cover, and waited. The main gate was only a couple hundred yards away. A rail fence led up to it. He left the shadows of the house and eased over the fence. From there, he crept along it and finally drew close to the padlocked gate. The lock probably contained a key pad that was opened with a combination of numbers.

It was impossible to get over or under it and a ten foot chain link fence ran the perimeter of the whole ranch. He sat back on his haunches in the ditch and tried to control his shivers. The wind drove the arctic temperature into his very bones. Should he return to the ranch house and try to listen to the gang's conversation? Or maybe he could disable the vehicles. Choices. Well, he had to make his move soon.

A saying flitted through his mind: *cold as death; stronger than steel*. Well, he was certainly as cold as death. Whether he was stronger than steel was yet to be seen.

***

5:47am, Saturday

Maegan froze. She'd heard a rifle shot up in the woods. It was close -- very close. She wondered who was shooting. She shrugged; she had things to do -- she couldn't go after every shot she heard. As she started down the hill toward the ranch, she stopped in her tracks. A woman's scream echoed off the hills. She hesitated.

At least she should try to see if she could help. Maybe it wouldn't take long. She hefted her rifle under her arm and started up the slope, angling away from the valley in a slow ascent toward the Rims. A half mile further, she halted to catch her breath. It had been raining, which was bad enough, and now the rain turned to snow. She slipped several times on the pine needles, catching herself in time to keep from sliding down the steep hillside. Wiping her face, she oriented herself with a large boulder that stood like a sentinel against the hill. The scream had come from that direction -- she'd bet her life on it.

Grimly she started out again, more slowly this time, using the brush and trees for cover, pausing frequently to listen. Was it Butch and that woman -- Gina Lindsey? Had they finally cornered her? Had they already shot her? What if Butch appeared? What would she say to him? Would he kill her, too?

She knelt, the dampness of the ground seeping through her jeans, and waited, straining to see through the fog of falling snow and lingering darkness. *Ah.* Just up there by the big rock, she caught the flicker of movement. She crept closer, her fingers aching with cold as she gripped her rifle. Then she saw him -- a man stood just to the left

263

of her position, a man with a large stomach. As she inched closer, careful not to break any twigs or rustle the branches, she realized he was so totally focused on something on the slope below that she could have been an elephant trampling around and he wouldn't have heard her.

It wasn't Butch. There was someone lower still than her position -- another man. Two men. Were there three? Yes -- the slender form of a young man appeared briefly on the slope above her and disappeared behind the rock. She turned her gaze back to the man who stood not twenty yards away. He was looking down the hill.

She heard someone talking -- a woman's voice. The man she was watching turned slightly. She ducked down and crept forward. When she peered again through the branches again, she knew who he was -- Sheriff Dugal.

"All right! Let's finish this." The words drifted to her from the unseen man below. Butch. She didn't dare try to get lower to see him. There were more words, then silence.

Dugal lifted his weapon and sighted. She could almost see his finger tightening on the trigger. The woman would die. Butch would be shooting, as well -- two shots. One of them would connect. If they missed, they'd fire again. A younger man was out there, too, and she knew who he was -- Waldo Clayton. She'd seen him at the ranch several times with Dugal. She brought her attention back to Dugal. Lifting her rifle, she sighted on him. *What kind of prison sentence do they give people who shot police officers?* This was Montana -- would it be hanging? Yet she had to do something to save that woman down there.

She pulled the trigger. Dugal stood absolutely still, then he jerked upward, cried out, and fell face forward down the slope. She lost sight of him. Someone yelled. She scuttled down the hillside and drew up behind a good-sized rock.

Peering around it, she saw Butch. He fired once into the bushes where she'd been, and then whirled, studying the woods on either side of him, his rifle still at his shoulder. His face was mottled red, his hair standing on end. He was in a killing rage and wouldn't stop until he'd finished the job. Now there was another person to kill. She took some satisfaction in the thought that he didn't know who it was that had fired that shot.

She had her sights fixed on his heart and was squeezing the trigger, when someone burst from the gully in front of her and plunged into the bushes. *The woman.* Maegan dropped back and launched herself at the girl.

They landed together on the piney slope. Maegan rolled a few feet and got to her knees, staring at the woman she thought was Gina. But this girl had short, dark hair. Not red. Not like the girl she'd seen in the hospital.

The woman lunged to her feet like a frightened animal. When she turned and faced her, Maegan knew it was Gina. She'd dyed her hair.

Maegan crawled through the bushes. "Gina? Gina Lindsey? Is that you?"

Chapter 35

A Sunday School Lesson

From Gina's Blog, 5:52am

"Oh my gosh! Maegan!" I twist around, pulling the girl with me into a heavy growth of elder bushes. "Yes, yes. It's me. How did you get here? Was it you ... yes, of course it was." I see Maegan's rifle and the expert way she handles it. "You saved my life."

Maegan smiles, a really beautiful smile, and shakes her dark head. "Well, we're not out of danger yet. You spoiled my shot to take out Butch. Let's get out of here, where we can talk."

I nod and glance up. "You got Dugal, though. That was a good shot."

"Is he dead?"

I shake my head, fighting waves of exhaustion. Everything seems dim and unreal like I'm in a dream. "I don't know."

I start off again, angling down the hill, toward the head of the valley. After a bit, I glance back at Maegan. "Where are you going? I've got to get help for Jesse. We crashed his plane up there on the top." I'm still struggling to stay on my feet and concentrate on putting one foot in front of the other.

Maegan stops. "Gina, wait up. We have to decide what to do."

"What do you mean?"

She wipes her nose on her sleeve. "My car's parked at the other end of the valley, over by the highway. If I tell you where it is, and give you the keys, will you be able to drive out?"

I limp over to a log and sit down on it, studying Maegan. She seems changed -- she's not the same frightened young woman I'd seen at the hospital. "What's happened? Where have you been? Do you have Jilly?"

Maegan rests with one foot propped on a log and shakes her head. "It's a long story, and I have to get back to the ranch. Butch is taking the people out. I can feel it. They're closing the operation down. He might even kill them all. And I promised Jilly I'd ..." Her voice broke.

I want to wrap my arms around her, but I know she wouldn't like that. "Hey," I say in a low voice, "that was extremely brave of you to come up here for me." My voice must have sounded weak, because she looks at me with raised brows.

"Coming up here was the least I could do for you." She stared into the treetops. "I want to confess something ... it was me who tampered with the four-wheeler and made you have that awful accident. I could have killed you." There were tears in her eyes. "You see what being around someone like Butch does to you? It makes you a ... murderer."

I reach up and touch her arm. "Oh, the MP on the cigarette lighter you dropped. Your last name must start with a p."

Maegan nods. "Yeah. Peters." The wind groans through the trees and I wonder if they will topple over. She says, "You need to tend to those wounds and get something to eat. You're done in." She straightens and looks around. "I ... I guess I'll take off, if you're okay."

"What's your plan?"

She shrugs. "Don't know till I get there and see what's going on. I can get in the back gate if they haven't changed the combination. From there, I guess I'll sneak around. I also know where the cameras are. If I'm lucky, I'll get past them and rescue the workers."

"You'll need more than luck." I hear the words coming from my mouth. I'm not sure where they came from.

She gives me a strange look. "Are you ... one of those religious people, like at the camp?"

I smile and stand. "You mean a Christian? No, not really. At least not a functioning one. Are you?"

"Not at all. I didn't even know about religion until I went to their meetings. They talked like they were so sure of things, like they really believe they're going to heaven when they die."

I nod. "They *do* believe they're going to heaven because they've put their trust in Jesus." I shake my head. "I can't believe I said that. My aunt is a Christian and my Dad was one, too, and I guess they taught me some things I haven't forgotten." I chuckle like I'm prepared to laugh it off with her if she finds it funny.

She pierces me with an intense stare. "I guess I could face Butch again if I had that kind of faith." She says it so wistfully that suddenly I'm wishing I could tell her how to get it. "What do you need to do? Get baptized, like the Catholics? Or give money to the church?"

I sigh and close my eyes, harking back to my childhood days. Sunday School. The smell of mold in the church basement and Mrs. Graham's perfume. Funny I can remember her name. Flannelgraph stories of the Prodigal Son and Noah's Ark. I remember helping her put all the little animals on the board.

She shifts her feet.

"Sorry. I had to remember. It's been so long." At last I know the answer to her question. "The Bible says you get to heaven purely through faith. You just pray and ask God to forgive your sins because of what Jesus did for you on the cross."

I rub my forehead. I'm way out of my depth and I'm longing for a warm meal, dry clothes and a little sleep. Yet I can't evade her questions -- to answer them the best I know is the smallest thing I can do for her.

She repositions her rifle and sniffs. "Well, I have to go." She casts me another glance. "What did Jesus do for me? What's a cross?"

I can't believe I'm having this conversation out here in the middle of nowhere while two guys are stalking through the forest, intent on murdering us. "A cross was the Roman form of capital punishment. Very cruel. Haven't you seen The Passion?"

She shakes her head.

I continue in a low voice. "They killed Him for crimes He didn't commit. He died because He loves you -- He loves all of us. And His death paid for your sin. You have to pray and ask Jesus to forgive your sins, and He does. That's what they say."

She nods, staring off down the valley like she's thinking about it. "Okay. Take it easy. When you get out, call the sheriff ... Mike Crosby ... and get him up here."

"I can't." I take a couple of hobbling steps away and look back at her. "They're intercepting his calls. I'll try to get into town and see him personally." I glance at the stormy sky. "If this wind gets worse, I won't be going anywhere. The road will be closed."

"Get going, then," she says with a dazzling smile and I admire how truly beautiful she is with her dark, snapping eyes and white teeth and olive complexion. "See you later."

She turns and heads down the hill, her head bent, watching her steps, her rifle clutched securely under her arm. The snow's turned to rain now and I'm cold and wet. I want to call out to her, to stop her, to talk some more with her, but the words die in my throat and with tears stinging my eyeballs, I head east toward the highway.

I don't take more than ten steps before I hear the report of heavy rifle fire. I drop behind a boulder. It was close, very close, just above me. I look down the slope and see Maegan lying on the ground. Even from where I am kneeling, I see a dark red stain seeping onto the snow.

"No!" I choke on my cry and scrabble down the hill. In about ten seconds I'm turning her over. There's a gaping wound in her chest and blood is pouring out of it. She's having a hard time breathing. I cradle her head in my arms while tears pour down my cheeks.

"Maegan! I'm so sorry!" I know there's nothing I can do. Even now death is creeping across her face.

She struggles to speak. "I bet ... they thought ... it was you. You ... better get ... away." A thin trickle of blood comes from her mouth. Her eyes glaze, but she recovers, and opens them wider. "Pray for me, Gina. The ... prayer. Please." She reaches up and feebly tugs on my arm.

I'm crying so hard I can hardly talk. I manage to say, "Dear Jesus, forgive my sin." I wait. She nods. "Please accept my soul into Your kingdom. I believe in You." I see her lips moving. I don't know if what I said were the right words, but it's all I can think of, and they seem to calm her.

She nods again -- a very slight movement of her head. Her words when they come are wispy thin, a mere thread. I lean closer to hear. "It's ... okay." She tries to sit up. Can't. "Hey ... the ... code is 102551." She tries to smile. "His birth date. I ... " She turns her head a fraction. The grip on my arm falls away. I feel for a pulse.

She's gone.

I don't have time to grieve. Or even to bury her properly. I promise myself that when this is over, I'll return and recover her body. Now I have to flee. I gather up her rifle and the shells she has in her pocket. After that, I straighten and glance around for cover. There, just below me, is a fallen tree -- freshly fallen, from the looks of it. I dash over to it and manage to conceal myself in the branches and the other brush that's growing around it.

I hear them before I see them. They are laughing. Whittier arrives first, and soon after, Waldo makes his appearance. They see the body and hurry over to it. Both stand and stare at it for a time in total silence. Whittier lets out a string of cuss words.

"It's Maegan! Not Gina!" He looks up. "She's around. Look at the prints. She was here a minute ago, I swear. C'mon, Clayton. Get the lead out. We're wastin' time here, and we can't let her escape."

Waldo's still staring at the body like he can't pry his eyes away from it. I hear him sniff. He wipes his nose on his sleeve and glances at Whittier. "Don't you think one killing's enough for a mornin', boss? I'm cold. I'm headin' back to the ranch for a cup of coffee."

Whittier grabs him and whirls him around so their faces are only about three inches apart. "You'll do as I say or I swear I'll shoot you and let you lie just like this. You're in this all the way, Clayton. Don't forget it. Now, get out there and start trackin' that no-good little narc, y'hear?" He shoves him away.

Waldo stumbles and then regains his balance. "Yes sir."

Evidently they don't see my tracks to the fallen tree. They start off, Waldo leading, going east. Maybe they assume I'd be heading toward the Anderson ranch. I have a sneaking feeling that Waldo *had* seen my tracks and was taking Whittier away from me.

Pretty soon they're lost to sight in the trees and underbrush. The snow's turned to rain and the wind's picking up. I glance one more time at Maegan's still form and turn away. Now I'm facing down the valley, to the west, toward Whittier's hidden ranch, the one he must have bought from the Andersons.

It can't be more than a mile away. The clouds and fog lift just enough for me to see across the valley. I can't see the ranch but I know from the rock formations where it's located. My knees hurt, I'm weak from hunger and lack of sleep, and my head feels like someone hit me with a two by four.

As I carefully take each step, making my way down the hill and into the valley, a rage rises behind my eyes, almost blinding me in its intensity. Someone's going to pay for these murders. Someone's going down. And it isn't going to be me.

***

4:24am, Saturday

Tim awakened abruptly to heavy pounding. He rolled over and as he lurched out of bed, he glanced at the luminous dial of his clock. *4:24am.* Someone was trying to bash in his front door in the middle of the night. The knob rattled and then the pounding began again. He leaped into his jeans and pulled on a pair of socks.

"Tim! It's me! Open up!"

He groaned. Only one person in the world had that voice. "Coming!"

When he unlocked the door, Bobbi didn't pause a second, grabbed his shirt front and yanked him outside onto his small porch. It was snowing.

"You have to come! Now!" Her face was blue from cold -- he wondered how long she'd been outside -- and her eyes were bulging.

"Why? What's wrong?"

"It's Gina. I just woke up from a ... a nightmare. She was dying. Someone shot her. We've got to go, Tim. We have to look for her."

Tim straightened his shirt and stepped back inside out of the snow. "I'm not goin' anywhere without my boots, Mom. Come on in. You've had a bad shock, but it was just a dream." He motioned for her and she came without protest, almost like she was sleepwalking. For the first time he noticed she was only wearing her flannel nightgown and thin slippers.

"It wasn't a dream. It was from God. I know. It ... it was awful."

He smiled. "Go get dressed. Call the Andersons and find out if they've found the plane. Then we better get them sheep in. After that, I'll drive you wherever you want to go."

She knew he referred to the ewes and lambs they still had in the pen by the barn. She nodded and turned back to the house.

A few minutes later, she trudged to the calving shed. She'd lived through more spring blizzards than she could remember, but this one had snuck in so quick it scared her. It took all her strength to open the barn door. She propped it open and herded the sheep inside. When she went to shut the door, the wind slammed it so hard she checked to see if she'd lost any fingers.

The door reopened. It was Tim. His shout reached her through the gloom. "Is this all of them?"

"Uh-huh. Good thing they were close by." She tossed hay into the feeding trough.

"Did you call over to the Andersons?"

"Nobody answered." She straightened and leaned the pitchfork against the wall. "That seems odd, of course it's early."

He nodded. "I called Mike. He hasn't heard from Gina, either."

She shook her head. "I'm headin' back to the house to get the prayer chain goin'. That is, if the wind hasn't taken out the phone lines."

Tim eyed her cynically. "Your gossip chain, you mean?"

"It's not gossip," she huffed. "She could use our prayers, don't you think?"

A smile danced across his face. "You could be right. You manage the prayin' and I'll finish up here." He followed her out into the wind and carefully latched the barn door. "I can have the chains on the truck in no time."

She clutched her jacket tighter around her chest and hurried back to the house. It made her sick to think that Gina was in trouble in this lousy weather. Well, she wasn't going to stand by and let them get Gina, like they'd gotten Elton. Not if she could help it.

She'd made coffee and toast by the time he came stomping into the house. They ate, not saying much, knowing each other too well to have to talk. He dumped the rest of the coffee into a thermos and got on his jacket. She bundled into her winter parka and tied on her work boots. They got in the pickup.

As he turned the ignition, he said, "Where'd you want to go?"

"To the Andersons."

"But no one answered. They ain't there."

"They might've been asleep. He'll be up by now and might have news."

He snorted. "He has news, all right. News he's keeping to himself." He pulled out onto the driveway.

She noted that the wind had picked up. They'd been predicting sixty-mile-per-hour gusts.

He said, "We might not make it very far if the wind's blown trees onto the road."

"Just go as far as you can." She clamped her jaw and stared straight ahead into the blizzard. She wasn't going to back down, not when Gina needed her.

Out on the main road, she prayed as he drove carefully around two trees that were partially blocking the way. She figured the power would be out soon, and the sky, instead of lightening in the east with the new day, was dark and foreboding. Maybe they would all die today. Maybe it was the end of the world.

She shook off her morbid thoughts and turned up the heater.

Tim geared down for a hill and said, "What can we do at Anderson's? What if Bryce took Jesse to the hospital?"

"Myrtle will be there."

"How would she have gotten out in this weather?"

Bobbi shrugged and cleared a little patch of condensation off her window. "I don't know. All I know is that I need to be close to where Gina is. And I feel like she's over there." She waved her hand to the west. "Somewhere not far from where they crashed that plane."

Tim sighed deeply and stepped on the gas.

An hour later, they pulled out onto the Alzada highway. They hadn't gone far when a tree crashed across the road right in front of them. He slammed on the brakes, skidded to a stop and stared. "Well, we won't go any farther than this. Are you going to walk the rest of the way?"

Bobbi already had her door open. "You bet. It ain't more'n three miles. You comin'?"

He reached behind the seat and got his rifle. "Walking is better than sittin' in a cold car and freezing to death. Maybe we can get some coffee when we get there."

Bobbi smiled at him. "I knew you'd come through for me. Thanks, Tim. Just keep praying for Gina. She's in over her head and she's in danger. I can feel it in my bones."

He settled his rifle into the crook of his arm and led the way across the fallen tree.

Chapter 36

Deadlocked Gate

Saturday, 6:01am

Chance jerked and straightened. Lights were approaching down the road. Someone was coming. He scrunched down lower into the bushes and waited, gripping the rifle with stiff fingers.

A big red pickup slowed and stopped outside the gate. Someone got out from the passenger side. Chance couldn't see his face, and assumed it was one of Whittier's men. The man unlocked the gate and got back in the pickup as it slowly pulled through the opening.

Chance grinned. The man didn't want to wait beside the gate. Score one for the weather! He eased from the bushes and the instant the pickup cleared the gate, he slipped past it and like a wraith flattened himself on the ground in the far ditch as the man returned to lock it.

He waited until the truck pulled down the driveway and disappeared behind the house. He stood. Now he had to walk back to his pickup. As he started out, he knew he was in trouble. The cold was beginning to affect his thinking. After an hour or so, he fought the urge to lie down and go to sleep. Forcing himself to take step after step, he carefully planted each foot like he was climbing a steep stairway.

How much time did he have before they came after him? If Yasus and Manuel could contain the two men successfully for a few more hours, he had a chance. How feasible was that, though? What was far more probable was that the drug cartel's killers would discover he'd escaped and act quickly to either remove the people from the ranch or kill them right there. Time was running out, but even though he knew that, he couldn't hurry.

His first steps turned into a slow shuffle. He felt like he was swimming in mud, his legs were logs. He had to keep shaking his head to clear it, realizing that all his mental tricks would fail after time and soon he'd slump down on the ground in the melting snow and give up. Just go to sleep.

The wind howled down off the hillside, battering his body like a living thing. To avoid detection and the wind, he aimed higher and found himself among the trees below the butte. Here it was harder walking -- he had to avoid boulders, go around clumps of tangled bushes, over fallen logs, and through streams that rushed headlong toward the valley.

The urge to lie down almost overwhelmed him. He found himself praying out loud, even humming *Jesus Loves Me*. Just as he feared, nothing worked as he went on. The deadly cold seeped into his very being. His steps slowed. With a groan, he forced himself to keep going, but now he didn't know where he'd left the truck. Everything looked the same. How could he find it? A bank of low lying fog crept into the valley floor. Desperation swept through him: he had to find his truck -- without it he would die. *Well, then, I'll just die.* Hadn't he done enough? Maybe his task on earth was finished.

But he couldn't die. Gina needed him. Those people back at the ranch needed him. Even his father would be devastated if he died. In his mind's eye, he saw his father as clearly as if he stood before him -- his sandy hair in its usual crew cut, his blue eyes sparkling with the adventure of life, his white teeth flashing behind a wide smile. He was dressed in khaki shorts and a polo shirt and carried a briefcase.

"Hi, Dad." Chance drew to a halt and smiled at him. "Funny thing that you're here. What's that you say? How'd I get into this fix? Well, I'm looking for Stan's killers." He paused, realizing it wasn't his dad, after all.

A stranger stood before him, dressed in faded jeans, work boots, a heavy flannel jacket and a cowboy hat. He held out a cap from a thermos. It was steaming.

"Oh, thanks." Chance took it, not even thinking to ask who he was or what was in the cap. He drank. It tasted like slightly fermented fruit juice and it was hot. It warmed his body as he finished it off. He handed the cap to the man who stood there, regarding him with sober eyes.

"Thanks. Hey, I didn't get your name." A bank of fog rolled up the hillside from the valley floor, bringing sleet in its wings. Chance pulled his jacket tighter around his body and looked again at the stranger.

The man was gone.

Chance studied the landscape for a moment, then started off, determined to find his truck before the warmth of that drink wore off. He couldn't find any footprints in the snow where the man stood just a few moments before, and he was too tired and muddled in his thinking to allow that fact to sink in. With new strength, he strode down the hillside and in a few moments came to a gully. There, behind a screen of bushes, was his white pickup. It was the most welcome sight he'd ever seen.

Getting in, he started the motor and turned the heater on full blast. He had to get out of his wet clothes or he wouldn't be of any use to Gina or the people held captive at the ranch. He got his duffle bag out of the back and changed quickly into dry clothes. After that, he found a bottle of water and fished an energy bar from the glove compartment.

Just as he started to unwrap it, he spotted someone approaching from across the valley -- a lone figure. The wind was buffeting his Silverado, sending tumbleweeds rolling across the field. The rain came in a deluge. He could hardly see through it. Well, one good thing about the weather -- they wouldn't be taking those people out by plane. Not until the wind let up some.

He could see the figure better now. It was a woman. He waited as she drew nearer. She faltered once when she saw his pickup, then came on steadily.

He saw that she was limping. There was something familiar about her. He couldn't place her, not when he was nearly brain dead, but he was sure he knew her. She was slight of build and her dark hair, plastered close to her head from the rain, was cut short. She carried a backpack and a rifle. She stumbled and caught herself. Wiping a hand across her face, she doggedly closed the distance. He resisted the urge to get out and take her elbow or offer her a ride on his back. She didn't look the sort who would accept help.

It wasn't until she walked up to his open window, lifted her face upward, and said in a matter of fact tone, "Hi, Chance. Fancy meeting you here," that he knew who she was.

Gina!

***

From Gina's Blog, Saturday, 7:14am

The journey from the edge of the forest to the valley floor where Chance sits in his pickup is the longest I've ever endured. Nearly dead with cold and hunger, drenched with rain, aching in every nerve, and shivering from the shock of Maegan's death, I focus on the white vehicle and tell myself I can do it.

But I almost don't. Almost call for help. I wonder in a sort of detached, listless way, why he doesn't get out. Oh, yeah. I'd dyed my stupid hair. He doesn't recognize me. The rifle feels like it weighs as much as an elephant and my feet weigh two tons each as I stagger forward. Even my backpack, as light as it is without much food or water in it, bears heavily on my back. I stumble and almost fall.

Whoa. Concentrate, girl. You can't arrive at his pickup looking like an idiot. I almost laugh when that thought crosses my mind. At this point, what does it matter what Chance McNeil, or whatever his name is, thinks about me? Strangely enough, it does. I see surprise on his face when I greet him.

He nods. "Jump in."

Jumping is out of the range of possibility. I open the door, take off my backpack, and *crawl* into the cab. I wipe my nose. "How'd you get here?" Like most of our conversations, this one seems to be off on the wrong note. Why is it that we're always at each other's throats, almost like we have to defend ourselves? I lean toward the heat.

"An angel." He isn't wasting words.

I shoot him a quizzical glance and notice he's shivering and his skin is gray. "Oh, really. Why're you trembling?"

He casts me a strange look, almost like he's trying to smile and can't quite achieve it. "I'm cold. Changed when I got here. But I'm still freezing. Long story. What're you doing?"

Even with the heat, I know he's into hypothermia, and it's dangerous.

"Mine is a long story, too. The short version is that I went flying with Jesse and we crashed up on the Rims. I walked down the cliffs this morning and three men attacked me with the intent to kill. Maegan saved me, but she got shot. She's dead." My voice wobbles and I stare out the window. "We'd better head over to the Andersons. You need to get some hot food. And a shower." He looks at me again, this time with his brows raised. I nod firmly. "Yes. You may have to swallow some of your masculine pride and get help from someone. It's either that or die."

"I ain't gonna die, and we can't go back. It's too late. They'll kill those people, you know. They killed my brother. They'll do anything."

I stare at him. "What people?"

"The Mexicans. You know about them. I broke into the place last night. Got caught like a blinkin' fool. Put me in the basement with them ... about fifteen, two families. Even little kids. I overheard them talking ... the guards in the other room ... and they mentioned Whittier was up on the cliffs, aiming to kill you. I promised the people I'd come back and help them escape. Then I got out." He turns to me. "Listen. You have to go back to the Andersons and call the state police. Call your captain. Call someone. I'll see what I can do back at the ranch."

"I'm not going to the Andersons, if you're not. You *have* to get something warm in you. You'll die if you don't. Do you hear me? And if you die, what good will you be to those people in there? How can you bring your brother's killers to justice? You have to listen to me. We'll *both* go to the Andersons ranch and get some food in our bellies and some rest. After that, we'll do what we can do for those people."

"There's no time, Gina."

We stare at each other for the space of about ten seconds.

I know he isn't going to change his mind. "What about something to eat?" I challenge. "You'll starve."

He grins. Color is creeping into his face and his eyes are clearing. He holds up an energy bar and after a search in the rear seat, pulls out a package of smushed crackers. They're the kind with cheese and peanut butter between them that you put in lunches. "Breakfast. Care to join me?"

I sigh, and after digging in my backpack, I find a battle-scarred apple and a bottle of water. I hold the water up like you would a glass of wine. "Cheers."

He smiles. Beneath all the grime and scrubby beard, he's actually cute. Well, sort of cute. He has a nice smile and I have to admire his perseverance. As we eat, we don't talk much. His speech improves, and he's not shaking, which could be a bad sign. Yet I don't see his body stiffening like it would if he's in the last stages of hypothermia.

"What are you doing here?" I straighten on the seat. "And who are you? I think I deserve some answers before we go any further. How do I know I can trust you?"

***

Chance finished off a cracker and stared out into the storm. "I told you. I've been looking for my brother's killers. And I've found them, I think. What's wrong? Are you okay?"

"I'm fine." She hugged herself, shivering. "Who are you, Chance McNeil? I've asked over and over but you keep shutting me out." She shot him an intense look. "This time I want the truth."

He cleared his throat, trying to find the right words. "Okay. I'm Chris Marshal. I used to be an FBI agent. I've been on my own these last two years, tryin' to get evidence on that gang of scoundrels. I couldn't tell you before because I didn't want to endanger you or the investigation. Also because my dad is running for state legislature."

He saw the tension drain from her body. Her eyes softened. "I want to believe you, honest. Yet my track record with cowboys is shaky. Look where trusting Jesse got me. I found a package of drugs in his plane. Heroin."

He whistled. "Whew. The hard stuff, huh. I suspected as much when I saw that lab." He took a deep breath. "So you don't feel like you can trust me. Ask your Aunt Bobbi. I spent weeks looking for your uncle. Ask the folks over at the Bible camp. I've got a pretty good track record there. If you can't believe me after all this time ... " He looked into her wide, green-gold eyes. "I promise you, Gina Lindsey, I've told you the truth and I'm not going to let you down."

"Most promises aren't worth a hill of beans." A tiny smile flitted across her lips.

He leaned closer. "Did you hear what I said about the people in there? Whittier's taking them out as soon as the storm clears. I have to get back and try to save them."

"Just you? A cavalry of *one?* How much do you think you can do against the kind of guns we faced at the ranch? Have you called in back-up?"

"Not yet. I'm a little leary about trusting people, too." He turned on the windshield wipers. "I'm takin' you out of this. I mean it." He spoke through gritted teeth, desperate to convince her. If he didn't have to worry about her, he could focus better. "And you're wounded. There's blood on your head. You're tired and ready to drop. By the way, what'd you do to your hair? I like red."

"Deal with it." She grinned impishly and his heart flipped over. She was too darned good looking for her own good.

He stared out the windshield, told himself he couldn't go there. "Now, if you're ready, we'll go over to Andersons so you can make that call."

***

I grin at him. "I don't need to make a call. I already did. I had service for a few minutes and got out to 911. Dispatch probably radioed Mike. So he knows our position."

"What'd you tell them?" He rubs his forehead.

"Just about the plane crash."

"But not this location ... not anything about Whittier?"

I shake my head. "No."

We sit there and think for a bit. I turn to him. "Let's try it again. Give me your phone. Mine ran out of batteries. You have one, don't you?"

He sighs and rummages around in his glove compartment. "It's in here somewhere. You're not going to get service, so this is a waste of time."

I open the phone and let out a whoop when I see I have service. "See? I don't have to go to Andersons." I give him a glittering smile as I dial. Mike picks up on the first ring.

I say, "Hi, Mike. You'd better get the troops into Long Valley behind the Anderson ranch. I've found the drug operation. It's behind their place about three miles, and it's owned by Randy Whittier. Dugal's in with him, too. There was a little ... shootout in the hills. They tried to kill me."

"Did you see Whittier's face, Gina?"

I hear disbelief in his tone and it makes me mad. "Yes, sir, but it was dark and snowing. I recognized his voice and Chance ..." I stop because I don't want Whittier's gangsters to hear anything about Chance if they are intercepting this call. "Maegan ... do you know her? Máegan Peters? ... anyway, she came and killed Dugal just as Dugal and Whittier were about to shoot me. Then they shot her and I got away." I pause for breath. Silence on his end.

"Is she dead?" Mike's voice is scratchy. He keeps cutting in and out and I know I'm losing the connection.

"Yes. Get out here as soon as you can. There are about fifteen Mexican people the gang is trying to remove from the ranch. They may kill them."

"Let me get this straight. Dugal's in with the drug operation ... and this other woman's dead ... Randy Whittier's ... the drug boss. Can you verify ... facts? Did you see Whittier's ...?" He asks it again, his voice sounding like he just ate alum and is spitting it out in my face.

"Yes, sir. I know it's him." Again I don't tell him what Chance overheard. "Let's just say this is an eye witness account." My tone matches his. I figure it's time he faced the facts. "Your phone line is compromised, sir. They're getting information from it. They may even be listening to this conversation."

There was a longish pause. The wind shakes the pickup like a large dog shakes a toy. I glance at Chance.

"I can't ... get out ... you'll ..."

"Sheriff, I'm losing you. I know the roads are closed. Get a chain saw!" The line is dead and I'm talking to air. I snap the phone shut and hand it back to Chance. "All right, let's go. I'm with you all the way, cowboy. So you better get used to it."

He hesitates; I see more arguments forming. I stare him down and he sighs, puts the truck in gear and we start off down the rutted road toward Whittier's hidden ranch. I want to offer to drive because he's still suffering from hypothermia and he's teetering on the edge of collapse, but I know he won't accept my help. And, to be truthful, I'm not doing much better than he, as he so kindly pointed out. Besides which, I'm still struggling with the issue of trust.

The truth hits me like a sledge hammer: this has been my problem all along. I've closed the door to relationships because I can't trust people. Maybe it started when Mom left us. Maybe it's a pride issue. Maybe I'm just so darned stubborn I can't accept help.

We sit in stony silence, bouncing over the potholes and avoiding fallen trees as we wind our way down the valley, closer to the Whittier ranch. Before we get there, he pulls into a gully that affords a little cover. He stops.

"Okay. Let's do this. How do you propose to get in?"

"Maegan's last words. The combination for the key pad. 102551."

"And then what?"

I shrug. "No plan. Play it by ear."

"Huh. That's not how I operate."

"Well, we can't plan much until we see what the layout is."

His jaw is set and he's staring straight ahead as if to block me out. "The *layout* is that the ranch is locked up and on full alert."

He opens the door and steps out, gripping his rifle. I follow suit and stand beside the pickup, getting my bearings. The wind is definitely worse. Storm clouds block the sun, and my face stings with pellets of sleet. I'm cold and tired, but something is rising in me -- I want this finished; I want to end it *now*.

We advance through the storm, stopping now and then to listen and chose our next steps. The snow that fell earlier is almost gone. Yet I think the rain and wind is colder than the snow. I follow Chance as we make our way closer to the ranch, following a line of brush that leads to the main gate.

There, we hunker down behind a thin line of bushes only a few feet from the entrance. It's closed and locked with a key pad. I don't see any cameras, and there are no lights at the house.

"Power might be out." He whispers.

I nod. "Or they're lying low." I'm more than surprised to see the house. It's huge, like a lodge at a fancy resort. Big picture windows look down the valley. A wrap-around deck gives it a western feel. At least I don't see any dogs. I grip the rifle, glad I have it. Yet if they have the kind of firepower I faced in Spokane, this weapon is little more than a toy.

I study Chance. Despite his assurances, I'm still not sure about him. What's his angle? Was he truthful when he said he's on his own, or was that a ruse? Is he only out for revenge? Is he from a rival gang, set on taking out as many in this mob as he can? He said he'd lived in Columbia, long enough to get connected to the drug cartels.

It's an ugly thought and he's never done anything to provoke it, yet I'm at the stage where I don't trust anyone -- wouldn't even trust Aunt Bobbi if she appeared.

Chance's jaw is clamped shut. His hands grip his rifle until the knuckles are white. His body is tense, his gaze focused. He's the picture of a man on a mission -- a mission to kill. I've seen the signs of a man working himself up to the kind of rage that precedes a shooting. Yet I know that police officers who are trained to protect and care for people have difficulty killing.

It's getting lighter. I nudge him and say, "We have to get in soon. They're going to make their move as soon as it gets light."

He nods. "Okay. You come close behind me. We'll stay low and try to unlock that gate before they spot us. Cover me and if I'm shot, get back to the truck and hightail it over to Andersons. They'll be after you in no time."

I don't reply. My throat closes up and my heart is thumping so hard in my chest I think surely he can hear it. He's close enough to smell, to touch. I long to tell him I trust him, like him, value him. But there's no time.

With a glance at me, he slips from the ditch. I'm on his heels.

***

Saturday, 7:51 am

Whittier glowered at the satphone. He was supposed to get a call from the boss and he was the last person on earth Whittier wanted to talk to right now. When he'd returned from the cliffs, he discovered that Chance had escaped from the basement. Jim and Rowdy, held by the Mexicans for a couple of hours, had eventually overpowered them and gotten free. Whittier made sure the basement door was double locked. The Mexicans wouldn't get out now and no one was going to get in to rescue them.

He sent two men, some of the gang his boss had hired from Denver, to search for Chance, but they'd returned empty handed. He shrugged, shoving down his impatience and fury. He couldn't spare time to worry about that idiot.

The weather was giving him fits, too. He paced the office and glanced again at the phone, dreading the call, longing for a beer.

He remembered drinking beer at the Number 3 Cafe in Camp Crook with Elton last fall. He shuddered. *Why do I have to think of Elton now?* He couldn't resurrect the man, anymore than he could Sabrina Phillips or Maegan Peters. He shook his head, disbelieving. When had he turned into a killer? So many tiny steps, he couldn't pinpoint the actual moment he'd crossed the line that culminated in murder.

This waiting was the worst part. If he could've transported the people out right away, it would've been fine, but the storm ruined his plans and he still hadn't taken care of Gina Lindsey. The phone rang, and he pushed the button. "Yeah?"

"You still sitting on your duff, Butch?" It was the boss.

"Yes, sir. We're waiting for a window in the storm. Should have one soon."

"Soon as the sky clears, fly them out. All of them."

"But that's fifteen people. We'll overload the plane. I'll have to take them in two trips."

"To hell with overloading! Make it work. Do you hear me?"

"Yes, sir."

"Fine. My men will watch for you in Baker in about an hour."

"Not possible, boss. I won't get out in an hour."

"I don't want to hear any excuses! Call me when you get your window. Otherwise, we'll have to take care of the problem the other way."

Whittier knew the boss's "other way" was murder. Hunting down people in the woods and killing them was one thing -- murdering them in cold blood as they sat confined in a room was something else. Could he do it?

He groaned and wiped his face. What would he tell Susan? How could he face his kids and grandkids if this came out? How had he become so entangled in this web of crime? More importantly -- how could he get out? There was no way out.

"Okay, boss."

"And how about the girl? Did you get her?"

"Not yet. We almost had her. Another woman shot Dugal and she was aimin' for me. We'll get them both. Don't worry."

The boss blistered the wires with a string of expletives. "Another lose end. I'm comin' over there. I've been waiting in Baker, but by God I'm not waiting another blasted second. You get your act together, mister, or you'll end up dead, too." The line went dead.

Whittier ground his teeth as he strapped on his revolver. He picked up his submachine gun and turned to the door. The two-way radio at his belt buzzed.

He yanked it off and pushed the button. "Yeah?"

"We got some action at the front gate. What'd ya want me to do?"

Whittier's first reaction was to tell them to shoot and kill. Yet he hesitated. "We'll show them some western hospitality -- like hot lead for breakfast." He smiled and strode to the front windows, peering out into the darkness. "Let them come. I want you to fade back to the sheds. You hear?"

"Yes, sir."

Chapter 37

The Key

Saturday, 7:35 am

When Tim and Bobbi arrived at Anderson's house, they discovered that it was dark and empty. Bobbi took off her coat and boots and flipped the light switch. No lights came on. Tim stood near the door, glancing out into the eerie darkness.

He shifted restlessly. "I think I'll drive down to Whittier's ranch and see what's goin' on, Mom. Maybe I can help. I can use one of their trucks."

Bobbi nodded wearily and settled on the couch, drawing an afghan over her. "I'll wait here. Bryce will come soon. Just be careful."

Tim found an old black pickup with the keys in it and drove slowly down the rutted road toward Whittier's hidden ranch. He'd been there many times before -- at big parties Whittier threw for his friends from Colorado and Seattle and for locals who wanted a part in the action. Even though drugs and alcohol flowed freely at those parties, Butch didn't give anything away. The price Tim had paid was to become Whittier's errand boy, hauling the drugs out of the county.

He turned into the Whittier spread and beeped twice at the locked gate in front of the house, wondering if anyone would come out to open it as he didn't know the combination. The house looked dark and deserted, as did the rest of the ranch. Even the yard lights were extinguished. Had Butch cleared out? What about all his equipment and workers? He beeped again and a man emerged from the house, bent over from the wind and the rain. In a few moments, he had the gate open.

It was Jim, the black guy. Today he was wearing a white bandage around his head. Tim nodded and drove through to the house, wondering what happened to him. He parked in front beside Butch's big red truck, got out and turned to ask Jim what was going on. Jim had disappeared. Shrugging, Tim mounted the steps and opened the door.

The inside of the house was as empty of people and voices as the outside. Tim felt his way through the living room in the dim light. He called several times. No one answered. Shivers raced up and down his arms. This was too bizarre for words. A floor board squeaked behind him.

He half-way turned and saw movement from the corner of his eye. He ducked, but it was too late. A blow fell, landing solidly on his head, and he knew no more.

***

From Gina's Blog, Saturday, 8:21 am

We're in! I can't believe it. After Chance unlocked the gate unchallenged, we enter, sliding sideways into a row of poplar trees that are edged with a row of laurels. The big house is silent and dark. Whittier's red Dodge Ram truck and a four-wheeler are parked near the front porch. The wind moans low and snow eddys into drifts as Chance and I cautiously approach. The rifle is ready in my hand; Chance's gun nestles in the crook of his arm.

I grimace as the snow crunches noisily beneath our feet – surely they've heard us by now. Why hasn't any shots been fired, I wonder as we drew closer to the house, flitting from shelter to shelter. Is the house a trap?

"Back door." Chance starts around and I trail after him, ready to fend off the dogs, if there are any. We arrive without incident at the back. He steps up on the deck and tries the handle. When he comes back, he whispers, "It's unlocked. Doesn't seem to be anyone around. Maybe it's booby-trapped. Are you coming? Or do you want to stay out here?"

I draw a deep breath as I'm cast back in time. I'm in that dark, narrow hallway in a stinky New York apartment building again.

After a bit, I open my eyes, pushing down my queasy stomach and the jitters. "Yeah. Let's do it, partner. I'll cover your back."

He bends his head briefly. When he looks up, a smile lightens the features of his rough-hewn face. "All right."

On our hands and knees, we enter the back door. All I can see is the bottoms of his boots. I tell myself to breathe, but it's so stuffy in here I think I'll suffocate. My nerves are on edge and goose bumps scurry up and down my arms. I'm sure someone's going to come charging around the corner and begin blasting away at us.

We crawl down the hall. I'm dragging my rifle and it scraps along the tile floor, loud enough, I think, to wake the dead. My breath comes in gasps. What is that noise? A footstep? Someone clearing his throat?

I almost wet my pants when something soft and furry rubs against my face. It's a *cat!* I try to push it away, but it returns and rubs on me again. I follow Chance through the big kitchen and into what I guess is a dining room. The floor squeaks under my weight. Now the cat's gone into the kitchen, and it's meowing. Poor thing. Probably needs to be fed.

In the living room we cautiously stand up. Light comes in the big picture windows and I glance around. This is quite a place -- a big stone fireplace, a baby grand piano, and enough couches to seat half the population of Ekalaka. "Whew! Whittier didn't spare any expense on this place," I whisper.

He nods, shining the slender beam from his pen light around the room. The house is empty. It feels like a tomb. I can almost hear the ticking of a bomb. Would Whittier blow his own house to hide evidence? Are there explosives planted in this place?

He turns to me. "Let's go downstairs and look around."

I follow him, finding my footing with the scant light of his flashlight. In the room at the bottom of the stairs, he flips on the light switch. I blink against the bright glare and see a desk and screens for the surveillance cameras. They are all blank now and there are no computers on the desk. There is a row of file cabinets against the wall. I open several of the drawers. They are empty. Whittier made sure he didn't leave any evidence.

The door leading to the underground room is open. We enter and look around. On the far wall, another door is hanging wide, a dark tunnel gaping behind it.

"They've gone." His voice is full of despair. There are piles of bedding and garbage from food wrappings littering the floor.

We return to the kitchen. "I'm about starved," I say, glancing around. "Surely there's something in here we can eat." We rummage through the cupboards and refrigerator and find milk, cheese, and bread. It doesn't take long to wolf it down.

"Now let's find out what's goin' on here." Chance leads the way to the front door. We step outside.

He's gazing into the shadows that cling to the edges of the yard and the barn. I know he's thinking of the attack we'd received at the Lindsey ranch. "You keep watch. I'm going to look around. Holler if you need help."

The wind is bending the tops of the big pine trees and screeching around the corners of the house. It's stopped snowing for now. They'll get the plane in the air soon. *Hurry, Chance! We don't have all day!*

A heavy gun report sounds from the trees and in the same instant, the *thud!* of a shell lands on the house above my head. I fall to my knees. Peering around the corner, I raise the rifle to my shoulder. *There! A movement by the shed!* I squeeze off a shot. The assailant fires back twice. The shots go wild. I wait, the sights to my eye, my pulses racing.

Hold your fire, girl. He'll come out. I can almost hear Dad's quiet voice. My hands are sweaty in the cold. I'm schooling myself in patience when a man ventures into the open space between the shed and a row of bushes. I aim and pull the trigger.

He screams and falls. The next instant, Chance bursts from the shadows and runs to the man. I join him.

Chance puts a booted foot on the black man's chest. "This is the one I called the Linebacker. Gina, I think he's one of those that beat me up that night."

I'd shot the man on his upper right leg and he's bleeding profusely. "We'd better get him into the house. There might be some more of them around here."

Chance whips off the kerchief he has tied around his neck and applies it to the man's thigh. We lift him, helping him limp to the house. Once inside, we make him sit on a chair in the kitchen. After Chance binds his wound with some dish towels, he turns to me. "Can you find something we can tie him up with?"

Linebacker glares at us. "You gotta help me. I'll bleed to death!"

Chance shrugs. "Tough luck. You shoulda thought of that before you chose which side to be on."

I find a roll of duct tape in the supply closet. Chance tapes him to the chair. "He can cool off here while we round up the others." He shakes his head at our captive. "If I was you, I'd pray that we get back real quick. The longer we take, the greater your chances of bleedin' to death."

Linebacker's oaths singe my ears all the way out the front door. We step outside.

I take a deep breath. "You weren't very friendly in there, Marshal. I need to give you some etiquette lessons."

He laughs and gets on the four-wheeler. "And I'll have to teach you how to shoot. If I'd shot, we wouldn't have injuries to worry about."

"The light was bad and he was running in the ..." My protest dies in my throat as I see someone moving stealthily toward the house from the barns. A slender young man slips from the shadows and glides toward us. My heart's pounding hard. I bring up my rifle and train it on him, and Chance lifts his rifle, too. The man stops about twenty feet away and raises his hands.

"Hi, folks. Comin' in clean." His cheerful voice is at odds with his disheveled appearance.

"Waldo?" Chance lowers his gun a fraction. "What's going on? How'd you get here?"

"Followed Gina down the hill after I ditched Pyscho-Man." He grins again and nods to the house. "I mean Whittier. Don't worry. I don't want to shoot anybody, not for the world."

Chance's voice is sharp. "What's your angle, Clayton?"

"I came with Dugal. Whittier called him and told him to come and give him back-up. I thought they was going to arrest someone. I didn't know it involved … takin' out Gina. I'm sorry I came at you like I did, Gina. I truly thought I was capturing a ... bad person. And then Whittier shoots that other young girl by mistake." He shakes his head ruefully. "That's when I figured I was done with him. With all of them." He shifts his feet and looks at the ground. "Sorry I've been on the wrong side. I guess I've known ... about Dugal, him being a dirty cop, I mean ... but I didn't want to admit it and figured my job was on the line."

"I'm glad you finally saw the light, Waldo." Chance sits on the four-wheeler and twiddles nervously with the key. I know he wants to get going.

Waldo gives us his first smile. "Anyway, I volunteered to clear the road so we could get out after Dugal arrested her. My plan was to call Sheriff Crosby from the truck. That was when Dugal spotted Miss Lindsey beside that big rock and I saw that he was goin' to get a real good shot at her."

I stare at him. "So it was *you* who killed Dugal!"

"Yes. I know that other girl shot, too. Both shots connected. I didn't mean to kill him, but … it happened. Should I bring in his body?"

"No. We need you here. One of Whittier's killers is in there, taped to a chair, wounded. You can guard him in your spare time. Find a land line and call the sheriff in Ekalaka and tell him what's goin' on. Glad to have you on our side, buddy. You can set up here as situation chief. Get a fire goin' in the fireplace. I imagine we'll need some heat when we get back."

Waldo nodded. "What's your plan?"

"A little reconnoitering so we can keep a plane from taking off."

"Can you use another man?"

"We don't want too many out there." Chance glances at me. "Looks like the storm's tapering off. I hope we're in time. We're heading out to the airstrip." He nodded west behind the ranch buildings. "If Mike comes, send him out that way. You ready, Gina?"

I nod and clamber onto the machine behind him. In the distance, I hear a motor whirring. I can't place it at first, but then I know. *The plane!* "Chance! They're getting the plane out! We have to hurry!"

He nods and turns on the ignition. It roars to life. I wrap my arms around his waist, wondering if I can do this. My head still hurts and everything else feels like it's broken and splintered -- my leg, my ankle, my ribs. I'm hungry, too. The food I'd eaten helped, yet it won't take me far. Waves of exhaustion sweep over me and almost drag me down. I push it away and refocus. *What kind of a cop are you, Gina?* I grit my teeth as we roar away from the house in the direction of the airstrip.

When we arrive at the strip, a plane is taxiing out, gaining speed. Chance drives onto the tarmac and slows down. I leap off the machine, shouting, "He's getting away! We can't let him do this!"

A rifle booms from the hangar and a bullet pings off the airstrip. Chance abandons the four-wheeler and dives toward a tower built beside the runway. "Take cover, Gina! Get down!"

Unheeding, I stand mesmerized as the plane draws closer, gaining speed, its lights blinking in the semi-darkness. It's lifting off, not twenty feet away! The plane wobbles but steadies, gaining altitude and speed.

A man is sitting in the front passenger seat. I think it's one of Whittier's ranch hands, the one they call Rowdy. Susan Whittier introduced me to him the day I was at their nursery. He holds up a briefcase and I recognize it. It's my evidence briefcase! I even see the Mt. Rushmore sticker I stuck on the side of it after my vacation there. So they found my car and the evidence and they're getting away with it. All of it.

A woman's terrified face is pressed to the glass of the rear window. One of the Mexican women! Is it Jilly's mother? The wind slams into me at that moment, shrieking in its fury, almost knocking me down. The plane lifts off.

Disregarding the rifle fire behind me, I run a few steps down the tarmac and scream, waving my arms. The scream dies in my throat, and I return to the four-wheeler, crumpling down on it. Despair washes over me. It's worse than when I failed at that op in New York that cost me my job. I'd pinned so much on this -- all the people I wanted to help, and I'd failed them all.

Tears don't come. My pain goes too deep for that. I grind my teeth and grip my jacket in both fists, bending over until my forehead rests on the steering bar. *What kind of a cop are you, Gina?* A failure. A nothing. A nobody.

Christ died for you, Gina. He loves you. He wants you.

The words invade my consciousness like the waft of sweet perfume. I'm back in that hospital room with Dad. He's trying to tell me something. His cold hand grips mine. I'm surprised at how much strength he has. His eyes are bright -- too bright. And his lips are forming his last words.

They come in a mere whisper. I'm bending down, so close I can smell death on his breath. "There's something I want you to know. I ... I love you. And ... I forgive you. Gina, you ... are a fine cop, a wonderful ... person ... believe me. *I love you.*"

With that, he closes his eyes. His hand falls from mine.

Now I stifle a sob and lift my head, the despair gone. In its place, peace is sweeping through my soul like sunshine after the storm, like a drink of cold water in the desert. I take a deep breath and look out on the windswept landscape like I've never seen it before. The plane is still visible against the dark clouds. Snow stings my face.

"Thank You, God. Now help me find the key to this ... this situation. The key ... "

I drop my gaze to the dash on the four-wheeler. There it is, right in front of me. The key to the four-wheeler. Chance had turned the machine off, but left the key in the ignition. I turn it on and the motor throbs to life. Balancing the rifle between my knees, I grasp the handles and twist the throttle.

The last time I drove one of these things, I paid for it with an injured ankle. Yet I have to do something. In a few seconds, I'm speeding down the runway in pursuit of the blinking lights in the dark sky.

***

8:47 am

Tim opened his eyes and after a few blurry moments realized he was sitting tied to a chair in the office at the hangar. The roar of a plane taking off sounded distantly through the metal sheeting of the building. He was alone. The chair squeaked and wobbled as he pulled against the ropes binding him.

Shots rang out. *Who's shooting?* Figuring this was his chance to escape, he tugged again at the rope, but they'd done a professional job. The ropes held. Well, there was only one way to do this. He'd seen it in a movie once. He flung himself sideways and crashed to the floor, the wood of the chair splintering apart, nails screeching.

The movie hadn't shown that a person could hit their head on a cement floor this way. He lay stunned for a few minutes. When his head cleared, he kicked the rope off his legs. The back of the chair remained intact, and the rope held fast around his wrists.

The door burst open. He got to his knees, fear striking his heart. Yet he relaxed when he saw who it was. Chance! "Whew. You're a plenty welcome sight, my friend."

Chance took one quick look around and leaped over to him. "Tim! What're you doin' here, bud?" He sliced through the rope with a knife. "We gotta git outta here. Those two guys are comin' back. Can you walk?"

"Yeah," Tim said, rubbing his wrists and ankles. "I think they were going to hold me as a hostage if Whittier didn't get away. He's comin' back, you know. He only took half the people. Couldn't fit the others in the plane."

"Where are they being held?"

Tim motioned to the rear of the hangar. "In the back. There's another room."

Chance led the way to the door of the office and cracked it open. He peered into the darkened hangar. "You got a gun?"

Tim shook his head. "They took it from me. Where's Gina?"

"She took the four-wheeler and went after the plane. The little idiot."

"Sounds like Gina."

"We have to get out of here." Chance checked the hangar again, creeping out on quiet feet, catlike, into the gloom.

Tim followed him. They hid behind a stack of barrels. He whispered, "Hey, what's the plan? I don't want to ... "

At that moment one of the guards burst through the hangar's outer door, and behind him came another man. Both carried rifles -- Tim noticed they were Israeli made mini-submachine guns. He shrank against the wall.

The older man, the one with a salt and pepper beard, bellowed when he opened the office door. "Hey, Latch! He's gone!" He blistered the air with oaths. "I told you not to come outside! Now look! He's gotten away. What d'ya think the boss'll say?"

The younger man advanced to the office. "Shudup, Tank!"

When they entered, and the door snapped shut behind them, Tim and Chance sprang to their feet.

"Show me where the people are held," Chance said in a low voice.

Tim sprinted across the open area of the hangar and motioned to a door. "In there. You goin' to spring them now?"

Chance shook his head. "No. Let's get outside. I got a prisoner over in Whittier's house. Let's aim for it. Waldo's holding down the fort there. We can come back for the people after a bit."

They burst outside and found refuge behind a truck. Tim looked at Chance with raised brows. "Clayton? Dugal's deputy?"

Chance nodded. "He saved Gina's life. He's come over to our side."

"What about those two back there in the hangar?"

"We'll take care of them later. C'mon."

Tim trailed Chance, wondering what he'd missed while he was a prisoner. He'd died a thousand deaths tied to the chair while Whittier got away with the people and Gina's evidence. Not only that – he'd heard them say they were aiming to kill her. And they still might. They might kill them all.

He thought of Gina on the four-wheeler and shuddered. It wasn't over yet – not by a long shot.

Chapter 38

The Last Stand

From Gina's Blog, Saturday, 9:09 am

I cut across the meadow toward the big house, keeping the plane's lights in view. It's having trouble. Something is weighing them down. I'm guessing they overloaded it with the Mexican people, Whittier's files and maybe some of the drugs. The storm's not finished, either. The wind tosses the little craft about like a toy boat on a stormy sea. The plane wobbles, the engine sputters, and catches.

It begins snowing again -- this time the white flakes come straight across, driven hard by the screaming wind. It blinds me. I drive on, even when I can't see the lights overhead. Roaring past the lodge, I head down the valley on the road. Good thing Whittier's following the valley and not turning directly north over the cliffs. Gritting my teeth, I accelerate, bouncing across a low ditch and landing in the pasture.

We're still a good two miles from Anderson's place, I figure. The plane's flying low; it can't gain any lift. Whittier circles, probably seeking an updraft that would take him over the treetops and the cliffs.

I follow the erratic course of the aircraft, swerving past clusters of trees and low bushes. Once I splash through a creek. Gaining the road again, I turn up the speed to full throttle, bumping over the ruts and holes, riding it like a pro. Somehow I don't feel like a pro. Every leap and rattle sends pain shrieking from my knees and the wound in my chest. It doesn't help my headache, either.

Incredibly, I'm gaining on the Cessna. It veers north and I cut across the field once again, but a dark green wall of forest looms ahead. A barbed wire fence appears in front of me. I swerve sharply, almost rolling the machine, and follow the fence line, closing the distance between me and the plane. In a couple of minutes, the plane will be gone. I have to stop it. *Now!*

Accelerating as fast as I dare, almost losing control over the uneven ground, I get just below the plane and stop. Raising the rifle, I aim and shoot, once, twice, three times, hoping the bullet will find the gas tank or the engine. The plane continues on. My heart sinks. Whittier's won.

Suddenly the craft falters, descends rapidly and disappears from view. Why don't I hear a crash? Now I'm more concerned for the people on board than I am that Whittier might get away. I gun the four-wheeler and cresting a rise, see the plane lying near a creek. It looks like a wounded bird, one wing crumpled and twisted around a sturdy box elder tree. Cartons and equipment lay around it, spewed from its rent side. Flames ignite from the nose and begin to spread. I get as close as I dare, turn off the four-wheeler and, oblivious of the pain in my knees, race toward the screams that fill the air.

Wading through the high grass to the hole in the fuselage, I call to the shadowy forms barely visible through the smoke. "Come to the back! This way! Hurry!"

Two women and several children crawl toward me. I help them out. The others arrive. I count them. Eight. They're scratched and bleeding, but they're all able to walk. One girl's arm hangs at an odd angle and she cradles it against her chest. A man approaches me, his eyes shining. He's weeping and seems unaware of it. He grasps me around the shoulders and gives me a hug. I nod uncomfortably and disengage myself as soon as I can.

After I direct them to the shelter of a box elder tree near the creek, I turn back to the burning plane. I see Whittier as he unbuckles his seat belt and climbs over the passenger seat, over Rowdy. He crawls out the door and falls to the ground, blood flowing from a head wound.

The fire is mounting higher, flames are creeping toward the cabin where Rowdy sits, pinned between the seat and the instrument panel. His head lolls to the side and shattered windshield glass covers his body.

"We have to get that man out before the gas tank explodes!" My words make no impression on Whittier. I grasp the side of the plane and heft myself up, thinking -- this is the second time in less than twenty-four hours that I've pulled someone from a crashed airplane! The metal burns my hands, but I don't let go. Fingers shaking, my face scorching from the heat, I reach inside and yank at his seat belt, knowing the plane is going to blow any moment.

He has a knife. I cut the seat belt with it. Glimpsing my briefcase beside his left knee, I snatch it up and toss it out the window. Lifting him out, I dump him on the ground. The two Mexican men pull him away from the wreckage, while Whittier crawls behind us, collapsing on a space of bare ground. An instant later, an ear-splitting blast hurtles debris in every direction.

The girls cover their heads with their hands as flames engulf the plane. I am on my knees trying to shield the children from the blast, but then I get up and begin dragging boxes and cartons behind the tree. One of the men helps me. When we're finished, we both fall, exhausted, into the snow.

Whittier pulls himself to his feet and looks at me. "You ... shot us down! I ought to call the police ..."

"Why don't you just kill me and finish the job?" I stand and face him, pulling my cell phone from my pocket. "Calling the police is actually a good idea, Mr. Whittier. If God grants me a little service and power, I think I'll do that." I open it. *Service! A tiny bit of power!* I dial Mike's phone.

He picks up on the first ring. "Hello?"

"About time you answered your phone, sheriff."

"'Bout time you called, Lindsey. Where'n hell *are* you?"

Despite the cold, despite the crying, shivering people, despite my throbbing knees and head, I smile at the sound of his voice. "We're standing in middle of a field, sir. Just past the Anderson's ranch. I have Randy Whittier and one of his men here. I also have eight cold, scared people here -- his workers, or I should say slaves. Whittier was trying to get out them of the county in his plane. It crashed and is burning. When you come, you should see us waving at you in the light of the flames. We could use an ambulance."

He chuckles. "I'm five minutes away, so keep waving. I'll call the EMTs. Good work, officer."

A glow of satisfaction warms my body. I snap the phone shut. There's no time to revel in Mike's approval, though. Whittier is shuffling toward the road.

I tug my rifle from the four-wheeler. "Stay by the tree, Mr. Whittier," I call to him. "I'm a damned good shot, even in a snowstorm."

He turns slowly, his hands widespread. "You win for now, Lindsey. But I'll fight you in court. I can hire the best lawyers in the state and you won't beat them. I was just taking the people out to their work assignments. Got the proof of that."

"You do that, Mr. Whittier." I laugh grimly. "For now, though, I need you to stand over here while I check on Rowdy, whom you so rudely abandoned." I step over to the still body and feel his neck. "He's dead."

"I didn't … it's not my fault. It's yours." Whittier waves at the smoldering wreckage. "You shot down the plane."

"And you overloaded it and took off during a storm." I see lights flashing out on the highway. "Why don't you tell your story to the sheriff? I don't think you'll talk your way past him."

Whittier turns and starts away in a shambling dogtrot, heading to a row of low bushes by the creek.

"Don't be a fool, Whittier!" My voice carries across the meadow over the roar of the fire. "Stop or I'll blast a hole in your leg!" He stops. "Now get back here."

He returns, muttering under his breath.

Mike and Ty arrive in two vehicles -- the patrol car and the county's police pickup. They get out and begin walked across the snowy field, toting their rifles. After they cuff Whittier, I collapse onto the seat of the four-wheeler, my knees shaking. I still get the old after-op jitters.

One of the Mexican women approaches me shyly. I recognize her as the one I'd seen at the nursery a couple of days ago. "You know *Yilly?*" she asks in a low, musical voice.

I nod and smile. "*Si, Senora.* I have seen Jilly."

She beams and pats me on the arm. "Where she is?"

"She is safe. You must be her mother. *Madre?*"

"*Si.* Rosa Manteo. Where is *Yilly?*"

I try to explain that she is at a Bible camp and that she is safe, but I see she does not follow me. One of the boys, I think they call him Ramone, translates for me. Her smile breaks out like the dawn of a new day and she gives me a gentle hug.

Warmth floods me from her embrace and spreads through my being. I lift my eyes and smile into her eyes. I'm basking in her appreciation, yet as I gather my rifle and climb into the police car, I know the peace I feel is because of God.

He opened my eyes and showed me the key. He granted that I should remember Dad's final words, the words that make all the difference to me for now and always. *I love you.*

***

Saturday, 9:35 am

Whittier's lodge echoed with moans and curses.

"Linebaker must still be alive." Chance flashed a grin at Tim as they entered. Waldo had allowed the man to lie down and washed his wounded leg, wrapping it again with some real bandages he'd found. It wasn't necessary to tie him -- the man was unconscious and wouldn't go anywhere even if he was awake.

Waldo poured coffee into two mugs, which he'd made over a roaring fire in the fireplace.

Chance accepted it eagerly. The liquid burned his tongue, but the warmth was heavenly. "We can't take too long, Tim. So don't get comfortable."

"What're we goin' to do first?" Tim paced the living room. "We gonna let those guys get away scot free?"

Chance shook his head. "No, we have to get the people out of the hangar. After that, we gotta find those men and bring them in. I just wanted to make sure everything's okay over here."

"How about Gina? Where is she? Don't you think we should go help her?"

Chance sighed and rubbed his forehead. Too many choices. He gazed out the window down the valley where both the plane and Gina had gone. It was snowing, coming straight across like a blizzard. Suddenly he felt old and tired. He didn't want to go out into that again.

"Gina's okay," he said slowly, turning to Tim. "She's got a rifle. Our biggest priority is gettin' those people in the hangar to safety."

Tim nodded. "Well, if we have to, let's do it. The sooner we start, the sooner it's done."

"Okay." With a backward glance at Waldo, Chance set his cup down and opened the front door. The wind caught it from his grasp and slammed it against the wall.

Tim closed it and led the way to the black pickup. "Might as well drive. Saves time."

Chance climbed into the passenger seat and buckled his seat belt. "I think this time we're in for a rough ride. You ready?"

Tim's smile came naturally, brightening his eyes. "Yeah, man. I was born ready."

***

From Gina's Blog, Saturday, 10:12 am

When Mike turns toward Whittier's ranch, I'm a little disappointed. I want to go to the Anderson's place to find out how Jesse's doing and where he is. I sigh and resign myself to wait a little longer. Whittier is bound and sits in the back seat of the police car, glowering at us. Ty's following us with the Mexican people loaded into the pickup.

Mike glances at me and says, "Sorry I didn't believe you when you called. It's ... hard to think that about a fellow officer, as I'm sure you know."

I nod, blinking back sudden tears. "I understand, sheriff. It's hard to deal with, but it's a part of life, I guess. Have you heard anything about Jesse? He was knocked up pretty badly. I just wondered if anyone's found him."

Mike nods. "His dad found him and took him up to Baker hospital. Bobbi called. Said she and Tim had gone with Bryce to look for you up on the Rims. She said they'd searched and came back to where Bryce was parked and found he'd already left. So they assumed he'd found you. She called again just after I got your call. She's at the Andersons. I told her that you seemed to be okay."

I chuckle. "Well, that's not quite the truth, but I think I'll live."

"Do you want me to take you to the hospital?" He looks at me in alarm and must have noticed my bloody and torn clothes for the first time.

"How would you get there?

He grins. "Wal, I got out here, didn't I? I could get back."

I shake my head and stare outside. "No, let's finish this. I have a feeling it's not over yet."

"You're dead on about that," he says grimly.

We drive into the Whittier ranch and he pulls up outside the house. I cover the prisoner as we unload him. Opening the door, I smell coffee brewing. "Ah. Just what I need -- coffee. But how..."

"Cowboy coffee." Mike prods Whittier into the house. "A far cry from Starbucks, I can assure you."

"Anything hot will be wonderful now." I glance back as the Mexican people follow us up the steps and into the house. A bright blaze in the fireplace illuminates the living room where Waldo's tending the fire. He has a grill over it and a pot of coffee is perking. The Mexicans group together near the fire. Some of them lie down on the floor.

A woman rises from a chair in the far corner and comes forward.

I blink several times before I recognize her. "Aunt Bobbi?"

She runs across the room and hugs me close. "Oh, Gina! I was so worried! The whole county's been prayin' for you! We looked for you almost all night. I'm glad I convinced Bryce to bring me up here." She motions to a still figure standing by the fire.

Bryce tips his head silently. "Howdy."

I nod to him. "Hi, Bryce." Then I turn to Bobbi. "Sorry I didn't get a hold of you. I ... couldn't. After the plane crashed, I took off to get help. I got lost and almost fell off the Rims. I spent the night up there and this morning. After that, I found my way down the valley. I'm so sorry I couldn't call you."

I didn't say anything about the cave or being shot at. Not now. We're both crying by this time.

"That's okay, sweetie. I had a dream that you were in trouble, that you were dying. So Tim and I went lookin' for you at the Andersons." She wiped her nose on a tissue. "Can you believe what they've been up to around here? Randy Whittier! Who'd ever have thought he'd be involved in something like this! Do you think he was duped into it?"

"No, he knew all along exactly what he was doing. You knew who was growin' drugs, didn't you?" I sink into a chair near the fire and rest my feet on the hearth. The warmth feels so good! Mike sends Ty back to get Rowdy's body.

Bobbi sits near me, but looks away like she's ashamed. "I'm sorry about that, Gina. Yeah, I kinda knew it was Randy when you brought out that cigarette lighter with his initials on it. I'd seen him have one like that. And the logo -- that was his ranch's logo from a long time ago." She lays her hand on my arm like she wants to assure herself that I'm really there.

I shake my head. "Why didn't you say something? Especially since I've been looking into Elton's death?"

She shrugs. "I don't know. I wasn't sure, and people around here, well, they stick together, you know?"

I glance up at Bryce. I can see weariness and tension on his face. "How's Jesse?"

He grunts. "He'll make it. They're keeping him for a couple of days." A grin flits across his face. "Unless he checks himself out. He's that strong willed."

I want to ask about the heroin, but keep my mouth shut. The time would come for that. About then someone burst into the front room. It's Tim and he looks like he's seen a ghost. "We need some help! Now!"

Mike stands up. "Whoa, there, fella. Who're you talkin' about and what's goin' on?"

Tim glances around the room frantically like he's trying to gain support, yet he doesn't didn't focus on anyone, not even me.

He staggers a step further inside. "Chance and me. We've been over at the hangar, looking for those two dudes that were with Whittier. We found 'em, all right. They're holed up in the hangar and after they sent some blistering gunfire our way, they shouted that they were goin' to kill the Mexicans that are there if we don't back off and give 'em a free ticket out of the county."

"That so." Mike straightens. "Wal, I figure we can deal with two. You say there's only two?"

Tim shakes his head, his face a pale shade of gray, his eyes wide. He's trembling. "No, I didn't, sheriff. A helicopter landed just a few minutes ago. It's the big boss of the operation. He's come to get his drugs and people out, I suppose. Anyhow, he's brought three or four other guys with him. Chance is hunkered down over there, keepin' watch. It looks like its goin' to be a war. We're goin' to need every last man to help."

"Huh." Mike looked around. "Wal, who's with me?"

Waldo stood. "I'm ready, if you'll have me."

Mike nods. "Shore." He glances at me. "Gina, send Ty on over when he comes back, okay?"

I don't answer, just pull myself off the chair.

Bryce steps forward. "Count me in, too, sheriff."

Mike shakes his head. "I need a man here to watch these fellas and direct traffic. I called for an ambulance. I'm hopin' the EMT people will be able to git here purty quick. I appreciate your help, but you're needed here. You can tell these people," he nods toward the Mexicans, "they can go on over to their homes. We know where to find them when we need them."

He turns to Tim and checks his rifle. "Wal, if they want a war, I guess I'll give 'em one. Let's go, men."

"Hold on." I hobble over to him. "I'm going, too, sheriff. I've been trained in hostage taking situations, and I won't be left out of it. Not now."

I can see he's thinking of all the arguments he has for saying no and I wait patiently, clamping my jaw tightly shut, prepared to be just as stubborn as he. Finally he grunts and says, "All right. No heroics. Stay close." He lifts his eyes to Waldo and Tim. "The same goes for you gentlemen. You hear?"

They nod soberly.

Bobbi, from behind me, says, "Gina! You be careful, girl!"

I manage a half smile. "Careful's my middle name, Aunt Bobbi."

I follow Mike out to his car. Silently, we all pile in. I know it won't take long to get to the airstrip. It's probably not even a mile from the house. I grip my rifle and try not to think about Israeli-made Uzis and Maegan's still form on a snowy hillside.

Chapter 39

Roberto

Saturday, 10:52am

Chance was cold. It seemed he'd been cold for a very long time and didn't know when that status would change. He shifted and peered around the metal garbage container that stood about twenty yards from the doorway of the hangar. He'd crept here after the last volley of gunfire, hoping to arrive in one piece and undetected.

So far no one had shot his way. He'd sent Tim to the house to get help after a copter landed and four men disembarked from it. Three of them looked like gangster type individuals or soldiers in a revolution with their submachine guns, belts of ammo, and two-way radios strapped to their bodies. The fourth was slender of build and he walked with a determined stride. Even though he couldn't see his face, Chance marked him as the boss.

After they'd hustled to the hangar, they'd shouted out their demands -- that the cops pull back and give them free access to flee the county. Or else they would kill the seven people left in the hangar. He'd felt sick when he heard that. Why hadn't he rescued those people when he'd the chance? He'd been too busy, too preoccupied, and hadn't thought that they might be in further danger.

It was a bad mistake, but he couldn't go back. He could only deal with what he had before him now -- an ugly situation that had no easy way out. He wished fervently that it was finished. After blowing on his hands, he checked his rifle again. He still had plenty of ammo, yet he knew their weapons outclassed his.

Well, he was ready. This was his last stand. If he survived this, he'd have enough evidence to take this gang of cutthroats to court and get life sentences and maybe even a few hangings. Was this boss the same as the one in Columbia that he'd seen through field glasses, the one who'd murdered his brother in cold blood? He'd gotten a fuzzy picture of the man, yet it wasn't clear enough to identify him. He wondered what he looked like, who he was.

Now it was raining again. It wouldn't be long before they decided to make a break for the helicopter and get away, and he decided that when they did, he'd risk everything and stop them in their tracks. He glanced over his shoulder in the direction of the house. When would Tim come back?

He was certain that the gang's threats were not empty ones -- they *would* kill. He thought of the two families, of the pretty teenage girls and the little boys, so full of life and promise, of the older lady, the grandmother. Which ones got on the plane Gina was following and which ones were left behind? He couldn't allow the people in the hangar to be killed, like his brother had been; like Sabrina and Maegan and Gina's uncle had been.

Too many killings. Too much blood. There had to be an end to it.

The clouds were lifting. Suddenly he heard the throb of a motor. It drew closer. He cast a glance over his shoulder and saw the sheriff's car pull up about two hundred yards away at the end of the airstrip. Four people got out and began dashing toward cover, hunched over. The large one would be Mike. The two slender fellows he guessed were Tim and Waldo. The fourth was Gina.

"No, no, no!" He ground his teeth in frustration. Why had Mike allowed her to come?

Gina looked straight at him. He motioned for her to go to the left of his position, to hide behind some low-roofed sheds. She tipped her hand and started in that direction, but a blazing blast of gunfire blistered across the tarmac, cutting her off from the sheds.

She ducked behind the police car. The other three men found shelter behind a stack of wood that stood almost directly across from Chance's position to the right.

"Hold your fire in the hangar!" Mike's bellow cut clearly and authoritatively across the cold air. "This is Mike Crosby, sheriff of Carter County, and I order you to cease fire and come out with your hands up!"

"In your dreams, buster!" A voice boomed out from the hangar, along with raucous laughter. The speaker didn't show so much as an eyelash from the big empty doorway. "We don't care who you are or what your fancy title is! We're in charge here! We order you to go back to the house and get inside. Stay inside for an hour. If you don't do that, Mr. Sheriff, we'll blow the brains out of these here kids we have! It's your call. Get back! Now!"

Chance could see that Mike had been busy while the gangster was talking. He'd gotten Tim to creep off to the right, behind a screen of bushes, and keep circling around the hangar, while Waldo made a run for a pile of railroad ties closer to Chance. Both made it to their locations -- Chance lost sight of Tim. Waldo was lying flat behind the ties, his rifle clutched firmly in his hands.

There was silence for the space of about one minute.

A voice came again. This time it was a different man -- the voice was cultured, smooth. Chance knew it was the boss. "You have one minute to pull your guys back, sheriff. We are not fooling around or playing games with you. I know you're getting your men into position. The first body will appear in front of this door in one minute's time if you do not pull back. He is a seven year old boy by the name of Roberto. This is the last warning you will have from us."

Sweat trickled down Chance's face and into his eyes. He swiped it away and kept his rifle aimed at that gaping doorway. It was the only target he had. Gina was making her move -- this time with more finesse. There were three large oil drums near the police car and she'd managed to crawl to them. From there, she'd gotten to a low log fence that ran around the perimeter of the air field. It didn't offer much shelter. After that, she dashed to a box truck that was parked only twenty feet away from him.

She eyed him with desperation. "We can't let them kill those kids!" she hissed.

He shook his head impatiently and looked at his watch. Only twenty seconds to go. His stomach was tight, his muscles bunched and tense, his breathing deep and slow, like he was going to make a very long dive into the sea.

"Chance!" Gina pled with him with her eyes.

He swung his eyes back to the doorway. A little kid was shoved into the opening. The boy fell in a heap on the ground and began wailing like a wounded rabbit. Chance half stood, and crouched again, his rifle up, his pulses racing.

The voice came again. "Ten seconds, gentlemen. You're going to see him die."

Chance aimed and pulled the trigger. His shot boomed in the still air. He'd aimed for a window near the door where he figured the man was standing. The shot pinged off the metal siding and the window smashed into smithereens.

Silence. Five seconds. The boy tried to crawl away, but he was held by a rope around his waist and was pulled back into the doorway. Chance glanced over at Mike and Waldo. He heard the purr of another vehicle and he knew it was Ty in the sheriff's pickup. Ty parked out of sight from the hangar in a screen of trees and bushes. Good man.

Mike caught Chance's eye and motioned toward the hangar. Chance knew he meant *charge it*. But the little boy would die, even if they got inside, even if they shot the men in there. There was no way they could save him. No way. He shook his head

He heard a movement.

Gina stepped out from behind the truck. "All right! We'll move back, guys! It's not worth the life of a child. You hear me? Stop this murdering and killing. I'm tired of it. Just let those people come out and we'll back off."

"Gina! Get back, you little idiot! They'll kill you, too!" Chance wanted to pull her down forcibly but he wasn't close enough.

She paid him no attention at all and seemed as cool as a cucumber. The minute was gone and she had their attention. She lifted her voice. "Did you hear me in there? I said ..."

"We hear you, Miss Lindsey. I don't see what this affair is to you." From out of the doorway stepped a man. He was not large or muscular. In fact, he looked like a teacher or a librarian -- slender and short with graying hair and glasses. He wore a heavy wool jacket and carried an Uzi under his arm. The submachine gun was pointed directly at the little boy's head.

"Now we're in a fix, aren't we?" he said conversationally.

Gina gasped and staggered backward, almost like she'd been shot. "Cap! Captain Matthews! What are you doing ..." Her voice faded. She shook herself. "You're the mole."

He laughed like she'd told a good joke. "No, Gina. I'm the boss *and* the mole. Now get your friends to listen to reason. We really don't want a messy pile of bodies in the back room and I thoroughly dislike killing children."

"You killed my brother!" Chance called out from his hiding place. "And it didn't bother you too much then!"

Cap glanced in his direction. "Is that Chance I'm hearing? Hello, Chance! Or should I call you by your real name -- Chris Marshal? Been busy these last years trying to round up my gang? Well, it's done you no good because we're going to get out of here and disappear, just like we did last time. So you might as well give up. You can't win. It was a *chance* you had to take, but you lost. Again." He laughed.

Gina's face was the color of old paper and Chance could see even from where he knelt that she was trembling. She held up her head and stared back at her old boss.

"All right, Matthews. You've had your joke. Now let the little boy go and we'll get out of your way. All we ask is that you spare the lives of those people in there."

Cap grinned at her. "Yeah, and what assurance do I have that you're going to do what you say? You have a hostage you want to send over?"

Mike spoke up at last. "You ain't gittin' a hostage, you scumball! Just send those people out that door, pronto-like, and when I have them in custody, we'll drop back and give you your hour."

Chance saw indecision flit over the man's face and he noticed something else. The boy had stopped crying. At first Chance thought he was absolutely still, but the little guy was moving ever so slowly toward the side of the doorway. An inch at a time on his hands and knees. A thrill shot through him. Roberto was smarter than they thought. This might give Chance an opportunity.

Cap was getting angry -- and dangerous. "You are not calling the shots here, sheriff. I am! Send over a hostage or we shoot the boy and the other six. Two of which are women. What's it to be? I'm losing my patience with you."

There was silence for a space of about thirty seconds.

Cap called out again. "And call off the lap dog you've sent around to the back door! Now!" He stepped back inside the building.

Mike lifted up. "Tim! Fade back! Game's up! Come on in, Tim! Do you hear me?"

Tim's voice came from the back, muffled like he was eating cotton, "Yes, sir. Coming in."

Chance caught his breath. Matthews had seen only *one* person circling to the back. What about Ty? Where was he? He was nowhere to be seen. Chance let out his breath and peered around the garbage bin at the boy. He'd almost gotten out of the doorway. In another couple of minutes, he could be rescued. Gina had seen Roberto's movements, too. She glanced at Chance and gave his a surreptitious thumbs-up. He nodded.

He had to make his move. He studied the layout of the hangar and realized there were only two windows-- the one he shot out on the left of the doorway and another one further down on the right side of it. If he could get close to the building, then duck underneath the window, they wouldn't see him.

He dashed across to the truck Gina sheltered behind. From there he sprinted in a low crouch to the side of the hangar. Now he was in position to do something about the little boy if she could keep them busy for awhile longer and if Roberto didn't give him away. The boy's progress had slowed because he was almost clear of the doorway and he must have known he was in the danger zone of being detected. Now his movements were those of a snail on a warm rock.

He looked up once and saw Chance, not fifteen feet away, on the ground below the window. Dropping his gaze immediately, he froze for a few seconds without uttering even a grunt of surprise. Chance cheered for him silently. Smart little kid!

The others were still talking about hostages and Waldo offered to go in. Mike was balking at it, and Gina was pleading that they send the people out. Cap was getting more and more frustrated and disturbed.

Chance blocked out everything. He didn't feel tired, tense or cold. His whole being was centered on the little boy who cowered only ten feet away. Ten feet. Could he make it? He *had* to make it. At one point, he held up his hand to halt the kid from advancing any further. Any moment now, they'd see what was happening and yank him back. Chance withdrew his knife from his belt, ready to slice the rope and snatch the boy in one swift movement.

From the corner of his eye, he saw Waldo stand up and begin to move forward.

"Get those people out here!" Mike bellowed.

Gina dropped down and was covering the doorway with her rifle. Good. At least he had some cover. There was more discussion about the prisoners in the back. Matthews ordered that they be brought out. Chance heard the men inside shuffling their feet, muttering curses; he heard the clank of metal on metal, the boss's repeated command.

He was reaching out and was just touching Roberto's shoulder when a cry from inside the hangar echoed on the air.

"Hey! The kid's getting out! Get him!"

Chance leaped toward Roberto, landed on him, covered his body with his own, and made a quick, sure slice on the rope that held him. The knife did its work and the rope fell away. Chance reared back and pulled the boy with him, still shielding him with his body.

Gun fire erupted all around him. He was too late. He groaned inwardly even as he reached for his rifle, even as he tried to protect the little boy, even as he knew that all his efforts had amounted to nothing. He couldn't save Roberto, even as he couldn't save his brother's life.

A bullet pierced his body. High on his chest. He screamed and rolled, still holding the boy, aiming for the stack of oil drums. Another bullet struck. His leg. He lost count of them, but knew he was hit multiple times. In a dim hazy world of pain and sorrow, he collapsed at last behind the barrels and sank into a pit of darkness that seemed to have no bottom.

The last thing he heard was Gina's cry. "Chance! He's been hit!"

***

Virginia Ann Work

From Gina's Blog, Saturday 11:29 am

It seems to me that all hell let loose once the first bullets start to fly. I hear the booming of Mike's big 50-aught caliber rifle and the popping of Waldo's smaller 2500 Carbine. The roar of the Big Bore 45-aught caliber rifles from the hangar seems to shake the ground, and the sharp *ratta-tat-tat* coming from the Uzi submachine guns adds a bizarre higher note.

I add my little 30-aught caliber rifle shot, but it sounds like the popping of a bee-bee gun in the midst of all that heavy fire. Chance rolls with the boy and gets to the oil drums and I'm afraid they'll catch on fire. I know he's been hit. I have no way of knowing how badly. That he was able to roll, that the child seems safe, that he'd gained the oil drums is reassuring. What *isn't* reassuring are the big guns that are barking from the hangar, cutting through our meager defenses like a hot knife through cheese.

I have to move. Mike and Waldo drop down behind the stacked wood and they're safe enough unless the gang circles behind us. I start hearing fire from the back of the hangar and know that Ty is back there. I feel like cheering, but I know it's way too early to celebrate.

Glancing around, I jig and jog in short spurts of crouched dashes back to the log fence and from there I find refuge behind another vehicle -- this time a pickup. The fire seems to be concentrated on Mike's position. Chance's leg is protruding from the stack of oil drums -- it doesn't move. The boy peeks out toward me with a blackened and bloodied face.

I motion him over to me. He waits for about five seconds and makes a dash to me. I grab him and pull him close. I can feel his heart pounding.

"It is okay," I say with an attempt at a smile. "Okay."

He shakes his head and points to Chance. "Not okay, missy. He dead."

"No. He's okay. Honest." I want to run to Chance's side, but of course I can't. I say the first thing that comes to mind. "You stay

315

here. Here." I open the cab door and help him inside. "Stay low. You will be okay."

He nods, the little trooper, and crawls up on the seat, keeping his head low.

A good thing, too, because in that instant the windshield shatters into a million pieces. I grab him and hold him close. He squirms free and smiles at me.

"Okay, missy. You go get 'em."

I nod rather weakly, and patting his shoulder, return to the fight.

Only this time there's gunfire coming from behind us, from the trees that grow on the fringe of the air strip. A big gun. I remember the friendly fire at Lindsey's ranch. Is this fire friendly, too? Or is it one of theirs? But Mike and Waldo -- and even I -- would have been picked off easily if the man behind that rifle wasn't friendly. And we're still whole and in one piece.

One of the men in the hangar makes a break, heading toward the trees. The gun behind us sounds again. The man jerks upright and falls to his face. Mike sprints to the oil drums and from there to a position near the doorway. He stands, aims and sprays rounds of fire into the building. I hear someone scream.

Suddenly their guns are silent. I hear a familiar voice calling out, "Hold your fire! We're coming out!" It's Cap.

I watch as they come with their hands held high. Cap, followed by an older man with a gray beard, a younger man with the red cap, and two others. Mike and Waldo soon have them handcuffed and lined up on the side of the hangar.

I rush over to Chance. His blood is pooling around his body. My cry brings Mike. He turns Chance over. Feels for a pulse. Looks at me and shakes his head. "There's nothin' we can do, Gina. Come away. We'll get him later." Mike's tears run down his cheeks as he tries to pry me away.

I shake off his hands. "No! God, no! I can't let him die! Please! Please." I kneel beside him as Mike returns to his work. I comb my fingers through his hair. "I ... can't let you go! Please don't leave me, Chance!" There's too much blood. His face has lost color. I lift an eyelid. No response. No life.

Tears won't come. I feel drained, dead, numb. I want to shake him, to see the twinkle in his eyes, to hear his voice, his low chuckle. I lean close to his face, my voice a low murmur. "Oh, God. Please let him live."

Dimly I'm aware that Ty is bringing the prisoners from the hangar out into the open area, that they've rescued Roberto from the pickup, that the people are shouting joyously because of their freedom and reunion.

I can't move. Can't breathe. It's like I've died, too. *"Please, God."*

That's when I feel movement beneath me. The softest of sounds, a little breath or a sigh, comes from his lips. I sit up. With shaking hands, I start CPR. Breath in, out. In, out. I cry for help. Mike arrives.

"I ... I think he's still alive. I think I found a pulse and his chest moved."

Mike takes over. I put pressure on his bleeding wounds. Ty takes off his boots, elevates his feet.

"Get that copter in the air!" Mike yells when Waldo arrives and helps with the CPR. Mike's shirt is bloody and he looks wild, like a madman. "I think we might save him. We need him at a hospital! Pronto!"

"I think Cap can fly," I say.

Mike whirls to Cap, who stands with hands behind his back. "All right. You're gonna do somethin' good for a change. But don't forget, I'm covering you. Don't you make one false move, y'hear? You git that bird in the air. We're makin' a fast trip to Rapid. Move it!" He unlocks the cuffs and gives him a little shove.

Cap raises his head. It doesn't take him more than five seconds to gather his thoughts and run to the copter with Mike following close behind with his rifle. Five minutes later, Chance is loaded and the copter is in the air.

Tears blur my vision as the copter diminishes to a tiny speck in the sky. Clasping my hands to my chest, I wonder -- will he make it, or will be he declared DOA? I don't know. I start making my way to the police car. Yet I don't know if I can get there. Everything is fading; the world is dim, unreal. I stumble and Ty catches my arm.

Under my breath, I find myself pleading with God, *"Please, God. Please help him."*

Chapter 40

Miracles

From Gina's Blog, Saturday 12:28pm

The lights are burning brightly in the lodge. I drop onto a couch and set my feet on the hearth where a fire warms my body. Whittier and the man we call the Linebacker are in the corner of the big room, manacled and waiting to be transported. The only other gruesome reminder of our experiences is the sheet-wrapped body of the young man, the one they called Rowdy. I accept a cup of coffee from Aunt Bobbi. I figure it's about the best thing I've ever tasted in all my life.

I sip the coffee and watch as the Mexican people are reunited. After their greetings to one another, they gather around me briefly, chattering a mile a minute in Spanish. One word keeps reappearing. *"Gracias! Gracias, senorita!"*

I laugh and shake their hands and try to tell them through my tears that it wasn't just me, that lots of other people had a hand in freeing them. They don't care. They're just happy to be alive. They troop out and head for their own houses down the lane.

Aunt Bobbi plunks down beside me, her worried, red-rimmed eyes and sagging shoulders saying more than words as to what she's been through these last few hours. "I'm so glad you're safe, dear! What happened?"

I sigh and shake my head, not wanting to remember the blood and killing. "It's a long story, Bobbi. I'm just glad we're all safe. Everyone, that is, except Chance."

"Where did they take him? I heard he was shot, that he almost died."

I nod. "He did. They took him to Rapid. I don't know if he's ... going to make it, but I prayed for him. Maybe God will do a miracle." I'm surprised at what I say, so I chuckle like it's a joke.

The import of my statement doesn't escape her. Her eyes light up and she grasps my arm. "Gina! You prayed! So you ..."

"Yes. I believe in God, but I don't want to talk about right now. I'm so tired I could curl up right here and go to sleep. When do you think we can go home?"

Bobbi rubs her eyes. "Well, pretty soon. As soon as Tim gets done with his statement." She glances at Tim who's writing at the dining room table. He and Ty are working together. "Why did Randy do this? What's it all about?"

I sigh, cradling my cup in my two hands. "It's all about money, Bobbi – more money than you can imagine. Randy sold his ranch to an organized crime ring in Colorado to keep from losing it. But the money he got from the marijuana wasn't enough. He started producing heroin, too. I found out tonight that the big boss in charge of it all is my captain from Spokane. Jed Matthews." I shake my head, still unable to believe it.

I remember that he'd only been captain of our DEA squad for three years -- that there'd been some talk about the unethical way he'd gotten the job. Now I knew he must have forged his papers and paid off the people who hired him.

I continue, "Randy bought this piece of land from the Andersons and built this place. Whenever anyone learned too much and threatened to expose them, they were killed, like Sabrina Phillips and Maegan." I wince, hoping she wouldn't ask about Maegan. I don't want to go into that tonight.

"And Elton."

"Yeah." I take a deep breath. "Aunt Bobbi, I know you don't want to hear this, but I saw where he died. Up on the Rims, in a cave ..."

The door opens and two EMTs from Ekalaka come in. One of them, an older man, looks around and says, "We got a call. Where's the wounded?"

Making my way over to them, I motion to Linebacker. "He's injured his leg and he'll need an escort. There's also some wounded people down in the Mexican homes. One girl broke her arm, I think. Also, Mike wants you to take this body in." I point to the sheet-shrouded form. "I think they called him Rowdy. Hey, Ty. Can you help with this?"

Ty looks up. "Yeah."

I return to the couch and say to Bobbi, "I'm glad this is all over with. Everything, that is, except ... Uncle Elton."

Bobbi sniffles. "Yeah. You did great, Gina." She turns to me. I see distress and old grief in her eyes. "What were you startin' to say before? About findin' the place where Elton was ..."

"Yeah. Well, after the plane crashed, I helped Jesse as much as I could and then I took off to get help. I climbed down cliffs, thinking I could get to a ranch in the valley. I fell and landed on a kind of shelf. And found a cave. I slept in there and when I woke up, I saw where a bullet scoured the rock walls. I also found blood and a piece of a flannel shirt. I'm so sorry, Bobbi. He must have been killed there."

She covers her face and her shoulders shake with her sobs. I don't know what to do or say. I put my arm around her shoulders, trying ineffectually to comfort her.

She raises her head. "It *could* have been someone else ..."

"Yeah, I suppose so, but ..."

The front door bangs open. A man enters, holding a rifle. His face is shadowed under the rim of his hat; his clothing and boots are crusted with mud. He just stands there, not saying anything. I know him, yet I can't place him. Something about his stance seems so familiar. *Who is he?*

Suddenly the ground seems to move, the world shifts, my thoughts tumble about like rocks in an earthquake and I can't keep my mouth shut because I remember who he is. I muffle a gasp with my hand to my mouth and look at Bobbi.

Her face is as white as bleached cotton. She slowly rises to her feet. Her voice is a strangled cry like a mewling lamb. *"Elton?"* She takes a stumbling step in his direction. Her voice rises. *"That you, Elton?"*

"Bobbi!" The rifle clatters to the floor and in the next instant he's running across the room to grasp her in his arms.

Silence envelopes the room. Bobbi and Elton can hardly speak as they rock back and forth, murmuring endearments. He holds her face in his hands and kisses her forehead, her eyes, her lips. Their embrace seems to last forever. I turn my eyes away, hoping to give them a little privacy.

Hearing a strangled sob, I turn to see Tim. He's standing there staring, his jaw slack, his face purple. Like a sleepwalker, he crosses the room and touches his father's arm. "*Dad?* Is it you?"

"Tim!" Tears thicken Elton's voice, and he draws Tim and Bobbi close. "Yes, son, it's me!"

Whittier sputters, tries to stand, and falls back into his chair, swearing. "But you're supposed to be ... "

Elton turns on him and I think for a moment he's going to attack him. "You left me for dead, you sorry piece of scum. You deserve what's comin' to you." He leads Bobbi and Tim to the fire.

Bobbi turns to me. "And here's Gina. She came to help look for you, honey."

I stand and receive his hug and thanks.

"It was you, wasn't it," I say, wiping my eyes. "The friendly fire, I mean. Both times. At the ranch and just now, out at the air field."

He nods and a smile cracks his weathered face. "You got it, Gina."

"You saved the day. I hope you know that."

"It was the least I could do." He turns back to Bobbi and they sink down beside me on the couch. Tim sits on the arm rest, his arm still around his dad's shoulders like he's not going to let him get out of sight.

"And you left that note in the bedroom, too, didn't you," Bobbi says, touching his face tenderly. "Warnin' me about trusting the neighbors."

"I had to, Bobbi. I was so afraid you'd ... so afraid that I couldn't save you."

"Why didn't you show yourself? Come home? If you was alive, why didn't you come back? All that time I was grievin' and thinkin' you were dead."

I can hear anger in her tone. She pulls away from him.

"I couldn't, darlin'. Not until I'd done what I could to bring Whittier to justice. I had to appear to be dead. Then they'd let their guard down. I stayed in that old cabin up the valley."

"I thought someone might be in there," I say. They look at me. "When Jesse took me up on the Rims, riding, I saw the cabin and I thought I saw smoke coming from the chimney. I just put it down to a hired hand living there." I pause. "How did you survive, Uncle Elton? You were shot and left for dead."

He stands and turns his back to the fire, weariness etched on his face. "Wal, that's somethin' only the good Lord above knows. It was a miracle, that's for sure. Whittier shot me and left me, yes. But I didn't die. I came to after awhile and crawled outside. That's when I remembered I had a cell phone on me. I had service, and called Desiree."

"Desiree!" Bobbi stiffens and glares at him.

Elton nods. "Yeah. I knew if I called you and went home, they'd try again and get me the second time. So I called Desiree and found out she was in Ekalaka. She came over and found me and helped me to her car. She took me to Rapid and got a private doctor to fix me up. By that time, I was out of it. I guess my brain was scrambled a bit, because I had ... amnesia or something like it ... for about three months."

He pauses and returns to the couch, reaching for Bobbi like he needs her to understand. "She put me in a nursing home under a different name because I told her I needed to disappear. When I recovered, she helped me get money and an apartment. There never was anything ... wrong goin' on, I swear, Bobbi. She was pure gold in all she did for me."

Bobbi nods. Her expression is one of relief and yet she is struggling to understand and forgive. She sighs and stares at the fire. "All that time ... I was hurtin', you know. Hurtin' bad."

Tears streak his face. I'm surprised because you don't see grown men crying very often -- not in this country. He rubs her back. "I know, sweetheart, yet there was nothin' I could do about it. I swear. I wanted to catch Whittier. Can you forgive me? I kept watch over you lots of times, most nights, hiding out there in the windbreak."

She turns to him and begins sobbing against his chest.

About that time, I stand up and walk out to the kitchen. Tim follows me.

"So how about that, Tim?" I say, striving to be light and jolly.

His face is mottled red and white and his hands are shaking. I know he's ambivalent about it all. "I don't know. I just don't know."

"But he's back. Surely you're glad for that."

"Yeah. Whatever." He turns away from me.

By this time, I've about had it with his snotty attitude and temper fits. I grab him and whirl him around to face me. "Tim, you have your dad back. I know you've had issues with him in the past, but you need to forgive him and move on with your life. Besides, your Mom needs you. You're a grown man and you should be thinking about someone beside yourself. So get over it and face your responsibilities like a man." I pause for breath.

His eyes widen but he doesn't say a word, only steps back a pace and turns a little to the left like he's edging to the door.

"And it's time you got right with God, too," I finished lamely, hardly even thinking by now what I'm saying.

He flares at that. "Oh, like you're the one to preach at me about God, Gina! You've been a rebel all your life."

I smile at him and see surprise in his light gray eyes. "But this rebel's come home, Tim. I ... I've given my heart away. This time to the right Person. To God."

He doesn't know what to say. Tears well up in his eyes. I grab him again and give him a big hug. "Love you, cuz. Now and always."

"Yeah ... you, too, Gina," he chokes out.

We're both crying. I pull away from him and hand him a kleenex, then laugh shakily as we blow our noses. Tim finishes his report, and I see that Bobbi and Elton are ready to go home.

Chapter 41

A Penny's Worth of Thoughts

From Gina's Blog, Saturday 1:34pm

After I point out to Waldo where I'd come off the Rim Rocks so they can find Maegan's body, I drive to Andersons with Bobbi, Elton and Tim and get the Jeep. The storm's letting up -- I see some blue sky overhead. From Andersons, I call the camp and arrange for Jilly to be brought over to her family. Myrtle has a big pot of chili ready for us, so we sit down and eat.

After we're finished, I drive over to the Lindsey ranch, feeling like I could crash for a year.

Mike calls soon after we arrive. He says that he's coming back, and that Chance is in surgery. His voice is grave when he says, "We don't know if ... he'll make it, but I can't stay here any longer. I have a lot of work to do. I got Cap in custody down here, and some of the officers are drivin' me back. We're goin' to comb that place for evidence because I shore want to throw the book at Whittier."

I clear my throat, happy and sad and fearful all in the same moment. "That reminds me. Be sure to find Chance's pickup. We left it in some brush about a quarter of a mile away from the ranch. He has all his evidence in it. I'm sure you'll be able to find it." I pace the kitchen where Bobbi's preparing a light snack. "I'll come down and sit with him for awhile. Don't have anything better to do."

He chuckles. "Okay, sounds good. See you later. You come into the office and give your statement, y'hear? You and Tim both. I'll get Chance's later."

I smile. "Will do that, sheriff."

As we eat, I tell them I'm going to drive down to Rapid. Tim offers to come with me and help drive, but I can see he doesn't want to leave his dad. "No, I'll be okay," I say, standing stiffly, trying hard not to show how much pain I'm in.

"You better get some treatment yourself when you're down there, Gina," Bobbi says tartly, not missing anything.

I'm so tired I can't argue. "Okay."

After I turn in the yellow Jeep at the Rapid City airport rental and reclaim the Honda pickup, I make my way to the hospital. I didn't get nearly enough sleep in the cave last night, yet I have to be here. Who else does he have?

To my surprise, I find some people in his room -- a man dressed in khaki pants and a white polo shirt and wingtip shoes, and a woman who looks like she just stepped out of a beauty parlor, wearing white shorts and a crisp green blouse. Both look up when I hesitate at the door. The man has Chance's smile and eyes. The woman doesn't look like him at all.

"I ... uh, I'm Gina Lindsey. A friend." I glance at the still figure on the bed that's attached to machines that whir and bleep.

The man stands up. "I'm his Dad, Josh Marshal, and this is my wife, Brenda."

I shake hands with both of them, and they attempt to make me feel welcome. I'm not comfortable, though. I look down on Chance's still face. "Has he ... come to? Spoken?"

Mr. Marshal sighs and sits down, looking at his son rather mournfully. "No. At least not since we've arrived. We just got here a few hours ago. Where are you from?"

I exchange information with them and give them an abbreviated version of how he was shot. After awhile, I excuse myself to get a cup of coffee. As I walk down the squeaky-clean hospital corridor, I wonder, does Chance really need me if he has his dad and step-mom? I don't want to get close to his folks right now; I don't want to explain everything. When I return to the room, I realize I have no choice except to speak with them. I sit stiffly on the hard plastic chair, listening to the breathing machine and the beeping heart monitor.

A half an hour later, they say they have to get something to eat and invite me to join them. I decline. After they're gone, I look around the room. No cards. No flowers. I find a Gideon Bible in the drawer of the bedside table.

Slowly I sit and open the book, flipping through it until I get to the Gospel of John. I begin reading and I'm drawn into it so entirely that I'm not aware of what's going on around me. Nurses come in occasionally; announcements are made on the intercom, carts wheel past his room. I'm oblivious to it all. Has this always been in the Bible? How come I've never seen it before? The words are beautiful, magical, throbbing with life and vitality.

As I continue the Apostle John's book, I find myself crying out for God, for His love and grace. I identify with Nicodemus, the religious leader who came to Jesus that night. Like him, I'm locked in my own world of rationalizations, pre-conceived ideas and narrow viewpoints.

This book is like looking into a window to my heart. When I prayed to Him on the four-wheeler, I felt new life flowing into my soul. He answered me. It was a beginning. John 3:16 says He will give me eternal life if I put my faith in Him, that I'll be *born again*.

I close my eyes. *Dear God, here I am, Gina Lindsey, Your lost little girl. I've been running away from You for a long time because I was hurt and lonely and scared. Now I want You in my life. Please forgive my sins, Lord. I believe in You. Thank You.*

I open my eyes. Nothing has changed -- I still hear the beeping machine at Chance's bedside, the announcements over the intercom, the squeak of nurse's shoes in the hall -- yet everything has changed. It's like one of those kaleidoscopes -- you twist it just a fraction of an inch and the whole scene shifts into a beautiful pattern.

My life has shifted. The pieces have fallen together; the deadlock has been blown away. I can't believe it. I've found God, or to put it better, He has found me, and it isn't anything like I'd imagined. I'm breathing heaven's air; my burden's rolled from my shoulders; I'm standing on solid ground. Yet even as joy floods my heart, a question pesters my consciousness like a little kid pulling at your jacket: *what now? What else does God have for me? What work does He have to do in my heart before I can be free from my past?*

I sigh and close the Bible, stroking the cover gently. I can't face these issues yet. I don't know what they are and I'm too tired to look deeply into my heart to find the answer. Not now.

When Chance's folks return, I place the Bible carefully in the drawer and return to my chair, wondering what I'll say to them for the next several hours.

I discover that Josh Marshal is an accomplished talker and I remember Chance saying he is in politics. He asks insightful questions and leans forward slightly, watching my face, listening intently to my replies. Before I know it, I'm telling him my life history. His wife, Brenda, studies her professionally painted fingernails as if she's bored and is thinking about what color she'll have them painted next.

Around ten o'clock, I get up and find the vending machines. I choose a sandwich and a can of pop and a Hershey candy bar. As I eat at the sterile formica-topped table, I find myself drooping like a wilted daisy, wishing I was home and in bed. I throw away most of the sandwich and decide to head on back to the ranch. Chance isn't aware of what's going on, and I can't do anything for him here.

When I step into the room a little later, I realize immediately that there's been a change. His eyes are open. Josh is standing beside the bed holding his hand while tears roll down his cheeks. He says, "Chris! I'm so glad you've come back to us!"

Chance nods and attempts a smile.

Brenda looks over Josh's shoulder and is making little murmuring sounds like you would to calm an infant. Chance looks at me. I see surprise in his eyes.

"Hi," I say, coming closer.

He smiles and reaches for me. "Gina." It's a mere whisper of a word, but it's all I need to hear. "I ... didn't expect ... you." His eyes speak to me more eloquently than his lips.

I grasp his hand. "Oh, Chance. I'm glad you ... you're with us. I prayed so hard. It's a ... miracle."

His eyes open wider. "You prayed?"

I nod. "Yes. And God heard me."

"That's great." He looks again at his Dad, at Brenda. "Thanks ... for coming ..." His eyes drift shut.

I linger by his bed for a bit, and when the nurse says his vitals are strong, I tell his folks good-bye and start for home. As I drive northwest on the Norwegian Cut-off road, I make three resolutions: I'm going to read the Bible Bobbi gave me, I'm going to find what's hindering me from opening up to God, and I'm going to stay awake.

That's my biggest challenge and somehow I do it.

***

From Gina's Blog, August 10

I'm sitting on the back deck. Shep is asleep at my feet, twitching as he chases a rabbit or a squirrel in his dreams. Twilight is settling over the land, and the mourning doves are calling to their mates in the windbreak.

Most of my aches and pains have healed and I've gotten rested, tanned and lazy in the two weeks since the shoot-out at the Whittier ranch. I gaze off into the distance toward Lone Butte. The screen door squeaks open. I look up and smile as Uncle Elton comes onto the porch and sits on the swing.

Silence settles between us for a space of time, a norm for most conversations with him. I'm content with it now and allow it to linger for a few moments before I say with a deprecatory smile, "I don't want to get nosy, and you don't have to answer if you don't want to, but I have to know something." I take a deep breath and see a smile beginning to form on his weathered face.

I continue, "Bobbi's probably told you already that I sent off some mud samples I found on your boots to the lab in Pierre. They came back with marijuana traces. I was just wondering where ..."

"I'd been walkin'?" He chuckles and scratches Shep around the ears, then leans back in the swing and considers the new moon rising over Lone Butte. "Well, it's not somethin' I'm particularly proud of. Randy told me he'd invested in some new kind of plants. Said it would make him a mint, and he invited me to go with him to see the farm. He wanted me to invest in the business." He snorts and shakes his head.

"Wal, I went down to the South Pines. I thought at the time it was a strange place to grow the crop, hidden as it was in that narrow valley. I walked through those plants like a tourist and didn't know what I was seein'. Thought it was ginsing, or somethin' like that. I told him I'd think about it and came on home. After I'd talked about it with Bobbi, we decided not to invest that way."

Another silence ensued and this time I wasn't so patient. "And so?" I leaned forward, staring at him.

"A couple of weeks later, I was readin' an article in the paper how they'd caught some marijuana growers in Iowa, planting them underneath corn. All of a sudden I remembered them dang plants of Randy's and it just clicked." He cleared his throat and took a drink of beer. "I didn't know who to talk to, but figured it was Dugal's jurisdiction, so I went to him. Fool idea. Next thing I know, I'm lookin' down the barrel of Whittier's rifle."

He stood. "Do you want somethin'? There's some pie leftover. Think I'll get me a piece."

Bobbi's pie is not to be refused lightly. Yet I'd had enough sugar for the day. Probably for the week. "No, thanks, Uncle Elton," I say, grinning up at him. "I never suspected you of runnin' or growin' drugs. I was just curious."

He laughed and tipped his head. "I know, Gina. You can't stop bein' a cop, can you? And you're a mighty fine one. Just like your Dad. I have to say that."

After he leaves, I smile to myself. It's not often Uncle Elton praises someone and when he does, it's genuine. I stroll down to the corral and whistle for Cyndi. A low nicker answers my call and pretty soon I hear hoof beats. She comes up to the fence and shoves her nose between the rails, the greedy little bugger. I find a horse biscuit in my pocket and offer it to her.

I'd decided to stay on the ranch for the rest of the summer and the DEA in Spokane gave me administrative leave to rest and rejuvenate.

Chance was released from the hospital a week after the shoot-out. His dad paid for a ticket to Tacoma, so he flew home. I didn't get to see him before he left, and I've only heard from him twice, except for messages on Facebook. He says he's recuperating well and asked about Cyndi. In my mind, he seems more concerned about her than about me.

Jesse's back, too; I've seen him several times. He's busy with the water bottling plant. He insisted I come and tour it, explaining that they had to hire guards as someone tried to steal their "secret" to the healing water. I had to laugh; I guess he takes it seriously, though.

I've gotten through most of the book of John in my Bible reading. Yet there's still this big lump in my heart that I can't make go away. I've prayed that God will show me what it is, but it's buried so deeply I can't find it. *Patience, Gina,* I seem to hear. *Yeah, right,* I answer. As you've probably figured by now, I'm not the most patient person in the world. Yet God is teaching me a lot these quiet summer days on the ranch.

I won't bore you with the details of the court proceedings. Jed Matthews' case is still being appealed. Mike assured me that even if he doesn't get a hanging, he'll cool his heels in prison for life. It was harder to convict Randy Whittier. Yet with Elton's evidence and the photo card I salvaged from my singed briefcase, they were able to get a prison sentence of thirty years for him, which probably amounts to life unless he can get out on parole. I feel sorry Susan and the kids. She left the ranch and went to live with her folks in Seattle.

Maegan's funeral, at the church in Ekalaka, was bittersweet. There were many tears in evidence when I related how she'd prayed for salvation just before she died.

I wrote in my statement that I'd found a package of heroin in Jesse's crashed plane. When Mike faced the Andersons with that, Jesse and Bryce were genuinely surprised. Mike went back to Whittier and questioned him on it, adding that Chance found traces of heroin in the beakers in his lab.

Whittier confessed: he'd gotten one of his men a job with the Andersons and whenever Jesse got ready to fly up to Baker or to Rapid, they'd smuggle a package onboard the plane. It was an easy matter after he landed to have it picked up by one of their gang.

Bobbi and Elton had a hard time readjusting to life together and I'd heard them arguing a lot. The other night, though, jazz music wafted on the soft summer's breeze. I peeked out the office window.

They were out there in the moonlight doing a slow waltz, holding each other so close you couldn't tell if it was one person or two. I figure they're going to be okay.

I gaze up at the star-spangled sky, thinking about all that's happened. Miracles seem to blossom like the flowers in Bobbi's garden. And who would have believed it would happen here? I chuckle, thinking that the people in Carter County will have something to talk about for years.

***

From Gina's Blog, August 31

The fields are brown and there's a forest fire going somewhere down in the Short Pines. The ranchers are finishing up their haying and getting ready to harvest wheat. Elton's dived into his work like a fish that's been out of water too long.

I'm on the front porch when a white pickup pulls into the driveway and stops in a cloud of dust. I don't move, because I see a familiar cowboy hat on the man in the driver's seat.

Chance!

He leans out the window and calls to me with laughter in his voice, "Hey! You need a lift, miss? I might be goin' your way!"

I lay down my laptop and come off the porch. By the time I get to him, he's gotten out, and his arms are wide open. I run into them like I'm running home.

His scruffy beard's gone, and his hair's cut short. Even his fingernails are scrubbed clean and neatly clipped. He doesn't look like the man who rescued me from the snowstorm last April. Yet I know that in the ways that really matter, he hasn't changed at all. He's the same determined, honest, enigmatic and radical Christian man he'd always been.

After the hug, I invite him in. That evening, under a full moon, we walk down to the corral. I hear hoof steps and a snuffling sound. It's Cyndi. I heft myself to the top rail and scratch around her ears.

She likes the attention, and stretches her lips for the apple Chance holds out for her.

He pats Cyndi's neck and gives me a sideways glance. "You two gettin' along?"

I come off the fence and stand beside him, still rubbing her. "Yeah. She misses you. She told me she's upset with you for deserting her like you did."

He grins. "Is that so? Did you tell her I missed her, too, and that I had to take care of things? And that I've come back to her as soon as I could?"

"No. I think you better tell her yourself." His nearness is doing funny things to my heart. I tell it to be still; it doesn't listen to me.

A full moon appears over the butte and coyotes yap in the distance. Soft jazz music reaches us from the house and I figure Bobbi put it on for our benefit. The little match-maker! I look up at him and realize I really like him. Maybe more than like.

He turns to me and brushes a tendril of hair from my forehead. "I see your hair is red again. Did your temper come back with it?"

"You better not try me, cowboy, or you'll find out." I lay my hand on his arm. "Where's your scruffy look? I think I like it better than the city dude who's returned to me. So it's Chris Marshal, huh. Is that what you want me to call you?"

He chuckles and returns to Cyndi who'd shoved her nose through the rails. "Call me whatever you want."

Silence descends on us. After a bit, he turns to me and says, "A penny for your thoughts."

"Oh, I was thinking about my phone interview with the police chief in Spokane tomorrow."

"Don't you ever quit working? Do you realize what a success you've become? You even made the Tacoma paper."

I feel my face flush. "I just did what I had to do. And the interview's important."

"What's going on?"

"Well, I've been offered a job in the police department as a sergeant with their SIU, Special Investigative Unit. I'll need to take more training. I'm fairly excited about it."

"So you're going back to Spokane?"

I nod.

"But what about ... Lindseys ... I thought you'd want to stay around here and ..." He looks at Cyndi.

I can't resist teasing him. "My, my. I never thought I'd see Chance Marshal speechless."

He chuckles, wrapping an arm around me. "I ... thought you were going to take the deputy job Mike offered."

"Yeah, I thought about that." I bite my lip. "But I have my things, my horse, my friends, my job up in Spokane. I can come and visit here any time. It's not like I'm never coming back. With Tim leaving for school, they might need me more often."

"Tim's leavin' for school?"

"He decided to go into law enforcement. So I'll come whenever I get vacation time." I chuckle. "They can't get rid of me that easily!"

"I bet Jesse's glad about that."

"I haven't told him." I push away from him and reach for Cyndi's soft nose. "We've gone out a couple of times, yet I'm not sure about him. He's dating other girls, too."

He processes that for a moment, then says very quietly, "Oh. I hope he finds what he wants."

I laugh. "Well, knowing Jesse, he probably will. What about you? Has your dad put you to work in Tacoma?"

"I got offered a job in Alaska. Pays real good. I should be a rich man soon." There's a twinkle in his eyes.

A lump forms in my throat. *Alaska!* I shove my hands in my pockets.

"Now who's speechless?" He chides.

"I hear the hunting's great there."

"So I've been told." He draws me close again and tips my chin so I have to look into his eyes. "I'm praying about it and I'd like to go, but somethin' is pulling me back to my ranch in Washington."

"Really." I'm looking into his startling blue eyes, and wonder if he's fixing to kiss me. I pull away from him. "So you're going to live in Tacoma?"

"Tacoma! Why would I want to live there? I'm looking into becoming a border guard."

"No way! Which border?"

He laughs. "Canadian, Gina. I'll live on my ranch and drive from there."

The way he says my name sets my heart pounding again. "Then you'll be …" I take a deep breath. "We'll be …"

"Seeing each other in church on Sundays?"

I smile. "I reckon that's a possibility. And once in a while through the week, I hope."

His eyes sparkle with laughter. "Yes, I think we can work that out. In fact, I know of a nice ranch where you can board your horse."

I join his chuckle and give him a wink. "Oh, now I get the picture. You want me to do all the work, mucking out stalls and putting up hay."

His shirt tickles my nose with the aromas of clover and pine and leather. Lonely strains of a saxophone sigh on the wind. His arm encircles my waist and we do a slow waltz while the horse looks on, her eyelids drooping sleepily.

He kisses my forehead and breathes deeply, a smile on his lips. His voice is husky. "So, you never answered my question. Are you goin' my way, Gina?"

The intensity of his gaze scares me. I'm not sure I can be what he needs me to be; I'm not sure of myself. In fact, I'm downright scared of a commitment. He's not pushing things, though. We have time. I smile. "Depends on where you're going."

"Wherever God leads me, girl."

I snuggle close to him. "That's good enough for me, cowboy." As the music swirls around us, I find I'm not afraid. How can fear invade my heart when joy is flooding it?

After a few moments, we walk back to the house. I squeeze his hand and match my stride to his.

I'm ready to start the adventure.

Deadlocked

A Note from Virginia Ann Work

The creation of Gina Lindsey series is an interesting story in itself.

Back in 2006, I attended a writer's conference at Wheaton, IL and met Jolene Philo who is from Iowa. We became instant friends, and as we sat around the table after one of the meals, Jolene related to another friend how she and her husband lived for a few years in a remote rural village called Camp Crook. There, she said, she taught school and he was a counselor at a boy's ranch.

As she continued her tale, I perked up and began really listening. Something was very familiar about the details of the people in that area.

I asked, "Camp Crook, South Dakota? The one that's close to Ekalaka, Montana?"

She shot me a surprised look. "Yes.'"

I could barely speak and blurted out, "We used to live in Ekalaka!"

We discovered that my husband and I had moved to Ekalaka just after they left Camp Crook -- we'd only missed knowing each other by a couple of months! It was like we'd found a family we hadn't known.

The "capper" came a little later from the other lady sitting with us. She said, "You two ought to write a story about that area!"

"I like mysteries," I offered.

Jolene replied, "I do, too."

And just like that, we were immersed in a frenzy of excited planning and plotting, the ideas coming faster than we could write them down.

So began a partnership that lasted several years. Once we met in Rapid City and traveled to Camp Crook and Ekalaka to gather information and do some plotting. We stayed at Trails End Ranch camp, visited the Forestry station in Camp Crook, drove out to Camp Needmore and the Rimrocks, and were delighted with an afternoon exploring Medicine Rocks State Park.

When life and other writing projects took Jolene away from me and the book, I set it aside for a time until God called me back to it.

I love mysteries. I love to write. I love to serve God with this gift He has given me. Where God will take me in the next book -- and you, too, if you dare to come along on the adventure -- is anyone's guess. I can only look forward to the journey with joy and anticipation.

Virginia Ann Work (Ginger)
Chewelah, WA , November 2011
www.VirginiaAnnWork.com

Other Books By Virginia Ann Work

The Keys to the Kingdom Series
Sirocco Wind from the East
Mistral Wind from the North
Zephyr Wind from the West

The Jodi Fischer Young Adult Mysteries
The Mystery of the Missing Message
The Secret in the Silver Box

The Gina Lindsey Mystery Series
Deadlocked

Proof

Made in the USA
Charleston, SC
31 December 2013